The
Rakehell
of
Roth

The
Rakehell
of
Roth

AMALIE HOWARD

Entangled Publishing, LLC
10940 S Parker Road
Suite 327
Parker, CO 80134
Visit our website at www.entangledpublishing.com.

Amara is an imprint of Entangled Publishing, LLC.

Edited by Heather Howland, Lydia Sharp, Liz Pelletier
Cover design by Erin Dameron-Hill, EDH Graphics
Cover art by photographer: Kim Killion/KillionGroup
and guita22/123rf.com and fotoVoyager/GettyImages
Interior design by Toni Kerr

Print ISBN 978-1-68281-515-1
ebook ISBN 978-1-68281-516-8

Manufactured in the United States of America

First Edition February 2021

AMARA

For my golden girls, this one's for you.

CHAPTER ONE

Was it peculiar that she didn't *feel* married?

A forgotten glass of warm champagne in hand, Lady Isobel Vance, the new Marchioness of Roth, peeked up at the towering, silent gentleman beside her as they stood on the balcony. The Marquess of Roth could be a statue carved from marble instead of flesh and bone. Starkly beautiful. Impenetrable. Impossible to read.

Her *husband*.

A thoughtful frown limned his full lips, turning them down at the corners, and his gray eyes held less warmth than shards of flint. Hardly a doting bridegroom. Other than the exchange of vows, he hadn't said more than two words to her since they'd left the chapel. Isobel swallowed past the thickening knot in her throat and the feeling of unease growing in her belly.

Shouldn't a bride feel a modicum of happiness on her wedding day?

Then again, her nuptials to Lord Roth had been rather abrupt. Over the past few months in London with her aunt and uncle, the marquess had treated her with polite courtesy and charming indulgence. He wouldn't have found her disagreeable in looks, she knew. Most men didn't. Her sister, Astrid, had always bemoaned her beauty as a curse, but Isobel well knew that men craved beautiful things. In their world, beauty was coveted, much like pedigree.

And the Marquess of Roth was of exceptional pedigree.

Heir to the Duke of Kendrick, he was well-heeled, handsome, and young. A desirable catch, by all accounts. And he wasn't the lecherous Edmund Cain, Earl of Beaumont, who was twice her age and had been trying to lift her skirts since the moment she'd been old enough to marry, especially after compromising her own sister. Poor Astrid had quit London, only to fend off his return as earl nine years later—and his vile pursuit of Isobel—by wedding the dreaded Duke of Beswick.

Isobel had attempted to take matters into her own hands to secure a husband who *wasn't* the earl, but it had only been with Beswick's help that she'd been able to avoid the earl's trap altogether. Astrid's scarred duke had not only persuaded the Prince Regent to favor Roth's suit, but had also procured a special marriage license.

Gratitude didn't begin to cover what she felt.

She'd escaped Beaumont's clutches and secured an enviable match with a marquess. A man who was both beautiful and heroic. Noble and honorable. The perfect gentleman. Already half-enamored, girlish visions of a blissful future had danced in her head, full of laughter and joy, family and children. They would be rapturously happy.

Despite a few vague rumors of his aversion to matrimony, their wedding had been a boon, and what had caused him to propose hadn't been of interest to her, only that he *had*.

Now, however, Isobel frowned.

Why had he decided to settle down?

Roth didn't need her dowry. As far as she knew, he was in line for a very solvent dukedom. She'd heard the gossip that the marquess had the reputation of a notorious rake, but which young gentleman wasn't a bit of a rogue? Her aunt had always said that reformed rakes made the best husbands.

Isobel didn't know if that was the case with Roth, but she hoped his roué days were over. Her own father had been faithful to her mother, and though Isobel knew that many gentlemen of the *ton* kept mistresses, the idea did not sit well with her. Not that she would have any say in such things. A society lady was meant to do her duty and provide an heir, and even if her husband sought carnal diversions elsewhere, it was of no consequence.

With a face like his, it wasn't hard to picture the dashing marquess being surrounded by fawning, simpering women. She spared him a furtive glance through her lashes and promptly lost her breath. The man made the estimable Beau Brummell look like a shriveled toad. Tall, broad-shouldered, and superbly fit, he was every lady's dream. Hers as well, if her galloping heart had anything to say about it. Even in profile, his sharply edged masculine beauty made her cheeks heat. Sculpted lips, high cheekbones, thick, golden-brown hair curling into a wide brow, and glittering eyes the color of a glacier in a winter storm. His given name was fitting.

Winter.

Because at the moment, he embodied the frigid season.

Suppressing a tiny sigh, Isobel sipped at her warm drink and winced. She'd give anything for a glass of her sister's whiskey. Or some French brandy. Something with a little more bite to bolster her flagging confidence. Or ward off the chill of her iceberg of a husband. Perhaps he had other things on his mind, like matters of business?

She drew a bracing breath, determined to make the best of it.

"Are you well, my lord?" she ventured softly.

Slate-gray eyes fell to hers, confused for an instant as if he didn't know who she was or what she was doing there, as though she were some species of creature he did not recognize. But then they cleared, and recognition filled them. "Yes, of course. And you?"

"I'm well, thank you."

"Good."

Awkward silence spooled between them.

So much for brilliant conversation. Ducking her head, Isobel cringed and gulped the rest of her tasteless drink, her eyes darting to the revelry within the balcony doors. Lady Hammerton's ball was in full swing, and Isobel knew that Astrid would be there. A small comfort, at least.

"I…I suppose we should go in," she suggested.

The marquess gave her an unreadable look, though his mouth pinched with the barest hint of resignation. "Yes, the show must go on, mustn't it?"

She blinked in confusion. "The show, my lord?"

He leaned down to graze his lips over her cheek, the soft caress at odds with his mocking tone and taking her by surprise. Inhaling deeply as though scenting her skin, his nose drifted down the curve of her jaw until his mouth hovered over the corner of hers. Isobel's lips parted of their own trembling accord, in unspoken invitation, which he did not accept.

Kiss me, she wanted to beg.

She didn't. But shyly, she tilted her chin, trying to show him what she yearned for. With a muttered curse, the marquess reared back and stared at her with a strange blend of irritation and desire in those flinty eyes.

Isobel swallowed her disappointment. "Did I do something wrong, my lord?"

It felt like an eternity before that beautiful gray gaze landed on her, the brief hint of desire from earlier no longer present. Not one ounce of warmth came through his impassive regard. It wasn't irritation now, she realized, but forced indifference. *Why would he need to be indifferent?*

"No," he murmured. "This is simply new to both of us."

"Marriage?"

His lip curled. "Until death us do part, love."

The sentiment and endearment should have eased her, but the cynical way he uttered those words did not sound like the commitment and union they were meant to represent, though rather more of a curse. But then, once more as if in contradiction of himself, he lifted her hand and brought her knuckles to his lips. Ever so slowly, he brushed his mouth over her gloved hand, until she could feel her heartbeat throbbing in each fingertip. The gentleness of the caress undid any worry she had.

If he touched her like this, they were going to be just fine.

• • •

Winter sat back against the velvet squabs of his coach and settled in for the ride to his father's ancestral seat in Chelmsford, his family home and the only place he could take a wife.

Bloody hell. Not *a* wife. *His* wife.

God, how his sister would have cackled to see the great Winter Vance leg-shackled.

I shall never marry! His twelve-year-old self had puffed his chest. *Girls are annoying, just like bratty little sisters.*

Prue had paid his male posturing no mind. *Then I shall curse you, my favorite brother, to marry the most beautiful angel in the world!*

And here he was.

Married to exactly that.

Winter forced himself to focus on the task at hand. He couldn't go to his private estate, Rothingham Gable, for obvious reasons. For one, that particular abode was not prepared for a Lady Roth, given the week-long house party that had just been hosted there.

He had not even been in residence. Rutland and Petersham and the rest of their fast set had run the show, desperate for some wild country fun to offset the terminal boredom of the season. While he missed them from time to time, those days of endless dissipation were over. They had been since Prue's death. Not that anyone actually knew...or had noticed. People believed what they wanted to believe.

Winter slanted his new wife a glance. Her attention was caught outside the small window, her face held in pensive thought. Her profile was exquisite, perfect in its symmetry from the classic line of her forehead to her delicate nose and pink rosebud pout. Isobel was young, fresh out of the schoolroom, but he couldn't deny her exceptional beauty…or his irritating and inconvenient attraction to her.

Christ, he wanted to debauch that mouth right there on the balcony—take it from virginal pink to passionate red. The urge had taken him by surprise. The honeysuckle scent of her satiny skin had been an aphrodisiac. When he'd grazed the corner of her mouth and seen her undisguised longing, the bolt of lust tunneling through him had nearly brought him to his knees.

Just like it threatened to do now.

Ripping his gaze from her tempting lips, he let it drift down the elegant line of her throat. He imagined tasting the skin there, nuzzling her fluttering pulse beneath his lips, and inhaling more of her sweet, flowery smell. Winter bit back a groan. He would no doubt sample both later…when he'd be expected to do his marital duty. *Hell*. He'd have to hold himself in check. Make it perfunctory. And most of all, quick. The act was a necessary obligation, nothing more, because he had an inkling that this woman could be the end of him.

"Did you enjoy seeing your sister?" he asked, his voice rough edged. They'd called in at Beswick Park after leaving Lady Hammerton's. Her rousing entertainments had gone well into the dawn hours.

His wife startled, attention flying to him. "Yes, of course, my lord. Thank you for arranging the visit."

"Call me Winter," he said.

She flushed. "Winter."

His wife turned the full force of those ice-blue eyes on him, and for a moment, it felt like his skin had been seared by lightning. But that gaze also shone with no small degree of infatuation. It didn't take much to interpret the shy glances and the soft blushes whenever she thought he wasn't looking.

This was why it could never work.

He wanted sex and a warm body; she wanted sonnets and his soul.

The plain truth was that he'd needed to marry. An expedient wedding was the answer to Winter's problems *and* hers—and he'd jumped at the solution. His father's recent codicil stated if he wasn't married by his twenty-first birthday, he wouldn't get a finger on the rest of his inheritance until he was thirty. That was over a decade away! The social club he'd opened with his best friend, the Duke of Westmore, using the first portion of his inheritance, was in its infancy. Anything could happen.

Which was why marriage was a lesser evil—it paid to be prepared.

And Winter didn't have to court anyone, endure evenings at Almack's, or worry about matchmaking mothers, fortune hunters, and the like. Isobel Everleigh was the perfect choice for a quiet, dutiful bride. He did not intend to be another casualty to fate, love, or beautiful women. He'd seen too much of what marriage and dependence had done to his own mother and his sister to ever want that deadly yoke for himself. Love made people weak and foolish, and drove them to madness or worse.

And Isobel—as perfect a bride as she might be—was no exception.

Reluctant amusement built in his chest. Oh yes. His sister definitely would have laughed herself silly at his predicament that he'd gone and gotten himself wedlocked to a jejune, enraptured debutante with romantic starbursts in her eyes.

She's just what you deserve, Win, she would have teased. *The angel to your devil.*

Right now, his devil wanted to strip the angel bare. Make her writhe and moan. Corrupt her with sin.

"What's your home like?" Isobel asked, interrupting his depraved thoughts, her sweet voice flicking against his senses. He'd much rather hear that soft voice screaming with pleasure, head thrown back and eyes glazed, golden curls tumbling down…

Damnation. Stop.

Winter cleared his tight throat. "Kendrick Abbey is much like Beswick Park, I suppose. Rolling hills, manse, ornamental ponds, a lake, tenants, the usual." He waved an arm, guessing that she might share her sister's penchant for horses. "You can ride to your heart's content."

"I don't care for horses."

A frown creased his brow. "You don't?"

"One threw me when I was a girl," she explained with a pretty blush. "My sister insisted I get back on, but I was much too timid. They frighten me, really. To be honest, mounting such an enormous, powerful animal makes my pulse race."

Winter stared at her, his frown deepening as *his*

pulse kicked up a notch. Was she being facetious? At his look, his wife bit her lip, and his stare swung to that moistened, plump roll of flesh when she released it. Hell if he didn't want to taste it. Winter tore his gaze away and focused on the delicate slope of her nose. Yes, that was a safe bet.

When had it gotten so hot in the carriage? It was bloody sweltering.

He tugged at his collar. "What *do* you enjoy doing, then?"

"I like balls," she replied shyly, and the ones in his pants throbbed in approval even though they had nothing to do with the event in question. "I liked dancing with you at Lady Hammerton's very much."

"Did you?" His voice sounded choked, even to his own ears.

Nodding, Isobel's tongue darted out to wet her lips, and Winter dug his fingers into the bench. Everything she did and said was so artless and yet so deeply erotic he felt it in his bones. *Christ*, he needed to get in control! Oblivious to his deteriorating composure, she warmed to filling the silence with conversation while he descended into silent torture.

"I also enjoy playing the pianoforte, though I'm not very adept, I'm afraid. My sister accuses me of pounding the keys too hard at times."

Oh, bloody hell, there was no way she didn't know what she was doing to him with those provocative words—*mounting, balls, pounding*—but her pretty face remained earnest and sincere, not an ounce of artifice to be seen.

It was just him then, lost in the mire of obscenity. *Control, for the love of God, Roth.*

"Anything else?" he managed politely.

She brightened at his interest. "I enjoy embroidery. It's a wonderful, ladylike pastime. Though I do not enjoy getting pricked."

Winter made a strangled noise. It was no use. He was going to fucking *die*.

• • •

The carriage ride had been an absolute disaster. A complete and utter calamity. Despite Isobel's efforts, once more, to have a mature, adult conversation with her husband, she had failed spectacularly. The marquess had glowered at her as though vacillating between tossing her bodily from the coach, wanting to incinerate her with his eyes, and staring at her as if she were his next meal.

The last had made her uncomfortably hot.

Was this what her wedding night would be like? Hot, uncomfortable, and impossible to predict? While she wasn't in the least experienced, those hungry looks had awakened feelings in her she didn't even know she had—a choked sensation in her breast, overheated skin, blood that felt like thickened honey, and the outrageous need to throw herself across the coach and scale his huge body like a monkey on a tree.

Without a stitch of clothing.

Thank God her thoughts were private, though she was sure that some of them might have been visible on her face, given the tightening of his brow and his restless shifting on the opposite bench. Twice, out of the corner of her eye, she'd seen the heel of his palm grind into his lap, but she hadn't dared to let her eyes drift anywhere below his chin. It simply wasn't proper. At least her behavior was beyond reproach, even if her thoughts weren't.

Because those were *beyond* shameless.

It was a miracle Isobel had been able to keep her composure intact when they finally arrived at Kendrick Abbey.

"Are you well, my lady?" Winter asked after the footman helped her down in the well-kept courtyard. "You seem…flustered."

"The coach was rather warm," she replied, grateful for the bite of the crisp early evening air. "And I'm nervous to meet His Grace."

"Don't be. Kendrick isn't here. He's in Bath. He spends most of his time at his estate there, taking the waters. With any luck, it will just be Oblivious Oliver." At her questioning look, he shrugged. "My brother."

"Oh," she said. Isobel didn't know he had a brother, but there were a lot of things she didn't know about her new husband. She had years to learn, however. Grasping his gloved hand, she smiled up at him. He gave their joined hands a quizzical look but did not pull his away. Isobel took that as a good sign as she surveyed her new home and its occupants.

The servants were all lined up to welcome their new mistress, and she greeted each one of them, from the butler to the housekeeper to the footmen, with sincere warmth.

She would get to know each of them more later.

For now, Isobel followed her husband up to their suite of rooms, taking in as much as she could of the abbey's impressive interior, from its vaulted ceilings to its meticulously polished furnishings. Isobel was no stranger to fortune, but this took her appreciation of wealth to a new level. Her husband's chambers, though not the master, had a sumptuously decorated interconnecting bedroom. The decor was just as lavish as the rest of the house.

"Are you hungry?" Winter said. "I've asked Mrs. Butterfield to send up a tray for an early supper. I've also rung for a lady's maid to prepare you a bath." He paused at the threshold, his gaze unfathomable. "In the meantime, I must find my brother and take him to task for not being there to receive us properly. I'll return shortly."

Isobel gave him a soft smile, grateful for his thoughtfulness and equally glad he did not insist she accompany him. She was a bundle of nerves as it was, knowing their wedding night was forthcoming. A bath and a meal would help.

Hours later, she'd finished both, and despite eating the delicious fare alone—Winter had yet to return—Isobel couldn't relax. It was her first time in a strange place and finding herself eased was impossible. After changing into her night rail, she'd climbed into the huge bed. Would Winter prefer her under the blankets? Above them? In bed at all? In an attempt to distract herself, she tried to read from a book she'd packed in her things but couldn't concentrate. Her nerves were much too frayed.

Where was her husband? Would he come to her?

Stretching restlessly, she inched out of the bed and went to the window, where the full moon cast its silvery light over the gardens visible from her room. She and Astrid used to pretend to be fairies dancing under the moon when they were little girls. Like then, she had the urge to run outside barefooted, feel the grass beneath her toes, and spin around in circles until she collapsed with dizziness. The whimsical recollection made her smile.

The skin on her nape prickled and she whirled around, throttling a scream in her throat.

The Marquess of Roth stood at the connecting door, watching her.

Isobel blushed, realizing that the moonlight through the windowpanes rendered her filmy night clothes nearly invisible. She crossed her arms over herself, only to be stalled by Winter's rasped, "Don't."

Obediently, Isobel dropped her arms. Her nerves returned in full force when he approached, only stopping when he was an arm's length away, dark, tall, and foreboding. The moonlight caught his face, too, casting his angular features in silver shadows. He was dressed only in shirtsleeves, she realized breathlessly, and her eyes traced the strong neck disappearing into the opened collar. His shirt was untucked from his trousers, his feet scandalously bare.

"I was waiting," she murmured when he didn't say anything.

"I trust everything was to your satisfaction?"

Isobel nodded, suddenly shy. "It was. Thank you, my lord."

"Winter."

She bit her lip, unable to say his given name in so intimate a setting. He stared at her for what seemed like forever before closing the gap between them, and she gasped when his hands closed over her waist. One large palm slipped down to caress her hip. Sensations flooded her untried body, pebbling her nipples beneath the lacy night rail. She clenched her jaw hard. It was that, or give way to the vulgar moans clambering up her throat.

"Do you know what to expect?" he asked. "Did your sister or mother advise you of the wedding night?"

"Yes, my aunt explained," Isobel whispered. She would not admit the guidance she'd received from her Aunt Mildred was thin at best, though she had a general idea of the act and what it entailed. He would undress her. Impale her. Fill her with his seed. Even in her head, the process sounded awful. She swallowed hard, her muscles locking.

"Don't be afraid," he told her.

With that, he untied the ribbons at her throat and wrists, and the flimsy garment pooled to the floor. Isobel held her breath, fighting her blush, as he took her nude body in, his face hard as if hewn from granite. A muscle jumped in that rigid jaw.

"This first time might hurt," he said. "But I will try to make it as painless as possible."

In a show of effortless strength, the marquess scooped her up and carried her to the bed, and she scrambled backward before he shucked off his own clothing and climbed on top of her. There wasn't enough room to get a good view of anything, but good gracious, she could feel the hot brand of him on her thigh. Instead of making her frightened, it made her ache.

Was her breathing supposed to be this shallow? Her heartbeat so fast? The sharpness of all the combined feelings was making her light-headed. Her muscles tightened again, though this time it wasn't because of dread but excitement. Isobel had no time to process any of it before he bent toward her, his parted lips settling on her neck. Nerves forgotten, her skin burned at the erotic contact as his tongue swept over her flesh.

The slow sensual lick was vastly different to the chaste, perfunctory peck he'd given her in the chapel, or the almost-kiss on the balcony, but she wasn't complaining. He bit her earlobe, sucking it into his mouth, and her entire body shuddered. Good Lord, this wasn't even kissing, it was…it was…*devouring*. The idea of his mouth trailing down her body in a similar fashion nearly made her eyes roll back in her head.

Would he?

As if she'd demanded it, he continued his journey south of her jaw until Isobel moaned, her hands climbing up to wind in her husband's hair as she succumbed to his skill. Heavens above, she'd never felt more alive, more on *edge*. Every muscle in her body strained and shook as he reached the valley between her breasts, his lips wet and warm. She felt faint from the pleasure coiling in her stomach, her brain a muddled mess. Could a person die from such sensation? Surely it was possible.

One more lick, one more dangerously sinful bite, and she'd be done for.

A whimper broke from her. "Winter."

Cool air blew against the damp skin of her body when he broke away, a stormy gaze boring into hers. Was he going to stop? Pull away? He wouldn't be so cruel, would he? He'd *told* her to use his given name!

But with a fraught growl, his mouth descended to

where he'd left off and kissed its way down her body, lingering over each of her breasts until she was certain she'd go mad. By the time he lifted himself above her, she no longer had a rational thought in her head. She was a blinding mass of need and raw desire. When his body finally slid into hers, it pinched, but his careful preparation had soothed the way.

"Hold still," he rasped, his voice hoarse with strain as his breath sawed out of him. "Get used to me."

It wasn't his words as much as his thoughtfulness that melted her. Once she'd adjusted to accommodate him, Isobel sucked in air as he began to move, withdrawing almost all the way before easing back in.

"Is this too much?" he asked.

"No, you're perfect."

Winter stilled, but she didn't have time to feel embarrassed by the blurted admission before he repeated the motion, making her gasp. With each pass, it felt better. Sensation upon sensation built inside her with every stroke until he reached between them to caress a spot that made her see stars and she cried out as pleasure took her.

A few short thrusts later, and Winter groaned what sounded like her name, though she couldn't be sure, his huge frame withdrawing completely from her and then going rigid with what she imagined was the culmination of his own release. Breathing hard, he slumped forward, his large body blanketing hers. It was strangely nice, though the moment did not last.

Her husband lifted off of her. For an unguarded moment his eyes met hers, a flare of shock evident before he rolled away. Isobel did not feel slighted when he stood and reached for his trousers. She could only remember the tenderness of his touch, and the kindness he'd displayed with her inexperienced body. Her husband *had* to care to be so gentle and considerate.

Isobel draped herself in the warmth of everything she felt and smiled to herself.

One day, perhaps soon, she would tell him she loved him.

CHAPTER TWO

Oh how she hated that bloody, black-hearted jacka-napes!

The brisk morning wind teased the pins from Isobel's hair, blond tendrils lashing into her face as she galloped at a breakneck pace across the moors. She was in a fine froth, and she pushed her mare Hellion to go even faster. Faintly, Isobel heard a voice calling out from somewhere behind her, but she couldn't turn back now. Nothing but a grueling ride would cool the heat in her veins.

According to the newssheets she'd read that morning, her husband was up to his disreputable exploits in London again, while she, the poor, pathetic—and any number of other uncharitable descriptors—country mouse of a wife remained at home in pious, devoted silence.

Devoted, my furious foot.

Her maggot of a marquess had abandoned her here.

After their wedding, Isobel had assumed she and Winter would live together in Chelmsford. It was his father's ducal seat, after all, and his family home. Old bitterness, buried down deep, spilled through her. How foolish and utterly naive she'd been! Her *caring* new husband had bedded her and then left her.

That. Same. Night.

She'd gathered—albeit after a lot of weeping and the shattering of her rose-tinted spectacles—that her husband might not have held as grand an affection for her as she'd had for him. That what had seemed so special to her had not meant a thing to him at all, because right after he'd done his duty, he'd absconded like a thief in the dark.

Isobel snarled out an oath as her mare's hooves pounded the dirt, putting much needed distance between them and those dratted newssheets at the manor. It was a beautiful day with not a cloud in the sky, but Isobel hardly took notice, so intent she was on outrunning her fury.

In the beginning, she had thought Winter's absence would be for a day or two. She had waited like a besotted fool for weeks before Mrs. Butterfield had taken pity on her and explained that the marquess was very busy with his business in London and very rarely came to Kendrick Abbey. And if he did come to the country, he had his own estate in Chelmsford—Rothingham Gable.

Even then, she'd been so sickeningly naive, wondering why a husband would choose to leave his new wife at his father's ducal residence instead of his.

Perhaps he was performing restorations.

Perhaps he wanted to surprise her.

Perhaps, perhaps, perhaps.

She'd learned the unpleasant answer a few months later from a loose-lipped maid—her heroic, honorable, noble husband was apparently renowned for hosting wild house parties at Rothingham Gable. Bacchanalian revels, the maid had confided with suffocated giggles.

Of course, that had all been long before he'd been married, the maid had hastily assured her.

Of course, a heartsick Isobel had echoed.

Now, three years and five months later, with the barest minimum of correspondence from the marquess, she learned more about her vagabond husband from the London gossip rags than from the man himself. Isobel had had enough. This time, he'd purportedly engaged in a dawn duel. Over an opera singer of all things.

She scowled as she slowed and dismounted, letting Hellion cool off and graze.

How dare he disrespect her so?

As the Marchioness of Roth, she'd held her head high and pretended her callous husband wasn't such an empirical ass. She'd been patient. Honored her vows. Respected his wishes. Brushed off his antics as youthful folly. Buried the hurt that his coldhearted desertion had caused. Told herself that eventually, like all highborn gentlemen, Winter would come to his senses and require an heir. Then she would have a family, even if her rakehell of a husband did not want to be involved.

Someday.

Someday had never come. Swallowing her bitterness, Isobel paced back and forth, the rich smell of grass and earth doing little to calm her down. Even the cheery sound of laughter from the children of the tenant farmers down the hill didn't make her smile.

As year after year passed, she convinced herself that she wasn't bloody miserable each month she spent cooped up like some forgotten mare put out to pasture, with only her pianoforte and her useless accomplishments to keep her company. Isobel remembered with acute shame what she'd primly told her sister years ago: *a young lady should be accomplished in the feminine arts. Music, and dancing, and whatnot.*

Well, she was eating a large serving of crow and *whatnot* at the moment. No one had ever explained to her younger and vociferously green self what *whatnot* had meant. If it meant dealing with a husband who had dumped his wife in Chelmsford while he gallivanted in London and pretended he was an eternal bachelor, then she'd be an expert in the matter.

"He'll grow out of it, dear," Mrs. Butterfield had told her. "All men sow their wild oats."

So she'd let him sow. Acres and acres of it. But this was outside of enough.

A bloody duel. Over someone who *wasn't* his wife.

Isobel clenched her fists together, staring mindlessly over the tops of the tenant cottages to the spire of the village church in the distance. Clarissa, her dearest friend and lady's companion, had suggested that some of the accounts of gambling and indecent revelry might be false—salacious stories sold newspapers, after all. But even *some* stories had to have a modicum of truth to them. Isobel thought she'd become desensitized to her husband's antics, but clearly not.

Rage and hurt bubbled up into her throat.

"Damnation, woman!" Clarissa wheezed as she reined her horse to a lathered stop where Isobel stood at the edge of the rise overlooking the lake. "I never should have taught you to ride."

Her sweaty best friend dismounted, her dark mess of curls sticking out in every direction, and her green eyes knowing, full of sympathetic anger. Isobel's own eyes were dry as she greeted her. She'd shed enough tears for that pigeon-livered rogue of a husband. He did not deserve another drop from her, not a single one.

"I take it you read the newssheets," Isobel said. No need to beat around the bush. There was only one reason that her friend would follow her mad dash from the house.

Clarissa nodded and remained silent. After three years of shared confidences, particularly about the subject of the Maggot of Roth, she well knew when to let Isobel vent. She had enough opinions of her own about Isobel's scoundrel of a husband, but at times like this, she was the more level-headed of the two of them.

"They exaggerate everything," Clarissa said in a soothing voice. "You know this. Those abominable liars write what they want to write."

"Then why wouldn't Roth dispute them, if that were the case?"

"Perhaps he thinks them amusing? Men don't worry about those sorts of things."

"Those sorts of things," Isobel repeated. "He fought a *duel*, Clarissa. Over Contessa James of all people."

Clarissa pulled a face. "Maybe he's acting out," she suggested mildly.

"He's a grown man. How much acting out does he need to do?"

"Men mature differently than women," her friend replied with the patience deserving of a saint instead of her usual speak-first-think-later temperament.

"And he's never recovered from his sister's and mother's deaths—you also know that as well as I do. Everyone knows that it left him in a terrible state. It's the reason he and the duke don't get along."

"Grief shouldn't make a man an absolute steaming arse-rag."

Clarissa's eyes sparked with reluctant approval, her mouth twitching at the inventive slur. "Shouldn't have taught you to swear, either."

"You shouldn't have taught me a lot of things."

Clarissa was the daughter of the Duke of Kendrick's private solicitor, Mr. Bell, and the youngest of six, the other five all boys. From the moment she and Isobel had been introduced nearly three and a half years ago, they'd been inseparable, and everything Clarissa learned from her rambunctious brothers, she'd taught to Isobel.

And that meant *everything*.

Isobel had been so sheltered that when the incorrigible, boisterous, and entirely too bold girl had asked her with a saucy grin if she was *up the pole yet*, her eyes had gone wide and her mouth had gaped. "It only takes one time, you know," her new friend had said knowingly. "To get with child."

"No," a scandalized Isobel had stammered. "I don't think so."

"What were his kisses like?" A curious stare had followed. "Did you stick your tongue in his mouth?"

"No!"

"Then you're doing it wrong."

Isobel had stopped blushing after the first life lesson—one involving how babies were made. That had been eye-opening, to say the least. Not that she hadn't had a thoroughly erotic introduction to marital relations with her own clodpole of a husband, a union which had not borne any fruit of the newborn variety. By design, she'd learned since, as the marquess had withdrawn and spilled in the sheets. Perhaps, that, too, had been a blessing in disguise.

Though deep down, Isobel did not deny wishing for children of her own and a family to care for one day, blessing in disguise or not.

Thank God for Clarissa, the only light in what had promised to be a lonely and dismal existence. From then on, her self-ordained best friend had encouraged her to ask her anything, as in *anything*. And since it was much too shameful to voice certain inquiries out loud, Isobel chose to pen secret letters to which Clarissa provided answers in lewd, graphic, and gleeful detail.

After the first letter asking about what it was like to truly kiss a man, the impish Clarissa had replied with a scandalous masterpiece dedicated solely to the vagaries of kissing, including tongues, spit, and fish-faced puckers that had made the two girls dissolve into irreverent giggles.

Eventually, what had started out as naughty but instructive letters between friends had turned into a surprising windfall. Isobel's sister Astrid, an authoress herself, had taken one look at the stack of scandalously frank correspondence, burst into laughter, and sent them off to her publishing man of affairs. While Astrid mostly published essays about women's rights with the steadfast support of her own husband, her visionary publisher had seen opportunity with the *Dearest Friend* letters. That had been the start of *The*

Daring Lady Darcy.

All anonymous, of course.

Said publisher didn't want to go to prison.

Lady Darcy's instant success had taken them all by surprise. As it turned out, wicked advice to ladies of quality had been a shocking novelty, and the modest publication had risen to instant notoriety. From recipes to fashion to needlepoint, to physical and emotional intimacy, to scandalous erotic advice, there was no stone left unturned, no subject left untouched. The frank periodicals flouted decency, but readers were greedy for more.

"I should write Lady Darcy a letter on disemboweling unsuspecting husbands," Isobel said, then with a grin, she added, "And hiding a body without getting caught."

Clarissa cackled, eyes sparking with glee. "I'd have to do some research, but why not? I bet our readers would love that. What do you think of 'A Lady's Guide to Mariticide'?"

Isobel laughed with her friend, the hottest part of her anger draining away. She could always count on Clarissa to make her smile.

Thundering hooves interrupted their amusement.

"Your ladyship!" A panting groom rode out to meet them.

Isobel schooled her features into calm. "What is it, Randolph?"

"His Grace is in residence!"

Oh, good Lord, she had completely forgotten her father-in-law's arrival!

Strangely, Isobel had developed a fondness for the duke over the years. Having lost her own parents in a terrible carriage accident, she had gravitated to the stoic man. Besides her sister, who had her own life, Kendrick was the only family she had. Eventually, they had bonded over a shared love of music as well as their common bedsore of a connection—his estranged son and her equally estranged spouse.

Isobel stepped over to where Hellion was grazing. She glowered at Clarissa. "You could have reminded me," she accused without much heat.

"How could I when I forgot as well?"

"Some friend you are. Come on."

Clarissa shook her head. "Not a chance. You enjoy the Duke of Derision by yourself. He positively loathes me. Besides, I need to cool my horse and my sore behind after chasing your shadow for the last half an hour."

"He doesn't loathe you."

Clarissa's eyebrows shot upward. "He called me a witless pest, Izzy." Her eyes widened as she clutched at her chest with dramatic flair. "*Witless*. Me? Doesn't everyone know that I am the undeclared Goddess of Eternal Wit? For shame!"

Isobel snorted. "That's a mouthful."

"Well, you know what they say about more than a mouthful."

"No, Clarissa," Isobel said, her lips twitching, "what *do* they say?"

She tapped her lips with a finger. "Something I might need to consider for our next batch of letters. Speaking of, I should get started. 'More than a Mouthful' is a memorable title, don't you think? Or perhaps, 'Ladies Gobbling Bananas.'"

"*Clarissa*!" Heat flooded Isobel's cheeks. Sometimes her best friend was too much.

"What? It's a natural part of life, or so my brothers declare in secret. All men enjoy it, I bet." She wrinkled her nose. "Even the duke. Perhaps we should send him a copy and see if we can get him to crack a smile?"

"You wouldn't!"

Isobel pinned her lips between her teeth. If the duke had any inkling of her secret life as Lady Darcy, he would implode. As much as he cared for her, Lady Darcy's intrigues weren't the *done thing* for a lady of quality. The duke was a fastidious man who was a stickler for decorum.

That said, most people didn't appreciate her father-in-law. Underneath all that aloof, brooding reserve, he had a heart that beat fiercely for his sons, even though his firstborn seemed to be convinced the duke was the devil. From what Isobel could garner from the tight-lipped upper servants, they'd been on the outs since Winter was a boy…a divide that had only worsened in recent years.

Isobel sighed and mounted her horse. She wasn't sure she was up for company, but she turned Hellion around, stroking the mare gently. Hellion was the foal of her sister's prized thoroughbreds, Brutus and Temperance, and had been a belated wedding present from the Duke and Duchess of Beswick. At first, Isobel had been terrified of the horse, but the truth was she'd been so lonely that she'd learned to ride out of sheer necessity.

At least the mare had stuck around.

Because Hellion was *loyal*, unlike a certain fickle, spineless marquess.

Arriving at the stables in short order, she slid from the horse with a soothing word and a caress, and threw the reins to a waiting groom, before dashing toward the kitchens. With luck, she would have a few minutes to freshen up and change before greeting the duke.

"Goodness, watch out!" a voice exclaimed as she barreled to the stairs.

Isobel slowed, narrowly missing a collision with one of the Fairfax twins. Violet and Molly had shown up six months ago with a note from their late father's solicitor citing the duke as their guardian. Kendrick had read it without blinking and told Mrs. Butterfield to take care of it. He'd ignored his wards ever since, though he hadn't batted an eyelash at allowing them to stay. At two-and-twenty, they were only two years older than her, and Isobel suspected he might have done it for her sake. Outside of Clarissa, female company was in short supply.

"Sorry!" Isobel caught her breath before climbing the stairs at a more sedate pace. "I forgot the duke was back today and with everything this morning, I'm a mess."

Violet pulled a face, lifting the hem of her black bombazine mourning dress to follow Isobel. Molly, never a far step away, appeared beside them. "He doesn't look happy. He never looks happy. Maybe he saw those awful scandal sheets, too."

A fist clenched around Isobel's heart, mortification rushing through her. She couldn't deal with anymore pity, not even from the one person who could possibly understand. She and the duke had shared a lot over the years, but this was painful new territory.

"Honestly, you can't believe a word of it, Izzy dear," Violet said when they reached the landing. "The papers reported that I was an unremarkable, plain spinster, after two unsuccessful seasons, while Molly here was the rose of the hour, when we look *exactly* the same. How am I not a rose as well? No, no, I'm some anonymous, hideous weed." She exhaled a peeved breath. "My name is *Violet*, for heaven's sake. *I'm* the flower."

Molly rolled her eyes and gave a shrug that made her brown ringlets bounce. "Everything isn't a competition, Violet. But maybe if you were less thorny and more flowery, that would help your prospects."

"I am not thorny, you beast!"

Despite being identical, the twins couldn't be more like chalk and cheese, always at odds with each other. It usually made for good fun, but right now, Isobel had other things to worry about. "For the love of all things holy, stop bickering you two and help me change!"

After a quick sponge and spray of honeysuckle-scented water, it didn't take her, the twins, and two maids long to switch out of her riding habit to a pale green muslin morning dress. Her hair brushed and re-braided, Isobel made her way down the stairs to the duke's study.

With a calming breath, she knocked and entered.

In terms of coloring, the duke looked nothing like his eldest son. His hair leaned toward black instead of brown, and his eyes were blue instead of gray. However, the family resemblance was stamped in his high forehead and that proud nose. Not that she'd seen enough of her husband of late to compare otherwise. For all she knew, Winter Vance had put on ten stone and developed a set of jowls better suited to his excessive lifestyle.

"Your Grace, you've returned earlier than expected." She greeted him from the open doorway, watching as the tall, elegant man rose to his feet from behind the desk.

"We had good weather and made excellent time." The Duke of Kendrick frowned, a concerned expression on his face. "How are you faring, my dear?"

It was only then that Isobel saw the rolled-up newssheets on the desk, and all of her brave composure unraveled.

"I could shoot him in his rotten legs," Isobel muttered, bursting into tears. She'd sworn no more, but her body shook with the effort to contain them.

"Get in line," the duke said, offering his handkerchief. "Though I suspect you'd have much better aim than me."

Isobel dabbed at her eyes with a laugh. He'd been the one to teach her to shoot and bought her a pair of pocket pistols for her last birthday. She composed herself and took a seat, pouring a cup from the nearby tea tray instead of the bottle of brandy she wanted.

Kendrick eyed her. "You need to go to London."

"I cannot go to London."

"He refuses to see me," he pointed out. "He won't refuse his wife."

Isobel sighed. "We've had this discussion, Your Grace. I won't go and be publicly cast aside. We both know that Roth is more than capable of doing that. I won't set myself up for such a public rejection."

The duke flinched. A year ago, the wretched marquess had cut his own father—*a duke, no less*—dead at a ball. It hadn't done anything except pour salt in an old, raw wound between the two men, and the rumor mill had put it down to family intrigues that weren't as rabidly exciting as Lord Roth's other deliciously devilish escapades. Like his races in Hyde Park, bare-knuckle boxing, outrageous gambling, and illegal duels over opera singers.

"You must."

A slight frown drew her brows together. "Why do you want me to go so badly? I've been content here in Chelmsford."

She cringed at the lie. *Content* was a ludicrous stretch of the truth. If she didn't have Clarissa, and more recently, the twins, she would have gone mad ages ago. But Isobel had long convinced herself that her situation was better than many other *ton* marriages that ended in disaster. She couldn't hate her husband if she didn't actually see him, could she?

She silenced the voice screaming an emphatic *yes!* and turned back to her father-in-law.

"I would like to hold my grandchild before I die," the duke said.

Isobel's brows rose at the turn in conversation and tried to hide the instant ache his words brought on. "You do realize that your son needs to participate for that to happen." After years of fruitless waiting for her marauding husband to come to his senses, she'd long squashed that yearning, but it rose to torment her all the same whenever the duke mentioned grandchildren. "And you're not going to die."

"I will someday," he said. "My son is far from

happy. And I believe his happiness starts with you."

She felt a twinge at the sadness in his voice. "He doesn't even *know* me."

"Not yet," the duke said. "But *I* do, and you are perfect for him. He needs a woman like you. Someone with a backbone who won't take his shit."

Isobel gasped. Kendrick *never* swore. Perhaps he was as fed up with his son's antics as she was. She sipped her rapidly cooling tea and contemplated the stern-faced man sitting across from her. "And you think that's me?"

The duke studied her for a long moment. "What is it you want most out of life, Isobel?"

The question was one she'd put to herself many a lonely night abed. Isobel considered the answer. She wanted an enthusiastic, dutiful husband, and someday, a loving family like her sister and the Duke of Beswick had. She wanted companionship and friendship in a partner. She wanted a bit of adventure, passion, and maybe the chance to experience something new. And all of those things were out of her reach.

They would continue to be so long as she stayed in Chelmsford. Isobel fisted her hands in her skirts. Confronting Winter in town was daunting, but she knew she had to make some sort of stand. She deserved to be presented to society, not hidden away like some mistake. A part of her wanted to shake her odious husband until his teeth rattled, and then show him just what he'd been missing all these years. Flaunt her presence in his face.

Raise the daring Lady Darcy in the flesh.

Make him grovel. Make him sorry. Make him *beg*.

The thought made a dark thrill course through her veins. How often had she fumed to Clarissa about getting even? About pulling her husband up to scratch? This was her chance, and now, she even had Kendrick's blessing.

Isobel's hard gaze met her father-in-law's. "Very well, I'll do it. I'll go."

Because damned if she wasn't going to make him regret making a fool of her for so long.

CHAPTER THREE

It's better to regret something you've actually had the guts to do, Dearest Friend, than to regret not doing anything at all.
– Lady Darcy

Winter regarded the tempestuous beauty currently ensconced in his private chambers and sighed. It would be the third one his man of affairs, Matteo, had discovered this month. More than a dozen in the last six. Aline Montburn, the leading actress of the Covent Garden theater, was all sable curls and legs that went on forever. But for the same three reasons he hadn't been able to look at anyone else in over three years, Winter shook his head and departed the room.

She wasn't blond.

Her eyes weren't the color of the ocean touched by the sun in December.

And she wasn't his wife.

Following his marriage, his false reputation as a rake had prevailed. Given that he was an owner of The Silver Scythe—his wildly popular social club, though some would say it was more exclusive in its offerings than any other gentlemen's club in London—he'd had to uphold a certain public image for the sake of his devoted patrons.

Even if it was a lie.

His reputation as a rogue was a definite draw for membership, and he perpetuated the pretense for one reason only—to make money. He didn't want to touch a penny of his father's fortune, not if he could help it, not for this. His plans had nothing to do with the duke; they were for Prue.

Most of his old set, including Prinny and the Duke of Rutland, had expected him to be the same upon his return to London after his sudden nuptials—generous with his coin and always up to show his friends a good time. And he had been, but he'd never touched another woman.

He hadn't wanted to.

After barely a quarter of an hour with his sweetly responsive wife, every cell in his body had suddenly become partial to ice-blue eyes, creamy skin, and hair the color of sun-kissed wheat. And when she'd turned those shining eyes on him, he'd felt like he was the sun that rose in the morning and set at night.

No woman had ever looked at him as she had.

Like he was worth so much *more*. The way she'd lain beneath him, her gaze so trusting and ardent, and then, her words—*you're perfect*—had blindsided him. Shaken him to the core. God, she had been so sweet and giving in his arms, staring at him with such *hope*, he'd felt it to his bones.

The weight of her faith in him had been too great. Despite the primal and unexpectedly ferocious attraction to his wife, Winter understood that he had to end it before it began. Before he started to believe in the possibility of impossible things. Before she expected things from him that he was unable to give.

With a twinge of regret, Winter shook his head. It had to be done. His marriage to her had to remain one of impartiality.

No affections. No fondness. No *weakness*.

"The lady has departed, my lord," a musical baritone said from behind him.

Winter turned and looked over his shoulder as he tore off his coat and unwound his cravat. "No luck in convincing her to stay, Matteo?"

"Miss Montburn desired the main attraction, not the understudy, even if I am much better looking." He smirked. "Her loss."

"Indeed." Winter grinned at his friend. With his dark good looks, athletic build, and charismatic personality, most women who came to the residence didn't mind when Matteo turned on the charm. "Did you tell her you have more money than the king and your phallus is revered on three continents?"

A dark brow arched in amusement. "There are more important things than money, Roth." He left the second declaration uncontested with a wink.

Winter chuckled as Matteo retreated from the room. The man had his quirks, but Winter appreciated his dry humor, his deep intelligence, and his utter genius with numbers. They'd met during Winter's grand tour in Italy and got on so well that Winter ended up offering him a position as his man of business with an enormous salary just to get him to leave his beloved Venice.

He'd accepted both the position and Winter's friendship, and hadn't looked back. Over the years, he'd invested in several of Winter's projects and oversaw most of them. Matteo seemed to have the Midas touch, but to Winter's surprise, he gave most of his earnings away, claiming that he had no need for all of it. Even his villa in Venice had become a lodging house for people in need.

Winter had once asked him why.

Matteo had shrugged. "My mother was from a modest family. My grandparents threw her out with nothing when she was with child and she lived in poverty, making choices that no woman should have to make. It's no hardship for me to help when I have more than enough. Everyone needs a hand sometime."

That had given Winter the seeds for his own idea, for a fund in Prue's memory.

It had exceeded his every expectation.

Striding down the staircase, Winter met the butler's irritated stare. Ludlow didn't bother to hide his feelings that Winter's place was at his wife's side. But Winter had known him since he was a boy, and though he wouldn't tolerate outright insolence, he had a soft spot for the man who had smuggled him biscuits as a child when he'd been naughty, which had been often.

"Any correspondence, Ludlow?"

"The latest copy of *The Daring Lady Darcy* was delivered, my lord, along with the newssheets."

Winter perked up. He had no idea who the irreverent author was, along with the rest of the nobility—the wagers at all the clubs had grown intense—but those ingenious little periodicals drove business to The Silver Scythe's private rooms in twittering droves. Gentlemen, ladies, couples…all wanting to try Lady Darcy's scandalous advice. He grinned. If he ever met the author, he'd shake their hand and offer them a bottle of his finest whiskey.

Lady Darcy, the heroine in the letters, was both

delicious and depraved, and her written explorations titillated the *ton* to no end. With the lilting prose of a Jane Austen novel, the debauched content was more along the lines of John Cleland's *Fanny Hill*, a favorite of Winter's own collection of expurgated literary works. The author of *The Daring Lady Darcy* was anonymous, and rightly so. No sane gentleman courted a prison sentence for obscenity, and some of the scenes flirted in the realm of the offensive.

"Also," Ludlow went on, "Lord Oliver did call in earlier."

Winter groaned, his good humor waning. "Wonderful. What did my dear stick-in-the-moors brother want?"

The man was a gnat, always buzzing around, complaining about Winter's lifestyle and grumbling that their family's sterling reputation was being smeared. True, Winter wished he could walk away from his ducal birthright and stick it to his father, but he couldn't deny that his family name and wealth had opened many doors.

One of which was being able to use the first portion of the inheritance he'd received at eighteen to invest in The Silver Scythe. *That* venture had almost given the old man apoplexy, but Winter had earned money hand over fist, nearly quadrupling his investment in the social club during its third year. The profits gained in the last year had been staggering.

From a scandalously young age, Winter had devoted himself to a life in the pursuit of pleasure. He'd dropped out of Oxford, flaunted his name and wealth, and generally made a spectacle of himself whenever he could. He'd earned his disreputable reputation within the *ton*, and worked tirelessly to keep it.

Until Prue's death changed everything.

After that, admittedly, he'd struggled. For months he went through the motions, but the things that used to bring him pleasure only made him feel hollow. Days of debauchery no longer held any appeal, and wasting his life, even if to spit in his sanctimonious father's face, seemed like an insult to the memory of his sister. He went back to university and got his act together. Made a plan with Westmore to buy The Silver Scythe. Got married as insurance.

Winter still owned the outrageously successful club, but *he* wasn't the same.

"Lord Oliver said that he would return tomorrow," Ludlow said, and cleared his throat as Winter turned to leave. "I've also heard word from the servant grapevine that His Grace's residence at Vance House is being readied for the duke's arrival in town."

Winter froze mid-step. "My father is coming to London?"

"For the season. That is what I've heard, my lord."

"And what of my…er, Lady Roth?"

The butler's lips flattened imperceptibly. "Lady Roth is currently at Kendrick Abbey, my lord. Mrs. Butterfield writes that she is in excellent health, spends time with Miss Clarissa and the Fairfax twins, and visits with Her Grace, Lady Beswick, once a month. It is fortunate that they live only a short ride away. However, the duchess will soon enter her confinement with her second child, as you know."

Of course he knew. Beswick couldn't stop talking about his three-year-old daughter, Philippa, and he was over the moon that his wife was pregnant again.

Winter didn't begrudge the man his joy, but his notion of happiness differed greatly from the settled duke. An evening of happiness for Beswick included childish romps and bedtime stories, whereas for Winter, it involved financial accounting, gambling, a spot of whiskey, and the occasional pining for a future he would never have.

"Tell Matteo to send my congratulations to Beswick." He paused. "And purchase an extravagantly romantic bouquet of flowers for his duchess. Don't send a note. It will drive the duke crazy."

Winter smirked. The Duke of Beswick was possessive to a fault, and while his duchess had no eyes for any other, Winter loved aggravating his friend. The man wasn't called the Beast of Beswick for nothing.

Ludlow nodded. "And *your* wife, my lord?"

Winter balked at the question. He had no idea what kind of flowers Isobel liked. Or if she even liked flowers. What in the hell was Ludlow asking? He turned to face the butler, not fooled by his obsequious expression. "My wife what?"

"Any correspondence or extravagantly romantic bouquets for her?"

He detected a lilt of sarcasm in the butler's tone, but chose to ignore it. Winter hadn't written to Isobel in years. He blinked. Not ever, actually. He was certain Matteo sent gifts and messages for birthdays and special occasions, though.

Winter glared at the butler for making him feel guilty. "No. Call for my horse. I'm going out."

"You just returned home, my lord."

"Are you my keeper now?"

Ludlow's mouth had gone so thin, it was nearly

invisible. "*Someone* has to be."

"Now, see here—" Winter had had just about enough. He turned to give the man the blistering he deserved and stiffened as the front door to his house crashed unceremoniously open, letting in a burst of cool, fragrant wind.

A cloaked vision stood there as the enticing waft of flowers slammed into Winter. He couldn't see beyond the heavily-brimmed bonnet, and for a moment, he thought the actress, Aline, had changed her mind about a frolic in the sheets with Matteo.

But Aline was petite. This new arrival was not.

Ludlow rushed toward the door in greeting, and froze as the woman chuckled and said something to him in a low, sultry voice. He couldn't quite see the butler's face. He also couldn't catch the lady's tones to recognize its owner, but they were decidedly refined. Most of his callers were from the demimonde, but the occasional aristocratic lady still found her way to 15 Audley Street looking for trouble and a tumble.

He caught his breath as Ludlow took her cloak, and her bonnet was removed in slow motion. A skein of silken, wheat-colored hair shook loose and a heart-shaped face came into view with glowing pinkened cheeks. Full, luscious lips parted, and he exhaled as a pair of unforgettable frosted-ocean eyes met his.

Recognition and lust hit him like a runaway carriage.

Because the stunning, surprising, and gracefully elegant vision standing in his foyer was none other than his lady wife—the Marchioness of Roth.

What the bloody devil was *she* doing here?

Winter stood stock still in utter disbelief as liquid

heat unraveled in his groin, bursting through his veins like the fireworks over Vauxhall. He blinked, but the vision did not dissipate. Time had only fulfilled its promise with her youthful beauty, and the svelte changeling who now stood in his bride's stead was a radiant goddess.

"Husband," she said in a low greeting that went straight to his cock.

"What are you doing here?" he choked out.

A blond brow arched. "This is your home, is it not? And by extension, mine as well?"

"No."

The corners of those kissable lips drifted upward at his curt denial. "Whyever not? Surely you haven't forgotten you have a wife? Despite not having seen you in years, I hadn't expected you to be in your dotage at so young an age, my lord."

His jaw slackened. Winter was at a loss. He simply could not reconcile the confident virago who stood on his threshold with the demure, shy mouse he'd left behind three years ago. That girl had been unable to look at him without blushing. Without complete adoration glowing in her gaze. This *woman* looked like she could tear him apart with her eyes alone, chew him up and spit him out…spent, trembling, and gratifyingly wrecked.

To his utter dismay, the crotch of his trousers crowded to the point of pain, arousal shunting through him like a flood.

In three years, his attraction to her hadn't abated in the least.

No, it had grown like a furtive beast, feeding on the scraps of his memory. The fragrant scent of her, the slick velvet feel of her. The moans she made as she came apart, her body convulsing around his, and his given name a benediction upon her lips. He'd hoarded the precious fragments like a beggar hoarding coin.

Fuck, fuck, *fuck*.

"This is no place for a lady. You should be at Vance House," he told her in a hoarse voice. His father's ducal residence was a few streets away, which, while still not far enough away, was not here.

Disdainful eyes traveled the ostentatious decor of the foyer and then flicked to his disheveled form. In his current state, cravat missing and coat discarded, Winter knew he looked like he'd been well and truly corrupted by his evening activities, even though he had spent the better part of four hours at his club poring over tedious expense accounts. Hence his rumpled appearance, though *she* wouldn't know that.

A tiny grin touched her lips, throwing him for a loop.

Did she find something amusing?

"What's wrong with me staying here?" she asked innocently, though her arctic eyes warred with her soft words. For some reason, Winter had the feeling his wife was furious, though nothing showed in her calm demeanor…except for those eyes that glittered like sharpened ice, threatening to dagger him at any moment. The contradiction thrilled him and irritated him all at once, sliding under his skin like silk over a blade.

"It's a gentleman's residence."

"Naturally," his wife interrupted, retrieving her cloak and bonnet from Ludlow, who stood with his mouth uncharacteristically agape. She favored the butler with a sweet smile that made him snap to attention, a smitten look clouding his normally austere features. "You are right, my lord. I do intend to stay at Vance House." Her mouth curved more as she turned back toward Winter, the decadent curve of those plump lips knocking him like a hammer to the ribs. "Your father insisted, of course. But I wanted to inform you myself that I was in town."

Winter scowled at the mention of the duke, his eyes narrowing at the fact that his father had known of his wife's visit. "Why *are* you here, Isobel?"

"A marchioness should be at her husband's side, don't you think?" A pair of brilliant, jewel-hard eyes speared him, daring him to challenge her. "I'm here for the season."

"The season?" he echoed, his brain slow on the uptake.

"Yes." His marchioness smiled, that full pout twisting in a way that made him suddenly want to do untoward, debauched things to it. "We wouldn't want the *ton* to think you've lost your touch, would we, Winter?"

His eyes narrowed. "In what way?"

"That the Marquess of Roth can't handle his own wife."

The words registered like fired shots. Winter blinked. Did his prim, shy bride just insult his masculinity? But then something like excitement licked up his spine. Strangely, it was the most alive he'd felt in months. *Years*. A slow grin replaced his scowl. His demure kitten had grown into a feline with razor-sharp claws, but whatever game his little wife intended to play, Winter would see it won.

And then he would send her back to Chelmsford.

"Trust me, love, you couldn't be more wrong."

The Marchioness of Roth turned in a vicious whirl of satin skirts and glanced over her shoulder in the doorway, a sultry gaze boring into his, one that promised both satisfaction and destruction in equal measure. "Prove it then, *love*."

She made those four parting words sound like a gauntlet: *See you at dawn.*

Winter stood there, stunned, for several loud heartbeats after his wife had left, leaving shrapnel in her wake.

Ludlow pinned him with a gratified expression. "So, roses to Vance House, then, my lord?"

"Sod off, Ludlow."

From the look of his wife, he was going to need a lot more than roses.

CHAPTER FOUR

In matters of seduction, Dearest Friend, the easiest way to catch an unattached gentleman's eye is with confidence. Subtlety is for spinsters.
– Lady Darcy

Oh hell, oh hell, oh hell.

Isobel sat straight up in the unfamiliar bed in an unfamiliar room, her heart pounding from the dregs of her nightmare, trying to orient herself. She wasn't in her bedchamber at home, at Kendrick Abbey. She was at Vance House. In *London*. Where her scoundrel of a husband was actively sowing his no-good oats, as was evident from the dreadful shape she'd witnessed him in last night. And where she'd effectively called him out in no uncertain terms.

The nightmare was real, then.

She sighed and slumped back down. From the accounts she'd read in the scandal sheets, Isobel had fully expected Winter to be living a bachelor lifestyle. What she hadn't expected was the shocking, nerve-shattering effect he'd had on her. Or the fact that he had no jowls to speak of at all. And the tiny detail that three years later, he was still the most sinfully attractive man she'd ever laid eyes on.

Botheration.

She'd returned to the duke's residence seething after her spontaneous visit to Audley Street, and not much of her anger had drained away overnight. She was still furious. Her husband had looked like he'd just crawled out of bed. In the middle of the afternoon. *Whose* bed was a question she did not want to dwell upon.

Lamentably, Winter looked no worse for wear. In fact, those years looked unfairly good on his lanky frame—filling him out in places and hardening him in others. Isobel hadn't been able to calm the deep, pulsating throb that had roared to life in her belly at the sight of him...that rich brown hair hanging carelessly over his brow, those gray eyes that had swirled like liquid smoke in the gloom, even though the whites of them had been bloodshot.

Heavy carousing would do that, she thought sourly.

But even a pair of reddened eyes and disheveled appearance could not detract from his raw physical appeal. Those broad shoulders and towering frame, his gorgeous, fallen-angel face that promised wicked delights. A rush of heat swamped her as her nipples tightened, her core clenching. Isobel buried her head in the pillows with a stifled shriek.

Why couldn't life be easy? Was that so much to ask? She'd been promised he'd have rampant gout, thanks to a dissolute lifestyle, hadn't she?

What would Lady Darcy have done?

Isobel let out a dry laugh. The dauntless Lady Darcy would have stripped to her naughty, lacy undergarments in Winter's foyer and dragged the man to his bedchamber, whereupon she would have kept him abed for days, forcing him to make amends for three years of lost time with his tongue, his fingers, and his long—

She flung *that* errant thought away. As much as she could recall from her brief wedding night, Winter's sex was neither too long nor too short, too thick or too thin. She had felt the blunt, sleek pressure of it, then a pinch of fullness, followed by an intense friction, and the shocking dissipation of pleasure that had gripped her entire body.

And then he'd left, forcing her fertile imagination to invent Lady Darcy.

Isobel ran her palms down her concave belly to the sharp bones of her hips and sighed. Despite her loneliness and her bitterness, she had remained faithful to her vows. A wry smile touched her lips. Though, if she was being fair, she *had* gotten quite a bit of her frustrations out through Lady Darcy. That version of herself lived the life that Isobel had been cheated of…one of youthful desire and exploration. One of female pleasure and satisfaction.

It was the reason the letters were so popular, she knew. Women had questions. They were sublimely romantic. And to no one's surprise, they had many of the same needs as men and were largely unable to act on them. *Especially* if they were ladies.

She blushed. Good God, Winter would probably be horrified if he knew what kind of caprices her mind housed. Well, it was his own fault, really. That was the price of a banished wife's existence in Chelmsford. One had to use one's imagination, after all, and as it turned out, hers was puckishly creative.

Hers *and* Clarissa's.

She was not alone in her written crimes of passion.

Although living in Chelmsford had kept her insulated from the ways of the *ton*, even Isobel wasn't that green not to know that other highborn wives carried on discreet affairs when their husbands were away. The Countess of Mead, a headstrong woman, often boasted of her countless lovers, most of them her own footmen. Even that had been addressed in one of Lady Darcy's letters—cuckolding one's husband, a piece cleverly entitled "When the Cock Crows" that had scandalized men everywhere. The ladies had loved it.

But despite the occasional pang of latent desire from her written exploits, Isobel had no desire to make a cuckold of her husband. Atonement for his behavior, however, was another matter. Winter Vance needed to be taught a lesson, and in spite of her inexperience, Isobel wasn't a shy, naive girl anymore. She had an arsenal of information at her fingertips. Education in lieu of experience was one of life's greatest weapons.

Fate had given her a crate of lemons. She planned to drown her scoundrel of a husband in lemonade.

A commotion outside her bedchamber made her sit up just as the door burst open. "Rise and shine, my dearest friend," Clarissa cried gaily, followed by Violet and Molly. "We have gowns to purchase, hearts to slay, and deviant husbands to torture!"

"Not us," Violet grumbled. "We're still in mourning for Papa. Though we do plan to live vicariously through you two, won't we, Molly?"

"Not me," Molly said. "I intend to lose myself in the library and live vicariously through the pages. I should have stayed in Chelmsford."

"You don't mean that." Violet glared at her sister, and then turned back to Isobel. "Come on, Izzy, time to get up. Unlike Miss I-Love-Books-More-Than-People, I expect a full fashion show and all the details once you return."

"What do you have against books?" Molly yelled.

Isobel groaned, burying her head anew beneath the mound of pillows. "Must you all be so loud?"

"Of course we must." Clarissa dragged the bed-sheets to the side and then shoved open the curtains to the muted sunlight. She waved to an army of maids who bustled into the room. "You have an appointment with Madame Pinot for a fitting this afternoon."

Violet let out a delighted shriek, which made Isobel cover her ears.

"She is very hard to get in to see," Violet gushed, "but apparently, people move mountains for the Duke of Kendrick, and the chance to dress the mysteriously reclusive Marchioness of Roth, sister to the very outspoken, very contrary Duchess of Beswick."

"*Wonderful.* I loathe fittings."

"Liar." Clarissa poked her in the side. "You love fashion."

It was true. Isobel had always loved perusing the latest in women's couture, even though Chelmsford offered little in terms of entertainment, besides the occasional social assembly. Now that she had the chance to choose and wear some of the newest trends, she should have been thrilled. Instead, she only felt uncertainty. The emotion must have showed on her face, because Clarissa sat on the edge of the bed and squeezed her arm.

"Think of the plan, sweeting. A woman's style is part of her armory, and we must make sure yours is especially fitted for the occasion." Clarissa leaned in, her voice a whisper for Isobel's ears only. "Embody Lady Darcy. Make us proud."

"Lady Darcy isn't real," Isobel whispered back.

She huffed with an aggrieved look. "Nonsense."

"You're taking this much too seriously, you realize," Isobel said, sitting up and rubbing her head. The brandy she'd hunted down upon arrival at Vance House hadn't helped much to put her to sleep but had left her with a throbbing headache.

Clarissa winked. "Take that back, wench. I'll have you know I take sexual gratification very seriously."

"Goodness, Clarissa, the servants!" Molly said, glancing at the nearest maid who had gone pink-cheeked.

Isobel, too, was sure her face bore the same color. It was a common occurrence in proximity to Clarissa, who lived to shock and titillate. Though Lady Darcy was an amalgamation of the two of them, the character's predilection for the obscene came from Clarissa.

"Three years is a long time by anyone's standards, Izzy," Clarissa went on with a dismissive wave. "At least that's what my brothers say. It can cause physical deformation for a man supposedly. In coloration, too."

Isobel's mouth dropped. "You are jesting."

"I never jest about sexual organs."

One of the maids made a choking noise.

"*Clarissa!*" both twins burst out.

Her eyes sparkled as she winked, waggling her eyebrows. "I happen to be an authority on the subject."

"Who's the liar now? You don't know anything about…such things," Isobel huffed. But once the twins started giggling, that was it—their laughter was infectious. Clarissa was innocent in body, but her mind was unconscionably filthy. And she clearly had no problem corrupting friends and maids alike. Likely another consequence of being a chronic eavesdropper with five older brothers. "Unempirical knowledge does not make one an expert."

Clarissa waved a careless arm. "Be that as it may, we have a plan, and we must see through said plan. Seduce Lord Roth forthwith, and perhaps get Lady Roth up the pole, too."

"You wish to get with child, Isobel?" Violet asked, wide-eyed.

She squashed the ugly ache that spiked in her breast. "One day if that's in my future, but right now, my only goal is bringing the Maggot of Roth to heel."

"Just show him a little leg and he'll be humping it in a hurry," Clarissa said with a grin. "Woof, woof."

"You are truly dreadful."

Trying not to snicker, Isobel allowed the scarlet-faced maid to tend to her. She knew she'd rue the day she'd confided in Clarissa about her plan, and she should have known from the subsequent scream of "Long live Lady Darcy!" but she couldn't have done any of this without her best friend. Once Clarissa set her mind to something, she completed it without fail. Which meant by the end of the season, Winter Vance would be a man-shaped puddle at Isobel's feet.

As far as becoming *enceinte*...well, as unlikely as it was to happen, a baby would not be unwelcomed.

At least, Kendrick would get the grandchild he hoped for.

• • •

The fitting at Madame Pinot's was delightful. Isobel was impressed with the efficiency of the women who worked there, as well as the Frenchwoman's boundless knowledge of all things fashion. Isobel was certain she'd left a considerable dent in Kendrick's accounts, but the duke had insisted that she avail herself of his credit. For Clarissa, too.

Oliver would blow an artery once he was informed of their purchases. He was stingy to a fault and hated his older brother Winter's spendthrift ways. The thought of aggravating his stuffy, stuck-up self, made Isobel nearly chortle with unabashed delight. Oliver resented Winter with a passion, which had somehow extended to Isobel simply by default of being his wife. As a result, he was insufferably rude, treating her with the barest modicum of respect, and that was only in front of his father.

It was, perhaps, the only thing she and her husband had in common.

"Why are you smiling like the cat who ate all the cream?" Clarissa asked as they sat in the carriage surrounded by a mountain of parcels. "You know the rules…share the cream."

"I'm thinking of Oliver's face when he sees those bills."

A wolfish look spread across Clarissa's face. "Damnation, but I should have commissioned a dozen more gowns." Her grin widened. "Shall we come up with a plan to spend more of the duke's money, then? Shoes, hats, gloves, even new jewelry, perhaps?"

"Clarissa, you are diabolical."

She canted her head in receipt of the compliment. "I try." She paused. "So, are you finally going to tell me what was it like seeing your marquess now that the twins aren't around?"

Isobel gulped, a dozen thoughts translating to her lips and resulting in only one. "He's an ass."

"Naturally." Clarissa smirked. "But is he still handsome as the devil?"

"Yes." Isobel didn't bother lying to her best friend. She could always see right through her anyway.

"I bet Oliver's peeved because Winter got all the good looks in the family," she said with a laugh.

Isobel shot her a glance. "Oliver's not ugly."

While he favored his mother's side with his rounder face and blond hair, there was still some resemblance between the brothers. If he wasn't such a condescending prig at heart, he'd actually be handsome.

"Yes, well he's a cad." Clarissa glowered at her. "Stop trying to redirect the conversation. I want to hear about what it was like to see dear Winter after all this time. Especially considering he's one of Lady Darcy's deepest, darkest fantasies. Well, at least the Izzy half."

Isobel went hot. "He is not!"

"Let's agree to disagree. Now spill it."

In a bland tone, Isobel recounted the details of her visit, watching Clarissa's eyes get wider and wider.

"Your eyeballs are going to roll out of their sockets," Isobel warned.

Clarissa gaped. "I cannot believe you actually went to 15 Audley Street."

"Why?"

"Derrick says it is a den of depravity. And Derrick is the seediest of all my brothers. Trust me, I've overheard him tell stories of the parties at that place. How do you think Lady Darcy gets some of her more creative explanations?"

Face aflame, Isobel made a gagging noise. "I don't want to know about *Derrick's* sex life."

Clarissa's nose wrinkled as her green eyes turned speculative. "Derrick did mention a week ago that it was strange that the marquess was never around." She frowned. "Don't you think that's odd? I mean what if Roth is no longer the rakehell everyone thinks he is?"

Wait, *what*? Isobel's heart stuttered in her chest at her friend's complete turnabout. Had she forgotten that he just fought a blasted duel? Isobel's irritation sizzled back to the surface. "What about Contessa James, then? He doesn't want to be married, Clarissa. He's made that more than clear. He left me alone in Chelmsford for *three* years. A leopard doesn't change its spots, no matter how much one might wish it to. Roth is a complete mutton monger!"

Clarissa's lips twitched at the inventive insult that the man was addicted to wenching, but she shrugged. "People can change."

"I think too much shopping has addled your mind."

• • •

They didn't speak the entire way back to Vance House. Isobel was fuming. Coming to London with a plan to take down her husband was a far cry from allowing herself to believe he had been miraculously cured of being a complete scoundrel. Yes, his sister's death was tragic, but that didn't change who he was. It was *after* Prudence's death that the rotter had chosen to leave her and abandon her.

Winter Vance deserved what was coming to him.

She glanced over at Clarissa, whose face was openly remorseful. Isobel sighed. She could never remain angry with her friend for long. The carriage rolled to a stop, and just as Isobel opened her mouth to apologize, the door was pulled open. Her groom stood there, his pale face wreathed in worry.

"Randolph? What is it? Is it Hellion?"

"There's been a fire, my lady," he said. "Hellion is safe, but others in the mews have not fared so well. Someone left a lit cheroot and the hay caught fire. The blaze was contained, but the smoke is still thick."

She descended and made to dash around the back of the residence to the mews, but the groom cleared his throat and blocked her way. "It's not safe, milady."

"Randolph, move," she said with a glare when he wouldn't let her pass.

Clarissa tugged on her sleeve. "He's right, Isobel. The men will have been instructed to keep anyone away for safety. Especially the lady in residence."

"But *Hellion*…" Perhaps it was silly, but Isobel *needed* to see her mare. She needed to hold her, make sure she was all right. Hellion had become so much more than a pet to her. The horse was family.

"I know," Clarissa soothed. "Randolph has told you she's fine. Listen to him."

Isobel bit her lip and nodded. The groom, seemingly mollified that she would stay put, disappeared back to the stables.

But the worry would not leave her as they entered the house.

Struck with an idea, she raced upstairs then discarded the dress she'd been wearing, shucked on a pair of old trousers, a linen shirt, a brown coat, and worn boots that she'd used to train Hellion at Kendrick Abbey. All things she could get dirty.

Clarissa gasped as she made to leave her chambers. "Izzy, what are you doing? You cannot run down willy-nilly to the mews dressed like that. This isn't like in Chelmsford where you could do as you please. It's not proper. Even *I* know that."

Isobel knotted her hair and tucked it into the tweed cap she held in hand. "There," she said, ignoring Clarissa's disapproving glare. "I look like a boy. No one in society will know and all proper female reputations will be guarded from infamy and shame." Isobel glanced down at herself with a grin. "Never thought I'd thank the heavens for my nonexistent chest and stick-figure body."

"If I can't stop you, at least wear this." Clarissa fumbled in her pockets and handed Isobel a gray square of cloth that had ties on the sides. "The maids use it for dusting."

Isobel narrowed her gaze. "Why do *you* have it?"

"I might have nicked it to do some snooping," Clarissa said, cheeks pink.

Snooping where? The only people in residence were the two of them, the twins, and the duke, and Oliver, from time to time. Curious, Isobel wanted to press the issue and Clarissa's obvious secrets, but she also wanted to check on Hellion. She narrowed her eyes on her friend. "This isn't over. Confessions on the snooping when I return."

"Isobel…"

"I know, I'll be careful, I promise."

She fastened the cloth and raced downstairs to the kitchens before jogging to the mews. As she'd expected, no one spared her a second glance. She was dressed like every other servant running around and carrying buckets of water. The men all had rags tied around their noses and mouths. The stench of smoke was heavy in the air as Randolph had said. She located him where he stood next to a smoking paddock and tapped him on his shoulder.

"What are you standing around for, boy?" he snapped. "Get a bucket and get to work."

Isobel realized he would not recognize her behind the cloth that obscured most of her face and the cap kept her eyes in shadow. "It's me, Randolph."

His round eyes widened as he took measure of her and matched her voice to the image she presented. "My lady!"

"Just call me Iz," she whispered. Randolph's mouth opened and closed like a fish, and Isobel sighed. "You've seen me in breeches for years, Randolph."

"But you're in *town*, my lady." He lowered his voice to a horrified whisper. "And the *duke* is in residence."

"Well I couldn't wear a gown, could I?" she said. "Now stop being dramatic and take me to Hellion. You won't get into trouble with the duke, I swear it. Kendrick won't even know."

"And your husband?"

She scowled. "Take me to my horse, Randolph. I won't ask again."

Randolph stared at her as though waging a mental battle, but then with a terse nod, he obeyed her command without another word. Isobel knew she was treading a dangerous line, and she understood the man's trepidation around the imperious Duke of Kendrick, whose strict observance of propriety was well-known. Isobel suspected the duke had an inkling of her wardrobe misadventures in Chelmsford, but Randolph was right. London was a whole different beast. Here, she was Lady Roth, first and foremost, with a reputation to safeguard. And ladies of quality did not run amok with the servant classes while dressed in men's clothing.

But Isobel forgot everything as her eyes fell on Hellion, and instantly, she went to her mare, crooning softly under her breath. Thankfully, the horse seemed fine as Randolph had said, though a little more skittish than usual.

"Did we lose any others?" she asked him.

"One," he said. "Though he was old and his heart likely gave out."

Still saddened, Isobel stared over at the smoking and charred end of the stables. "It was lucky that the fire was contained so quickly. It could have been disastrous."

"We had more than luck on our side," Randolph said somberly, and moved away to assist a man with a ruined piece of timber.

Isobel stared at the blackened, collapsed corner of the mews. The fire had been fierce, and so many horses could have perished, including her beloved Hellion. She stroked the mare's glossy flanks, grateful that she'd escaped injury.

A sudden commotion in the yard made her whirl around as a tall man strode into view. She blinked in silent shock, every muscle in her body going tight.

No wonder Randolph had been skittish.

Why was her dratted husband *here*?

Isobel swallowed hard at the sight of him, though this wasn't the suave marquess she knew. His jacket was missing, as was his cravat, the long, tanned column of his throat damp with grime and sweat. Thickly muscled forearms were visible from his rolled back shirtsleeves and flecks of ash streaked his brow.

It was obvious he'd been neck-deep in the burning mews. Surprise rippled through her. She didn't take him for a man who would get his hands dirty, but here he was. Covered in soot.

He made no bones about heading straight toward her, and she opened her mouth to explain her unusual attire.

"You, there, lad—fetch me a cup of water."

Isobel froze in place, mute. Goodness, did he not recognize her? Her hand almost lifted to the cloth at her face and hung in midair like a sparrow without a home.

Winter speared her with an exhausted glance. "Did you hear me, boy? Water, please."

Mindful of her disguise, she lowered her voice to an imitation of rough gravel. "Aye, milord. Right away, your lordship."

She raced off to procure the water from the kitchens, returning to where he stood, stroking Hellion with a thoughtful expression. Mercurial gray eyes landed on her after he emptied the cup. "Whose horse is this?"

Isobel hastily ducked her head. "Her ladyship's," she said, unable to keep the thread of pride from her voice. "Lady Roth. This beauty here is called Hellion."

The man visibly started, his throat working as he studied the mare belonging to her as if the horse harbored secrets that only her mistress would know. Shock and intense curiosity warred on his face. Isobel suspected he wasn't normally this transparent, and he wouldn't be...not in front of *her*. Then again, to him, she was just a stable boy. No one of consequence. There would be no need to hide his expressions.

Fascinated, Isobel peeked up at him from beneath her cap. It was like getting a glimpse into something forbidden and she couldn't help the delicious thrill that filled her. When his attention swung back in her direction, she quickly bent her head to hide her eyes. They were distinctive enough in color that he might recognize them, and Isobel did not wish to be exposed. She wanted more of this intriguing insight into her husband.

"I thought she was afraid of horses," he murmured.

Isobel shook her head. "Not anymore."

"And you are her groom?"

"In training, milord." She paused. "For Mr. Randolph over yonder."

"What's your name?"

"Iz. Like the verb." Isobel almost swore and inwardly kicked herself. Lowly servants wouldn't know the first thing about grammatical concepts, but luckily, he was too distracted to notice her slip. Winter was staring at a man who was heading toward him, rage in every ground-covering step.

Isobel's heart sank as she took stock of the arrival.

Oliver. She was already pushing her luck with one Vance brother. Two of them together spelled disaster. To her gratitude, Randolph had returned to her side, and she shifted behind him just as Oliver swung a wild punch at his brother's face. Winter moved out of the way, his eyes glinting dangerously.

"What the hell was that for?" he snarled.

Oliver shoved the end of a cheroot in his face. "This was the culprit that started the fire. The brand *you* favor."

"Along with half the gentlemen in London." Winter arched an eyebrow. "You expect me to believe, brother, that that cigar end survived when half the mews did not? I've been here breaking my back to save the building and all the horses."

"Getting the authorities," Oliver snapped.

Isobel snuck a glance at Winter's face and almost recoiled at the leashed violence she saw there. "And no, *brother*, I was not here smoking in the mews, so whoever started this fire either had something to prove or another agenda. Where were *you*?"

Oliver's face went puce. "How dare you? Are you suggesting—?"

"Enough, Oliver, I'm too tired to argue." Winter cut his brother off with a weary gesture. "I arrived earlier to check on my two horses stabled here—with Kendrick's permission, might I add—only to discover a corner of the mews already on fire."

"And Lady Roth?" Oliver couldn't help taunting in a smarmy voice that made Isobel want to kick him right in the teeth. "Did you come to see her?"

Notwithstanding her deep-seated urges to take her odious brother-in-law to task, Isobel was also curious

as to what Winter's response would be, and was prepared to make a mad dash for the house to change
into a gown should he answer in the affirmative. She
was disappointed, however, when the marquess
ground his teeth, turned on his heel without a word,
and walked back the way he'd come.

Apparently, such a trifling question did not even
deserve a response.

CHAPTER FIVE

If in any doubt of your own dancing skills, depend on exceptional manners and witty conversation. And be free with your compliments. Men adore hearing how wonderful they are.
– Lady Darcy

Ensconced in the opulent card room at The Silver Scythe, Winter stared at his current hand of cards and decided to fold. He was bored out of his mind. Perhaps *bored* wasn't the right word.

He was agitated, anxious, on edge.

Rattled.

All because his wife was in town. His gorgeous, desirable, and unwelcome wife whose name had been on everyone's lips for the better part of a week. And she was on the best of terms with his *father*, of all people.

Winter had wrongly assumed the straitlaced Duke of Kendrick would take one look at the green country girl with no outstanding lineage that his disappointment of a son had married and purse his lips in everlasting disgust. Instead, he'd done the opposite and taken her under his wing. Winter hadn't expected them to become allies, let alone come to London together for the season. *That* was simply not cricket. The development had blindsided him.

Notwithstanding the tiny fact that his wife had turned into a deuced temptress.

Even now, his blood fired at the thought of her.

"Roth," the Duke of Westmore said, clapping him on the back. "Surprised to see you here."

"Oh? Why's that?" Winter drawled, staring in disgust at his new hand of cards, which wasn't any better than the last. His luck had turned and landed in the communal chamber pot, along with what was left of his flagging humor.

"Saw your lady wife over at the Beddingford bash. She looked spectacular. The fops have already proclaimed her an original, an incomparable, this season's everything." Westmore's grin was all teeth. "Wherever have you been hiding her?"

Winter experienced an urge to punch the man in his smirking mouth, and then caught himself. He must be out of sorts. Wulfric Bane, the Duke of Westmore, was one of his longtime friends and didn't deserve missing teeth because Winter couldn't seem to control himself whenever anyone mentioned his wife. Her beauty, her charm, her bloody incomparableness.

"I *haven't* been hiding her," he snapped. "She prefers the country."

Until now, apparently.

In truth, he hadn't given her a choice, though he hadn't been completely cut off from updates as to her welfare. Mrs. Butterfield had sent him meticulous reports. In the beginning, they'd come regularly, and then had dwindled after Winter had strongly suggested to the housekeeper that he didn't require them with such detail or frequency. Too many reminders of her had done more ill than good.

"I didn't even know you were married, Roth," another man across the table said, Viscount Something or Other. "Who's the lucky chit?"

Winter's eyes narrowed on him. Perhaps he *would* be up for fisticuffs if the viscount kept flapping that hairless, weak-chinned gob of his. "No one you'd know. She never had a season."

"Wasn't she the younger Everleigh heiress?" Westmore interjected, sitting in an empty seat and either oblivious to—or purposely ignoring—his friend's brewing foul mood. "I seem to recall hearing about a scandal a few years ago with the Duke of Beswick making quite the scene at Lady Hammerton's Christmastide house party." He paused and grinned. "Now *there's* a lady with a few secrets beneath those skirts. They don't make them like Lady H anymore."

"She's older than Medusa," Winter muttered.

Westmore guffawed. "True, but the things she could teach, as you well know. Nothing wrong with a woman who knows her way around a man, I say."

"A few generations of men, at least."

Winter tugged on his cravat, the cloth tightening like a guillotine made of guilt. He wasn't even sure why he was denigrating Lady Hammerton. Though she was old enough to be his mother, she was a good sort, and he'd married Isobel in the chapel on her estate with her backing, after all. And they'd spent some time together after one of his club's infamous charity auctions.

"I bet anything she's Lady Darcy," Westmore said.

He arched a brow. "Not likely. Lady Darcy's much too innocent to be that old harridan."

The men around him broke into raucous laughter and Winter gave a careless shrug. Perhaps *innocent* wasn't the right word. Lady Darcy's deeds would put a courtesan to shame, but something about the erotic letters—despite their salacious content—struck him as decidedly whimsical. No seasoned widow could ever sound so…*hopeful*.

"Speaking of innocent young ladies," Westmore said with a sideways glance at Winter. "Back to the delectable Lady Roth and the latest *on-dit*." The smirk on his lips said he knew exactly what he was doing, the shameless bastard. "Do tell, Roth—is she anything like our daring Lady Darcy?"

Winter's groin clenched. The thought of Isobel on her knees, reenacting one of Lady Darcy's more memorable correspondence, those pink lips parted and ready to take him, had Winter's eyes nearly rolling back in his head.

Fucking hell.

No, she was a lady, and without reservation, the type to lie there and submit. He couldn't fathom his decorous little wife doing anything so filthy as some of those letters had detailed. No matter how fast his imagination flew. Despite being a monk for the better part of three years, his memory was still perfectly functional.

You could teach her, a voice whispered.

The thought licked at his starving senses, and he shook his head to clear it.

"My wife is none of anyone's bloody business!" he growled.

"Since when is England's ultimate bachelor married?" another drunken lout burst out, nearly spilling his drink all across the table as his squinty gaze fell on him. "Is she a looker? She must be if she snared *you*. Thought you'd always sworn off wedlock, Roth?"

Winter scowled. God, he was surrounded by drunkards and profligates. He stood, ignoring Westmore's gratified look.

"Where are you off to?" the duke asked innocently.

Reaching for his gloves, Winter signaled the factotum. He bit the words through his teeth. "To retrieve my wife."

"I expect a full accounting!"

"Go sod yourself, Westmore."

Outside the establishment, he directed his waiting coach to the Beddingford's residence. He'd received the invitation weeks before but hadn't accepted. Winter didn't do *ton* events.

Besides, he'd been ousted from too many ballrooms to count. Thank God he wasn't on the recently married Marquess of Beddingford's *persona non-grata* list. At least, not yet. Despite his reputation, the perfidious *ton* had welcomed him back with open arms when news of his own wealth had spread. Winter huffed a disgusted sigh. It'd been so long since he'd ventured into a Mayfair ballroom that Winter had no idea what he would be walking into.

Gritting his teeth, he descended the carriage with a purposeful step and strode to the crowded foyer. His nostrils flared as the warm, overly perfumed air reached him. It was a crush, one that made him want to turn tail and race back to the informal, casual comforts of Covent Garden. He gave the servant near the majordomo his name, and didn't wait before availing himself of a whiskey from a nearby footman.

Gulping the drink, he surveyed the glittering crowd over the balcony at the top of the marble staircase—a dazzling display of immaculately groomed men and preening females garbed in every hue imaginable. There was no way he was going to find a woman he'd set eyes on once in three years in that mêlée.

But in that, he was wrong.

Isobel's presence drew him like a magnetic force.

His heart rate accelerated as his gaze fell on the slender, statuesque woman dressed in an ice-blue gown that was almost white in the middle of the bright ballroom. The lace-overlaid silk rippled around her as if it were alive with each elegant turn of the dance, and set off her blond hair and sun-kissed complexion to perfection.

Every fluid movement of her body suggested grace and an underlying litheness. From what he'd gathered from her groom earlier, she obviously now enjoyed horseback riding. Winter had the sudden image of her straddling him with those long limbs, her head thrown back in complete abandon. Once more, his cock decided to make its presence known, but his arousal slaked considerably as his gaze settled on her dancing partner…his father.

"The Marquess of Roth," the majordomo intoned.

Conversation came to a screeching halt, heads swiveling in his direction, and then resumed at a fever pitch. Winter arched a sardonic brow at the rampant attention suddenly directed his way before heading down the stairs. By the shocked whispers rising toward him, he was clearly preceded by reputation. A chuckle rumbled through his chest. There was only one person who could one-up his notoriety. If only Lady Darcy were real, they would have made quite the entrance.

Winter knew the instant Isobel's eyes landed on

him, a visceral throb roaring through his body as if she'd somehow slid a palm over his skin. But before he could lock eyes with her, she twirled away, severing the raw connection.

He stopped to pay his respects to Beddingford and his new marchioness. "Good to see you, Roth," the marquess said. "I admit, I was surprised to hear your name."

"Don't worry, my good man," Winter said in an amused drawl. "I promise to behave. Now, introduce me to your better half."

Beddingford's besotted expression nearly made Winter's stomach turn. "Allow me to present my beautiful wife, Lady Beddingford."

"A pleasure, my lord," the lovely brunette said. "I've heard a lot about you."

Twinkling brown eyes without the usual judgment he'd come to expect met his, as the marchioness offered him a regal nod. She was a beauty, one he did not recognize though she looked vaguely familiar.

"Have we met?" he asked.

Beddingford let out a laugh. "No, and thank God for it. We all know of your repute with the fairer sex. I would not have stood a chance."

Lady Beddingford patted her husband's arm, her warm brown eyes shining with affection, and joined in his laughter. "Of course you would have." She shot Winter a mischievous glance. "And while the devastating Lord Roth may set all the ladies' hearts afire, mine only flutters for one particular marquess. Besides, Lord Roth is married, is he not?"

"Ah, yes, Roth, what a colossal secret you've kept from everyone," Beddingford said. "If Lady Roth hadn't arrived in London with the elusive Duke of Kendrick on her arm as her very vocal advocate, no one would have believed her claims."

Winter's mouth flattened. He curbed the violence of his words for the sake of the lady present. "If I recall, my marriage was announced quite publicly three years ago at Lady Hammerton's yule ball. It wasn't a secret. You were there, too, Beds."

The man colored at the old nickname with an apologetic glance to his wife. "Yes, well, but then you returned to town without the new Lady Roth. So everyone assumed that you had cried off the thing, or annulled it, or whatever."

"No."

To Winter's surprise, Lady Beddingford cleared her throat and grinned up at her doting husband. "Now that that misunderstanding has been cleared up, I must hear about this nickname, darling. *Beds*, is it? It sounds too intriguing for words."

"My dear—"

"Don't make me ask Lord Roth," she teased with a laugh. "I'm sure he'll be only too happy to share some of your wild stories as young bucks."

The man's eyes nearly fell out of his head. "He most certainly will *not*."

Winter laughed as Beddingford abruptly steered his wife toward the ballroom floor with a panicked look on his face. He couldn't recall seeing his old friend ever looking so infatuated with a woman. Then again, Beddingford had never kept pace with the rest of their set. He'd attended all the requisite balls and maintained a decent reputation, whereas Winter had done the opposite. Anything to destroy his father's perfect illusion of the Vance family. The man had sent his wife to her death and his only daughter into addiction. The cold devil deserved everything that Winter had given him.

His gaze wandered to where his father was escorting Isobel toward the refreshments room, and Winter's jaw clenched. Shouldn't his wife come to receive him? Shouldn't his perfectionist *father* encourage her to do so? It was a deliberate slight, one which Winter did not intend to rise to, no matter how provoked it made him.

"Lost, Winter?"

The voice came out of nowhere, but then his brother's form materialized to his left. "Good God, Olly, can't find anything better to do than stalk my every step?"

"I was invited. And it's *Oliver*."

"Obnoxious Oliver."

His brother made a strangled sound. "I see you haven't lost your inflated sense of cleverness. Good to know that Father will eventually put his faith elsewhere, at least in the matter of the ducal estate."

"Yes, yes, you'll inherit the bulk of whatever's unentailed, if he has anything to say about it. Everyone here knows how rich you will be, I'm sure."

Oliver scowled. "Everyone who *counts*."

Winter glanced over his shoulder, wondering how and why their relationship as brothers had gone so terribly wrong. There were two years between them, but it could have been twenty. Oliver had been born with a tree-stump up his arse and a granite boulder of a chip on his shoulder. He would have been the perfect choice to be the next uptight Duke of Kendrick, not Winter. But the stringent rules of primogeniture could not be overturned, sadly.

And unless Winter died, blood made him Kendrick's heir.

His brother's mouth tightened. "Why are *you* here, Winter?"

"I was invited."

The fulminating tension between them solidified to something resembling stone. Stone about to shatter. As though sensing the mounting danger, anyone standing on the edge of the ballroom and looking at them had given them a wide berth.

"Gracious, you two, you're frightening away all the eligible young men," a lively feminine voice cut in. "And what's an unmarried girl without prospects to do if your incessant glowering chases them away?"

Winter turned, his smile shifting into the real thing as Clarissa strolled toward them. He hadn't seen her in years, though Mrs. Butterfield had reported that Isobel had taken a strong liking to Mr. Bell's daughter and they'd become fast friends. That had been another development he hadn't expected.

Clarissa was *Clarissa*.

Wild and unrepentant as a girl, forever chasing after her boisterous brothers on the parklands at Kendrick Abbey, and always wearing an impish grin on her face. Clarissa was the complete opposite of the recalcitrant, shy woman he'd married. He frowned, touching on the more recent impressions of his kitten-turned-tiger wife. Now, the two women seemed to have a lot more in common.

A dangerous amount, it seemed. Winter wasn't sure whether that was a good or bad thing. He remembered the rebellious, openly challenging look his wife had given him, and revised his initial assessment. Definitely bad.

"Lord Roth, how lovely to see you," Clarissa said, her green eyes dancing. "You look well. Better than well, actually." She accepted his kiss on her gloved knuckles and turned to Oliver. There, the smile withered on her face, a guarded look replacing it. "Lord Oliver."

"Miss Bell," Oliver intoned flatly with a curt bow, and Winter eyed him in surprise.

His brother did not even look at Clarissa, his gaze trained pointedly on the ballroom floor. The strain blooming between them eclipsed the ugly tension that had been there before. Winter's eyes narrowed. It seemed he'd missed more over the past three years than what had gone on with his own wife. He suddenly had the distinct urge to stir up trouble. Payback made for an excellent distraction.

Grinning to himself, he turned to Clarissa. "Are you here for the season as well, then?"

"What's left of it," she said. "Along with the dreary dregs of the marriage prospects, that is."

Winter couldn't help noticing with inhuman delight that her gaze veered toward his brother before fastening elsewhere. So there *was* something there.

He nodded sagely. "Dregs, indeed."

"Have you seen Izzy?"

"Don't you mean Lady Roth?" Oliver interjected, his tone oozing disdain. "If so, then unless she has already moved on, I believe she is near the refreshments room."

Clarissa's mouth went flat before it was overtaken by a sugary sweet smile. "Why, are you offering to escort me there, Lord Oliver? How truly gallant of you." Her disparaging tone matched his, suggesting that she didn't think he was gallant in the least. It would goad the pretentious Oliver into fury, Winter knew.

"No, I was merely answering your question."

"Figures, then," she replied.

His lips curled. "What does?"

"You aren't a gentleman."

Winter felt like he was caught in the middle of a furious tennis match, just barely dodging the ball whizzing back and forth. He waited for a break before clearing his throat. "Actually, Oliver was just saying how much he wanted to dance. It's truly fortunate that you arrived, Clarissa."

Identical glares pinned him in place. He grinned.

"This looks fun," an amused voice said.

Winter's hilarity faltered as he looked into the cool blue gaze of his wife. She was even more stunning up close, but he kept his instant response at bay, even as he reached for her hand and drew it to his lips. "My lady, how lovely you are this evening."

She inclined her head. "Thank you, my lord."

Every inch the regal marchioness, she glowed. Even her flaxen hair shone, coiffed in elegant curls that framed her face to perfection. Winter scowled, wondering why he was cataloguing his wife's assets. He should be thinking of ways to scare her back to Chelmsford. She'd challenged him, after all, and he'd accepted. Here was a perfect opportunity to rise to that challenge, to prove he bloody well could handle his own wife.

A dance, then. Something to unbalance and shake

her off that perfect pedestal.

He'd meant to goad Oliver with the dance comment, but perhaps he could hit two birds with one stone. The tension between Clarissa and Oliver was too good to pass up, and he needed to unsettle his irritatingly composed wife.

A dance would be that stone.

"I was just saying how much my brother wanted to dance with Clarissa. I believe I hear the strains of a waltz." Ignoring Oliver's pinched expression, he extended an elbow to his wife. "Shall we, then?"

Isobel's eyes widened, her gaze flying to Clarissa, whose face looked like she'd come upon a steaming dung heap in the middle of the ballroom, before returning to Winter, who kept his expression purposely innocent. "You wish to dance? With me?"

"We're all dancing."

"No, we are not." Clarissa's furious denial came through clenched teeth.

"No," Oliver snapped at the same time.

Winter laughed loudly, drawing as much attention as he could. "It's delightful to note that the cause of *this* scene is not me." His voice rose to a dramatic stage whisper. "A refusal to dance by the favored son of the Duke of Kendrick? An unmarried woman's reputation in peril?" Winter's gaze slanted to Isobel as he threw a dramatic hand to his chest. "Gracious, who or what could possibly be the cause of such a delicious *on-dit*?"

Now three pairs of murderous eyes glowered at him.

Several bystanders inched closer the minute the hint of scandal had reared its wicked head. Despite his claims to the contrary, he *would* be at the center of it, Winter knew. The wildly improper Rakehell of Roth, surrounded by his straitlaced brother, an unmarried female, and said rakehell's beautiful, mysterious wife? Gossip would fly faster than fire.

"Dance with him," Isobel said to Clarissa in a low voice.

"But—"

"He's right. The gossip will be insufferable if you do not," she said calmly. Her hard gaze turned to Oliver as she said the one thing that would motivate him. "Do not shame the duke, Lord Oliver. His eyes are upon you right at this moment."

That frigid stare impaled Winter next. He lifted an eyebrow as she took his measure, her disdain of his methods stamped in her expression. With a huff, she turned in a swirl of silvery skirts and moistened her plump lips, her thick fringe of lashes falling to her cheeks in a demure look that didn't fool him one bit. Every single eye in the place watched as he strode after the one woman who apparently did not swoon at his feet and collapse in a mindless heap from his attentions.

Moving into place on the ballroom, they lined up and she placed a stiff palm in his.

"Well, you've gotten your way and what you wanted. Happy now?"

"Not yet," he murmured huskily. "But I intend to be once you tell me why you're in town."

For a moment, her outward composure slipped, her cheeks pinkening even as her body hitched slightly as if she meant to storm off and leave him there. A succinct and incendiary cut direct. In her place,

Winter would have done it, just to fuel the gossip mill. But he did not know what was truly behind this little game his wife was playing and why she'd come to London. A gleam of fury glinted in her wintry eyes. For all their iciness, she was burning at the seams. Like her horse. *Hellion*.

Winter vowed to talk to that young groom and find out more about his mistress. Perhaps the lad would give him some insight. Something he could use to turn the tables, because right now, he could only bluff his way through it with so much bravado. He was holding on by a thin thread, his body on edge and bracingly alive. Even now, he fought a primal urge to pick her up, fling her over his shoulder, and bear her to his lair like a bloody caveman. For a moment, he almost considered it. That would set the *ton's* tongues to wagging.

"Are you going to stand there and ogle me for the rest of the evening?" she snapped as the first few strains of music began.

"I do love a woman in control. So direct," he drawled, leading her into the first turn. "It appears you've grown up, kitten."

"Don't call me that."

"Why? It suits you."

Her lips pinched. "If I am a feline, what does that make you? A slobbering, oversexed hound?"

He wanted to laugh at her tart-tongued reply, but there was too much at stake. Winter's smile was slow and practiced, his voice lowering for her ears only the next time they came together. "I've been called many things, I assure you, but slobbering isn't one of them. Unless of course, I'm lodged between a woman's thighs."

Isobel's mouth opened in a soundless gasp, one elegant, gloved hand flying to her lips. "You…you unspeakable—"

"Rake? Scoundrel? Roué?" he supplied helpfully. "I've heard them all, love."

"I'm sure you have," she muttered.

Suddenly, a spark of blue fire appeared in those wintry eyes. A purposeful, hard stare brimming with resolve. It coasted over his skin and inched down his spine to settle low in his belly. Winter experienced the same sensation he'd had that first evening in his foyer when she'd announced her intention to be in London for the season.

Of some invisible challenge being tossed down.

"I suppose there's only one thing left to do, then," she said.

He arched a brow. "What's that?"

"Give a hound something to chase."

A coy, playful smile curved her lips as she twirled away on the ballroom floor, throwing such a sultry look over her shoulder that made every inch of him— *every extra inch*—rise up at rigid attention. Thank God he hadn't worn silk or something equally flimsy. The attendees at the ball would have gotten an eyeful. As it was, he was lucky the buttons to his falls weren't bursting loose from the sudden intense pressure at his groin.

"You're playing with fire, kitten," he growled, catching her by the wrist, once she returned to him.

She pinned her bottom lip between her teeth and stared up at him. "Then I'd advise against getting burned, Lord Roth. Or scratched."

Hell on a fucking stick.

Damn but she roused his blood.

A cocktail of excitement and lust coursing through him, Winter grinned, relishing the sport ahead. His saucy minx of a wife was in for the lesson of a lifetime.

CHAPTER SIX

Dancing is a sneaky way to test the merchandise. This is no time to be shy. Performance on the ballroom floor is indicative of performance in the bedchamber.
– Lady Darcy

Isobel had not thought this through.

She was locking horns with a master of seduction, while she was a mere novice. Even with Lady Darcy cheering her on in the background, she felt out of her element, flailing in the deep part of a lake just to keep her head above water.

Her husband's strong arms grasped her around the waist, hauling her much closer than she'd expected in the next few steps, his other gloved hand tightening around hers. They could be naked for all the protection the layers of fabric between them provided…on their hands and elsewhere. The heat of his body burned through them like paper, scorching her, threatening to incinerate her.

Good God, she was out of her mind. For her, getting burned *wasn't* worth the risk, not with a man like Winter. He'd laugh and leave her in ashes.

Isobel knew the waltz well enough, as she'd been forced to learn the steps with an overeager Clarissa. But by no decent stretch of the imagination was this lewd, burningly brazen display it.

"Lord Roth, that's a bit too close," she grit out. "We're supposed to be twelve inches apart."

"It's supposed to be this way," he replied, his low rasp at the shell of her ear doing unimaginable things to the rest of her as he guided her effortlessly across the floor. The blackguard. He knew exactly what he was doing. "You haven't been in London long enough to know it."

"I have," she said. "You're being vulgar. People are staring. Cease this and release your grasp at once."

"No."

She clenched her teeth. "I will leave you here."

His grin was slow and seductive, his hand tightening on her waist. His fingers were so hot that Isobel feared they'd leave scald marks on her skin. "You won't."

She stiffened at his tone. "How do you know?"

"You don't want to embarrass my father, who is watching us like a hawk as we speak."

The fight left her body in a rush as her wandering gaze found the duke, who was indeed watching them with an unreadable expression on his stoic face. Isobel suppressed a frustrated sigh. Of course the blasted bounder was right. She could not—would not—shame Kendrick.

"I do not think you are familiar with the waltz," she snapped. "None of the other couples are dancing this closely."

"None of them have my skill."

"Is that so?" she returned, determined to ignore the imprint of his long-fingered hands and the shivers tracing over her skin like butterfly wings.

"I've had lots of practice."

She wanted to roll her eyes and punch him in his conceited head, but settled for a bland smile instead.

"So I've heard."

He remained silent for a few more beats, his hold loosening marginally as though he knew she wouldn't flee as she'd threatened. And after a moment of wary internal debate, Isobel let herself relax into his expert lead. There was something so freeing about dancing, notwithstanding the fact that if one had a talented partner as Lord Roth clearly was, it felt as though she was barely touching the ground with the tips of her jeweled slippers.

This was one of the things she'd missed. The balls and the dancing. She'd had the barest glimpse of a season with her aunt and uncle when they'd all but forced her to accept the Earl of Beaumont's suit. Isobel had relished every bit of the social life in London for the short time she'd been here, despite her revulsion for the earl himself.

As if her thoughts conjured his visage, on the next turn, Isobel's eyes caught on a gentleman who could have been Beaumont's very twin standing at the edge of the ballroom. She faltered a step before reason could intervene. The earl was no longer welcomed in England, so it could not be him. The last she had heard, he'd fled to the Continent in disgrace, his title and fortune having been stripped by the Prince Regent.

And yet, her eyes scoured the edges of the crowd, just to be sure.

The man, had there actually been one, was gone.

"What is the matter?" Winter asked.

"I thought I saw someone."

"Who?" He frowned and glanced around the ballroom.

"No one," she said, meaning it. "I made a mistake."

Her second mistake was to look at up at Roth, hearing the almost protective note in his voice. The breath *whooshed* from her lungs, that intense gray stare burning into hers...as tangible as the strong arms banded about her. Isobel swallowed, her cheeks on fire as her nerves sizzled with awareness. One smoldering look and she was ready to wave a white flag. Beg him to kiss her. Tell him to do *anything* he wanted. The concern in his gaze melted into amusement as his sinful mouth curled in gratification.

"See something you want, kitten?" he purred.

"I told you, don't call me that."

"Why not?"

Isobel narrowed her eyes in affront. "I'm not a housecat."

Something like agreement flashed in his eyes as he studied her, his gaze falling from her eyes to her lips, and then back up. "No, you're not. You're a tigress."

That gray gaze of his darkened, swirling with storm clouds and smoky desire. Desire *she* had somehow put there. Desire that now transferred liberally to her, making her breasts tighten and her body feel distractingly achy. God, the man could incinerate drawers with a glance, and right now, she was on the verge of going up in flames. She licked her lips, her pulse ratcheting as she stumbled on the next step and gripped at him for purchase.

"Problem, kitten?"

"No." Isobel nearly stomped on his instep in frustration at the nickname. He would only keep saying it to provoke her if she gave him a response. "The floor was slick just there."

Winter's smile was all teeth. "Slick, is it?"

The low rasp of his words, as intended, shot straight to her throbbing core. Blast it, she couldn't do this! A few filthy words and victory was in his grasp. Isobel's breath hitched, her entire body slumping like a rabbit caught in an inescapable snare.

"You'll never win, you know," he taunted. "This game you're playing."

The *never* made Isobel's spine snap straight. Being dismissed by him in such a flippant way made her see red.

Chin up, she told herself fiercely. *You came to London with one goal.* She didn't come here to lose… or to go down without any semblance of a fight. She'd be damned if she'd turn tail and run just because her shameless flirt of a husband could seduce a doornail. He wasn't immune from her touch, either, and that gave her power.

Unhurriedly, she let her hand slide down his arm, shaping the well-defined muscle, and felt his entire body stiffen. "It's cute that you think this is a game, Winter."

His eyes darkened at her use of his given name, and Isobel hid her smile. Careful not to call attention to her next move, she purposefully drifted off balance on the following turn, forcing them to almost collide with another couple, and let her knees buckle. The momentum shoved her side into his hard chest.

"Oh, I do beg your pardon," she said over her shoulder to the other couple before peering up at him, eyes wide and guileless. "Sorry, my lord, there must have been more…slickness."

Those full lips parted on a sharp inhale when he yanked her upright, a heated stare meeting hers as her hands gripped his waist…and a rigid length jutted into her belly. Isobel swallowed her gasp, her body going hot. Blast! If she wasn't careful, she'd be a pile of cinders by the end of the wretched dance. But she would take him, too. He'd burn with her.

That was the thing with flames—they didn't care who they consumed.

Pull yourself together and focus!

Remembering why she'd deliberately stumbled in the first place, Isobel drew her gloved knuckles down his hard waist, dangerously close to the straining bulge in his trousers, while pretending to find her footing. His choked exhalation made her bite back a gratified grin. She wouldn't be one half of Lady Darcy if she didn't know what the state of those trousers indicated.

Letting all the pent-up yearning she'd buried for three years show in her eyes, she took in a protracted breath that made her bodice rise and tighten. Winter's gray eyes went almost black as they dropped to the creamy display of her rose-tinted décolletage. Thank God—and talented seamstresses—for creative padding. Her modest bosom had never looked better.

Winter swallowed, his throat working compulsively.

Isobel nearly burst into a wild giggle. So Clarissa's long ago quip about heaving breasts and men's inability to resist them *was* true! At the time, she'd told her friend that she was reading far too many penny romance novels, but it appeared that Clarissa's pennies had been well spent if Roth's smoldering gaze was any indication.

Isobel quickly searched out her friend. Unlike the moral-smiting excuse for a dance she was forced to endure, Clarissa and Oliver were locked in a stilted embrace, both their forms wooden, their faces carved from marble.

Poor Clarissa. Isobel would have to make it up to her somehow.

But she had bigger problems to worry about…as in the man currently at her mercy. Isobel's gaze slanted back to Winter. His face remained tight with strain. *Good*. She shifted again, inviting another tormenting brush of her body against her husband's muscular thighs.

Unfortunately, despite her purposeful machinations, his fingers felt as though they had branded through the layers of silk into her skin, and her bones were so molten that she could barely hold herself upright. Desire was a two-edged blade. Every movement of their bodies sent the flames between them burning higher. She couldn't give up, but neither could she escape unscathed.

After an interminable time, the music finally stopped, but Winter did not release her.

"You are a tease, Lady Roth," he murmured and the low hum of his voice went straight to her heated nether regions. The arrogant smirk that followed, however, made her temper rise.

"It takes one to know one, does it not?"

Isobel yanked her hand out of his and whirled away, leaving him there. His husky chuckle followed as she made her way to where the Duke of Kendrick was waiting. He arched an eyebrow that reminded her of his son's. The resemblance made her scowl.

She lifted her chin. "I wish to leave."

She also wished for a cold bath.

One preferably housed within a glacier.

In the depths of the Arctic.

Kendrick didn't bat an eye. Just inclined his head, offering her his arm without comment. By the time they had located a sullen Clarissa, retrieved their cloaks, and called for their carriage, both Isobel's temper and her desire had cooled considerably. And as soon as they were en route to Vance House, the pressure in her lungs finally eased and she felt like she could breathe again. All it took was to be out of view of her husband.

Winter had met her eyes across the ballroom as she'd been saying her goodbyes and *winked*. It had made her even more determined to beat him. Perhaps Clarissa would have some more ideas. If her friend ever spoke to her again, that was. Clarissa had not uttered a single word since her dance with Oliver, and the coach was fraught with uncomfortable silence. Thank goodness Winter's brother had chosen to stay. His presence would have made the journey intolerable.

It wasn't until Isobel had bid the duke goodnight and she'd changed into her night rail that she was able to corner Clarissa in her bedchamber, already huddled under a mound of covers.

"Will you never speak to me again?" she asked the lump.

"I am sleeping, Isobel."

Isobel sighed at the curt use of her full name. "I'm sorry you had to dance with him, but it could not be helped."

A head popped up, green eyes blazing with fury. "You know how I feel about that man. Dancing with him was worse than purgatory. Worse than being dragged behind wild horses over a bed of nails without a stitch of clothing. Worse than...than..."

"I get it."

"No." She shook her head and gave a shudder. "No, you don't."

"It was one waltz, Clarissa," Isobel said, sitting on the edge of the bed. "I'm sorry, but too many people were hanging on, ready to make a scene. If you want to blame someone, you can blame me, but we both know who was truly at fault. Winter instigated the whole thing. If Oliver had left you high and dry with that rancid look on his face, people in the ballroom would have wondered what was wrong with *you*." She lifted her hands in a helpless gesture. "And you do wish to secure a husband out of all this, don't you?"

"Men stink," Clarissa muttered, but she shoved the covers back in silent invitation.

With a grateful smile, Isobel scooted up and tucked in beside her best friend. "They do, don't they?"

Clarissa turned to face her, a small grin overtaking her morose expression. "Speaking of waltzing, I thought Winter was going to deflower you then and there in the middle of the ballroom floor."

"He already deflowered me, remember?" she said dryly.

"Pollinate, then." She sighed. "Honestly, watching

the two of you was the only way I could endure dancing with that dreary prude, Oliver. You should have heard him raging on and on about Winter's proclivities. I almost told him that he would benefit from letting loose a little and taking a page from his brother's book, but that man was truly born to be a vicar, not anything else. Those two could not be more polar opposites—the pervert and the prude."

"Was it *that* bad?"

Clarissa rolled her eyes with a dramatic sigh. "Think of the worst possible thing you've ever endured and multiply it by a thousand. That still won't cover it."

"What happened between the two of you?" Isobel asked, curious. "Surely you used to be friends growing up. You were friends with Winter, weren't you?

"Yes. We all were." Clarissa's eyes grew distant. "Unfortunately, Oliver never outgrew his childhood rivalry with Winter. It got more serious the older they became, and when Oliver got Winter injured when they were fifteen, I decided enough was enough and confronted him about it. He accused me of being nothing but a naive little girl, in love with a boy who could never love her back, and then told the duke awful lies about me." She pursed her lips. "I was never in love with Winter. He was like another brother to me. But Oliver could never get past his own biases. The man's a bird-witted cod's head who can't see past his own nose to what is right in front of him."

Reading between the lines, Isobel gasped in disbelief. She couldn't even focus on Clarissa's creative name calling, though she would agree that Oliver was the worst kind of fool. "Good heavens, Clarissa, did you *fancy* Oliver?"

"Hush, you'll wake the twins."

"Stop evading and answer the question or maybe I will wake them and let them in on the juicy secret."

"Don't you dare!" Clarissa set her lips into a scowl. "When I was a girl, maybe. Now, I despise him. And the feeling is nauseatingly mutual. Let's talk about something more interesting than Lord Tight-Arse before I get angry all over again."

"Is it?"

"Is it what?"

Isobel smirked. "Tight."

Clarissa's cheeks went crimson. "Shut up."

Laughing, Isobel narrowed her eyes as a thought occurred to her, given what she'd just learned and the fact that Clarissa might still harbor feelings for a man she claimed to hate. "Wait a moment," she said, her suspicions deepening. "About that snooping mask you had in your possession the other day…"

Clarissa groaned. "You were supposed to forget that."

Isobel shot her with an unblinking stare. "Confess, wench."

"Fine, very well. It *is* Oliver, if you must know. It's only to get information, you see. I'm worried about him with Winter. He's up to something and I'm determined to prove it."

"So let me get this straight—you're spying on Oliver to *protect* Winter? That poor excuse for an explanation has more holes in it than a fishing net."

Clarissa nodded, but kept her eyes firmly on the ceiling. "It's true."

Isobel didn't believe that for one second. Clarissa was up to something. She rarely did anything without a thorough scheme. "So what do you think he's planning then?"

"I think he intends to discredit Winter somehow. I found notes in his room on The Silver Scythe and information about a meeting with an earl about a sum of money owed to him."

"What's The Silver Scythe?"

"A gentlemen's gaming club, I think." Clarissa gave another ferocious blush, her hands twisting in the folds of her night rail. "At least that's what it looked like."

"Clarissa Gwendolyn Bell," Isobel said in a hushed whisper. "Have you been to this gentlemen's club?"

"Only the outside," she replied, her blush going deeper. "I followed Oliver there once without his knowledge."

Wide-eyed, Isobel chucked her friend in the arm. "You heathen! I must insist that if you return, I have to accompany you. Did you discover anything else in his room?"

Clarissa shook her head. "It's not enough that he covets Winter's downfall; I worry things will get out of hand. I've never seen anyone so consumed with hostility, and it's gotten worse over the years. Oliver can't move past his own bitterness."

"And Winter? Have you told him of your concerns?"

"Not recently. He thinks Oliver is irritating but harmless."

Isobel frowned. Oliver might be, but there were many other men who were far from harmless, who went out of their way to destroy people in pursuit of their own selfish desires. She and her sister had dealt with one firsthand.

Now she was the Marchioness of Roth, protected by the powerful Duke of Kendrick, if not her own husband. Astrid had the same protection as Duchess of Beswick.

The Earl of Beaumont was firmly in their past.

CHAPTER SEVEN

Subterfuge is an excellent tool in the waging of the seduction wars.
– Lady Darcy

"Aren't you my special beauty," Isobel crooned to the mare as she moved the curry comb in a circular motion down the horse's hindquarters. Hellion loved being groomed, and here in London Isobel could only do that dressed as Iz the groom without causing a ruckus about a lady—*gasp*—doing manual labor and kneeling in the dirt.

Randolph hadn't stopped scowling since the moment she'd raced down to the stables, dressed in her breeches, shirt, cap, and mask. "My lady," he'd chided. "You cannot keep doing this. What if you're recognized? It will be my hide *and* yours if the duke discovers such tomfoolery."

"I'm wearing a mask," she insisted. "No one will recognize me."

"There's no fire anymore. Why are you even wearing a mask?"

Isobel had shrugged. "I can say I'm disfigured, like the Duke of Beswick. That I suffered injuries to my face as a child. No one will question it as long as you back me up. Say you will, Randolph. Please." She wasn't above using bribery to get her way, but Randolph already knew she had a stubborn streak a mile long. She went the route of cajolery. "I'll put in a word with the duke about the head groom position at Kendrick Abbey once Rodney retires."

His eyes had narrowed, but then he'd sighed in resignation. "If the duke finds out, I had nothing to do with it."

"I promise he won't."

Grumbling under his breath, he'd walked away, and Isobel had resisted the urge to hoot with triumph. She'd thought she would love the glamour of London, and she did. But she also missed the quiet spaces of Chelmsford and the freedom to be herself. Even if it meant donning a pair of ratty old breeches and spending time in a stable yard.

"There, sweet girl," Isobel murmured to Hellion. "Doesn't that feel nice? I've missed you."

In town, she barely had time for herself, much less the mare. The invitations came in a deluge. Clarissa was thrilled, of course, but the thought of all of the endless socializing was overwhelming. Not to mention the interminable intrigues of who had the biggest fortunes, who was sleeping with whom, who planned to offer for whom, and who was getting jilted. Add in the cat-and-mouse game she was playing with her husband, and Isobel was ready to scream.

She couldn't get a handle on him. Isobel bit her lip. The dratted attraction was insufferable. Those eyes of his hadn't lost their piercing quality, his smile still inspired wickedness, and his well-defined, masculine form made her own body sit up and take notice.

Honestly, the constant state of arousal was tiresome.

And on top of that, Lady Darcy's clever methods of dealing with such sexual frustration were losing their efficacy. Such was the fate of being awakened with heart-pounding fantasies one didn't need. Isobel wished she could go back in time, put herself back to sleep in dear old Chelmsford, and forget about her desirable, irresistible, maddening rake of a husband.

He was the whole reason she'd *needed* to become Iz for the rest of the afternoon.

She'd come to London to prove to him—and herself—that she wasn't a country mouse he could ignore. To teach him a lesson and leave him wanting, just as he'd left her. If she truly wanted to channel Lady Darcy, she needed to retake the power he'd snatched from under her, and to do that, she had to up her seduction game. Her cheeks flushed.

The question was, how *did* one seduce an utter horse's arse?

Hellion pranced and gave a whinny at her suddenly aggressive strokes, and Isobel gentled the motion. "Sorry, girl."

Isobel shoved thoughts of Winter from her mind. Grooming Hellion was tiring, and by the time she had gone over the horse with a soft brush and combed out the mare's mane and tail, she was breathing heavily. The hard, mindless work was exactly what she'd needed to release the build-up of tension and fretfulness simmering in her veins. Maybe she should inform the other half of Lady Darcy that vigorous activity cured sexual frustration. Somewhat.

"There you go, my girl," Isobel said, using a damp washcloth to gently clean the mare's eyes and nose. "You look a treat."

The horse nudged her as if in thanks, and Isobel gave her an apple.

After re-stabling the horse in her pen, Isobel refilled her oats, then moved outside to cool off. She was boiling in the coarse, ill-fitting clothing and her sweat-dampened mask. She longed to tear off the face covering and dunk her head in a bucket of water but didn't dare to, not after Randolph's warnings. Even though she couldn't see them, there were eyes everywhere. Isobel splashed carefully, and then sat under a shady tree to munch on a second apple she'd tucked into her pocket and watch the men patch up the burned corner of the stable.

The repair was nearly complete, and the workmen laughed and joked with each other. She snickered to herself at some of the bawdier jokes, but it was nothing she hadn't heard before, not after being around Clarissa's raunchy brothers. She missed those rascals terribly, too.

Isobel was so engrossed in her thoughts that she didn't hear the heavy footsteps approaching until their owner was right on top of her. God above, it was Lord Roth himself.

"Are you looking for someone, milord?" she asked, peering up at him and taking a large, noisy bite of her apple beneath the loose hem of her mask.

"I'm looking for you, as a matter of fact."

"Me?"

Isobel froze at his tone, her breath catching. Did he know who she was? Had she been discovered after all? She opened her mouth and shut it. Even if he had, she didn't know what she would say. Instead, she waited, shocked to the gills when he squatted down beside her. She hunched down more, keeping her face hidden. Thank God she reeked of horse and sweat, enough at least to not smell like a woman.

Or his wife.

Aside from breasts, Clarissa had elucidated that men were also exceedingly particular about scents. Isobel fought the urge not to inhale *him* and failed miserably. His own natural scent of pine and wintry air set her heart to hammering and her traitorous blood on fire. Dear God, why did he have to smell so deliciously divine? Like a forest covered in freshly fallen snow.

"Why is your face covered?" he asked.

"Burns, milord," she lied. "When I was nine."

Winter nodded, and Isobel was stunned he was so easily satisfied by the explanation. Then again, he was friends with the heavily scarred Lord Beswick, so perhaps he understood what it was like for a person to live life under a mask because of a facial disfigurement.

"How is your charge? Hellion, is it?"

"The mare's well, milord. Just gave her a good rub down."

"And her mistress?"

Isobel hid her surprise with a shrug. "Also good, milord. She took Hellion out to Rotten Row this morning. The horse doesn't get nearly enough exercise as she did at Kendrick Abbey. She gets restless."

Much like her owner.

Isobel took another healthy bite of her apple, chewing loudly and hoping he'd take the hint and go away, but no such luck. Her husband leaned back against the tree beside her, and she fought not to ogle the splendid expanse of fawn-covered thigh that stretched precariously close. One long arm reached out to drape over his knee. Isobel could hear every rustle of fabric as it tugged against his well-muscled body—a masculine frame she remembered far too well.

With him so near and so accessible, Isobel had the sudden, mad urge to climb into his lap and fit her softer curves to his harder angles. God, she was a wanton. Maybe she needed to curry three more horses. Or dunk her feverish idiot body into the Serpentine.

"So Iz-like-the-verb," he said, and Isobel stiffened. Drat, he *had* been listening. She'd have to be careful. Just because he wasn't acting like a giant prick didn't mean that he didn't have a working brain hiding behind a veneer of kindness and civility. "How long have you been Lady Roth's groom?"

Isobel felt his eyes settle on her but kept her chin angled down, head bowed, and shoulders slouched. He wouldn't insist she look at him in light of her false condition. Some men might, but deep down, she knew he wouldn't.

She considered the safest answer. "I've helped with Lady Roth's horse for three years, milord, and afore that, I helped Lady Beswick. I came with the horse from Beswick Park."

He pondered her reply for a minute and then rose, handing down a coin that she took in one grime-covered fist. "I need a favor from you."

And there it was—the reason he'd sought her out. "What's that then, milord?"

"Keep an eye on your lady for me. If you see anything odd, report back to me."

She frowned, wondering where his sudden

nosiness was coming from. Maybe he wanted to know if she was getting ready to leave. Or was it more? She knew he'd noticed her alarm during their dance at the ball when she'd imagined she'd seen Beaumont—was he just being considerate? "Cor, are you expecting trouble, milord?"

"Can't be too careful."

He handed her a card from his coat that had his name and his address—the house she'd visited. 15 Audley Street. Isobel's mouth curled, but she tucked the cardstock into her pocket.

Winter tilted his head. "Is she a good mistress?"

"Lady Roth? She's the best."

"The *best*? That's a ringing endorsement."

As she peered up at him from beneath the darkened brim of her hat, his full mouth tilted into an unguarded smile that lit his eyes to silver. Isobel stared, fascinated at the difference in the man. The few smiles she'd caught sight of had been pale imitations of this one, and for a brief heartbeat, she was dazzled stupid. She jerked her head down, knowing that if he saw *her* eyes, her secret would be out.

"She's kind," she mumbled, feeling strange talking about herself. She had no idea how servants would view her, though she always tried to be caring and thoughtful. "A decent mistress with a big heart."

"That's good to know."

Isobel's breath stuttered out. Good to know so he could break it? Stomp on it? Toss it aside? She had no intention of letting this man get anywhere close to that vulnerable part of her.

In that moment, she had an absolutely brilliant idea. It was devious in its simplicity, because now she had a way of planting the seeds for her next moves in this game they were playing. She would use *Iz* to water the ground. Appeal to his male pride.

"The marchioness is fond of you, milord," she said casually.

Winter froze, his brows rising. "Is she?"

"She speaks of you often. Not to me, of course, but to her horse. She's very partial to Hellion. I accompany her, so I overheard. She called you a handsome devil," she added hastily.

Blast, she was trying too hard!

He'd gone quiet, and when she dared peek up, he was staring thoughtfully at the house, a small smile on his lips.

Good Lord, was it *working*?

"See you soon, Iz," he murmured.

Watching him leave, she couldn't help being captivated by the slight glimpse she'd gotten of the true Winter. The man behind the mask. It might not be physical like the linen slip covering her face, but he wore one just the same. He reminded her of the soot-covered man she'd seen here in this very spot a handful of days ago, who hadn't minded toiling alongside servants to save the lives of the animals housed inside.

Something in her chest ached.

Terrible men didn't do decent things.

Frowning, she stared down at the gold sovereign he'd tossed to her in her palm—a fortune to any servant. Isobel could have been invisible for all the attention he'd paid her since she'd arrived in London. And yet, he would task a humble stable hand to report back to him on anything odd? The man she knew of didn't do anything without an agenda, so why was he being protective over a marchioness he obviously did not care for? It was baffling. Then again, she could hardly say she *knew* Winter at all. This was the most she'd ever spoken to him beyond the guise of courtesy.

Three years of marriage and she hardly knew her own husband.

"You're playing a dangerous game, my lady," Randolph said in a low voice, making her nearly jump out of her skin. "Lord Roth will not be pleased to discover your true identity, nor will his father for that matter."

Isobel suppressed a shiver. Should he discover the extent of her deception, Lord Roth would be livid. So would the duke. But being Iz, the grubby little groom, offered an opportunity Isobel had not expected. A way to take the real measure of her husband, as well as a very clever way to *win*.

She would drop hints here and there, convince him that his wife still carried a *tendre* for him. Seduction might not be her forte, but she was good at reading people. She wanted to know what made him tick. And she was more curious than she had any right to be. She'd glimpsed a vulnerability in his eyes that she'd never been privy to before. Was it some kind of weakness? Or was it something she could use in her plans? Either way, it was an opportunity she could not pass up. Not while her future hung in the balance.

She gave Randolph a forced grin and flicked him the gold coin. "Don't worry your grumpy little head about it, because he won't."

"I hope you know what you're doing, my lady."

Isobel swallowed the knot of nerves coiling into her throat along with the words that rose to the tip of her tongue. *You and me both.*

CHAPTER EIGHT

A woman's tools for seduction are many, Dearest Friend—the most effective are the eyes, the lips, the twist of a fan, the tilt of a head. If all else fails, flaunt the girls.
– Lady Darcy

Winter studied the flat silver case of his preferred cheroots and frowned at the charred, destroyed roof of the mews, visible from the western corner of his father's library. It was even more interesting that Oliver had been the one to produce the smoking end of his brand as evidence of Winter's wrongdoing. Almost as if he'd been waiting for the opportunity.

Of late, his brother's tactics were becoming tiresome.

Winter sighed. Things would have been so much simpler if Oliver had been born first. Then he would be the duke's heir and all would be well with the world. How many times had Winter simply wanted to disappear? Start a new life without the ducal guillotine hanging over his shoulders? But it was a cowardly thing. He knew that. As much as he wanted to escape, he had held back from doing so, if only to honor his birthright for the sake of his mother.

You will be duke one day, she'd said to him. *You must be wise, my little knight. Wise and brave. And guard your heart from those who will use it against you.*

I shall, Mama, he'd whispered back solemnly.

She had loved his father, but the duke had not loved her in the same way. Unable to endure marriage to a man who did not return her affection, she'd died from a broken heart. Winter had vowed to never let anyone have that kind of power over him.

His brother had assumed that Winter would sooner die before marrying, and that had been true... until a girl with ice-blue eyes had needed rescuing. For some bone-deep reason, he'd wanted to be the hero. The worthy *knight* who saved the princess.

Maybe because he hadn't been able to save Prue.

Despite his claims to the contrary, it hadn't at *all* been about the codicil when he'd set eyes on Isobel and heard about her need for a husband. However, the marriage that had started as a means to an end for both of them was shifting.

Dangerously.

To let her in would be to lose who *he* was. And he couldn't risk that.

With a sigh, he set down the cheroot case, raking a hand through his hair as he walked closer to the wall of windows at the far end of the study. Movement caught his attention when a sliver of yellow flashed in the maze at the foot of the landscaped gardens. He cracked open the window and caught the musical trill of female laughter and another glimpse of golden skirts.

He heard the lilting voice of his wife on the air. "Don't be such homebodies, Violet and Molly! The fresh air is good for your constitution."

"Cozy libraries suit my constitution," one of the twins groaned out, Winter didn't know which. His distant fourth cousins, Violet and Molly, were Kendrick's wards since their father passed, which struck him as faintly ironic. The man could barely parent his own children, but had welcomed two more into his home.

"First to the center wins the prize," Isobel trilled. "Hurry, Clarissa!"

"This maze is the devil's armpit! And that sodding prize you promised better be worth it!"

Winter grinned at Clarissa's colorful reply. He remembered thinking similar thoughts about the hedged maze as a lad when he and Oliver would play hide-and-seek during their rare childhood visits to London. His amusement faded as he thought of the well at its center and the time he'd been shoved in, though no one had been around.

Ludlow had been the one to hear his frantic cries. The ten-year-old Winter had told his father that he'd tripped and fallen in, but he had not imagined the shove of child-sized fists against his back while he'd tossed a farthing into the well's depths. Oliver couldn't have been more than eight or nine. It had been a step up from the toads in his bed or the angry wasp nest in his boot, but Winter had always put it down to sibling jealousy.

Though, after he'd broken his leg from a loose cinch on a saddle at twelve and was set upon by thugs at Eton a few years later, Winter could no longer discount his brother's hostility. After Oxford, the antagonism had gone in a different direction...more in the vein of smearing his character and booting him from the duke's favor.

Another giddy peal of laughter distracted him, and

suddenly he was of the mind to head down to the maze. He strode from the study, taking the stairs to the garden two at a time. With sure steps, he cut through the hedgerows in a matter of minutes, slipping through secret gaps in the borders at precise intervals until he was at the center.

He approached the ornately bricked well and stared at the bucket hanging at the top of it. How many wishes had he and Prue made in that old thing? He'd give his fortune to the well to have one more day with her, but his sister was gone, and no amount of wishes could bring her back.

Winter sucked in a shallow breath and banished the swell of memory. The rustling of skirts and the pant of breaths as someone drew nearer made some of his tension fade.

"I can spot the gable of the well over this hedge," he heard his wife sing out.

A frustrated female shriek echoed farther away through the thick hedgerows. "That's it! Come on, Molly, I'm done. I'm much too hot."

"I give up, too, because I think I'm back at the start," Clarissa yelled. "You win. I'll be drowning my sweaty self in a vat of lemonade in the kitchen. Or whiskey. I'm sure the duke has some hidden some-where with sons like his."

"Quitters!" Isobel tossed back.

"We're not quitting," one of the twins whined. "It's called survival. And today, the dratted hedges have bested us. What would we have won anyway?"

"A wish, of course."

Clarissa's derisive snort drifted through the foliage. "If wishes were horses, poor men would ride."

"So cynical, Clarissa."

"Mistress of Cynicism, get it right! Shall I send a servant to fetch you?"

"No, thank you. I'm not a loser."

Clarissa's voice came through again, though fainter this time as if she'd already departed the maze. "You say that to my face, Isobel Helena Vance!"

Isobel's laughter brushed over Winter's senses like a summer rain. "I'm quaking in my boots, Clarissa Gwendolyn Bell!"

He grinned at their banter and folded his arms, propping his hip along the edge as a breathless, radiant woman came tumbling into view. His wife. Once more, he was struck speechless by her beauty. She'd always been beautiful, but now she was *luminous*. Golden hair askew, red-cheeked with grass stains on her dress, she'd never looked lovelier.

"Oh," she gasped, coming to an abrupt halt, her gaze focusing on him and then blinking rapidly as if she doubted her own mind of whom she saw. "What are *you* doing here?"

Winter's mouth curled into a smirk. "Perhaps you wished for me to be. This is a wishing well, you know." He gave a suggestive wink, his tone dripping with innuendo. "It knows our deepest thoughts and desires, even before we know them ourselves."

Her eyes flared, but then she composed herself and smiled. "Then you should be bearing a large jug of water because I'm parched!" Her already rosy cheeks bloomed as she approached to peer over the side of the well. Glittering blue eyes met his, determination rising in them at the look of bold challenge in his. "And if this well was privy to my innermost thoughts as you imply, the bearer of said jug would have been wearing much less clothing or none at all."

Winter blinked.

Did she…did he just hear her say she wanted him naked?

He felt his mouth fall open, his turn to stare in mute stupefaction. "I beg your pardon?"

Her answering smile was full of mischief, lighting those singular eyes from within as she peered up at him. "Gracious, Roth, are you *blushing*? A wicked rogue like you going red over a few bawdy words? Color me shocked."

"You think me wicked?"

Pink rose in her cheeks. "Aren't you?"

"Only when it suits me."

She licked her lips and pulled a corner of the lower one between her teeth. The sight of it let loose a flood of instant lust in his veins. "And does it suit you now?"

Bloody hell. Was she *flirting* with him? "Who are you and what have you done with the timid Lady Isobel?"

"She grew up, and she was never timid, my lord." Her laugh rang out between them. "You simply did not know her."

His appreciative gaze slid from her glowing face to the embroidered bodice of her walking gown to the tips of her muddied boots. "Indeed."

The push and pull between them had begun when she'd barged into his home, and had only increased during that teasing dance of theirs—like weapons being drawn and paces being counted in a duel unlike any other. And now, it seemed as if she were preparing to take it up another notch.

Perhaps he had underestimated his little country wife.

One knee perched on the surrounding bench, Isobel propped her hands on the crumbling stonework and stared at him, her pert nose wrinkling. "Do you have a farthing, my lord?"

With a lift of a brow, he fished in his pockets for a coin and handed it to her. He watched in silence as she closed her eyes for a second and then flicked it over the edge until there was the tiniest answering splash. She stared down into the depths before turning and sitting on the bench, a smile playing about her full lips.

"What did you wish for?" he asked.

She smoothed her dress, flicking off a few errant leaves caught in the fabric. "If I told you, it wouldn't come true, would it?"

"You did use my coin, so perhaps I have a vested interest in the boon it purchased."

Her brow pleated. "I don't think it works that way. You gave it freely."

"Let me guess, then. You wished for new jewels. Or a new horse."

"Do you think me so shallow, my lord?"

Her earlier words came back to haunt him—clearly, he *didn't* know her at all. What she truly desired, what she valued, or even what she would hope for while standing at the edge of a wishing well. Suddenly, he *wanted* to know all those things. Would she covet material things or perhaps wish for something else?

Isobel was an enigma, one that fascinated him despite his qualms about falling into the very trap he feared. He frowned as he studied her serene face. Though she seemed calm, those pretty eyes of hers glinted with a fierce strength.

"Why are you here, Isobel?" he asked instead, pushing off the bricked surround of the old well, his gaze holding hers.

"I wanted to see London."

"What's wrong with the life you have in Chelmsford? You have everything there you could ever want."

"I don't have you."

Winter blinked, her words crashing through him like a gale-force wind. "But you do. I'm your husband. You're the Marchioness of Roth. What more do you want?"

"Is it so hard to believe that I'm here for *you*?"

He prowled toward her, but she did not flinch away as he came to a stop in front of her neatly arranged skirts. His wife glanced up at him, the picture of ladylike decorum. Wanting to crack that perfect composure, Winter bent so their faces were level, his arms grasping the top of the bench on either side of her, his body caging hers in. He thought he heard the tiniest gasp, though her expression remained quite unruffled.

Ice-blue eyes seared into his, but she did not stop him when his nose grazed her temple. Winter inhaled, the scent of fresh grass and honeysuckle tickling his nostrils. She smelled like warm summer evenings on the lake. Out of the corner of his eye, Winter saw her bare fingers curling into the folds of her skirts, and he felt a beat of pure satisfaction.

He trailed his nose down, his lips grazing the shell

of her ear. Christ, her skin was just as he remembered…like the softest silk. A shallow exhale broke from her lips, but still, Isobel didn't move away.

"Yes, it is hard to believe, so tell me the truth," he said, licking her lobe before sucking it into his mouth.

"I did," she replied breathlessly.

He bit lightly, not enough to hurt, but enough to punish her for the lie. Her gasp was reward enough for him to soothe the sting with a gentle swipe of his tongue. "Ready to be honest, or do you wish for more incentive?"

Her sudden hesitation gave him pause. The lust simmering in his blood flared to a boil. He pulled away, his hot gaze fastening to hers. Pure need churned in their blue depths, her pupils blown with the same desires that dominated him. His stare dropped to her plush parted lips, and for a moment, Winter wasn't sure who was the seducer and who was the seduced.

"Christ," he muttered, shifting backward.

Isobel took in a lungful of air as though it was the first time she'd breathed in hours. Purpose grew in her gaze, eclipsing the remnants of passion. Her slender throat worked before she drew a deep breath. "Very well, if you want the plain truth of it, I intend to win you back."

The words detonated between them like a hidden landmine.

That, Winter had not anticipated.

He'd expected her to prevaricate and say she was bored, or she wanted a diversion, or Clarissa was on the hunt for a husband. Not this. Not a bald admission of wanting to win *him*. Winter hissed a breath through his teeth. He desired her, too, but that was beside the point. Want was a fluid word—she wanted a spouse and he wanted someone to fuck.

Those two things were vastly different.

Winter resisted the urge to step away and scowled, his arousal well and truly doused. His father had to have put her up to this. Was that why they'd come to London, to ambush him as a pair? Because Kendrick was desperate to secure his ducal legacy?

He felt the usual anger unfurling inside of him. Rage at his father's selfish desires, anger that he continued to use whomever he saw fit to gain his own ends, powerlessness to stop him. It was the same old story over again, only this time Isobel was the pawn.

"Did Kendrick put you up to this?" The words emerged as a growl.

"What? No, of course not." She cleared her throat. "We might have discussed your absence, but this is what I want, Winter. My husband is what I want."

His given name on her tongue did unconscionable things to him, made his blood heat and desire storm through his body. For a second, all he could think about was hearing her moaning it, sobbing it, screaming it to the heavens. Anger twined with desire, and it was only by the most valiant of efforts that he held himself in place instead of bending her over that bench, fisting his fingers in the golden skeins of her hair, and giving in to his basest desires then and there.

He doubted his sweet, innocent wife would approve.

He'd only taken her once in the customary way that wouldn't terrify a virgin. However, even thinking of her in such an erotic position—back arched, bodice down, and breasts filling his palms—was enough to inflame his blood anew. A small whimper escaped her lips as though she could sense his depraved thoughts…and his thinning control, held only by the smallest of tethers.

Winter's gaze snapped up. Her nostrils flared, pupils dilating while her body tensed, preparing itself to flee as though cognizant of being hunted by something innately dangerous. But instead of bolting as he fully expected her to, she held her ground, chest rising with shortened huffs. He tore his gaze away from the rosy flesh of her bosom, drawn up to where the tip of her tongue slipped out to sweep those plump lips.

He wanted to do depraved things to that rosebud mouth. Kiss it. Fuck it. *Own* it.

Christ, what the hell was wrong with him?

"No," he bit out. "*No.*"

"No to being a husband?" she asked, breathless. "I'm your wife. It isn't unreasonable for me to want you in my life, or the next step that comes with any marriage…a family. A child. Or are you incapable of it?"

His head flew up at that, ice spearing through him.

She frowned. "Don't you require an heir?"

His jaw clenched tight, the words a much-needed bucket of reason to his ruthless desires, bringing his sanity back like a sharp slap. "You are mistaken, Isobel. I do not want children. I am not in need of an heir, as I have Oliver, and Lord knows how much he craves the title."

"Then why did you marry me?" she asked. "You don't want a wife or child and wish to live the life of an eternal bachelor. You can't stand being in my presence to even have a civil conversation. Clearly we are unsuited, so why did you even bother?"

Winter stilled. None of the answers that sprung to mind were appropriate: *I wanted to bed you. I failed my sister. I wanted to be the hero, a better man.*

He looked away. "You needed a husband."

• • •

It hurt to hear it—the bald truth of *why* the man she'd been infatuated with had married her—but after a few pained heartbeats, Isobel pulled herself together. Now wasn't the time to fall apart or to berate herself for being foolishly naive.

Because what he said *was* true. Her need of a husband had been the catalyst—a solution to escape betrothal to an unsuitable earl. What she had not expected was trading one form of the devil for another. In this case, someone who had no desire to be a husband, to be a partner, to be anything but an attention-seeking git.

Who did not want a wife nor children, apparently.

She'd come to terms with being ignored and cast aside as a wife, but the feeling of bitterness spreading in the pit of her stomach at his blatant refusal to build a family, damaged her more than she would have imagined. The picture of such a future seemed entirely too bleak…and devastatingly lonely.

Where on earth had she gone wrong?

Had she been so thoroughly mistaken in taking him for an honorable gentleman? She remembered his smiles and his devilish charm. He'd danced with her and flirted, and she'd fallen for it stock, lock, and barrel. What girl wouldn't? But in hindsight, her own infatuation with his looks and personality might have blinded her to the truth of what lay beneath.

Because he was not *that* man.

Isobel pinned her lips, feeling his heated stare track the movement, and another burst of answering warmth bloomed within her. Winter might not desire her as a wife, but he keenly desired her as a woman. Then again, if all the tomfooleries printed by the gossip rags were true, he chased anything in a skirt.

Even her…his objectionable wife.

She ground her teeth together, the desire draining out of her limbs. She wasn't naïve—she knew men like Winter had needs, and from what she'd seen at 15 Audley Street, she hoped he'd been smart and protected himself. Even the Prince Regent was rumored to have contracted syphilis. The rogues of the whole Carlton House set were infamous womanizers. Lady Darcy had done an illuminating exposé on sexual health, including the use of French letters, English riding coats, sponges, and the like, that had been quite eye-opening. All thanks to Clarissa, her unsuspecting brothers, and an enormous amount of blush-inducing research.

A butterfly landed on her skirts and she studied it, wanting to touch its gossamer wings, but knowing the moment she tried, it would fly away. Eventually, the delicate thing took to the skies in search of sweeter pastures.

Isobel loosed a bitter breath. Winter wasn't a butterfly, and neither was he delicate.

With a nod, she sent her husband an even stare. "I needed a spouse, but I did not expect to be held prisoner in the country."

"A prisoner?" he scoffed. "In a sprawling manor worth a bloody fortune?"

"Your *father's* estate," she said softly.

His mouth tightened as he uncurled that broad body of his and rose easily to his feet to move past the well. "I don't see you complaining. You seem to have gotten rather close to the duke, after all."

"By necessity, I assure you."

He huffed a laugh over his shoulder. "Hedging your bets, my lady?"

It took a moment for his meaning to register, and when it did, Isobel nearly screamed. *Oh, that cockle-brained cur!*

Was he honestly suggesting that she was angling for his father? How dare he be so crass? Isobel wound her fists into her skirts, thankful that he'd risen and couldn't see the disbelief and fury on her face. Of *course* he would assume something so utterly wrong.

God, he made her want to kick him!

She couldn't fathom what an ass he was in her presence and yet so gentle in the company of Iz. Then again, he had nothing to prove with a humble groom. No mask to wear. No games to play. No meddling wives to chase away. Her eyes narrowed. That seemed to be exactly what he wanted…for her to be angry. To quit London. Quit *him*.

Well, two could play at that game.

"No, I'm not after your father," she said, standing, her eyes finding him where he now stood at the edge of the clearing near a cluster of blooming rosebushes. His hooded gaze rested on her, but he kept his distance, as though he didn't trust himself. "But if I were, why would that bother you? You seem to *hedge your bets* at every opportunity here in London."

A strange noise emitted from his chest, and after a beat, she registered it as laughter. Cold, hollow, unfeeling laughter. "That's a husband's prerogative, darling. And you shouldn't have come to town if you did not wish your delicate senses to be offended."

"I'm not blind," Isobel snarled. "I can read, and the newssheets reach Chelmsford just as well." She stalked toward him and stopped just short of her skirts brushing his boot-clad toes. "Trust me, I'm well aware of your reputation, and my senses are inured to anything you have done or can possibly do."

Her lungs ached after the outburst and she breathed in heavily, the air charged between them. Winter's face was unreadable, his lips a pressed white line and his fists knuckled at his sides. A muscle leaped in that chiseled jaw. He was predatorially still until he spoke, the low rumble making a quiver of sinful awareness ripple through her. "Are you?"

"Am I what?" she echoed.

A hand lifted to brush a stray tendril of hair from her brow. "Inured."

Drawn by the huskiness in his voice, Isobel's body nearly swayed into his touch. Her gaze was imprisoned by a molten gray stare so full of wicked promise that her breath stuttered and her mouth went dry. His thumb drifted down her cheek to graze across her jaw and then her bottom lip. The intimate gesture immobilized her. She could almost taste his skin.

"W…what are you doing?" she stammered.

"Disproving your brave words."

Isobel gulped as his thumb pulled decadently against her lip, unsure whether to lean in and lick or rear back and bolt. The rough graze of skin against skin made her head spin. She wanted to suck the probing digit into her mouth and bite him as he'd bitten her earlobe.

Good heavens, where had *that* thought come from?

"That wasn't a challenge," she said, proud that there was no audible strain in her voice. "It was a statement of fact. Why do you think I came to London? I read that you'd fought a duel for some opera singer, and I thought if you were so hell-bent on living your most glorious life then I would get on with mine. If you do not require me to beget an heir, then this discussion is moot. I'll find another way."

Winter's stormy eyes narrowed to pinpricks, as if memorizing every dip, every curve in her mouth. Her lips tingled, and she licked them, catching the tip of his thumb in the process. His fingers firmed on her jaw, eyes flaring, when he leaned down as though he intended to replace his fingertip with his mouth. For an agonizing second, Isobel thought he might kiss her, but then he yanked away with a growl, his hand falling to his side.

"What did you mean by that?"

She frowned at his emphatic words. "By what?"

"That you'll find another way?"

She tossed her head and stared at him, her chin jutting in challenge. "I've made no secret that I want to start a family, Winter, and I will do that with or without you. There are many children in need of care. I always wanted children of my own, but I know better than to expect this from you. You've made it perfectly clear that this isn't what you want."

Air hit her flushed cheeks when he whirled toward the maze's exit. Winter glanced over his shoulder, jaw working, an ugly chuckle breaking from him. He turned to face her, and the awful look on his face made her entire body brace for the impact of his reply. "You're right, Isobel, it's not. I would make the worst sort of father, worse even than my own."

Isobel took a step toward him and halted at the ice in his stare. "He's not the same man you knew, Winter."

"And you think three years makes you an expert? I've dealt with him my entire life, been a living pawn on his chessboard—one to be moved and discarded at will, so trust me when I say without a shadow of a doubt that *you* are mistaken."

"So that's it, then?" she bit out. "You'll walk away from me?"

Her cheeks heated at her boldness, but he only shrugged. "By law, I already have, dearest. Wedded and bedded as they say. Go back to Chelmsford where you belong. Or stay in London if you prefer. But there's no way in hell either of us will ever share the same bed again."

Her temper pricked at his stony dismissal, and she gave in to it heedlessly. "And why, pray tell, is that?"

"One and done, love."

Stung, Isobel glared at him, fingers knotting into her skirts as she fought the urge to rail and scream. It wasn't *her* fault she was inexperienced. It was sodding well *his*! And yet, he was blaming her for it. Her eyes narrowed as something Clarissa had shared came back to her—a suspicion that Winter didn't engage with women at his own assemblies, and hadn't for the better part of five years. She loosed a breath. *Could such a rumor be true?*

"Care to make a wager on that?"

Winter's eyes glinted with amusement. "I don't make wagers for sport, but if I were a betting man, it wouldn't take much to have you running back to Chelmsford with your tail between your legs within the month, *wife*."

The gauntlet fell between them, striking nerves in her body she didn't know she possessed. Making her temper boil with indignation. He expected she would flee his very presence like the mouse he accused her of being? Well, she was no mouse. Not anymore.

"I'll wager that the only thing between my legs, darling, will be you," she countered saucily, her chin hiking with resolve as she stalked toward him. "And you'll beg me for that honor."

His eyes smoldered beneath his brows. "Is that so?"

"Count on it."

Then Isobel did the one thing she knew he would not expect. She shoved herself up to her tiptoes, grabbed his lapels, and planted a hard kiss on his stunned mouth before slipping between the hedges.

CHAPTER NINE

Don't be afraid to be selective. Explore the menu. Be adventurous. No one wants to be stuck eating spotted dick for the rest of their lives.
– Lady Darcy

Three days later and Winter could still feel the warm press of his wife's lips, taste the tart sweetness of her mouth. The kiss had been chaste, the arousal it had spawned had not been. He'd been in a coil for some time following, forced to cool his ardor on that bloody bench in the maze until he was in an appropriate state to return to the house. It had been an eternity since he'd kissed a woman…or allowed one to kiss him.

She'd been all flashing, icy blue eyes and repressed temper, standing there like an angry angel lording over a mere mortal. And mortal Winter *was* in her presence. Never had he wanted to grovel more and plead that she have her way with him. Say yes to everything she commanded. Lay himself bare at her feet like a devoted disciple.

Winter almost grinned at the recollection of her sinfully erotic boast that he'd be begging to be between her legs. Little did she know he already craved it with a vengeance. Those sleek thighs of hers haunted him. He'd had to relieve himself almost every night since that kiss…something he hadn't done so often in years.

There was only one thing to be done about it—he

had to make her leave and get things back to normal. Get his life back on track. She wanted a husband? He would give her one…the one he knew she'd never accept. And he knew just the way to do it.

"Matteo," Winter called.

He appeared on silent footsteps, garbed in fitted trousers and an exquisitely tailored coat. The man had exceptional taste. "Yes, my lord?"

"Send an invitation to Lady Roth to accompany me to The Silver Scythe this evening. Instruct her that my carriage will arrive for her at ten sharp."

Matteo's deep brown eyes widened. "Tonight?"

"Yes."

"Might I remind you, my lord, that it's *masque* night."

Winter smiled. He was well aware of what night it was, especially in the private section of the wildly popular gaming club that catered to specific members. All highly confidential and consensual, of course. His valiant little wife would never recover.

"I am aware. Extend the invitation."

The man bowed. "As you wish, though it is not much notice, and she will require a mask and a gown."

Winter arched a brow. "A man of your talents shouldn't find that too hard of a problem to address, now, should he?"

"I will visit Madame Pinot," he said.

Isobel had visited the celebrated modiste herself upon arrival in London for the season, so her measurements would be on hand. He'd only recently received the bills, sent on from Oliver with a nasty note about the astronomical amounts for both Isobel and Clarissa.

The figures hadn't daunted Winter—not to a man of his own personal wealth—but the itemized garments had left him wound as tight as a spring.

Gowns, slippers, chemises, night rails, silk stockings, lace-embroidered drawers. He'd been unable to function for a good hour just from the sheer torture of imagining Isobel clad in lacy undergarments with violet ribbons that teased her porcelain skin.

"Matteo?"

The man turned. "Yes, Lord Roth?"

"I want her in purple."

After dressing, he made his way downstairs to the morning room where Ludlow had placed his pile of usual correspondence. He sifted through them while sipping on Matteo's own brew of strong Italian coffee. As always, the social invitations arrived in droves. He couldn't accept them all of course, nor was he inclined to, but he'd been particular about knowing where his wife and father would be. Now that he knew why she was here, he tossed them all to the side.

He'd rather sit in the gaming room at his club with a glass of whiskey and a hand of cards. Matteo had long since taken over *masque* night in the private portion as majordomo. But tonight would be different. Tonight, Winter would be experiencing it through the eyes of his soon-to-be-shocked-senseless wife.

He couldn't wait.

Briefly, he wondered how her opinion of him would alter, whether she would look at him with censure and disgust, in much the same way that Oliver did, and something in his chest gave a small twinge. He shook himself hard. What she felt about him didn't matter. What mattered was that she would return to Chelmsford.

After breakfast, Winter settled into his study to go over his many accounts and investments that spanned countries and continents.

Contrary to popular opinion, even a fake libertine still had to work.

• • •

Isobel stared at the handwritten note with a mixture of fascination and distrust. Her gaze panned to the gorgeous man who had delivered it. She'd caught a brief glimpse of him when she'd first arrived in London standing on the landing at Winter's residence, but that glance had barely done him justice. He was tall and well-built with olive skin. Brown eyes gleamed over a strong nose and wide lips. He was nothing compared to Winter, of course, but Isobel still had a pair of fully functional eyes. Without a doubt, he was very handsome.

"What is your name?"

He bowed. "I am Matteo, Lady Roth."

"And what purpose do you serve to my husband?"

"I am his man of affairs, business partner, sometimes valet, and friend, among other things," he replied. "Lord Roth wishes to have your reply, my lady."

She let out a breath. "What exactly is The Silver Scythe? A social club?"

His mouth bowed into a smile. "I will let Roth educate you on its many mysteries."

Something in the way he said the last two words

made a frisson of nerves wind down her spine. Clarissa had mentioned The Silver Scythe before. It'd been the place that Oliver had met with the unnamed earl that Clarissa had visited when following him in secret.

Isobel felt the beginnings of interest blooming. She was certain the sudden invitation had something to do with her parting challenge in the maze. It was a feint, and one intended to make her lose.

She glanced down at the elegant cardstock. "It's a masquerade? I'm afraid I don't have anything to—"

Lifting an arm, Matteo nodded and signaled to the coachman waiting at the entry with several large boxes in his arms. "With Lord Roth's compliments."

Isobel frowned, recognizing the inscription of Madame Pinot's shop. "He's thought of everything, hasn't he? I don't know what to say," she murmured.

"Say yes, my lady," Matteo said, dismissing the man once the boxes were in place on the low table.

She had no other choice. Saying no was tantamount to admitting defeat. She might as well run back to Chelmsford exactly as he'd said, with her tail tucked meekly between her legs. Isobel drew a breath and straightened her spine. She would do what she must.

"Have you known his lordship long, Matteo?" she asked, slipping the cover off one of the boxes and inhaling sharply at the first peek of shimmering amethyst satin shot through with silver thread. It was the most magnificent color she'd ever seen. The nerves in the pit of her stomach coalesced into warmth.

Focus, she commanded herself. This was all a

game, nothing more.

"I've known Lord Roth for eight years."

So five years before they'd been married. She'd been right in guessing they'd met during his travels. "He's been a good friend to you?"

A fierce intelligence gleamed in the depths of the man's eyes as they burned through her, past her whispered question to the unvoiced fears fluttering within. "Roth is a decent man, my lady. Complicated, but steadfast at the heart of it."

"He says he doesn't have a heart."

To her surprise, Matteo chuckled, a pleasant sound that made her own lips curl in return. "That sounds like something he would say. I suppose you will have to find out for yourself whether he does or not."

"You won't tell me?"

"Some Cupid kills with arrows, some with traps."

"Shakespeare?" Disbelieving laughter burst from her. "I'm quite sure that neither love nor Cupid are words in my husband's vocabulary." She shook her head, her voice low as she replaced the cover on the box. "The only trap I fear is going to this club and making a complete fool of myself."

"That will never happen. I look forward to seeing you, my lady."

"You'll be there?"

"Yes." He bowed. "It was my honor, Lady Roth."

After Matteo left, she mulled over what he'd said. He had to be addled if he believed a man like Winter would ever become prey to a cherub's arrows. If he did indeed have a heart, it was walled up behind layers upon layers of iron and stone, and fortified by sheer mulishness.

Isobel signaled for the waiting footman to ferry the boxes up to her chamber, where she knew her very curious friends would be waiting, having no doubt attempted to eavesdrop on the conversation. Sure enough, they fell upon her in a frenzy the moment she reached the top of the landing.

"I'm surprised you three did not tumble down the staircase," Isobel teased. "In a sweaty, drooling pile."

"Dear Lord, stop stalling, woman, who *was* he?" Molly fairly squealed, which was rather unlike the dour twin who usually scoffed at their frivolity.

Clarissa fanned herself. "Good gracious, he was so beautiful that I almost clubbed him over the head and dragged him to my lair to have my wicked way with him."

"You'd have to fight me." Violet sighed.

Isobel twisted her lips in amusement at the girls' calf-eyed expressions. "He's Roth's man of affairs."

"What did Mr. Tall, Dark, and Delicious want?" Molly asked, breathless, wide eyes tracking the footmen carrying the stack of boxes from the modiste.

"What are all those for?" Violet frowned. "I thought all the orders had already been delivered?"

"These are from Roth." Isobel ushered the wide-eyed girls into her chamber, dismissing the waiting maids. "I've been invited to The Silver Scythe. For a masquerade tonight."

There was dead silence in the bedroom. Clarissa, Violet, and Molly looked like mirror-images of each other—slack-jawed and shell-shocked.

Clarissa was the first to react. "Holy buzzard ballocks!"

Isobel giggled. "Buzzards have those?"

"Stop trying to change the subject, wretch," she said in a gleeful whisper. "You're going to a masquerade *there*?" She dragged Isobel over to the bed and the other two followed. "Gracious, Izzy, I've asked my brothers about that place and it's rather worse than we imagined."

Worse?

"Like a brothel?" she asked, her stomach climbing into her throat. She knew of Winter's reputation and that he ran with an indecently fast set, but this was beyond the pale.

"No," Clarissa said, eyes gleaming. "*Worse*."

Isobel's brow pleated as she stared at each of the young women in turn. Molly and Violet both sat on the edge of their seats, their eyes like saucers as she was sure hers were. *What could possibly be worse than a brothel?*

Clarissa was practically shaking. With what, Isobel didn't know, but it couldn't be good if her friend could barely speak. "Part of it is a normal gaming and supper establishment, but I've heard from Derrick's own mouth that another part caters to members with…specific needs."

The way she said *needs* made Isobel's skin prickle. "Well, go on, don't keep us in suspense."

"Spanking and torture and the like," Clarissa blurted.

Molly burst into snorts. "Spanking like a child? Are you serious?"

Clarissa scowled at her. "Don't laugh. It's the truth. Apparently, some men—and some women, too—like to be switched." Her voice went breathless. "It's a thing. A sexual thing. Some of them like to be restrained as well, and they pay for the privilege, believe it or not." She gave a dramatic sigh and threw herself back into the bedclothes. "I'll bet Lady Darcy would have a go at hitching a lover to the bedposts with a pair of her silk stockings."

Isobel's cheeks went red-hot at the image. "Clarissa!"

"What?" her friend replied, her own cheeks stained pink. "As long as both parties agree, who is it hurting?"

"If word got out, they'd be branded as immoral deviants," Molly said. "I've read about that."

"There are worse things," Clarissa shot back.

Molly tossed her head. "Such as?"

"Murderers and thieves for one, half-wit," Violet said smugly. "Don't be a wiseacre, Molly."

"I am *not*!"

But Isobel wasn't listening to their bickering. The heat that had climbed into her face was now descending elsewhere into her body. Considering that she was one-part Lady Darcy, the scandalous direction of her thoughts couldn't be helped. On torturous cue, the picture of a dissolute Lord Roth, wrists banded tight and legs splayed wide, spun into her brain.

No, he would likely prefer the reverse. In her head, the image shifted and she was the one helplessly tied while a devil with sable locks and a powerful chest loomed over her. A gasp wrenched from Isobel's lips as her thighs clenched with helpless desire.

"Have you heard of such things before?" she choked out.

"Not much, though apparently it's been a pastime of Prinny's lately," Clarissa said. "All rather hush-hush of course. Rumor has it that he's been a frequent visitor to Marylebone where he visits with a woman by the name of Theresa Berkley and her merry band of mistresses."

Isobel's eyes widened as Molly and Violet gasped and covered their mouths. "Truly?"

"You three are actually surprised?" Clarissa scoffed. "That roué will do anything in the pursuit of pleasure, even being flogged while tied to a wooden steed."

Molly's mouth fell open. "Now you're jesting."

"Heard it straight from the horse's mouth."

"Which horse? And how did you manage to do that?" Violet asked. Isobel was curious, too. It wasn't like men were open about bawdy talk in front of gently bred ladies.

Clarissa grinned. "Easy. I told Harold he had no idea what a Berkley Horse was, and of course, he went straight to Derrick who couldn't wait to set him straight about the nature of a good flogging. A bunch of gossiping fishwives, my brothers."

Isobel shook her head. "One of these days, they'll catch you, and what will happen then?"

"I'll cross that bridge when I come to it. For now, they are a boundless treasure trove of salacious information."

"Forget your brothers, you twits," Violet said with breathless exasperation. "Open the boxes so I can see the dress before *I* have to flog someone!"

Isobel sniffed as she reached for the first of the boxes and opened it. She parted the sheets of delicate fabric. "No one's flogging anyone. That's not my cup of tea and it shouldn't be yours, either. It's not proper." Though it didn't explain why ribbons of heat curled through her veins and converged in an insistent pulse between her legs. She ignored it and lifted the delicate gown from its confines.

All of them let out matching *oohs*.

The dress was fit for royalty. Yards and yards of rich satin the color of shimmering amethysts gave the illusion of liquid movement. The stitching was so fine, the seams nearly invisible. Tiny seed pearls and crystals adorned the bodice and the hem. It was almost too lovely to look at, much less wear. The other boxes contained a pair of slippers, ivory gloves, a cloak made of some velvety-soft fabric, and an intricate mask.

She pulled it out. Designed in shades of purple to match the glimmering hues of the dress, feathers and diamonds studded its stunning surface. It would cover half of her face, shielding her identity from view, and for that she was grateful. Unlike the usual masks, it did not have a handle, but a pair of silk ribbons that were meant to tie around her head.

"I don't know if I can do it," she murmured aloud, pressing the racy mask to her face and feeling a different kind of heat diffuse through her body.

Clarissa moved to stand beside her, humor replaced by solemnity. "Then don't. You're in charge."

"But then I lose." She bit her lip, a finger tracing one violet plume. "I'm here to make him grovel, and if I can't even wear this dress, what hope do I have of winning this ridiculous wager I've made to have him begging for my attentions?"

"You can do this, Izzy," Clarissa said. "And you have us behind you all the way. Show that husband of yours who wears the trousers!"

"This is a gown and I'm in over my head," she said, staring at her three friends.

"Then you swim," Violet said brightly.

Molly frowned. "Or sink."

"Shut *up*, Molly!" Clarissa and Violet cried in unison.

But they were both right—one of the two would happen. Isobel stared at herself in the nearby mirrored glass, barely recognizing herself beneath the mask. As rakish as he was, Winter would never let any real harm befall her nor would he suffer her reputation to be ruined. If she had to guess, this outing was meant to teach her a lesson and have her running back to Chelmsford.

She'd been the one to throw down the challenge, after all.

Now she just had to strap on her big-girl stockings and see the wager through.

CHAPTER TEN

Dearest Friend, the erotic art of Mr. Thomas Rowland-son provides a wealth of practical instruction. Gather your smelling salts and your pearl necklaces. Do not say I did not warn you.
– Lady Darcy

The vision in violet ascending the steps of The Silver Scythe could not possibly be real. Winter had been unable to form any coherent sentences since he'd collected her at Vance House. In the carriage, apart from a soft greeting, she had remained mostly silent. Nerves, he gathered. He felt them, too, batting around in the pit of his stomach. Though he had no inkling of why *he* was nervous. This was meant to unbalance *her*.

But the minute he'd seen her, the tables had turned.

Fuck, he should have instructed Matteo to dress her in a sack. Though he had a sneaking suspicion that his wife would make that look appealing, too. And that tantalizing mask that drew attention to her piercing eyes and luscious pout. Hell, it made him want to see her in it alone, wearing nothing else. As a result, he'd been as hard as stone even before her sultry honeysuckle scent had filled the carriage. For him, the short ride had been torture.

Thank God, she hadn't wanted to talk, because he was sure he would have spouted a load of nonsense. By the time they arrived, however, he had composed himself enough to remember his manners, offering his arm as he led her into the marble foyer of the sumptuously decorated converted mansion. He was particularly proud of his little club, which he'd bought years ago with the Duke of Westmore, and together they had transformed the place from rundown supper club to extraordinary, invitation-only oasis for the wealthy and connected. No expense had been spared for comfort. Or pleasure.

Membership was thriving and business could not be better. One day, he hoped to offer Kendrick a grand tour of what went on behind closed *private* doors. The duke would keel over. His brother, too. Oliver only knew of the non-secret part of the club, though the fact that a duke's son was a gaming hell owner galled both of them to no end. Never mind that the establishment brought in hundreds of thousands of pounds. Vice was a profitable business.

Instead of entering the main hall after divesting themselves of their cloaks, Winter led Isobel up a side staircase barred by a black velvet rope. A silent man stood there, who let them pass without a word. Winter saw his wife worry her lip with her teeth, and he hid his smile. Good, she was uneasy. He wanted her to be. They reached the top of a jutting alcove that looked over much of the first floor.

Following her wide-eyed stare, he let his gaze trace the decor, feeling another surge of pride as he took in the rich fittings of the gaming room—felted card tables, mahogany furniture, and thick-piled Persian carpets. Elegantly dressed men and women occupied the space, some playing, others mingling. Most of them were easily recognizable, since none of them wore masks. It wasn't required, not in this part of the club.

People came to The Silver Scythe to see and be seen—the crème de la crème of the aristocracy. Lords, ladies, princes, princesses, maharajas, sultans, politicians, old money, new money. Wealth was power, and the power in this room spilled from it like overflowing wine.

"Would you prefer to use another name while we are here?" Winter asked his silent wife, though her eyes were drinking in every detail below.

She blinked owlishly up at him, her pale blue eyes glittering like gems from the depths of the purple mask. "Why would…*oh*!"

"You don't have to, but some of our more reticent members prefer to have a *nom de guerre,* if you will."

"Lady Darcy," she said without pause.

Winter wanted to laugh. Isobel was the furthest thing from the infamous Lady Darcy. For one, Lady Darcy would be dripping in confidence, armed only with her wits, her charm, and a smile. He also itched to tell her that there were likely already at least three such named women in attendance below, given the rage for the anonymous author.

He arched a brow. "*You* know who Lady Darcy is?"

Blue eyes met his with a hint of fire in them. "Doesn't everyone?"

"And yet you still choose that name?"

Isobel came to a halt, forcing him to stop at her side, just in front of the supper room where tables were set with sparkling crystal glasses, silver cutlery, and the finest of china. She took a minute to scan the room, her expressive eyes flashing with admiration. "Does that shock you, my lord? That a lady of my delicate sensibilities would read such a scandalous periodical?"

"Not at all," he said as he turned them down a wide velvet-paneled corridor. Winter nodded to the enormous man guarding the door at the end, and they were granted entry. "One has to learn somehow. She's as good a teacher as any, I suppose."

A blush of color rose in her cheeks. "She is rather blunt."

"Refreshing, I would counter."

Isobel peered up at him. "Are you an admirer, Lord Roth?"

"Of Lady Darcy?" he asked and she nodded. "I find her wit and candor energizing, though I suspect that the true Lady Darcy is an old biddy with nothing but time on her hands and a wealth of stories beneath her belt, giving advice to poor unsuspecting misses. There are bets in the betting book at White's and here as well as to her identity. Some say she's a man."

"Truly?" She shook her head, a small smile playing about those plush lips. "I disagree," she went on after a protracted look. "I think Lady Darcy is newly married with a scoundrel of a husband, and she invented her *nom de plume* as a means of curiosity and escape."

Now it was his turn to stare, one eyebrow rising. "A bit close to home perhaps?"

"You don't believe she could be me?" Isobel asked.

This time he did laugh. Loudly. Enough to draw the attention of several masked guests sitting in tucked-away alcoves. As he steered them past after a brisk nod of greeting, Winter glanced at his wife's lovely features visible beneath the mask, sweeping down her neck to her swelling décolletage. The rich color made the silver flecks in her eyes glow and the creaminess of her skin seem even more luminous.

"No," he said finally.

"Why not?"

He led her down another mazelike hallway, this one lit with golden sconces and set with paintings of a distinctly erotic nature. He wondered if she'd noticed. Winter paused in front of a particularly suggestive garden scene by Thomas Rowlandson. He didn't have long to wait before the sweetest gasp left her parted lips, her eyes arrested on the piece.

A pink tongue darted out to wet her lips before a quivering palm rose to rest on her breast. Her skin turned a delectable shade of pink as he bent forward, his mouth so close to her ear that he could feel the heat of her skin.

"That's why," he whispered. "You're much too innocent, little beauty."

• • •

Oh, dear God. Isobel felt so unbearably hot that she was sure she would swoon. Her throat felt dry and her heart pounded against her ribs like a demented thing. The painting in front of her was lewd, depicting sexual congress between many frolicking partners in a public garden, and it was indecent, horrifying, and scandalously arousing. But that hadn't been the catalyst to set her off.

That had been Winter's gravelly rasp against her

ear that had nearly made her eyes roll back in her head. She'd *felt* his lips graze her ear, and Lord help her, she wanted to feel his teeth graze over her skin. Feel him suck that sensitive lobe into his mouth as he'd done before near the wishing well.

No, the fire shooting through her body was a direct result of *him*, not because of filthy art that she and Clarissa had already pored over in scandalous delight. For research, of course. Isobel reached for her fan and realized too late that she didn't have one. It hadn't been provided with the dress. Her gloved fingers curled into fists at her sides. She wasn't *that* innocent, she wanted to declare to Winter, but her mouth refused to cooperate.

Everything refused to cooperate.

She could only stand still like a rabbit caught in the sights of a very, very hungry wolf. Willing her body to move, she breathed out and wrenched her eyes from the painting, only to fall on another that was twice as bawdy. She snatched her gaze away.

Good Lord, there were filthy paintings everywhere the eye could see, and all she could feel was her husband's huge frame against her back, caging her in. Her senses were battered on so many fronts—visual stimulation, his body bracketing hers, the deeply masculine scent of him, the rough cadence of his breathing. The only thing missing was taste and the feral need brewing inside of her to turn and seal her mouth to his.

She needed to take control of a situation that was quickly spiraling out of control.

She had to take charge.

Isobel found her voice. "These are interesting. It's

certainly not Ackermann's," she said, referring to Rowlandson's printer on the Strand, The Repository of Arts.

"Indeed."

She didn't have to turn to feel his surprise that she was familiar with the artist or his body of work. Score one for her. She needed to retune this game of theirs. Winter's fingers gripped her elbow and her entire body tensed, but he only meant to lead her down the rest of the eye-opening corridor. Another black lacquered door stood at the end, for which he produced a large gold key and turned it in the lock. It slid open on noiseless hinges.

"Welcome to what we call the Underground, Lady Darcy," he said.

To the untrained eye, the club looked exactly like the rest of the mansion they had walked through. Sumptuous decor, exquisite furnishings, not a guinea spared, but Isobel *felt* the difference. The air felt silkier against her skin as if she were walking into a web of sin. Tingles exploded across her body in a rash of gooseflesh as she followed Winter, her own darkly handsome Hades, luring her into the depths of the Underworld.

No, he'd called it the Underground.

Isobel repressed a shiver. Not of fear…of something else. Some intoxicating combination of desire and dread. Panic warred with the promise of pleasure. But as she strolled with Winter past other masked people who paid them no mind, she wasn't afraid. For some mysterious reason, she trusted him. Foolish, perhaps, but there it was. He wanted her gone, but she felt it deep in her bones that she wasn't in any danger. And she was curious, oh so curious to learn about her perplexing, secretive, and dangerously attractive husband.

In here, Winter wore a simple gray mask. Isobel suspected that most people knew who he was from the subtle way their gazes slid his way. Or perhaps it was the prowling presence of him—the true predator in a field full of prey. Even in a place as dark as this one, he reigned. The Prince of Darkness, as beautiful and deadly as a fallen angel. And by God, some wanton part of her wanted to succumb to whatever he would promise.

Focus, Isobel. The game is yours. Be Lady Darcy.

"Where are we going?" she asked in a convincingly stable voice.

"Have you eaten?"

She shook her head. "No."

"Then dinner."

She couldn't possibly eat a single bite. She was much too hot. Too wound up. But when they entered a large salon with an intimate corner cubicle set for two and delectable scents reached her nostrils, her stomach gave an obnoxious grumble. Thankfully, with the low strains of music in the background, it hadn't been noticeable. Perhaps that was why she was feeling light-headed…she was simply hungry.

Though hunger pangs didn't usually strike between her legs.

Isobel nearly giggled at the thought.

There were no chairs but a luxuriously padded bench seat that curved into the wall, much like the one in a carriage, which forced them to sit side by side. When they were seated, her gaze canvassed the space. Like the previous supper room she'd glimpsed, this one left no stone unturned in terms of extravagance. Unlike the previous dining room, however, these occupants all wore masks. It made a fluttery feeling emerge in her belly, that sensation of being in a forbidden place. It excited her.

She paused, remembering what Clarissa had said, and panned the room again. Beside the masks and the overindulgence, nothing seemed out of the ordinary. "I have to admit, my lord, I'm surprised. This all seems rather tame."

"Look again," Winter said.

Isobel acquiesced, this time, taking in details her eyes had missed before. Naughty but gorgeously wrought sculptures, much like the crude paintings in the entrance corridor, graced the edges of the room. Her eyes lifted to the cherubic mural painted on the ceiling that boasted a distinct lack of clothing and a definite lack of morality.

It was only then she saw that the footmen wore practically nothing. They were dressed in black and gold livery, but beneath their open jackets, hints of bare skin were visible. She'd been too intent on the food before, though now she gasped. As wine was poured by a particularly handsome servant with a roguish smile—and a gaping jacket showcasing his well-defined chest—Isobel caught her breath.

Gracious, it was beyond scandalous! How had she not noticed? Clearly she'd been distracted by her husband. She opened her mouth and then closed it. They were all gorgeous, every single one of them, and they all screamed lust. Or maybe that was just her. Her mouth gaped as that very same footman led a scantily dressed older lady from a nearby table to a door at the far end.

"Are they…? Do they choose to do this?"

"Of course. And everyone who works here is compensated handsomely. Anything goes as long as it's consensual." His gaze tracked hers. "Jorge has worked here since its opening."

"What are they going to do?" she blurted, her cheeks flaming hot.

Winter lounged back in his seat. "Whatever they want. Now, please, enjoy the meal."

Dinner was efficiently served by more of the stunning footmen. Isobel ate and moaned as the exquisite flavors danced in her mouth—cream of turtle soup, followed by braised beef loin in wine, roasted pheasant, and a delicate fish in a beurre-blanc sauce. Isobel tried a little of everything, another sound of pleasure escaping her lips at first taste of the rich dessert served at the end. Dear God, she'd died and gone to heaven.

She glanced up. Winter's eyes were glued to hers, his sharp cheekbones flushed, probably from the wine he'd consumed. "Good?" he rasped.

"Divine."

"The chocolate is imported from Spain. It's an aphrodisiac to enhance sexual pleasure."

Isobel nearly choked on her mouthful. She'd had drinking chocolate before, but this was something else. A rich, layered torte that melted on her tongue and tasted like carnality on a plate. Who knew that food could be so sensual?

Or perhaps it was the searing look in her husband's eyes as she licked a stray crumb from her lip. The growl that ripped from him went straight to her lady parts. Wanting to torture him just a little, she scooped the last bite and raised her fork to his lips.

"If that is truly its purpose, perhaps you should have some as well."

Watching her, he accepted it, opening his mouth and curling his tongue around the tines. The tension between them shot through the roof. Her chest tightened and her nipples pebbled against her dress. But Isobel wasn't the only one affected. Winter's eyes were so dark with need, his pupils had nearly swallowed the gray irises.

"So, besides fare fit for the devil himself, what else is here?" she asked, wiping her mouth with her napkin.

"Whatever one desires."

Isobel swallowed, the words lost in her tight throat as he angled his body toward her. The moment was interrupted, thankfully, when a masked gentleman stopped and claimed Winter's attention. Air flooded her lungs as though they'd been held prisoner.

"Sorry to interrupt, Roth," the man said. "Just a quick matter of the auction. Apologies."

An irritated Winter glanced at her. "This won't take a moment, Isobel."

"Please," she murmured.

They clearly knew each other. The man seemed vaguely familiar to her, but she could not place him. As her eyes wandered over the other diners and the footmen, a wicked idea came to her.

Time to take back the reins.

Removing her glove, she slid the hand resting on her lap beneath the table to Winter's knee. The embroidered tablecloth hid the movement from view.

The only outward sign that he'd noticed her daring act was a slight intake of breath. He kept his attention focused on the gentleman. Heartbeat thundering in her ears, she inched up his rock-hard thigh, marveling at the muscle she felt there. He was not a man prone to laziness, if evidenced by his corded strength.

But his deliciously muscular thighs were not the goal.

That prize rested at the top of them. According to Lady Darcy's detailed instructions—knees, thighs, groin— in that order. Save the trophy for last. Men liked to be teased, but not *too* much. A firm handhold was best.

Isobel bit her lip—she could barely muster up the courage to inch upward, much less worry about grip. She was attempting to stage an epic seduction when she had no blasted idea what she was doing. She'd never touched a man *there*.

It's a body part, she told herself, *like a knee*.

Gathering her courage, she resumed her exploration, freezing when her marauding fingertips encountered the rock-hard ridge in the crotch of his trousers. Isobel nearly choked on her inhale. It was nothing like a knee at all! She steeled herself and inched forward, knuckles sliding along its impressive length. Her husband put the male organs on display in Rowlandson's lewd drawings to utter shame. Her mouth went dry as her fingers learned his shape.

Giving her wine a nonchalant sip with her free hand, she peered up at the men who were still in quiet discussion. Winter gave no sign that he was affected by her tentative exploration.

Time to change that. Step two: grasp firmly.

She filled her palm with him and did just that.

It was then that he lifted his own glass with a shaking hand and drained the contents, though he did not pull away or put a stop to her attentions. A gratified smile took over her lips.

Good Lord, he was thick and long, pulsing against her even through the layers of his clothing. She fisted him, gently squeezing and running her fingers along his thick staff to the tip. One fingertip traced the rounded crown, a bead of wetness soaking through the black fabric. A choked noise reached her ears and she shot him an innocent glance.

"Did you say something, my lord?" she murmured, drawing the gazes of both men. She froze, her hand in place, her thumb drawing tiny circles over him. His girth jerked in her palm, more fluid dampening her skin. Winter's face could be hewn from rock, though his eyes burned…with lust and the promise of retribution.

"No," he croaked.

The gentleman on the other side of the table wore a diverted expression, and Isobel felt a beat of alarm. Oh God, he didn't guess what she was doing, did he?

"I've taken up enough of your time. I'll leave you to your…dinner," he said with an amused twinkle in his eye, and walked off. Isobel felt a blush take over her entire body at the intonation of the last word. She refused to entertain any shame, however.

A heavy palm covered hers. "Just what do you think you are doing, Isobel?"

"You did say I could do whatever I desired," she replied saucily, with much more confidence than she felt. "Do you not like it?"

"Does it feel like I don't like it?" he growled.

She lifted her gaze to his, taking in his clenched jaw. "No."

• • •

That was because her innocent touch had nearly made him spill in his pants like a schoolboy. Christ, the boldness of her. Fisting his shaft while Westmore was standing there with that knowing smirk on his face. It wasn't hard to deduce what was going on under the table, if not from Winter's own monosyllabic responses to the rigid cast of his features. But he hadn't wanted to stop her—it had felt too good.

Even now, his cock begged for release. He was *so* close to spending in his trousers, held back only by pure will. He'd watched her the entire night so far, unable to take his eyes away. She'd taken in everything with unvarnished delight, consumed every bite of her meal with such pleasure that he'd been rapt. And unbearably, excruciatingly aroused.

He hadn't sported an erection in this club in years, and not for lack of opportunity. Sex and vice were rampant, just not for him. And then she'd touched him, working his weeping cock with a combination of inexperience and eagerness that nearly undid him. If Westmore hadn't been standing there, irritating the fuck out of him, he would have launched his own fingers up her skirts to return the favor.

God, this woman. What would she be like in the throes of passion? He thought back to their first and only coupling, which had been an experience he'd been unable to forget. Clearly, one time had ruined him for any other. But now he wanted her in every position imaginable—under him, above him, and every scandalous way in between. His staff swelled even more beneath their palms, causing an erotic exhale to leave her lips.

Damn, he wanted to fuck them both out of their misery.

No, *no*. He had to stay the course. Bedding her would be a mistake.

His cock would have to accept its sorry fate.

Winter cleared his throat and slid out of the seat. He felt her eyes dart to the prominent, *unsatisfied* bulge in his trousers, a blush staining her cheeks, but he made no move to cover up. It was just as well the wet spot from his excitement blended into the dark fabric, but his raging condition was *her* doing, after all. Instead of looking away as he expected her to do, his audacious little wife lifted her chin and looked her fill. Yet again, he found himself at a loss for words.

Who *was* this woman?

Before either of them could speak, her gaze was drawn to the far end of the room where a raised stage sat. Lights were extinguished by efficient servants, drawing everyone's eyes to the front. "Goodness, isn't that your man of affairs?" she asked.

"Matteo, yes. He's the master of the evening," Winter answered, his throat thick with lust.

"What's he doing?"

"Watch," Winter said.

Matteo took the stage and welcomed the guests. "The bidding for one hour of Lady Darcy's time will start at a hundred pounds. She is an expert in flogging, both performing and receiving. Dedicated to her passion, Lady Darcy is willing to…"

Isobel froze, her eyes blasting to his, though not with surprise at the woman's name, which matched hers. "What is this?" she whispered.

"Exactly what it looks like. An auction."

"But…it's…she's…" she trailed off, her eyes flicking back to the woman who now held a crop in her capable hands. The bidding had already increased to several hundred pounds. This Lady Darcy was in high demand. Twin flags of color lit his wife's cheeks.

Winter's mouth curled. "Do you wish to participate?" Her gaze panned from the stage back to him. "Tell me, kitten, would you offer yourself up for auction wearing nothing but a switch and a smile?"

So many emotions crossed her beautifully expressive face, it was fascinating to watch. Panic, alarm, intrigue, lust, shyness, resolve. But her reply… Her reply was pure seduction.

"With the right incentive, why not?"

He blew out a strangled breath, his body and brain tangling on the knife edge of reason. All he wanted to do was yank her into his arms and savage that cocktease of a gown to pieces. Claim her until they were both spent and unable to breathe. Rid himself of this unspeakable obsession once and for all. But Winter knew that would be a mistake he would be unable to recover from. He scrubbed at his face with his palm.

This whole evening had been a fucking terrible idea.

"Come," he growled. "I'll take you home."

The tension between them in the carriage didn't abate but was heightened by the confined space, his erection straining toward her as if it had a mind of its own. A mere two feet and a few paltry layers of clothing separated them. Six buttons and a flip of her skirts, and he could sink home. Groaning, Winter tugged at his cravat, focusing on anything but the accident waiting to happen sitting opposite him.

"Did I do something wrong?" she asked softly.

"No," he bit out.

"You're upset."

What man wouldn't be with an erection the size of the English Channel that showed no signs of deflating any time soon? "Just leave it, Isobel."

She leaned forward. "You're angry with me."

Winter's lips flattened as he crudely cupped his distended cock, nearly hissing at the sensitivity. Blood roared in his ears. "No, I am not angry, but unless you intend to get on your knees here in this coach, *wife*, and put that mouth to better use, you'll stop asking questions."

Her eyes sparked, but for the rest of the ride, she remained blessedly silent.

CHAPTER ELEVEN

Solitary practices or vices, also known as erotic self-stimulation, will not stunt your growth nor will it stop development of the organs or create artificial maturity. That is simply ridiculous. It is your body, Dearest Friend. Learn it. Love it.
– Lady Darcy

Isobel's thighs clenched over the sleek, powerful muscles of her horse as Hellion galloped down Rotten Row, kicking up thick clods of dirt in their wake. Sweat gleamed in patches on the mare's hide, matching the perspiration that gathered on Isobel's own neck and scalp. The dirt trodden track wasn't the wild fields of Chelmsford, but it would do. And Isobel needed the release.

Unless you intend to get on your knees and put that mouth to better use…

God, the sodding words were on repeat in her head!

Crazed laughter bubbled through her. What she really needed was a different kind of ride, but this would have to do. Squirming in the saddle, Isobel pushed the horse harder. It was a risk to take Hellion out dressed as Iz, and rather different from grooming her in the privacy of the mews, but there was no way a highborn lady would get away riding astride in London without censure, and she'd been desperate for a bracing round of vigorous exercise.

Limbs trembling with exhaustion after the final run, she cooled off the horse as they returned at a much slower pace to the mews near Vance House, where she dismounted, only to be approached by Randolph with his usual scowl. He seemed surlier than normal. The reason for it was made evident when he nodded over his shoulder to the man who waited at the entrance to the stables.

Her husband—the object of her frustration.

She let out a shaky breath. Isobel hadn't seen Winter since that disastrous evening at The Silver Scythe several nights ago. Though Clarissa and the twins had hounded her for days, she'd been tight-lipped about the experience. Admitting she'd felt her way around her husband's groin didn't strike her as something she wanted to share. In truth, she rather regretted her boldness, especially the tense ride home when his vulgar suggestion had stunned her into silence. A part of her had wanted to do as he'd asked—and shock him in return—but the truth was, even with Lady Darcy's direction, she wasn't *that* bold. No matter how intrigued she may have been by the idea.

Now, the marquess sat on the fence like he didn't have a care in the world, his gaze tracking her movements. She handed Hellion off to Randolph, ignoring his look of reproach, as she made sure the cloth over her face and her cap were tucked in place. Isobel almost rolled her eyes. If he continued to act like a mother hen, he'd be the one to expose her true identity, not her.

"Top o' the morning to you, milord," she called out to Winter, drawing a look of disgust from the older groom. Heavens, it was turning out that her whole life was full of masks. "Randy said you were waiting for me?"

"Ran*dolph*," the older groom growled, half lifting his palm to cuff her in the ear for her insolence and then thinking the better of it with a slight squawk of alarm. Isobel bit back a grin—it would have been what she deserved if she truly was a boy. Which she wasn't. She really shouldn't tease him so.

"Any news to report?" her husband said, dismissing the other groom with a flick of his hand.

Assaulted by the crisp scent of him, Isobel couldn't suck in a lungful of air for a handful of heartbeats. Nearly gasping, she thrust her fists into her pockets and bit her lip beneath the cloth. She needed to focus on planting the seeds of Lady Roth's secret love, not attempt to absorb him through her nose. "Her ladyship has been distracted during her outings."

"Distracted?"

He perked up at that, and she grinned beneath the mask. He was much easier to bait than she'd expected.

"Well, blushing and carrying on, mostly about you, milord. She's gone all doe-eyed, nattering on about falling for the wrong man. Winter this and winter that. Though Lud knows why she's on about the weather. It's sodding June."

Winter chuckled, the seductive sound winding through her like music. God, she loved his laugh. It was both deep and wicked, lighting places inside of her that needed to behave. Heat gathered between her legs where her breeches pressed and rubbed, and she wanted to shove her knees together to relieve the ache. But a motion like that would not escape his notice, and it wasn't like she wanted to draw his attention there. She was missing a crucial bit of equipment for her disguise, after all.

Isobel was grateful for the face cloth, though, because at least it hid her flaming cheeks. She felt Winter's eyes on her, traveling from the cloth-covered mounds of her nose and chin, and tracing up to her ear, which was covered by her cap. Oh, hellfire, her *hair*! Had she tucked every strand in after her ride? Given her breakneck speed, her hair would be a mess. Blond hair was common, but *long* blond hair would be a dead giveaway.

"How badly were you burned, Iz?" he asked.

"Not so bad," she blurted, the huskiness of his voice doing obscene things to her.

"It's a miracle you're alive."

His obvious concern for a humble groom surprised her. Once more, it did not match what she knew about him, that he was a selfish libertine who only cared for himself. She shrugged off the notion. He was only fishing for information.

"I shouldn't exist at all, milord." Wasn't *that* the truth?

He went silent, and Isobel didn't risk peeking up at him. With her track record, she'd fall into a lust-filled trance and tumble to the ground in a dead faint. "Besides that, has the marchioness seemed upset or overly aggravated or frustrated?"

All. Sodding. Three.

"Frustrated, milord?" Boys probably shouldn't squeak, but it was too late. Isobel cleared her throat, lowering her voice. "In what way?"

Winter let out a laugh, his fingers closing about

the fence post until his knuckles went white. "Never mind, you're much too young. Any visitors of late?"

"No, milord. Not to the yard, though mayhap, she receives callers. Lord Oliver for one."

"Ah, yes. My brother. What's he up to, I wonder?" Isobel felt his gaze land on her again. It was truly a wonder how in tune she was with him. "Does she receive him often?"

"Lord Oliver? Hardly," Isobel said before she could think twice. "Can't abide the man."

"Is that so?"

Isobel blinked, scrambling for a reason as to why she would know this. "She used to talk about him to Miss Clarissa when I accompanied them on rides in Chelmsford. A groom hears things here and there, you know. Neither of them seems to like him, though he appears to be favored by the duke."

"Favored, indeed," Winter murmured and hopped easily off the fence. "You'll let me know if you see him again."

To her surprise, he leaned in slightly, nostrils flaring. As before, she didn't dare meet his eyes. Or breathe. Or move a muscle until he'd righted himself. What was *that*? Unless she was mistaken, he'd bloody well sniffed her.

"Honeysuckle."

Fuck. The coarse oath burst in her head.

"Lady Roth visited Hellion earlier," she prevaricated, putting as much disgust in her voice as she could muster. "Her perfume makes my nose itch."

"Makes something itch," she thought she heard him say, but he'd already strolled halfway across the yard.

When Winter left, Isobel breathed out, lifting her arm to sniff at her own skin. There was no flowery scent there. Still, that had been much too close. From Randolph's thunderous expression, it seemed he agreed.

• • •

Winter swallowed a groan. The striking contemporary art on display in the great exhibition room at the Royal Academy was doing nothing for him. No, instead his attention was fixated on the two women walking arm in arm ahead of them, perusing the paintings and stopping to converse here and there. One was Clarissa, and the other, his wife.

The tempting minx was under his skin, her scent in his nose, her image burned into his brain…the feel of her elegant hand stroking him. Lust drizzled into his blood, threatening to enflame parts of him that needed to behave in public. He could not get the sensation of her caressing him so boldly out of his head. And now that her groom, Iz, had let slip that she was more enamored of him than she led anyone to believe, it seemed he couldn't stop thinking of her. He was fucking *obsessed*.

"You should do something about that," Westmore murmured at his side.

Winter suppressed the violent urge to punch the duke in the teeth. God knew why he'd invited the man in the first place once he'd discovered from a very obliging Ludlow where his bride had planned to go today. It was crowded enough that she hadn't seen him yet, though he knew it would only be a matter of time. For now, he enjoyed watching her, at least when Westmore wasn't provoking him with asinine comments.

"About what?" he said.

"Your wife." The duke grinned. "I can feel your frustration from here and it's making *my* ballocks ache. The devil knows why you didn't let her work that sap out at the club when it's obvious she wants it. Bed her and be done with it."

"She wants a child." He frowned. "She said she expected it when we married, but now she knows that I won't. I can't give in."

Westmore shrugged a shoulder. "What's the problem?"

"You know how I feel," Winter said, glaring at his friend. "It's what Kendrick wants, and I'd die before ever giving that man any satisfaction."

They stopped in front of a portrait of children painted by Sir Thomas Lawrence. Westmore pursed his lips, and Winter prepared for the rubbish that would no doubt come spewing forth. "This could be you…a parcel of brats, being painted by a celebrated artist."

"I do not want children."

"Because of Kendrick or because of you?"

Winter's eyes flicked to the woman in the sunflower-yellow dress, an indescribable urge taking hold of him. In another lifetime, he might have considered such a thing. If he didn't revile his father so much. If his whole life hadn't been about stamping out the insufferable Vance blood from his veins. He moved on to the next painting, one eye trained on the swatch of yellow.

"You know why."

A firm hand grasped his arm and steered him into a deserted corner of the hall. "This is not the time or the place, but you have to let it go, Roth," Westmore said. "Prue is dead. Denying yourself a family will not bring her back."

"How dare you?" Winter seethed, yanking his body back.

"I dare because no one else will, you arrogant jackass. You don't listen to Matteo, you barely speak to Ludlow, and now, you're refuting a possible future of happiness with a woman you're clearly obsessed with—and married to, might I add."

"You know nothing."

"I know enough," the duke countered, keeping his voice low, though they were already garnering attention from others. "And I know *you*. Let it go, my friend, and allow yourself a chance to be fucking happy."

Winter's nostrils flared, fury pouring through him in hot waves. "Prue never got that chance, did she?"

Westmore loosed a breath, the pity in his gaze too much to bear. "So you'll prefer to be angry and alone in some obscure way to punish yourself for failing her and in some fuck-you to your father, instead of being content with a wife and a family?"

"Yes," he gritted out. "And don't pity me. I choose this. For my mother. For Prue."

A hand squeezed his shoulder. "We both know Prue would not have wanted this for you. It would have killed her to see your heart so consumed with bitterness." He paused, obviously conflicted to go on. "And there are things about your mother you don't know."

"What are you talking about?"

Emotions chased across his face, but resolve remained. "I never told you but years ago, the duchess tried to seduce your father's solicitor and she threw a fit when he refused her. Prue saw it all. That was when things took a turn for the worse. After Mr. Bell made it clear that he would go to the duke if she didn't cease her advances, the duchess tried to discredit him, but Kendrick wouldn't hear of it."

"You're lying."

"And then she punished poor Prue for no reason at all, simply for being in the wrong place at the wrong time."

"Why haven't you told me this before?"

Westmore shrugged. "Because Prue asked me not to. She didn't want you to lose your mother's love as she had."

"Do Clarissa or her brothers know?"

"No, I don't think so."

Agape, Winter stared at his oldest friend, shocked to the core at the revelations, but before he could answer, a commotion from the other room reached them. A high-pitched scream filtered through the air, and then he was pushing past the duke, his long legs taking him around the bend to where the crowd was the thickest. His eyes searched desperately for yellow and found none. Relief was fleeting. The odds were slim that Isobel or Clarissa were in that mêlée, but he had to make sure.

His heart shriveled as he heard the sound of Isobel's voice. "Help. Get help, please!"

Fear punching through him, Winter shoved through the crowd with Westmore on his heels. He was mad with worry, growling at anyone in his path. "Get out of the way, for God's sake, or I will remove you bodily, so help me."

The violence in his voice must have done the trick, because the throng parted, and the sight that greeted him nearly made the strength drain from his body. Both Isobel and Clarissa were on the floor, but it was the sight of the red staining Isobel's ivory gloves that made his throat close. "Are you hurt? Are you bleeding?"

"It's not my blood," Isobel said, her eyes wild with terror. "It's Clarissa's."

Westmore took charge, calling for a constable and keeping the crowd at bay, while Winter skidded to a crouch beside the two women. There was a short but deep scratch on Clarissa's upper arm. Uncaring of being in public or propriety, he ripped his cravat from his neck and pressed it to her wound. She winced but didn't make a sound, even as he wrapped and tied the white cloth around the injury.

He examined his wife, scanning her body to make sure that she was not hurt. Other than the fear etched on her face, she appeared to be unharmed as she'd claimed. It didn't stop his heart from thundering in his chest, however. "What happened?"

"There was a man," she stammered, her hands trembling as she clasped them in her lap.

Winter looked around. "Is he still here? What did he look like?"

"No, he ran when I screamed. He was young with dark hair, and well-dressed." She swallowed hard, tears filling her eyes as they landed on an ashen Clarissa. "I saw the glint of something in his hand just before he grabbed for my reticule on my wrist, and then Clarissa pushed in, shoving him out of the way. He must have cut her somehow. And then he took off."

"A thief?" Westmore asked from where he stood, his large body partially blocking them from scrutiny, eyes narrowing.

It wasn't uncommon for thieves to frequent events open to the public. Flashmen were becoming more creative, dressing their footpad accomplices up in fancy clothing to take advantage of wealthy patrons in crowded settings. But something in Isobel's face made Winter pause.

"What is it?" he asked.

She bit at her lips, the nervous gesture telling. "He said something."

"He spoke to you?"

"Yes, at least I think he did. He said I would pay."

Winter rocked back to his heels, his eyes locking with Westmore's. That could only mean one thing—that the thief knew exactly who Isobel was. Fury and fear twined in his veins. It hadn't been an isolated incident by a random pickpocket. She had been *targeted*.

But by whom?

Ludlow had said that Oliver had received the invitation and he'd passed on the tickets to the women since he could not attend. Had his brother been involved somehow? Would he go to such extremes as to hurt his own sister-in-law? Winter's rage intensified to inhuman levels.

Fuck, he was going to throttle the lily-livered bastard.

His gaze caught Westmore's as he rose. "See them safely home."

"I will," the duke replied. "My carriage is in front. I fetched it when I sent for the constable." Westmore paused. "Don't do anything that will land you in prison."

"Wait, Winter, where are you going?" Isobel asked, her fingers reaching up to catch the edge of his jacket. But despite the clench at his name on her lips, Winter couldn't look down at her. He didn't want her to see the murder in his eyes or have her think it was directed at her.

No, his fury had its own deserving target.

"Stay with Westmore," he said, stepping out of her grasp. "You can trust him. He'll get you to safety after you've spoken to the constable and he'll summon a doctor to see about Clarissa."

Without looking back, he strode from the exhibition hall. The crowd cleared for him as if the deadly look on his face was enough to make people flee. Within moments, he was in his coach and on his way to Vance House.

He wasted no time storming into the foyer of his father's residence and throwing his cloak and hat to the butler. For once, it wasn't the duke who set him on edge. "Oliver, I know you're here!"

Servants scattered and scurried out of his way, eyes wide as if he were an unwanted intruder. For some reason, it made him angrier. He was a stranger here, yes, but it wasn't as though they didn't know he was the duke's bloody heir. Slamming the door to the study open, he found it empty, and then proceeded to stalk to the library, whereupon he found his prey, waiting as cool as a cucumber with a brandy in hand.

"To what do I owe the honor, dear brother?" Oliver drawled, lounging back in his chair. "I assume it must be quite dire to have dragged you here."

Winter pounded a fist into the mahogany desk. "Isobel was attacked at the exhibit. The exhibit *you* sent her to."

The fact that his brother goggled at him did not register until his response emerged. "*What*? How?"

His eyes narrowed. "You're saying you don't know?"

"No, I don't. What are you talking about?"

"Isobel and Clarissa were attacked at the Royal Academy today by a pickpocketing ruffian, and the attacker told Isobel she would pay." His anger surged to new levels. "Tell me you didn't have anything to do with it. Tell me and I won't beat you to a sodding pulp."

His brother stood, ashen-faced and mouth thinning. "I did not."

"Where did you get the invitation?"

Oliver's nostrils flared, but the hesitation that passed through his eyes was enough for Winter's wrath to flare. "An earl. A business acquaintance."

"You're hiding something. I see it written all over you."

"I would not hurt a woman."

Winter's fists clenched, itching to pummel his brother's pursed face. "Well, too fucking bad because Clarissa was stabbed."

"Stabbed?" he whispered. "How badly? Where?"

Oliver's reaction was almost comical, and if Winter was in a more rational state of mind, it would have struck him sooner that his brother's distress hadn't been for Isobel…it was for *Clarissa*. It was obvious that he harbored feelings for her. Deep feelings, if his horrified reaction was any indication. Given his response to the news, he would not have deliberately put either of them in danger.

It was the sole thing saving him from Winter.

"In the arm," he said. "She'll be fine if infection doesn't set in." Oliver went white, the blood draining from his face. Winter took brief satisfaction in seeing his coldhearted brother actually feeling some emotion for once, but then took pity on him. "Westmore is seeing to her and we've summoned Kendrick's physician. They should be here shortly."

The breath of relief Oliver exhaled was real. "Oh, thank God."

Winter turned to stalk from the room, but then stopped at the door. "You might not have had a hand in this, Oliver, but Kendrick won't be able to save your sorry arse if I find out you were in any way involved, mark my words."

CHAPTER TWELVE

Don't carry a torch for a man who does not want you.
It makes you look desperate and gauche. Have some
pride and set your sights elsewhere.
– Lady Darcy

After the exhibition, the following days went from bad to worse in the form of one buxom Italian heiress, Lady Vittorina Carpalo. An utterly unwelcome blast from Winter's past. He hadn't seen Vittorina in years, not since his time in Italy. She was spoiled and vain, and didn't care whom she had to ruin to get what she wanted. A handful of years ago, that had almost been Winter, and he'd only managed to escape her clutches by the skin of his teeth.

But now, here she was…on his brother's arm, crossing Vauxhall Bridge, heading into the gardens for the latest grand gala, with Isobel strolling a few feet away in deep conversation with Kendrick. The whole thing stank, and it wasn't a question of how, it was a question of why.

Why was she with *Oliver*?

Irritation hummed beneath the surface as he followed them past the pavilions and lush lawns with their marble statues and pillars, heading toward the supper boxes. Most of the lamps that made the gardens so special had not yet been lit—they would be following a whistle during supper when night fell—but the orchestra was already playing in the nearby rotunda.

Normally, Winter enjoyed visits to Vauxhall, considering the less than starchy atmosphere and the mix of social classes, but tonight he felt on edge. Not only because of Vittorina's unwelcome presence, but because of Isobel. When Ludlow had informed him that Lady Roth was accompanying the duke and Lord Oliver to the gardens, Winter had been torn.

He did not want to be anywhere near his father *or* his brother.

But he also wanted to keep an eye on his wife.

He had meant to stay away from Isobel, after ensuring that both she and Clarissa were healthy and well. The physician had pronounced Clarissa extremely lucky that the knife hadn't been a few inches lower or deeper. As it was, the cut hadn't needed stitching and had already closed on its own. Clarissa being Clarissa wore her wound proudly, loving the attention and the fact that she'd been in a knife fight. When Winter had drily remarked that being in a knife fight required actual fighting, she'd rolled her eyes and told him to mind his own business.

Isobel, on the other hand, was another matter entirely. She'd refused to leave Clarissa's side, and Winter knew that it was only because of Clarissa's insistence that she would be fine with the twins that Isobel had even ventured out at all. As far as he knew from servant gossip, it was the first time she'd been out in days.

Only to be pitted against a viper among women.

Christ! What had Oliver been thinking bringing Vittorina here? The question was, did his brother actually know who Vittorina was? It could be an unfortunate coincidence, but the truth was, he wouldn't put anything past his brother, despite believing his innocence in the attack at the gallery. This could still be a ploy to discredit him in the eyes of their father… or worse, Isobel.

There was only one way to find out.

"Roth, darling, how lovely to see you!" Vittorina squealed when he joined them.

Winter had to hand it to her. One would think they'd held each other in great esteem or knew each other intimately with such a greeting, when their parting had been one of threats and physical violence. The only thing he wanted to do was shudder with revulsion as her cloying perfume filled his nostrils.

His gaze flicked to Isobel, who watched the scene unfold with wary curiosity. His father's face remained inscrutable, though a brief emotion that Winter couldn't discern flickered in his eyes. Winter had long given up trying to read the man—or trying to please him—so he simply ignored the duke and faced the raven-haired jezebel prowling toward him.

"Lady Vittorina," he said, grasping her hand to keep her at arm's length. "What a surprise to see you here in London."

"Why so formal, *Winter*?" Calculating dark blue eyes met his when he bowed instead of kissing her knuckles. "And by the by, soon it will be Countess," she said with a tinkling laugh that grated on his every nerve. "I'm betrothed, you see. To a British earl."

Winter bit back the retort that she was finally in reach of getting what she wanted—an English title— and before he could ask who the sorry victim of an earl was, the supper whistle was blown. It made him feel marginally better that she was engaged, though the ravenous way that she was looking at him suggested otherwise.

From the pleat between Isobel's brows, she'd noticed, too. For the narrowest of seconds, Winter debated playing up the flirtation but changed his mind in the same breath. Nothing short of the devil could force him to cozy up to a woman like Vittorina. It would be like courting a spider, and he knew all too well the sly hazard of her webs.

"You must sit next to me," she chirped, latching on to his arm. "It's been so long, and I must know what you have been doing all this time. Years ago, I heard a laughable rumor that you had wed, though I could not countenance the most stalwart of bachelors ever settling down. However, there was no evidence of any marchioness. How have you been? You do look well, darling. I must say the years have been more than kind." Her gaze swept over him, unmistakable appreciation flaring in her eyes as her voice lowered. "I've missed you."

He balked at the look in her eyes and shrugged off her hold. "How is it that you're here?"

Vittorina laughed gaily. "Oh, Lord Oliver took pity on me when my plans with my fiancé fell through and invited me along. But I had no idea you were coming. And the duke of course, as well as his lovely companion, Lady Isobel."

The way she said it, as though Isobel and Kendrick were a couple, made Winter's blood crawl, and the irrational bite of jealousy he was beginning to hate reared its head. Isobel was *his*, damn it! It didn't matter if it was only in name. "Lady Roth," he ground out.

"I beg your pardon?"

"Lady Roth," he said. "My marchioness in the flesh. Enough evidence for you?"

It was worth it just to see the astonishment roll across Vittorina's face. He had no idea why Isobel hadn't been properly introduced and he didn't care.

"How…lovely." The sentiment sounded more like a curse, but Winter ignored her to move toward Isobel.

"Your Grace," he said to his father with a mocking bow.

The duke inclined his head. "Roth."

"I didn't expect to see you in a place like this, mixing with the plebeians. Has hell frozen over, I wonder?" Winter turned to his wife without waiting for any reply, his rigidity softening slightly. "My lady."

"Lord Roth," she murmured, her own greeting guarded.

"How are you faring this evening?" he asked in a low voice. "It's good to see you out and about. Any news on Clarissa?"

She canted her head. "She was the one who practically booted me out of Vance House, so you can expect that she's well on the mend." She glanced over to the stern-faced duke who had moved to the adjoining box to converse with an acquaintance. "I'm the only reason His Grace is here. He accompanied me this evening at his insistence, so you can cease to worry whether hell is in an unusually frigid condition."

"Good to know." With a chuckle, Winter arched a brow at his father's uncharacteristic kindness. In the past, Kendrick wouldn't have been caught dead in a place like Vauxhall. It was much too vulgar and uncouth for him, despite it being frequented by the Prince Regent and many other top-lofty aristocrats. And yet…here he was. For Isobel's sake.

His eyes narrowed on the man in question, and as if he'd felt the stare, a blue gaze connected with Winter's. To his surprise, the usual silent judgment he'd come to expect wasn't there. Instead, the duke looked almost regretful, those piercing eyes shadowed. For the first time in months, Winter truly took in his father's face. Kendrick wasn't old by any means, but he had…aged.

A shrill giggle cut through the air as Vittorina laughed at something Oliver said, and Winter caught the tail end of her remark. "The marquess and I go way back, and you know what they say—once a rake, always a rake."

He felt Isobel bristle, but she only worried her lip and clasped her hands together. Perhaps she hadn't heard. But then she lifted her eyes to meet his gaze and the frost there slammed into him like an icy blast. "Who, exactly, is that lady to you?"

He opened his mouth, but someone else beat him to it.

"His former betrothed," Vittorina drawled, eyes glittering with malice as she strolled over. "The betrothal *you* stole."

• • •

Isobel exhaled, the breath leaving her body in a wild rush. White spots danced before her eyes as the ground felt like sponge beneath her feet. Gracious, she would *not* swoon. Had Winter been engaged before marrying her? To *this* woman?

"We were never betrothed," Winter was quick to say. His gaze swung to his brother's, his fists clenching at his sides. "If you have orchestrated this meeting on purpose, brother dear, I have to warn you that it is in excruciatingly poor taste."

"I have no idea what you're talking about," Oliver said. "It was a favor to her fiancé, a recent acquaintance of mine."

When Isobel and the duke had arrived at the gardens, she had thought the lady had been a friend of Oliver's. Introductions had been made, and though it had struck her as odd that Oliver had introduced her informally as Lady Isobel before crossing the bridge into Vauxhall, she hadn't paid it much mind. Her brother-in-law rarely took it upon himself to acknowledge her, even in the presence of his father.

The beautiful woman gave a wolfish smile. "Call it what you want, *amore*. We both know what we were for all those glorious months. More than mere lovers." Though Isobel knew that the woman's venomous words were meant to wound, she still flinched. Lady Vittorina speared her with a vicious glare. "Trust me, the only thing missing was a betrothal ring."

"You're deluded," Winter snapped. "I would never have married you."

"Not even for your child?"

The silence in the box was deafening. Everything in Isobel's stomach threatened to come up as Winter went rigid. A muscle flexed in his jaw, his gray eyes going as hard as flint. "You were not with child, Vittorina."

"I was."

"Then it was not mine."

Isobel had had outside of enough. She turned in a whirl of skirts, catching Kendrick's eye before blindly rushing out of the pavilion to one of the many landscaped walks. She didn't care where she was going—she only needed to escape before she did something unforgivable…like shove Vittorina Carpalo right out of the supper box and cause a scandal that the duke and the rest of the *ton* would never recover from.

"Isobel!" Winter called from behind her, hot on her heels. "Stop, it's not safe."

She didn't listen. She kept moving, twining through people congregated on the paths, knowing the danger and not caring. Vauxhall was rife with pickpockets and criminals, stronger people preying on the weak, and all manner of unsavory elements. She pushed deeper into the gardens, her heart hammering in her chest and her lungs so tight that she couldn't draw a single breath of air.

A hand wrapped about her elbow, cutting her escape short in a grove. "Stop, Isobel. Please."

Her bosom heaved as she turned to face her captor. "What do you want?"

"I wasn't engaged to her, I swear it, and she was never with child. She's lying to rile you, can't you see that?"

Isobel sucked her lip between her teeth. "She's still in love with you."

"But I am not in love with *her*."

She had no idea why she was getting so angry. Winter was allowed to have a past, but something about the woman was getting under her skin. The bold way she'd looked at him, as though she had some prior claim of ownership had pushed Isobel over the edge. Lady Vittorina was everything she could never be—voluptuous, confident, sensual. All the things that Isobel was pretending to be.

She shook her head. "It doesn't matter. You were *with* her."

"*You're* my wife, Isobel, not her."

"Then why can't you act like it, damn it?" The violent outburst shot from her like lead ballast from a pistol. Her entire body trembled with the force of her emotion as she squared off against her husband, fists clenched at her sides. His eyes bored into hers, gray holding pale blue prisoner, the tension between them contracting and expanding like a live thing.

Isobel had no idea who closed the distance first, only that his lips were on hers, his tongue sliding across the seam and demanding entry. She gave it. She wanted it. Wanted *him*. Opening her mouth, Isobel welcomed him, meeting him stroke for stroke. Their teeth ground together as their bodies erased any space between them, his arms banded around her… her fingers knotted into the hair at his nape. She yanked. He groaned, his lips detaching for breath.

"Isobel—"

"Shut up and kiss me, Winter."

She tugged his head down and took his lips with hers, giving him no quarter. His tongue flicked inside her upper lip, making her gasp against his mouth. And he kissed her…stole all her air until she was breathless. *Senseless*. He walked her backward along the gravel path until her back braced against a lamppost near a deserted rotunda. Shadowy forms drifted around them, but she was safe in his arms.

Winter broke away, his full lips swollen from the intensity of their embrace and his gray eyes almost swallowed by black. "Hell, I don't do this."

He kissed her again, his teeth nibbling her lower lip and then drawing away to kiss down her jaw and throat.

"Do what?" she mumbled, her own lips tingling and senses dazed.

"Kiss women," he replied between kisses to her collarbone.

A dazed memory of their wedding night came back to her. Her new husband hadn't kissed her then, at least not on her lips. He'd kissed her neck, much like he was now. And he hadn't truly touched her lips during their wedding night either, but rather the corner of her mouth. And in the maze, she'd kissed *him*.

"You're kissing me," she said when he licked and bit his way back up to her lips.

"Yes."

"Why now?" she breathed.

"I don't know."

For a moment, he stared at her lips as though he was fighting an internal battle, one he eventually lost as he closed his mouth over hers with a growl. His tongue was almost violent, chasing hers and drawing it into his mouth, plunging and retreating in an erotic dance that made her core ache. A part of her understood what he'd meant…kissing was so intimate, almost as intimate as lovemaking itself. But now, he explored every inch of her as if he couldn't get enough, sipping at her lips and then devouring them with guttural groans that ripped from his chest. As if he were *starving* for her.

Good God, his hunger fed hers, made her blood molten. She couldn't get enough either—his sinful taste, his feel, his everything. Her needy fingers dragged down to his lapels, slipping underneath his waistcoat. She wanted to feel bare skin, but she would be content with the fine lawn of his shirt. Winter wasn't idle, his fingers chasing the length of her spine from her shoulders to the curve of her bottom, kneading and grinding her to him where she felt his arousal like a brand against her belly. His possessive touch made her mindless with need. He could lift her skirts and take her now and she would welcome it. He could tell her to go to her knees and she would drop willingly.

Minutes or an eternity passed before he tore himself away, panting. Isobel fought back a blush at the passionate intensity of their kiss. Anyone could have stumbled upon them, and despite the fact that Vauxhall Gardens was a favorite rendezvous for lovers, it was still public. From the nearby moans coming through the hedges, however, they weren't the only couple stealing a moment for themselves.

Silence spun between them, and then suddenly another whistle blew in the distance, indicating that the lamps that made the gardens so famous were about to be lit. Isobel glanced up as the first of the hanging multicolored lamps above them chased away the encroaching dark, followed by another and then another.

The full effect was magical, illuminating the trees

like a fairy-tale wonderland. Trailing her gaze, Winter glanced up, his heartbreakingly handsome face outlined in flickering blue and yellow light. His thumb brushed against her sore bottom lip.

"It's so beautiful," she whispered.

"Yes," he agreed, though Isobel knew he wasn't talking about the spectacle of the lights. She could feel his gaze trained on her. Her eyes met his, her throat tightening at what she saw there. Recognizing the melting desire in his eyes, she fought the urge to push to her toes and seal her mouth back to his, which made his next words a slap in the face.

"You need to go back to Chelmsford, Isobel. You don't belong here."

Stung, she recoiled. How could he be so cruel after the intimacy they'd just shared? But from his cooling expression, she saw the interlude now for what it had been—he'd been kissing her *goodbye*.

"And Lady Vittorina does?" she shot back bitterly.

"This has nothing to do with her," he said.

"Then what does it have to do with, Winter?" she bit out. "The fact that you don't want a wife in London putting a crick in your plans?"

"No."

"Why? Because you kissed me and that scared you?"

His eyes glittered, jaw going tight. "Because I don't want *you* here. Vittorina's presence only opened my eyes. I can't change and I will never be the husband you want."

The snarled words gutted her. Isobel poked him right in the middle of his chest, ignoring the way his eyes flared or the fact that his muscles were hewn from stone. She was beyond caring about decorum at this point. She was already too far gone to stop herself.

Too furious. Too jealous. Too *hurt*.

"You are a heartless bastard," she snapped, "and I wish I'd never met you."

CHAPTER THIRTEEN

Love is a competitive sport. Play or be played.
– Lady Darcy

She hated him.

He'd hurt her unconscionably. But it had to be done. Vittorina's presence had been a much-needed kick in the gut. She'd lied about being with child and almost trapped him, and now for whatever reason, she was here in London. Her appearance, though unwelcome, was the brutal reminder he needed that women could not be trusted. His mother was right—he could not let his guard down—and he foolishly had with Isobel.

Thinking back to what Westmore had revealed about his mother and her indiscretion, Winter frowned. The only way the duchess would have had any reason to be unfaithful would have been because of the duke…because she'd been driven to it. Maybe Prue hadn't seen what she thought she'd seen. Maybe she'd made a mistake. Either way, it didn't change what he had to do now.

Confront Kendrick.

It was disgustingly early, but he did not care. Winter scrubbed a rough hand through his hair for what seemed like the hundredth time and yanked on the cravat that was slowly but surely strangling him. Dismounting his horse in the mews behind Vance House, he threw the reins to the waiting groom. Randolph, or Randy, as Iz had cheekily called him.

His eyes scanned the mews for the young, scarred stable boy. Oddly, he'd taken a liking to the impertinent lad. The boy spoke his mind, and it was obvious that Randolph had his hands full with him. He'd caught the older groom scowling in their direction more than once.

The boy was a lowly groom, but he strutted around like an upper servant, and he had no qualms about talking to a lord of Winter's stature or reputation. He made a mental note to ask Beswick about him—the boy had mentioned being in the duchess's employ before becoming Hellion's caretaker. Winter wondered how bad the boy's facial scarring was. If it was anything like the Duke of Beswick's, he could understand the need for the covering. But he was of the distinct impression that the boy had bigger secrets.

"Where's Iz?" he asked Randolph.

"Iz, my lord?" The man's throat bobbed, brown eyes popping comically.

"The boy, the young pup who takes care of Hellion."

The groom's mouth fell open, his eyes shifting to the house in a panic. "Um…er…I…"

Winter frowned. "It's a simple question."

"Running an errand, my lord," Randolph burst out, his weathered skin the color of a pomegranate. "For special feed for her ladyship's horse."

"Very well. Why didn't you just say so?"

"Apologies, my lord," Randolph stammered with a bow. "Shall I give her a message?"

Her? Winter quirked a brow. Perhaps it was a mistaken slip of the tongue. The man seemed rather nervous. "No."

Without wasting further time, Winter strode from the courtyard toward the house. He took the steps two at a time, not bothering to announce himself. It was becoming too much of a frequent thing, these troublesome visits to his father's residence. First for Isobel, then for Oliver, and now for the duke. A handful of times in the last two weeks alone. It had to stop.

"Is the duke awake?" he practically growled at Simmons, his father's butler.

"Yes, he's in the breakfast room, my lord," the man replied, his sphinx-like face giving away nothing, unlike Winter's own butler. Ludlow could do with a lesson on minding his own business. The meddlesome servant had made no secret of the fact that he thought his master was lacking in his duty by ignoring his wife. But Winter had meant what he'd said to Isobel—he had no intention of changing his life.

Settling down.

Starting a family.

Becoming a duke.

His resentment bubbled over as he stalked through the pristine foyer toward the breakfast room. He wondered if Oliver was here and almost hoped that he was so he could crunch his fist into the worm's face. Winter did not wait for Simmons to announce him before crashing open the door, his eyes finding the duke sitting at the table near the window, perusing neatly ironed newssheets.

"Lord Roth, Your Grace," Simmons said, his voice holding a hint of reproach.

The duke looked up. "Ah, my prodigal heir," he said, folding the papers. "Thank you, Simmons, that will be all." Dismissing the two footmen in the room,

Kendrick rose and walked to the mantel, where he poured two glasses of whiskey before glancing at Winter. "Drink?"

"It's a little early in the day to imbibe, don't you think?" Winter drawled, tugging off his gloves.

"Says who? The ducal police?"

That dry humor did not sound like his father at all. Winter stalled, a knot forming in his throat. When was the last time they had spoken? It had to have been years, and only by distant correspondence or via Oliver. And Winter knew he could only trust his brother as far as he could throw him.

He watched the duke lift the tumbler to his lips. "Why are you here in London?"

"Can't a father want to see his son?"

"Answer the question," Winter said.

"For my daughter-in-law's sake," he said without preamble. "She never had a season."

His eyes narrowed. "She's already married."

The duke huffed a laugh when he resumed his seat at the table. "Is she? Because she hadn't seen hide or hair of her husband in three and a half years. I suppose we both wanted to see if he was in good health."

"You've seen that I am, so when are you leaving?" he asked with irritation, reaching for the second glass and downing its contents in one swallow. The liquor burned a scorching path to his suddenly unsettled stomach.

"Whenever Isobel is ready to leave."

The sound of his wife's name was like a blow to the chest. Winter turned and propped himself up against the desk. Though he could guess at his father's reasoning for wanting him back in the fold—the man had always been about the dukedom, after all—he wanted to hear the truth from his lips. "What prompted you to accompany her?"

"It's no secret that we've gotten close over the past three years." A sad expression twisted his lips, his fingers flexing on the crystal tumbler. "In some ways, she reminds me of Prudence."

The glass nearly shattered in Winter's fist. "Don't speak her name."

"Same humor, same cleverness, same capacity to love the unlovable." He eyed his fuming son. "Do you wish to throw that at me? Avenge your sister's memory? Trust me, I've punished myself harder than you know."

"She died because of you," Winter seethed. "No one was ever good enough for you, so she ran away, right into the arms of a fortune hunting swindler."

Kendrick sighed. "You won't believe me, not after all this time, but nothing on earth could have stopped her from running away with that man. She was already lost to us."

Winter growled with rage. "You could have done something."

"Prudence was determined to ruin herself. Your sister was willful, you know that." He drew a shattered breath, his voice thinning. "She'd discovered our deepest secret, you see."

"What was that? That you were a shitty father?"

"The only regret I have, Winter, is that I didn't tell you the truth sooner."

Winter expelled a hollow laugh. "What goddamn truth? That Prue was an addict? That Mother cuckolded you because of what you did to her? Westmore already told me about Mr. Bell, but I don't believe a word of it. You never loved her."

"That's not true, Son."

"Enough, Kendrick."

Winter swore foully under his breath. He'd had enough—all his father's truths were lies. He had no thirst for more. He needed a ride, a round at Gentleman Jackson's, something, anything to offset the tension coiling inside of him like a mindless beast.

He strode from the house to the mews, only to run into a familiar reedy figure tightening the cinches on his wife's horse. Winter resisted the urge to look for Hellion's mistress. He hadn't even thought to ask for her, so focused he'd been on talking to the duke. Perhaps she was out.

"Heard you were looking for me," Iz called out in a cool voice.

"Another time," he snapped.

But true to form, the young groom ignored him, giving the mare one firm pat before stopping to level him with a stare Winter couldn't see from beneath the brim of his cap. "I was about to take Hellion out for a gallop. You look like you could use one. Race you to the end of Rotten Row, old man. Winner calls the forfeit."

Winter's muscles bunched in anticipation. A bracing gallop was just the thing.

He mounted his horse while Iz mounted his, and they cantered together through Mayfair in silence until they came to the southern end of Hyde Park at the start of Rotten Row. It was much too early in the day for any real crowds, and by the time they arrived, Winter was a mess of undiluted nerves and conflicting emotions.

What truth could the duke possibly have to tell? What didn't he understand?

Besides, what difference would it make now? For him. For Prue.

"Ready," the boy said. "Steady. Go!"

And then they were off. Winter let himself go in the moment, giving in to the pure physicality of controlling a thousand pounds of racehorse muscle flexing beneath him. His purebred Arabian kept pace with Hellion, but Winter couldn't help marveling at the lad's skill on his wife's horse. The two of them moved as one like the wind.

One day, he hoped to see Isobel put the mare through her paces. It was a challenge to keep up with Hellion and her whippet of a groom, and just the effort Winter needed to grind his surging emotions to dust. Still, Hellion and Iz took the race easily by several lengths, and when he caught up to them, the lad chortled in triumph, pumping a fist into the air.

"Feel better?" Iz asked, trotting briskly past to cool down the lathered horse.

"Well done, you." Winter shrugged and pushed a smile to his face. "Thanks for the race. I needed that, so thank you."

"What's wrong?"

He swallowed, his throat working, the words spilling out of him. "I had a sister. She died."

• • •

Isobel wanted to weep at the unguarded, vulnerable agony on Winter's face, and before she could help herself, her fingers had reached over to tug on his sleeve. "I'm sorry, milord. Death is never easy."

"Are you familiar with it?" Winter asked, his gaze snapping to her hand.

Flushing, Isobel snatched it away. "Both my parents are dead." She blinked, worried about her impulsivity or that he might make the obvious leap to connect the similarities between his wife and Iz. She hadn't exactly been creative with her nickname. Winter might be distracted with his own concerns, but he wasn't stupid. "Consumption," she added swiftly, fighting a blush at the lie and grateful once more for her cloth covering.

The truth was her parents had died in an unfortunate carriage accident. Her sister Astrid had been convinced that it'd been foul play—an attempt by their unscrupulous uncle to inherit their father's vast fortune—but nothing had ever been proven. Their uncle's efforts to marry Isobel off to Beaumont had sharpened their suspicions, though he had not been successful. And his niece had married the intractable, complex man perched on the horse beside her, instead. She resisted another urge to touch him, keeping her hands firmly on Hellion's reins.

"I'm sorry for your loss," Winter said.

"It was a long time ago."

Side by side, they trotted in silence through Hyde Park for a while. She risked a peek at him through the gap in her mask and cap, but his attention was on the path in front of them as they cantered along the winding Serpentine. The lake glittered from the rays of the afternoon sun, a bevy of swans landing gracefully in the distance. If she wasn't so nervous about giving herself away, she would have stopped to stare. As it was, everything inside her was caught up in the man at her side.

"How did she die?" she asked.

"Opium," he murmured. "I couldn't save her. Oliver and I were too late."

"Is that why you don't get along?"

He didn't answer for a long time, and she wanted to kick herself. Damn and blast, she was Iz *not* Isobel. A groom, not his wife. She'd let her emotions overrun her. He would see through her for sure.

"We never have," he finally said. "Not as children, nor as men. Prue was the glue that held us together, and Oliver is driven to be everything I am not." His voice was so soft she could barely hear it. "He should have been duke, not me."

"No." It was out before she could curb her tongue, and she felt his gaze flick to her. "I mean, you're the firstborn. It's your right and duty."

"What do you know of duty, young Iz?"

She faltered, then tossed her chin. "I know that running away from it is never the answer."

"And do you know that from experience?" He made a tutting noise. "Were your parents local gentry in some country parish? You're educated, lad. A fool would know it. So why are you here apprenticing to be a groom? Running from *duty*?"

God, he was sharp. Or perhaps she wasn't as convincing as she should be. Isobel pinned her lips and urged Hellion into a quicker gait. Let him assume what he wanted. She risked exposing herself if she tried to explain. He caught up to her after a few minutes and, despite the earlier spike of tension, they fell back into silence.

"It's complicated." His low voice shivered through her. "With the duke and me. My father is a hard man. Autocratic and *ducal* to a fault. I could never measure up as a boy, and as a man, I vowed not to." He trailed off, but Isobel said nothing. This rare glimpse into her husband was more than she'd expected. He wanted to speak and he felt comfortable enough to do so. "My mother died of a broken heart. He could never love her as she loved him. And my sister…" He fought audibly for breath. "When she died, she took all the light with her. I blamed him for it. No one could measure up to his exacting standards, not my mother, not Prue, and not me. No one bar Oliver even cared to try."

She bit back a suspicious sniff, and a heavy, solemn gaze slid to her. "I don't know why I'm telling you all this. It's no burden for a stripling."

"I'm older than I look." Her voice emerged as a croak. "I'm sorry for your loss, too. But at least you have Lady Roth to shoulder your burdens. She cares for you."

"Does she?" His voice was so soft, she barely caught it.

"I heard it from her own lips, milord."

Once more they lapsed into silence as they took the last turn toward the eastern edge of the park to return to Mayfair. Within short order, they were riding back into the Vance House mews and dismounting, and for a moment, Isobel mourned the loss of privacy and the moments they'd shared.

"I must be off." A large hand came down on her shoulder, the light touch making her want to flee and nestle into him at the same time.

"What will you do?" Isobel asked. She didn't have to explain as his gaze went to the windows of his father's study.

"Duty is a noose, one I wish to avoid at all cost."

She shook her head, unsurprised by the return to normal, caustic Winter. "And when the title falls to you, what of your tenants? The people who depend on you."

"Oliver is much better suited to the task than a gambler, a rake, and a wastrel."

She stared at him from under her cap, careful to keep her face in shadow. His beautiful gray gaze glittered in the dappled sunlight, breaking down the walls of her heart. "You're more than that, milord."

"Who says? *You*?"

"Squire turned stable boy turned sage." She thrust her hands into her pockets and gave an insolent whistle. "You'd do best to listen, your lordship." Before he could answer, she peered at the house. "There's Lady Roth and Miss Clarissa now. Looks like they've been out spending your money."

In the moment he took to look over his shoulder, she slipped away.

CHAPTER FOURTEEN

Dearest Friend, they say that love and hate are two sides of the same coin. I say the fine edge between them is passion. And besides, a little hate-fucking never hurt anyone.
– Lady Darcy

Dratted masks. They were everywhere.

It was fast becoming an absurd metaphor. Or perhaps a warning, one Isobel wasn't heeding. Or maybe simply, this was the season for masquerades and they were the latest rage in the *ton*, because here she stood sipping a glass of lukewarm ratafia at yet another ball, garbed in a gown that cost more than a groom could make in a year, and yes, hiding behind a curved piece of gold-dusted *papier-mâché* attached to a rod.

Curse her life.

"Where's your marquess?" Clarissa asked, lowering her own mask.

"How should I know?" she muttered back.

"Testy, are we?" Her friend grinned. "Turns out I know exactly what's needed to fix what ails you. It involves hard, climbable muscles, sweet nothings"— she cut off dramatically—"better yet, no talking, though lots of nudity, sweaty skin on skin, panting—"

"Clarissa!" Isobel hissed. "We're in public."

"It's loud, and besides, no one is paying any mind to us."

But that wasn't exactly true, Isobel noted sourly. The guests had been staring at her from the moment the majordomo announced her arrival on Oliver's arm. Of course, the gossip fires had ignited shortly afterward, speculating as to Lord Roth's whereabouts and whether his wife was having a secret liaison with his brother.

Kendrick had cried off tonight's invitation, citing fatigue, but insisting that she and Clarissa attend, and he'd given Oliver a clear order to escort them. To Isobel's surprise, Oliver had acquiesced without a fuss. Which reminded her…

"What's going on between you and Oliver?"

Clarissa's eyes popped wide. "I beg your pardon."

Her gaze narrowed on her friend. "You turn rigorously polite when you're trying to hide something. Don't forget I know you."

Cheeks pinkening, Clarissa's mouth opened and shut, causing Isobel's suspicions to heighten. "Nothing. He's been solicitous since the incident at the gallery. He brought me tea."

"So there *is* something going on? You wretch, why didn't you tell me?" Isobel gasped dramatically. "Oh my God, you *like* him. You want to have his babies!"

"You're so childish." Clarissa's eyes fell away. "He's not so bad, not truly."

"But I thought you loathed the very air he breathed." To Isobel's stunned surprise, her friend went beet-red, which suggested she might be partaking of the same air of her former enemy. "Clarissa Gwendolyn Bell, what have you done?"

"Not here," she hissed, practically using her mask as a shield.

Isobel grinned and repeated her friend's words. "No one is paying any mind to us. Spill the beans before I'm forced to take drastic measures and find a drool-worthy shelf of muscles for you to climb, and I'm not talking about your crush on Lord Tight-Arse."

"Izzy!"

"Doesn't feel good now that the shoe is on the other foot, does it?" Isobel teased as Clarissa went from rosy-cheeked to flaming at the ears. "So, tell me, Clarissa dear, have you kissed him yet?"

"Kissed whom?" a deep voice interrupted.

Isobel nearly leaped out of her satin dress, her hands flying to her throat, only to see Oliver standing there with two refreshed glasses of punch, wearing an off-putting long-beaked plague mask. "Good God, don't do that! You nearly gave me heart failure."

"Kissed whom?" he repeated, his blue gaze tumbling to Clarissa, who was now attempting to impersonate a pickled beet.

For a second, his expression reminded her so much of Winter that Isobel nearly started. And even more curious, his cheeks were darkening with an embarrassed flush, too, though she suspected it might be jealousy. In hindsight, the tension between Clarissa and Oliver in the carriage on the way to the ball had been rather heightened—she'd been too busy mooning about Winter to pay them any mind.

"We were simply gossiping about future matches," Isobel fabricated quickly since neither of them seemed capable of speech. "See over there, Lady Sarah Truebow is dancing with Lord Henley even though she's been promised to another by her father. She secretly fancies him. But Lord Henley has been enamored with Lady Arabella for ages. Rumor is they've kissed in secret." She pointed discreetly to a young woman dressed in yellow with a feathery mask. "She, however, despite her daring, doesn't fancy marriage at all. It's all very dramatic. Our very own blue-blooded, highborn theater production."

Oliver's confused gaze met hers. "How do you know this?"

"Keen powers of observation, my lord."

"Where's Roth?"

Her humor evaporated. "How should I know? I don't have chains on the man."

"Someone should," he retorted.

The strains of the next set sounded and Isobel reached to take the glasses of punch from her brother-in-law. "Why don't you and Clarissa take a turn for the next dance? I'll be fine here for the moment."

Unlike the last time they were at a dance together, they both nodded shyly. Clarissa and Oliver. It boggled the mind. The two were like oil and water. Clarissa was bubbly and bright, and Oliver was sour and sullen. Stranger things had happened, Isobel remarked to herself as she watched her best friend blush prettily up at the man she'd apparently secretly pined for and also wanted to murder in the bloodiest of ways.

It made Isobel's heart squeeze.

If two people who were such opposites could find each other and meet in the middle, why couldn't she and Winter gain common ground? Then again, they weren't like oil and water—they were flint and tinder. Explosive and lethal. And he'd told her to leave in no uncertain terms, that he didn't want her here. Not that she'd expected to see him tonight, or the three previous functions since. He'd been avoiding everyone. *Her*, particularly, for whatever reason. Simmons had reported from Ludlow that Lord Roth wasn't unwell or under the weather.

Typical man. Burying his feelings deep.

And they went *deep*, as she'd realized. She'd asked Clarissa to confirm what Winter had confided about the mysterious Vance sister, and even her friend's face had gone tight.

"We're not supposed to know or talk about it," she'd said. "Prudence died from a self-administered dose of opium tincture."

Isobel had gasped. "Self-administered?"

"That was the gossip. She was ruined by a fortune hunter and fled to Seven Dials. When they found her, it was too late to save her. The family was never the same after her death."

The loss had shattered the only thing holding them together. And from what Isobel was able to gather, Winter had blamed the duke. It explained so much, but terrified her at the same time. A man who cut himself off from his family as Winter had done would be impossible to reach. It was no wonder he didn't want children.

"A beautiful woman shouldn't have to hold up pillars alone," a deep male voice drawled.

Isobel swiveled to face the enormous, tawny-haired man standing behind her, recognizing him as the Duke of Westmore, Winter's friend. "Your Grace, what a pleasure."

"Wulfric, please, and the pleasure is mine, I assure you," Westmore said, kissing her gloved knuckles. "I see our young heroine of the hour is feeling better after her experience."

Isobel followed his gaze to where Clarissa was dancing with Oliver. She noted with dry amusement that they no longer moved like wooden peg soldiers. Her attention returned to the duke. Taller than her husband, he was handsome and well-heeled.

"Any news on the perpetrator?" she asked, knowing that Westmore had taken it upon himself to work with the Runners to identify their attacker.

"No," he said. "Not yet."

His tone implied that it was improbable but not impossible.

"Is Roth with you?" he asked.

She shook her head. "I haven't seen him in days."

Compassion shot across his face before it disappeared. "I'd wondered if he might be here since he was not at The Silver Scythe."

"Has he been there, then?"

"Most nights, drowning in his cups and gambling until the wee hours of the morning." An unreadable jade stare met hers. "Alone."

Before she could pick apart his words for more, something flickered along her nape and the majordomo announced her husband's name. "The Marquess of Roth and Lady Vittorina Carpalo."

It was a cut she felt to her bones. She pasted a smile on her face and met her companion's stare even as the noise in the ballroom rose to a fever pitch. "I know it's untoward, but might I ask you to dance, Your Grace?"

• • •

Winter nearly missed one of the marble steps on his way down. If it weren't for the woman at his side, he might have teetered head over arse. His muddled gaze sharpened on the black-haired lady next to him who had accosted him in the street when he'd descended from his carriage. *Vittorina*. Why was she glued to his side like a leech? He hated leeches.

Winter scrubbed at his face with a bare palm, wondering where his gloves had gone. Had he lost them? Oh Christ, why was the sodding room spinning? He wasn't *that* foxed, was he?

"Winter, *amore*," Vittorina cooed into his ear. "Take my arm."

Even in his questionable state, he was aware of the curious eyes on them. He steered her out of the nearby door to a balcony, hauling deep gulps of air into his lungs to clear his head. He stalked to the balustrade, looking out at the dark gardens. "How many times do I have to tell you? I'm married and you are engaged."

"Edmund's not here." Hands slid up his back, twining around him. "You still want me, admit it."

"No, I don't," he said and left her there.

Once inside, he scanned the ballroom, his eyes falling on a bright head of golden curls and something in his chest settled. The fist squeezing his lungs released a little, though it flexed in jealousy when he registered her dancing partner. Westmore. What the fuck was the duke doing dancing with Isobel?

Without thinking twice, he ignored the buzzing chatter around him and cut through the throng of dancers. He spied Oliver, though to his surprise, was happily dancing with none other than Clarissa. Didn't those two hate each other? Winter blinked, wavering on his heels for a moment, and then remembered that Westmore was dancing with Isobel.

He shoved his way toward them, yanking on the duke's arm. "That's my wife."

The music sputtered as every scandalized eye in the ballroom centered upon them, couples bumping into each other as they gawked.

"Roth, what are you doing?" Isobel said, her beautiful face turning pink.

"I want to dance with you."

"You're causing a scene," she said. "And besides, I'm already dancing with someone."

Winter scowled. "Fuck off, Westmore."

The duke grinned and bowed. "Articulate as always, Roth."

With a smirk, he took his leave, and then Isobel was where she belonged—in Winter's arms. Music resumed and all was well with the world, until she smashed his instep with her heel, making him wince. "That's for showing up late and with another woman."

"She followed me in," he protested.

Her lips thinned. "And I suppose she also conveniently followed you out to the balcony? I have eyes, Lord Roth, and I'm perfectly capable of seeing." He was so intent on staring into her very beautiful eyes that he stumbled drunkenly on the next turn, nearly flinging her into the path of another couple. "Good God, sir, are you in your cups?"

"No. Not really. Maybe."

"Which is it?" she snapped, those wintry eyes lit with flames.

God, he loved when she fired up at him. Even now,

in the middle of a crowded ballroom, she put him through his paces. He inhaled as he guided her into a slightly clumsy turn. He was too distracted by the feel of her, the scent of her. She smelled of flowers and summer days. His gaze fell to her mouth, remembering the silken feel of those soft pink arches. Her sweet taste.

In the past, he'd never wanted to kiss anyone. For some deep-seated reason, kissing meant a level of involvement and care that he avoided, and over the years, he'd stopped doing it. And yet, all he wanted to do was kiss her, lose himself in her prickly softness, the tart sweetness that was hers alone. Mark every satin inch of her body with his mouth. Claim her as his.

Before he even realized what he was doing, he'd leaned forward.

"Roth," she said, eyes going wide with alarm. "What are you doing?"

"I want to kiss you."

Her cheeks bloomed, though fury still burned in her eyes. "Get ahold of yourself. You're foxed, and this is neither the time nor the place. You might be the notorious Rakehell of Roth, with scandal and vice as your playground, but I beg you, do not shame us both."

"You shouldn't care what people think."

"That's just it, Lord Roth, maybe *you* should."

And with that, she turned on her heel and left him in the middle of the ballroom floor. After a moment, he gave a jaunty bow to the unapologetic onlookers and strode away, ignoring the stares and the whispers. He was used to them. No doubt the gossip would be flying that his own wife had given him the cut direct. No more than he deserved, he supposed.

"That went well," Westmore said, handing him a glass of water.

"Where did she go?"

The duke arched a brow. "Retiring room."

"I've bungled it, haven't I?" Winter muttered, downing the water. "She'll despise me forever."

Westmore smirked. "Can't be any worse than how much she despises you already."

"Fair point."

He directed a waiting footman to bring him another glass of water, which he drank thirstily. The cumulative effect of four days of drowning his misery was taking a hard toll. But staying drunk had been the only way he'd been able to stop thinking about Prue…and Kendrick…and Isobel.

God, he was a sorry sack of shit. He didn't need anyone. He never had. No matter what one sweet-mouthed, sharp-eyed angel made him feel, it was weakness, pure and simple.

And weakness could not be tolerated.

CHAPTER FIFTEEN

Use your mouth. Well, for those things, too. But what I mean is tell him what you're going to do, how you're going to do it, and what you did, in explicit detail. He'll love it.
– Lady Darcy

A few days later, with barely two weeks left for her to win the wager, Isobel huddled with Clarissa in her bedchamber staring at the invitation on black card-stock with golden script. All it listed was a date and time, The Silver Scythe, and *charity auction & masquerade* beneath it. The thick card even had a special watermark on it, possibly to deter counterfeiters.

"Where did you get this?" Isobel whispered. "This looks fancy and exclusive."

"I stole it from Oliver's room."

Isobel met her friend's eyes. "What were you doing in Oliver's room, Clarissa?"

"Having a tea party, what else?" she replied with an eye roll.

"I think tea is a euphemism for something else with you two." Isobel stifled her snort. "We might have to title Lady Darcy's next letter: 'Adult Teatime, a short treatise on how to take one's tea, how to pour, and how to swallow like a lady.'"

She didn't see the pillow coming at her face until it was too late and she almost choked on her laughter. She sobered as she sat up and retrieved the fallen invitation. "Won't Oliver miss this?"

Clarissa bit her lip. "He's a little under the weather this evening and has taken to his bed early. I saw it the other day when we were…er…never you mind what we were doing, but I figured since he wasn't going to use it tonight, you could go in his place."

"Wait, did you steal this invitation from the duke's son?"

She threw a dramatic hand to her chest. "Theoretically, it's not really stealing if he isn't physically able to go, is it? It's more like bequeathing the invitation elsewhere. You're like his second, standing in for him."

"This isn't a duel, and using fancy words like bequeath doesn't change the fact that it's thievery."

"Fancy words categorically help."

Pursing her lips, Isobel shook her head at her friend's resolute face and stared down at the fancy cardstock, her fingers tracing over the edges. The idea of going back to the club was a titillating one, but there would be risks, unlike when she'd gone with Winter before. Still, a hum of excitement rose in her belly.

"What if Oliver wakes, feels recovered, and decides he wants to go?"

Clarissa grinned. "Then I shall use my imagination and distract him thoroughly. Don't worry, dearest, I am never without a plan. And it's always sisters before misters." She patted Isobel's shoulder when she didn't smile back. "Trust me, from what I saw earlier, he's not going to be in any shape to go out. You're safe."

"I don't know about this, Clarissa. What if they

know it isn't mine?"

"They won't." Her friend bit her lip as though she had more to say, and then blew out a breath. "You *have* to go Isobel. I think that Italian woman is going to be there. Oliver told me that when they were at Vauxhall, she asked him about some special charity auction at The Silver Scythe. I think this might be it."

"Why would Oliver tell you that?"

"Because I was digging for information on that hussy, what do you think?" She rolled her eyes skyward. "I asked him if her fiancé expected him to escort her anywhere else, and then promptly forbade him from doing so."

Isobel blinked. "And you didn't think to mention anything before?"

"You weren't exactly in the best frame of mind after that outing, if you recall." She shot her a wry look. Isobel had spent the entire next day in bed with chocolates and wine, being convinced by Clarissa and the twins of the benefits of not murdering her husband. "And honestly I didn't even know he had an invitation."

"It might not even be the same event."

Clarissa sniffed, lifting one shoulder in a shrug. "Even if it wasn't, put it this way…if that woman somehow managed to attend what is purported to be the most scandalous auction of the year at *your husband's club*, and you were not there, consider how you would feel." She waved the card like a precious trophy. "However, say there's one invitation about to fall into the palms of your sticky little hands, are you going to use it? Or are you going to turn tail and cower, and let some other jade paddle in your pond?"

"Harsh, Clarissa." Isobel winced at the choice of words, given that they were exactly what Winter had said about her hightailing it to Chelmsford.

Her best friend grinned. "I serve it cold."

"Revenge?"

She smiled. "Truth."

"So, you're saying I should protect my pond?" she asked.

Clarissa nodded. "Yes, definitely protect the pond, and most of all, bring that man to heel. He deserves to know what he's given up. Isn't that why you came to London in the first place? Well, here's your chance to win that wager and walk away with your head high." She grinned. "And make some tea while you're at it."

"You're obsessed with tea."

"All women are, even if they won't admit it," Clarissa said sagely. "Tea meaning sex, obviously."

Isobel stuck out her tongue. "I know what you mean."

"So, do you want this invitation or shall I put it back where I found it?"

Isobel drew a deep breath and reached for the black rectangle. "Never let it be said that I am a quitter. I have a wager to win."

Which was why exactly two hours later, Isobel found herself garbed in the very strange disguise of a female—albeit somewhat androgynous—highway-man. From the top of her wide-brimmed black hat, to the simple black cravat, ebony satin waistcoat, and raven superfine trousers and coat, to the tips of her polished boots, she exuded an air of mystery. Her blond hair was coiled into a knot at the base of her head, tucked into the hat, and her lips were painted a deep scarlet.

She stared critically at herself in the mirror. "I look like a walking riding crop."

"You are bloody gorgeous, woman," Clarissa said. "Mysterious. Sultry. The epitome of Lady Darcy." She wiped a mock tear from her eye. "Our precious, dirty little darling out in the world. God, our sweet baby grew up so fast."

"You're ridiculous," Isobel said with a giggle. "Are you certain you don't want to change your mind and come with me?"

She shook her head. "The invitation doesn't specify additional guests. We risk discovery and not getting in at all if two of us show up with one invitation. Best to play it safe just in case. I'm expecting a full account when you return."

"What will you do?"

Clarissa shot her a wicked wink. "Make tea."

"Oliver is ill."

"*That* part of him isn't."

"There's something truly wrong with you," Isobel said as a discarded chemise came flying toward her face.

"Good thing you love me."

Dodging the projectile, Isobel laughed wryly. "I do."

• • •

Sitting in his private office in The Silver Scythe, Westmore shot Winter his trademark smirk, only this time it made Winter want to punch him in his blindingly white teeth. "Soldier up, Roth. Let's see if you can go for half of what I got last year."

Winter rolled his eyes. The annual charity auction of gentlemen at The Silver Scythe was in full swing. While he had no quarrel about being auctioned off to a horde of hungry heiresses with money to burn, he couldn't be bothered to make more than the barest ounce of effort. They were lucky Matteo was willing to pick up the slack.

Three days' growth of stubble had made Winter take on the appearance of a buccaneer and his valet had insisted on a top to bottom groom. Now, hair neatly trimmed, face shaved, nails buffed and polished, and dressed in formal togs, he was the epitome of polished lordliness.

"Lord Roth. Your Grace." Matteo swept in, dressed to the nines with his usual elegance, tailored black trousers paired with an open crimson robe, and gold paint adorning his bare, muscular chest. The effect was as intended—completely shocking. "It's a packed house tonight. We are almost ready to close the evening's auction. All the others are completed."

"Jesus, Matteo." Westmore gave a mock groan. "The women aren't going to bid a farthing for us humdrum Englishmen with you parading around in that."

The man grinned and winked. "I can always dress you in some borrowed fare, Your Grace. Not to mention some body paint would do the trick. I'm sure the women would die for it. Your musculature is perfect."

"Next year," the duke promised.

"Devil take it, get a chamber, you two," Winter growled.

"What crawled up your arse, Roth?" Westmore asked.

Not a what. More of a *who*. But he didn't say anything. He had no idea why he was so irritable. Based on the monies tallied from the earlier auctions by other members, they were on track to exceed last year's donations to the shelter house in Seven Dials. He should have been pleased, but for the past few days, everything had felt out of sorts. Nothing seemed to *matter*.

And he knew exactly why.

After Vauxhall, Winter had distanced himself. There was no way he could give Isobel what she wanted. A husband who could love her back. Children. Hope for a happy future. She wanted a fairy tale, but Winter wasn't the hero of their story, even if he'd pretended to be once upon a time. The truth was, he was the villain—the evil lord who imprisons the princess.

"Do you think Lady Hammerton will be back this year, Roth?" Westmore asked. "She was the only reason you won last year, if you recall."

Winter shrugged, shoving his dark thoughts away. The notorious lady had paid an astronomical sum for him to sit for some portraits. Nude. Well, partially nude. He'd had to wear a large leaf-like cloth over his genitals. He wouldn't admit it to anyone, but he'd learned a lot from the raunchy, high-spirited widow, which was why he knew she couldn't be Lady Darcy. She'd also mentioned that she admired the chit, whoever she was.

In any case, it was Westmore's year to win. Since the inauguration of the first charity auction, they'd been neck and neck from year to year, pegs above all the other gentlemen.

"May the best man win," he said.

They didn't have many rules, but those they had were strict: no sexual conduct unless by consensual agreement and no breaking the law.

Winter watched from the sidelines as Matteo introduced the duke. The noise was deafening. Winter might be a rogue, but Westmore was in a whole other league. Within minutes, the bidding war had escalated into the thousands, with shrieks of excitement and anger punctuating the chatter. He almost laughed as Westmore strutted his way like a preening peacock across the stage at the end of the cavernous ballroom. It was a wonder the man was still unwed, but he'd never seemed interested in marriage.

A long time ago, Westmore had been a friend to Prue. In hindsight, his sister's death had hit the man hard, though Winter had been too wrapped up in his own anguish to notice. That was when he'd buried his heart and swore to never let anyone in.

Perhaps Westmore had done the same.

"Sold," Matteo shouted. "To the lady in the scarlet cloak, Lady J."

Winter's eyebrows crept up as the woman walked forward to complete the transaction. If he wasn't mistaken, the woman calling herself Lady J was actually Lady Jocelyn Capehart, the unmarried daughter of the Duke of Tyne. Her family and Westmore's had been at odds for decades. What was she doing *here*? His eyes met Westmore's and the surprise in them mirrored his. Nonetheless, she signed over the payment and it was a binding contract, meaning Westmore was hers for one night.

There was no time to dwell on it, however, as Matteo waved Winter out. Cheering filled his ears as he stalked across the stage, welcoming his guests with a smile. Even though it was a masquerade, some people chose to dress up, others chose to dress down, others wore magnificent costumes, and a daring few chose to wear the smallest amount of clothes possible. Everyone was encouraged to be themselves, or use other identities, if they so desired. As a result, there were quite a few Lady Darcys in the crowd.

Winter bit back a smile at how many of the so-called Lady Darcys resembled courtesans. He was still of the mind that Lady Darcy was part of the upper crust and wouldn't be caught dead at an assembly like this. Or maybe she *was* here...in disguise, wearing a symbolic mask like the rest of them.

• • •

Isobel's heart was pounding against her ribs as Winter appeared on stage.

God, he made her blood sing.

Tall and intimidating, the man was a handsome-as-sin devil, his brown, freshly trimmed hair falling carelessly over his brow, those piercing gray eyes scorching through the crowd. A small smirk graced his full lips, reminding her of how they'd felt on hers. Isobel clenched her thighs together, cursing the tight fabric that made her feel *everything*.

Every layer, every seam, every ridge.

She'd arrived with enough time to view a few of the last gentlemen up for auction. Many of the members, both male and female, had auctioned themselves and their services earlier, from what she could tell. The gentlemen auction, however, was the crème de la crème, and the last two to be auctioned would be Westmore and Roth.

Matteo bowed low. "As our last gentleman of the evening, I am honored to present Lord Winter Vance, the Marquess of Roth. As you can see for yourselves, Lord Roth is physically fit, can carry a passable tune, loves a glass of whiskey and a good book, enjoys wit and conversation, and is skilled in all the ways that count."

Isobel couldn't control the helpless clench of her thighs at the sultry smirk on Winter's face.

Matteo shook his finger back and forth at the squeals and sighs in the rapt audience. "However, as you all know, unlike the Duke of Westmore, Lord Roth is married and as such, his services tonight will be restricted at his discretion. He also reserves the sole right to reject any bid."

To Isobel's surprise, those statements didn't dim the enthusiasm. If anything, the sighs multiplied. Did the many hopefuls in attendance expect to convince the marquess otherwise?

"The bidding will start at one thousand pounds," Matteo said.

"One thousand, one hundred," an excited voice called out.

Another hand flew up. "One thousand, two!"

Isobel's eyes widened, a shocked giggle bursting out of her as she recognized the bidder. Good gracious, was that Lady *Hammerton*? The woman was ancient, but she lived with uncommon exuberance. It had been at her house party in North Stifford where she and Winter had exchanged marriage vows over three years ago.

Though Clarissa had explained that the scandalous auction was for charity, she couldn't help wondering what the winners did with their prizes. The majordomo had said that the gentlemen had right of refusal and the activities weren't carnal in nature, but she wasn't so sure, given the looks on some of the bidders' faces. What in God's green earth would Lady Hammerton use him for? It boggled the mind.

"Two thousand."

Heads turned in the crowd at the eight-hundred-quid leap, and Isobel gritted her teeth once the overconfident bidder came into view. *Vittorina.* Of its own volition, her gaze flicked up to her husband. The only sign he thought anything at all was the beat of a muscle in his cheek. She saw him glance at Matteo, but the man was too busy working the crowd into a frenzy, extolling Lord Roth's considerable virtues.

"Two thousand, one hundred," Lady Hammerton shouted.

An undaunted Vittorina tossed her head. "Two thousand, two."

Isobel frowned as the noise in the room swelled. The woman was out to win. She squared her shoulders, armed only with a name and a promissory note, and shifted into the rear of the room where the shadows cloaked her.

She cleared her throat. "Two thousand, three."

"Too much for me," Lady Hammerton said, though a knowing smile played over her lips as their eyes connected for a scant instant. Isobel cursed and hunched her shoulders. Had the old harridan recognized her?

"Two thousand, four," Vittorina said, a slight waver in her voice.

Isobel clenched her jaw. "Three thousand pounds."

"Three thousand in the back," Matteo said, dark eyes dancing. The bidding had already exceeded that of the Duke of Westmore. "Lady in green," he said to Vittorina, who craned her neck to see who had the audacity to out-bid her while Isobel shifted silently out of her view. "What say you?"

"Three thousand, one hundred," Vittorina said, though her throat bobbed nervously, her face going tight. Isobel didn't know the ins and outs of bidding, but she knew how to read people, and the woman was visibly anxious about the sum she had just offered. Three thousand must have been her limit.

"This is *my* pond," Isobel said to herself, and then louder, knowing she didn't have to go as high as she did but going anyway. She was making a point, even if it was only to herself. Go big, or go back to Chelmsford. "Five thousand."

The noise was thunderous as she shifted again from the spot where she'd called out the bid. The dark fabric of her clothing made it easy to slip through the crowds as people turned, desperate to identify the voice with the deep pockets. She saw Winter's eyes combing the crowd, silver igniting the gray in the stage lighting so that they seemed almost feral.

She'd lowered her voice, but something deep inside her warned that he *knew* who she was and that he would find her. Slowly, Winter's eyes panned toward her, and with every inch, her breath stuttered. Though she knew he could not see her clearly where she stood in the shadows, her heart fought against her ribs like a frantic beast. She felt it deep in her bones— that raw, elemental connection she only felt with him.

Did it go both ways? Did he sense her on a soul-deep level as she sensed him?

"Do I hear five thousand, one?" Matteo asked, his face bright with glee.

No one spoke, but the energy and excitement in the air were palpable.

"That's too rich for my blood," Vittorina snarled. "I withdraw."

Matteo clapped and rang a golden bell. "Sold to the mystery bidder in the back for the sum of five thousand pounds! Come forward, announce yourself, and claim your prize."

The room simmered down to a whisper as the crowds parted. Isobel took a deep breath and stepped forward, keeping her head low so that her face wasn't immediately visible. She felt it the moment Winter's eyes landed on her, and for a second, she was grateful for the dim lighting. She kept her voice low, its tones deep, offering no further clue to her identity.

"I fear the only name I can give you for now, sir, is Lady Darcy."

CHAPTER SIXTEEN

*Make the beast with two backs. Shakespeare came up
with that gem, not me.*
– Lady Darcy

Winter cursed the crowd, the gloom, and Matteo in
the same breath. While he was glad that Vittorina had
been outbid, the sum he'd fetched had been beyond
exorbitant, and he couldn't bloody see who had made
the tender. All he could make out was what looked
like a slender young man dressed in black. After
Matteo's invitation for the bidder to come forward
and make a claim, he'd heard the person say: *I fear the
only name I can give you tonight, sir, is Lady Darcy.*

He'd almost groaned.

Just what he needed. Though this Lady Darcy, unlike the other courtesans, seemed to be garbed in
men's clothing. A Mister Darcy, then. Perhaps, it was
simply a rich young man looking for guidance or advice. He'd been approached by such fledgling bucks in
the club before. Matteo neared, and Winter's irritation renewed. The man knew better than to accept
such large offers...they'd long since learned that
when it got to those levels, it was usually driven by
something personal. With Vittorina, it had been, but
he was unclear on the identity or motive of the bidder
in black.

"Why didn't you stop the bidding to confirm the
identity of the last?" he growled under his breath.

"You know the rules."

Smile faltering, Matteo frowned. "You did not give me the signal that it was of concern or that the pot would be limited."

That was true. He hadn't. "Apologies, you're right."

How had Vittorina even procured an invitation anyway? Winter knew that a few of the sought-after invitations were sold off for small fortunes, usually by very desperate men. Some were stolen. Westmore always made it a point to track down the transgressors, taking great pleasure in making them pay in some way or another, which was a huge deterrent for thieves, but it didn't always work.

Invitations were sent out to nonmembers only after careful consideration, and usually to those who had deep coffers and could afford future membership. Most of the peerage, especially the younger set, was obsessed about getting them. The names of the invitees were painted with a special watermark, but they'd been negligent about verifying names in recent years. Case in point were Lady J who'd won Westmore, Vittorina, and the mystery man in black.

Winter stood, aware that he was still being watched by an avid audience. The Duke of Westmore joined him on the stage. They both bowed to a thunderous wave of applause.

"Thank you for your patronage, esteemed guests." The duke grinned. "And if you desire membership, your applications will be personally considered. As you well know, we are the only club in London that allows female membership. Coin is king—pay the tithe and entry to your greatest fantasies will be granted. For now, let the celebration begin. Explore, gamble, eat, drink, dance, and be merry, my friends!"

They left the stage, moving back to the salon adjoining the staircase leading up to Winter's office. Winter tugged on his cravat, loosening the expertly tied cloth so he could suck in a lungful of air. Hell, he needed a drink.

"Well done, man," Westmore crowed, clapping him on the back. "Five thousand is a fortune."

"Indeed," he said. "Has the bidder come forward?"

"Not yet, my lord," Matteo said with an apologetic look.

A suspicious thought occurred to him and he slanted an arch glance at the duke. "Was this your idea of a jest?"

"No, of course not," Westmore replied. "I've much better use for five thousand quid." Winter let out a disbelieving noise. Five thousand was a drop in the bucket for the smug scoundrel, and they both knew it. Westmore paused, mouth twitching. "Though it's a bloody brilliant idea. I should have thought of it, just to toy with you."

"*Did* you put someone up to it?"

"Wish I did. Some other gentleman besides me is madly in love with you." He faked a dramatic sigh. "I might have to call them out."

"Did you see him?" Winter asked, ignoring his jesting.

"Side view," Westmore said. "He was tallish, lean, dressed in black. Might have worn a wine-colored cravat. Young. Kept moving through the crowds in the back and he wore a hat so I couldn't quite see his face."

Winter wished he had gotten a better look. At the very least, his view had been fleeting. He had felt a vague sense of awareness as if he'd known the man. Then again, in his particular line of debauchery, he crossed paths with much of the *beau monde* and the *demi monde*. And he hadn't gotten a clear look at the man's face. Well, he would know soon enough.

A commotion at the door drew their attention as Vittorina shoved her way through, eyes spitting fury. Her face—one that Winter had once considered beautiful—twisted into an ugly sneer. "Did you get a look at your bidder? It's a man." Her vicious gaze turned sharp with spite. "Tell me, Roth, does your wife know of your peculiar tastes?"

"My tastes are my business," he replied easily. "And we don't suffer those seeking to spread shame here."

Winter was about to order her removal from the club, when he was distracted by the presence of a new arrival. The man in black—the winning bidder. A discomfiting rush of visceral awareness hummed through him at the sight of a pair of scarlet lips and a slender but curved figure better suited to a siren than a man. He blinked, his jaw falling open at the long legs encased in snug black trousers above a nipped-in waist and pert breasts, recognition hitting his gut and descending straight to his hardening groin.

Bloody hell if the mystery bidder wasn't his fucking wife.

• • •

"This looks fun," Isobel said into the sudden silence. She removed her hat, tendrils of blond hair falling into her face, and was rewarded with the satisfaction of seeing Vittorina's face fall.

"*You* won the bid?" Winter burst out, as if he couldn't believe his own eyes.

She smiled, enjoying his expression, too, and the undisguised lust that had swept across his face the moment he'd realized it was her. "Is that any way to greet your wife, Roth?"

Westmore's loud laughter cut through the silence as he moved forward with a bow. "You look ravishing tonight, Lady Roth, or should I say, Lady Darcy." He shook his head, his eyes filled with mirth. "This cannot get any better."

But of course it could, because Vittorina found her voice. She closed the distance between them, getting into Isobel's space. "You do not know him like I do. He will come back to me."

"So you've said," Isobel replied easily, undaunted by the woman's proximity or threats. "Though I've yet to see any evidence of him falling into your arms."

"You're nothing but a country mouse he was forced to marry!"

Isobel lifted a shoulder. "That might be so, but at least that's a damn sight better than a woman who throws herself at a married man and can't take no for an answer."

Vittorina's eyes flashed with rage as she stepped closer. "Who do you think you are?"

Isobel drew herself to her full height, putting steel into her voice. "I'm the Marchioness of Roth, a fact you seem to have forgotten, and I don't like being threatened. Now get out of here before I have you tossed out on your arrogant, vain, unwanted arse. No one likes a sore loser."

Westmore's muffled snort was covered up by the sound of Matteo's laughter as Vittorina whirled with an angry huff and left.

"That was marvelous, Lady Roth. Christ, the expression on her face was priceless. She didn't expect the mouse to have teeth and claws." The duke let out a guffaw as he strode to the door. "I better make sure she leaves and doesn't cause trouble."

Isobel perused the salon, noting the dumbstruck look on her husband's face. She wanted to stick a finger under his chin and close his gaping jaw. In truth, his expression made her feel a hundred feet tall. Which led her to part two of this expedition—she had a wager to win. She cleared her throat, eyes flicking to Winter's man of affairs.

"Matteo?"

"Yes, my lady?"

She inhaled a confident breath, still channeling her inner Lady Darcy. Clarissa would be proud. "I wish for a moment with my winnings."

Matteo's grin was wide. "As you say, my lady."

And then they were alone…well, alone, surrounded by hundreds of people in the club, any of whom could walk into the salon at any moment. Isobel didn't care. There was only Winter. His gaze lashed to hers, and she almost quailed at the intensity of the conflicting emotions in them—shock, disbelief, humor, and most of all, lust. Bolts of heat shot through her as an answering desire coiled down her spine to settle between her legs.

Her core throbbed as their eyes locked, only intent on each other. The longer he stared at her, the more her body reacted. Her chest constricted painfully, the pulse between her thighs intensifying to dizzying levels. She shifted, the seam of her trousers rubbing against her sensitized skin and making her shudder.

Isobel licked her dry lips, her husband's eyes fastening there and darkening instantly.

"Winter."

"Come with me," he rasped.

He turned and climbed a nearby staircase that led to a small well-appointed workspace. "What is this?"

"My office?"

She blinked her confusion. "Your *office*?

"Westmore and I own The Silver Scythe," her husband said.

Well, that was news to her. In truth, it made her feel a little better if he'd been spending his nights here, and not in the private rooms she'd seen downstairs. A large paned-glass panel looked over the floor below, offering a bird's eye view of the club. Shucking her coat, she scanned the space, curious for more insight into her enigmatic husband. It was pristine, boasting a large desk, plain but plush carpets, and a sofa along the length of one wall. Framed art and objects hung on the wall, adding splashes of color and culture. From his travels, she assumed. A framed sketch in pencil and charcoal drew her attention.

She let out a gasp as she recognized the subject of the portrait—it was Winter, sprawled in a chair in all his bare-chested glory, wearing only a cloth designed to look like a fallen leaf. It was entitled *Adam in Winter*.

"That was Lady Hammerton's handiwork," he said, pouring himself a glass of whiskey. "Drink?"

"Yes, please," she murmured, her eyes tracing over the fine lines and the intricacy of the light and dark shading, and then froze. "Did you say Lady *Hammerton*?"

"The very same." He chuckled and handed her a tumbler. "She and your aunt Lady Verne are quite the pair. She sketches erotic nudes while her partner in crime is obsessed with needlepoint, specifically crocheting the male phallus."

Isobel let out a bark of laughter, grateful she hadn't yet taken a sip or she would have spewed liquid everywhere. She recalled Astrid mentioning something like that, but Isobel hadn't taken her seriously. "Those two are incorrigible."

"Gifted, too. I can vouch for Lady H, though I've yet to see evidence of Lady V's talent. However, Matteo has been a model and I've been told her work is rather…precise."

Isobel laughed and her gaze fell back on the drawing. Lady Hammerton had nailed the squareness of Winter's jaw, the strong line of his nose, and the sinful curve of his lips, hitched in a sensual half smirk. Isobel's gaze traveled down the slope of his shoulders to the expertly drawn bare chest. Each muscle was painstakingly detailed, down to the dark indent of his navel and the angled vee of his lower abdomen. Isobel's mouth went dry at the obvious hint of what lay under the scrap of fabric, and she blushed furiously.

"She's quite good," she said.

"She's a wicked old harridan who couldn't stop telling me how much she wished she were in her younger years so that she could put me through my paces." He sipped his drink and stared at her over the rim of his glass. "I'd never felt like such a piece of meat about to be gobbled in my entire life."

"Did she?"

He arched a brow, propping one hip on his desk. "Did she what?"

"Gobble you." Her tongue slipped out to lick dry lips, and his eyes burned silver. Good Lord, if he kept looking at her like that, she was going to make a fool of herself.

His eyes might have set her on fire, but he stayed put and shook his head. "Said she didn't seduce married men."

Isobel blinked. "Wait, this was recent?"

"She was last year's winner."

It shouldn't have been possible, but parts of her grew hotter and wetter. The scintillating thought that Winter might still look like that, only in the flesh beneath his clothes, was virtually impossible *not* to latch on to. And now, all she could think about was seeing him sprawled careless and indolent for her greedy perusal.

"I have to admit," she said, gaze panning between him and the portrait. "I never thought I'd be jealous of an old lady."

"Are you?"

She nodded. "Categorically. But I think it's time we remedy that, don't you?"

Consumed by a burst of lust that made her knees weak, Isobel moved away from the voluptuous portrait. She set down her whiskey and prowled over to the desk where her husband stood, not stopping until she was wedged between his long legs.

"What are you doing?" he asked in a low rasp.

She took his drink and drained the rest, licking her lips with a smack that made him inhale sharply. "Claiming my hard-won prize."

"Hard-won? With *my* money?" Winter laughed, the vibrations from his body rumbling into her, though he held himself like a statue. His hands now gripped the edges of the desk with such force that his knuckles went white. She smiled. Glad to see she wasn't alone in her ungovernable reactions where he was concerned. Isobel resisted the urge to rub herself against him like a cat.

"I assure you, it's my own money."

His eyes narrowed. "Where did you get it?"

Isobel couldn't tell him about Lady Darcy, not without Clarissa's approval. Or the fact that they'd made quite a fortune from the popular periodicals, which would account for the five thousand pounds she'd so easily squandered for one night with her marquess.

It was time to collect. Time to bring her husband to heel.

Instead of answering, she pushed to her toes and sealed her mouth to his.

CHAPTER SEVENTEEN

Dearest Friend, if you wish to learn about marital congress, also known as sex, tupping, fucking, prigging, basket making, rutting, rogering, strapping, or swiving, among others, go listen to a bawdy song. They are filthy but instructive.
– Lady Darcy

The silken press of her lips made Winter come unhinged.

One palm slid up her waistcoat-covered back, the other cupped her thigh beneath the tantalizing curve of her buttock, both holding her firmly in place. Those *fucking* trousers! They had made him wild with arousal to see those long, shapely legs so indecently outlined in that black fabric. He'd been sporting a mongrel of an erection the moment she'd taken off that hat and his brain had made the connection between voice and body.

The minute she had walked into the salon downstairs and he'd felt that first visceral, unmistakable tug, he'd known who she was. The bloody cheek of her! He should have put her over his knee the moment they were alone, but alas, she was in charge. Those were the rules, after all, and the time to say anything to the contrary was long past.

He was hers.

Officially bought and paid for.

Isobel moaned into his mouth, her lips parting and

that tiny pink tongue creeping forward for a taste. It recoiled wildly when it touched the tip of his and then crept back for more. And still, Winter didn't take control, letting her set the pace. He sat there and endured her sensual explorations until his skin felt like it was going to burst at the seams. Winter groaned as her teeth scraped his lip. He could taste the brandy on her tongue and a tart sweetness that was all her own. It made him want to taste her elsewhere.

Without warning, she pushed off of him, her pink mouth swollen and her light blue eyes hot with desire. "Let's make this last, shall we?" Her voice was husky and made his groin tighten even more.

He swallowed. "What, exactly?"

"Torture," she tossed over her shoulder with a saucy grin.

Hell, if she wasn't right. He was fit to bursting. Adjusting his painful erection with the heel of one hand, his needy eyes tracked her progress about the room, watching as she perused the items on a built-in bookshelf lining the wall near the entrance door to his office. He couldn't think of what rested on those shelves, all his brain could focus on was the sinuous arch of her bottom atop those long legs, the fabric stretching tauntingly with every step.

It was indecent and wicked, but his mouth watered with the need to sink his teeth into either of those perfect handfuls. God but she tempted him—with that pert, bitable rear, her tiny waist, and those perfect peach-like breasts that he also couldn't wait to get into his mouth. His cock jerked convulsively against his palm in enthusiastic agreement.

Christ.

If he wasn't careful, it wouldn't take much to spend in his trousers like a sodding greenhorn. Just watching her was a study in arousal. He shoved his hand down harder on the falls of his breeches, a raw growl rumbling through him at the intense sensation. Isobel's eyes met his from where she stood, concern in them.

"Are you well, Roth?"

"Quite," he bit out.

Her gaze fell to his palm-covered groin, and a blush stained her cheeks as if she was remembering the last time *her* hand rested over him. Then his vulgar words in the carriage. Winter let out a breath. She had to be a complete innocent if she wasn't aware of the effect she had on him. Then again, she *was* an innocent. He'd been the only one to have her. Unless she'd had a secret lover, which he highly doubted because Ludlow would have flung *that* in his face by now.

Pushing off the edge of the desk, he moved toward the relative safety and privacy of his chair. At least his inability to control his overexcited body would be hidden from view. Distracting himself with moving around some account ledgers on his desk, he didn't immediately see the thin book she'd removed from the shelf until it was much too late.

"Don't, that's not—" he began and then stopped when she opened the first plate of erotic illustrations, her cheeks flaming the color of poppies.

He knew exactly what she would see. Etchings upon etchings of Thomas Rowlandson's more risqué works. It was an art collection. Depraved and utterly filthy art, but it'd been a gift from Westmore when they'd opened the darker side of The Silver Scythe.

The drawings they'd passed in the corridor by the very same artist her first time at the club would be tame compared to these, which depicted sex in ways that would make a grown man blush. To his surprise, his sheltered little wife didn't immediately fling the book back, but continued paging through its contents, rolling her lips between her teeth, that sultry flush of hers in full bloom now.

"Interesting," she said, though her eyes didn't meet his as she replaced it and selected another. It was Cleland's, *Fanny Hill*, a flowery erotic novel about the adventures of a prostitute. To his eternal shock, a smile quirked her lips. "I've read this, though not this early edition, a later expurgated one."

Winter was well aware his jaw had hit the floor. But he almost groaned at the next book she chose— one of nearly a dozen volumes by the disturbingly violent and cruel Marquis de Sade— *La Nouvelle Justine*. It was a graphically depraved account of one girl's sexual encounters.

"Wasn't the Marquis de Sade imprisoned for these by Bonaparte?" she asked.

"He was."

She shot him a glance. "And yet you have them in your possession."

"I do." Despite the order to have the books destroyed by the Royal Court of Paris and the author's imprisonment, Winter did not feel the need to defend his possession of the volumes, though the subject matter was one of extreme debate. However, he couldn't stand to see any judgment in her eyes. He cleared his throat. "Hence the hard and fast rule of engagement at this club: permission and consent. As you might have gleaned, parts of this club cater to sensual play and fulfilling certain needs."

Isobel replaced the book and moved on to the adjoining shelves. "Like flogging."

He blinked. "Yes."

"I saw some of the earlier sales with members auctioning off their services. One Lady Renly who enjoys the occasional birch switch and the cane went for quite a high sum. I'm surprised the regent wasn't here to avail himself of your offerings."

Curious fingers trailed across a decorative paddle carved from onyx as well as a birch rod, and once more, when his cock leaped, Winter was grateful for cover of the desk. The last thing he wanted was for her to assume he was any kind of sexual deviant, not that she would, but some people tended to shy away from the unfamiliar. The thought that she was not the prude he expected slid like silk through his mind.

"Lady Darcy covered that subject in some detail in one of her letters," she went on. "She thought that switches were better kept green and in water for easier use."

Winter's groin tightened past the point of pain. He was aware. Those letters had brought on a slew of new members. He could barely get out a word as Isobel continued, oblivious to his worsening state.

"She was of the mind that the fetish probably had to do with all those young boys being sexually shamed and lashed at Eton or elsewhere," she explained. "Or perhaps it stemmed from wanting to escape the rigid rules of the *ton* outside of the bed-chamber?"

Hell, he wanted to put that well-informed mouth

of hers to practical use.

But then she chuckled, holding a familiar periodical aloft. "I see you're also a collector of Lady Darcy's work."

"I collect many things."

Pale blue eyes regarded him over the top edge of the volume. "You said you didn't think I could be her because I was too innocent. In truth, I fear you don't know me at all, Lord Roth." His mouth dried when she clasped her hands behind her back, causing the fabric of her waistcoat to pull tight over her breasts, as she sauntered back to the front of the desk. "Aren't you going to ask me how I'm here?"

"How *did* you get here?"

She grinned. "Clarissa stole Oliver's invitation."

That was why he hadn't seen his brother. "Is Clarissa here, too?"

"No." Isobel shook her head, propping her left hip on the desk and giving him her profile, her right leg swinging. One hand reached up to unknot her cravat. He was so distracted by the long, elegant lines of her exposed throat that he barely took in her next words. "She's at home playing nursemaid to your brother."

"Clarissa and Oliver?" Though he'd assumed as much at the previous ball.

She laughed with a nod, twisting the fabric of her cravat between her fingers. "Apparently."

"They detest each other, no?"

"Well, love and hate tend to walk the same path. Perhaps they have found some common ground." She pursed her lips. "You haven't asked why I stole the invitation and paid such an exorbitant amount for you."

"Why?"

Winter watched as she put her gloved palm to her mouth and pulled the tip of each finger with her teeth. His body throbbed as each slender finger loosened from captivity. He was instantly and viscerally reminded of the time she'd removed her glove beneath the table…and the indelicate torture his cock had experienced from her bare hands. Did she intend to do the same now? His breath reduced to pitiable pants.

"The reason is simple," she went on, tugging off the glove and discarding it, and then repeating the action with the second hand. "You wagered that I would flee London with my tail between my legs. And yet, here I am with nothing between said legs but a soaked pair of trousers."

Lust drove him straight up from his chair, evidence of his bulging erection be damned. "Isobel, you're—"

"Starting a dangerous game? Playing with fire? Biting off more than I can chew?" Her smile was pure seduction as it slid to his distended crotch. "You knew a girl, Roth, from three years ago who was unsophisticated in every possible way. Practically asleep. She's not anymore." She crossed her arms over her chest and licked her lips. "Now close that sinful mouth of yours, strip like a good lad, and show your mistress what she's won."

• • •

Isobel nearly toppled off the desk at his astonished expression. Half of her brain was excited by her boldness and the other was worried he'd see through her efforts. The racy books and whips in his collection had roused her to play the role of the provocateur. She might be innocent in body, but she had more than enough food for fantasy in her brain. In fact, her entire performance had hinged on the inner chant: *What would Lady Darcy do?*

"Isobel, what do you think you're doing?" Winter growled.

Don't back out now, she told herself firmly, even though every instinct was screaming at her to flee like the terrified kitten she was. *You're not a kitten! Or a cat or any foolish feline. You're a woman. Now act like it.*

She arched an imperious brow. "Did I stutter? I said strip. Show me what my five thousand pounds are worth."

Isobel pinned her lips, nerves coiling. Oh God, he was going to see right through her. Call her bluff. Laugh in her face. Call Matteo and have him escort her out, back to Vance House. Only he *wasn't* laughing.

His handsome face was tight with desire, his eyes pools of onyx and silver. Those long, lean fingers of his manhandled the edge of his desk. Isobel suddenly wanted them gripping her with equivalent ferocity, sinking into her flesh in carnal need. His broad shoulders bunched as he braced his weight against the mahogany, and his hips… She gulped at the sight of those grotesquely protruding breeches that did *nothing* to hide the mouth-watering, erotic outline of him.

Why her mouth watered, she did not know.

"This won't end as you hope, Isobel."

A beat of panic flickered through her. No, it

probably wouldn't, but now wasn't the time to waver or worry about what she had to lose. In this moment, he was hers. She would take her pleasure, use him thoroughly, and walk away, leaving him wanting.

At least, that was the plan.

"I'm not paying you to talk, Roth," she drawled, shaking out her loosened cravat. "And unless you wish me to tie this over your mouth, you'll do as you're told."

Shock crashed through his heated eyes, his cheekbones darkening from golden to berry. Dear God, the great Winter Vance was blushing. *Good*. She needed to keep him off-balance, to not see through her charade, though with each minute that passed, she grew bolder and more confident. Reassured by his obvious attraction to her, Isobel was reasonably sure that she could seduce him. And she was willing to wager her pride that Winter would not say no. She *hoped*.

Now she just needed to keep her wits about her and not become the seduced. She was mortifyingly aware of how sodden her trousers were between her thighs and how scratchy her shirt had become, the fabric abrading the sensitive buds of her nipples. Her feminine arousal equaled his, it seemed. She was wild for him.

But she also had a wager to win...which required patience and strategy instead of mounting him like an animal in heat. Her husband needed to *beg*. Isobel reached up and pulled the pins from her hair, letting the loosened locks tumble down her back. His subsequent groan was loud in the silence. If he clenched that jaw of his any harder, she was sure it would shatter.

"I'm waiting, Roth," she said, her voice low and husky.

"Isobel—" Her name was a cross between a warning and a desperate plea.

Undeterred, she flung the cravat at him. "Disrobe and put that over your eyes, or so help me, I'll put some of your wicked toys over there to good use."

A tremor rolled through those wide shoulders, and then he pushed off the desk, his eyes holding hers as he did as asked. His coat went first. Then his cravat, followed by his waistcoat. With every popped button and each discarded article of clothing, her pulse escalated. By the time he slid his shirt over his head, Isobel's mouth was so dry that she was ready to leap over the desk and gulp down that entire bottle of whiskey. But not before getting her greedy little palms all over that moral-smelting masculine body.

"More?" he asked in a low growl.

She could only nod, temporarily silenced by the overwhelming display of muscles. Lady Hammerton's portrait had not done him a lick of justice, because Winter was sculpted to god-like perfection. Her hitherto dry mouth flooded with moisture. Holy hell, he was *edible*, and she was going to consume him. After she got him to yield, of course.

His fingers had stalled at the waistband of his breeches.

"Why are you stopping? Disrobe means disrobe."

"And you?"

"I am the proprietress of the transaction," she told him, her brain's capacity to function reducing with every breath. "You are the performer."

A surprised chuckle burst from him. "Now I know

how a debutante feels on the marriage block. Or better yet, a Cyprian."

Isobel stilled, remembering what he'd told her about the rules of consent in the club. "Lord Roth, do you grant me permission to proceed?"

"I do." His gray eyes were so dark they were nearly black, but they shone with approval.

"And you accept *my* will in all things."

"Yes." The word was a primal growl that set her lady parts on fire.

"Good." She rewarded him with a sultry smile and strolled around the desk. "Bind your eyes."

Winter stared at her for a protracted moment, but then lifted his arms and wrapped the fine linen around the upper part of his face. Ragged breaths sawed past his lips, chest heaving as his clenched fists fell to his sides. God, she'd never seen a more beautifully made man.

And he was *hers*.

Isobel drew her own ragged breath into her aching lungs, ogling him without fear of him seeing just how desperate she was to drink him in. Freed of the hot press of his eyes, she traced a fingertip down his chest, watching as the muscle leaped reflexively beneath it, all the way down to his waistband that was still fastened.

"You disobeyed me, Lord Roth," she chided, knuckles brushing over his flexing abdomen. They leaped, too, along with other still-covered body parts. "I seem to recall telling you to get rid of these."

She let her hand drift lower, hearing his sharp intake of breath, her woolen mind dimly confirming that he was rock-hard everywhere, especially *there*.

The thick shape of him had been burned into her memory, but she wanted to *see* him.

Emboldened, Isobel unfastened his falls, allowing his eager erection to spring free from its confines, and nearly swooned then and there. Rowlandson might have some disturbingly erotic drawings, and she might have been able to keep a clear head while paging through the filthy pages earlier, but none of them could compare to the real thing.

Winter was as formidable and as beautiful there as he was everywhere else.

"Isobel." The three-syllable rasp of her name dripped through her like hot honey.

"Undress me."

He exhaled a groan. "I cannot see."

"Then feel."

• • •

Winter wondered if a man could actually die from need. His ballocks were so tight, his cock so full, with every muscle in his body straining for release that he was sure he was balancing on the very edge of death. But *hell*, what a way to go.

He could feel his wife's eyes on him, the lack of sight heightening every other sense—the smell of her, the sound of her own suffocated breaths, and now the *feel* of her.

As instructed, Winter reached out blindly, attempting to control the trembling of his hands when they contacted the front of her body. He fumbled with the buttons at first, but managed to get the first layer off and then her waistcoat. She helped with the shirt and then stepped away. The rustle of clothing reached him.

God, he wished he could see.

She shifted again, and then warm breath caressed his ear. "Put your hands on me, Winter."

At the sound of his given name, this time, he couldn't hold back the shudder that dissipated like lava through him. A shudder that turned into a full-on quake when his bare hands met soft feminine flesh. Her hips. Her *naked* hips. His greedy palm slid around the satiny curve, cupping the firm arse he'd drooled over before, her velvety skin making him harder than he'd ever been in his life.

"Sit," she ordered, pushing a palm to the center of his chest and urging him back into the seat behind him. Hell, he loved the sound of her voice. Her breathy commands. And then she straddled him, thighs bracketing his. Fuck this charade, he had to see her. Had to take her in.

Winter reached up to remove the blindfold.

"Take it off and this ends," she whispered, her fingers digging into his shoulders for purchase as she settled her weight over him.

"Isobel, please."

"No," she said. "I barely saw you our first time in Chelmsford, I had to *feel*. That's all you get now."

This was it, he really was going to die.

But he didn't die.

Not when she slid down onto him with a gasping moan, working his entire straining length into her ready warmth. Not when she began to move with short, erratic movements that told him she was as flustered as he. Not even when he had to force himself to think of anything—puppies, vicars, estate accounts—to not spill his seed instantaneously.

"How much do you want this?" she whispered.

"Badly," he grit out.

His cruel wife rose and stilled, hovering over his tip. "Then beg for it."

"Please," he groaned, mindless with pleasure as she swirled her hips, teasing him like the ruthless lover she was. Christ, she felt fucking glorious. The sensation of her body owning his, taking him *inside* and grasping him there, was beyond anything his frenzied dreams could have ever conjured. He'd fantasized about the heated clench of her body for years, been tortured by the excruciating push and pull between them these last weeks, but the reality was beyond imagining. He wanted to be lodged deep within her where he belonged. The latter part of the thought bludgeoned him, but he shoved it away before he could think too deeply on what it meant. It'd been in the heat of the moment, that was all.

She halted. "I'm not actually sure that you want this, Winter."

"I do. Use me. Fuck me. *Please*."

He could sense her gratification as she sank down like the tightest glove. It was heaven. With his sight taken away, all he *could* do was feel. She lifted and then drove down again. The clench of her body surrounded him like wet silk, her slick channel gripping and releasing him with every pass. His hands went up to fill themselves with her breasts, grazing over the hard buds and pinching them. Her gasp was his gift, make her speed up her movements.

But Winter could only let her take control for so

long. His hand slid to her back, climbed the knots of her spine and drew her body down to his until her breasts rubbed against the hair on his chest. His mouth found hers unerringly, licking into those delicious depths and finding that brazen tongue. He kissed her as she rode him, slowing her pace and drawing it out.

He would make every minute of this exquisite torture last.

Return the favor.

"Winter," she moaned against his lips, rearing back to pleasure herself against his groin at every downstroke, grinding against him. He wished he could see her face, but he could only imagine it. Head thrown back, lips parted, skin flushed with arousal. He slid his thumb down her soft belly to the apex of her sex, her keening cry his only warning before her body shivered and broke around his in powerful waves.

"Fuck!"

And then he was there with her, a scant moment later, chanting her name and growling like a feral beast as he yanked himself free to spend on his belly.

In the aftermath, they panted against each other in silence for what seemed like an eternity, but eventually, Isobel moved to shift off of him. Cool air settled upon the damp skin of his abdomen, and Winter reached up to remove the blindfold. By the time his eyes adjusted to the light from the lamps, Isobel had already donned her trousers and shirt. He watched in silence as she found her boots and fastened buttons, her face revealing nothing. "Isobel?"

That ice-blue gaze lifted to his. "I believe we had a wager, my lord, and I must say you beg so prettily."

She grinned, but it didn't quite reach her eyes. "Much more gratifying than me running back to Chelmsford with my tail between my legs, I assure you. I win, Lord Roth."

He could only gape as his wife winked and sauntered from the room.

CHAPTER EIGHTEEN

Take your pleasure by the horns, any which way you can get it.
– Lady Darcy

"Isobel Helena Vance, you *slept* with him?" Clarissa whisper-shrieked.

Isobel's eyes widened as she glanced around the lush gardens with its rows of brightly colored roses and verdant, neatly trimmed shrubs, but thankfully, there were no gardeners in sight to hear their salacious conversation. Which was why Isobel had suggested a walk after luncheon. Less risk of being overheard. And thankfully, the twins were still indoors—they would be unable to keep something this monumental a secret.

"Yes. Keep your voice down."

"As in goodnight sleep or tup-you-until-you-can't-walk sleep?"

Isobel bit her lip and blushed. "The second."

Clarissa screamed and launched across the garden bench, almost crushing her in the process. "Squeeze me sideways, Lady Darcy would be so proud."

Her blush deepened. "Trust me, this is *all* Lady Darcy's fault."

Isobel had nearly combusted recounting the events of the evening when she'd been awoken by a hurricane in skirts at the crack of dawn. Well, more around midday—later than usual for her—but she'd had an exhausting evening.

Even now, her body was still deliciously achy. Isobel's cheeks heated as she recalled how brazen she'd been. The power that had come with the interaction had been heady, though she was certain that Winter had let her do those things. He could have taken control quite easily at any point. In point of fact, he *had* during the act itself.

And the blindfold, dear God, the *blindfold*! What had she been thinking? Winter had loved it, obviously, and she had as well. However, though he'd been caught up in his pleasure, he'd still had the presence of mind to pull from her body at the last minute. In hindsight, Isobel had never intended to trick Winter in such a manner, but the perfunctory act had still stung.

She wasn't some doxy. She was his *wife*.

But if he didn't want children, withdrawal was necessary.

Isobel hadn't told Clarissa about that part. Or about the blindfold.

Thankfully, Clarissa had been too fascinated by the whole charity auction and the outrageously darker side of The Silver Scythe to push for the finer details. Isobel wasn't fooled, however. Clarissa would hound her for those later when she'd processed the rest. Perhaps Isobel would be able to fend her off with a convincing enough story, if she ever stopped blushing.

"So, the proceeds from this filthy man mart from a club that your husband *owns* do go to a charity?" Clarissa asked.

"A shelter house as I understand it," Isobel replied, biting back a grin. "In Seven Dials."

"That's generous. I suppose it doesn't matter

where the funds come from." She frowned. "Wait, Seven Dials? That's…a coincidence."

"What is?"

Clarissa shook her head, wrinkling her nose. "No, it's nothing. Never mind, I'm grasping for connections that don't exist." She grinned. "Tell me more about Vittorina the Vainglorious. Did she look like she swallowed a toad when you outbid her?"

"An entire bucket of toads," Isobel said. "And then she tried to imply that Winter wasn't into women."

Her grin widened. "Joke's on her because Winter is definitely into petticoat lane, also known as the temple of Venus, the fancy article, and nature's tufted treasure."

"Clarissa!" Isobel hissed, once more glancing around, and then decided to give her friend a solid dose of her own medicine in retaliation. "Enough about me. How was teatime last night?"

She was rewarded when Clarissa went a brilliant shade of red. "Fine," she mumbled.

It was Isobel's turn to grin. "Funny, I thought you were such a tea enthusiast. Don't want to kiss-and-tell, Clarissa dear?" When her skin color deepened to plum, Isobel pounced. "Good heavens, wench, what did you *do*?"

"He was asleep, so I had a peek," she rushed out.

Isobel gave a choked laugh. "And?"

"Suffice it to say that, ahem, it's true that curiosity silenced the cat. He's…not small."

"Must run in the family," Isobel said, and they both burst into uncontrollable giggles, drawing the attention of the gardener who had returned and was busy pruning a nearby tree. They watched him in silence, enjoying the warm afternoon air, until he moved on out of sight.

"So, what will you do?" Clarissa asked. "With Winter, I mean? Now that you've won your little wager and shown him who's queen of the castle."

She frowned. "Nothing. What happened between us doesn't change anything."

Clarissa's eyes brightened. "Oh, trust me, it will. Men don't like to lose. He'll come crawling to you on his own, and maybe give you some babies while he's at it."

Isobel's heart squeezed and a knot formed in her throat, but she kept her face calm. Little did Clarissa suspect that her husband would geld himself before doing that. She wrapped her arms about her middle. She hadn't been open with Clarissa about Winter's strong opinions on the matter, because it wasn't her place to divulge his private feelings, but his hard refusal of both being a husband and a father reduced the outcome of the game to something trivial. Bringing a man to his knees meant nothing if all she got out of it was a lonely future. Deep down, she wanted *more*. She wanted Winter...and a future with him.

Maybe she *should* cut her losses and go back to Chelmsford. She'd been such a fool, too focused on winning that she hadn't thought of what would happen if she actually won. Now, because she'd acted so impetuously, her reward was the same as her punishment.

"We should call on him today," Clarissa suggested, nodding hard. "That's what Lady Darcy would do. She wouldn't wait for him to start thinking, because Lord knows when men start using any part of their brain, things go belly up. She would take that bull by the horns and ride it into the sunset."

Isobel gave a choked laugh. "Lady Darcy has caused quite enough trouble."

Clarissa frowned and leaned in, her blue eyes concerned. "You're not going to give up, are you? You're not going to run because your blockheaded husband can't see what's right in front of him, are you?"

"I don't know," she mumbled.

"What do you want, Izzy?"

Isobel blinked. "What do you mean?"

Her best friend blew out an exasperated breath. "The question is exactly as it sounds—what do you want? For yourself. For the rest of your life." She pursed her lips. "For the next week, then."

Isobel exhaled. What she wanted was impossible… and brought with it a boatload of heartache. And her silly imagination was already pining for it. For *him*. She should have known she couldn't engage in anything physical without her heart having its say. It had taken every ounce of her control to leave that room as if the sex had been meaningless, when it had been the opposite. In truth, winning the ridiculous wager had meant nothing.

"I want the fairy tale. But for the next week, I suppose I just want him to see me."

"Then you have to fight for what you want and it's my job as your best friend to tell you when you're being a pussy-footing hector."

Isobel huffed. "Did you just call me a coward?"

"If the shoe fits." Clarissa stood and held out her hand. "What do you have to lose?"

Rather a lot, including the fate of her brittle heart, but she didn't tell Clarissa that. Instead, Isobel took her friend's hand and let her drag her back inside to get a cloak and bonnet, and have Simmons summon the carriage. Since Oliver had apparently taken the ducal carriage, they would have to settle for the plain black coach that was used for errands.

Within short order, they were in the conveyance and on their way to 15 Audley Street. Her emotions were tied up in precarious knots, and the closer they got to their destination, the more agitated she became. This was a bad idea.

"Why are you so nervous?" Clarissa scolded. "You're making *me* anxious."

"I don't know what to expect." She swallowed hard. "What if this is a mistake?"

Clarissa rolled her eyes. "We've already established that it's not. Stop falling back to old tactics. I know you, and you're looking for a way out. I think you like him and he likes you."

"He does?"

She gave an exasperated sniff. "He took you for a turn in Cock Alley, for heaven's sake."

"Clarissa!" Isobel bit out with a giggle, cheeks flaming. "That doesn't always mean a man likes a woman. It could be just sex."

"Fine, apart from the fact that he's hot for you and head-over-heels in lust, I think he cares about you. Trust me, that man has no eyes for anyone else when you're in the room. I saw it at the first ball we attended. You didn't see Winter's face at the exhibit, when he thought you were hurt. I've never seen anyone look at someone the way he looked at you...as though he'd almost lost something precious beyond measure. Anyone with a smattering of sense can see it."

"If you say so," Isobel said dubiously.

"I know so."

Still, by the time they pulled up to Winter's residence, Isobel's heart had settled into her throat. She was in the middle of calming herself enough to climb out of the coach when Clarissa gave an absurdly shrill squeal.

"Oh, there's Oliver! And he's looking so much better."

Sure enough, her brother-in-law was descending the staircase, his face wreathed in its usual dour lines. Didn't the man ever smile? Isobel couldn't fathom what Clarissa saw in him, but to each her own, she supposed.

Clarissa pushed past her. "I'll get a ride with him. That way, you can take this coach when you've finished and not have to worry about me."

"Clarissa, you don't even know where he's going."

She winked. "Oh, I'm going to convince him to take me to Gunter's for an ice."

Isobel watched as a bold Clarissa sauntered over to Oliver, tucking her arm in his and batting her eyes up at him. Isobel half expected Oliver to give his usual reaction and reject her, but instead, she was astonished to see her stern brother-in-law actually crack a smile. Clarissa turned back with a jaunty wave, giving her a thumbs-up, and then they both disappeared into Oliver's waiting coach.

Well, wonders would never cease.

Smiling, Isobel drew a breath, trying to drum up

the courage to go to the door, when it opened and her husband strode out. Hat and cane in hand, Winter looked utterly delectable. She sucked in a breath at the windblown, gorgeous sight of him, and ducked down. He took no notice of the plain coach, instead intent on flagging down a passing hackney. She frowned—why wouldn't he avail himself of his own horse or carriage?

"Follow that hack," she told her coachman before she could change her mind.

"Yes, my lady."

Her brain spun with scenarios. Where on earth was he going? It didn't take long for her to guess that the tightly-packed, run-down houses they rode past were in Covent Garden or spot the seven-road irregular square that gave the warren its name, Seven Dials.

After a few more minutes, the coach rolled to a stop and she peered out of the narrow window to see Winter descending the hackney in front of what looked like an old church. Her heart dropped to her stomach as a beautiful blonde joined him. Recognition was slow to hit, but when it did, she felt it everywhere like a blow she couldn't dodge.

Contessa James—the opera singer over whom he'd allegedly fought a duel.

She watched in horror as he kissed her cheek and the voluptuous singer flung her arms about his neck with a cry. Winter didn't detach, but hugged her back, in full view of passersby, and judging from the wolf whistles, there were a few. After their lengthy embrace, they disappeared together into the building.

Isobel's heart crumbled inside her chest even as she climbed down from the coach. Was it a bawdy house? Some kind of gaming hell?

"My lady," the coachman warned. "It's not safe here."

"I'll just be a minute."

Ignoring his protests, she crossed the street to the well-kept building, only to nearly crash into her husband on his way out. "That was fast," she said for lack of anything better to say.

His gray eyes widened with shock and then alarm. "Isobel, what are you doing here?"

"I could ask you the same thing," she bit out. Was that guilt slinking through his eyes? "Meeting the mistress you claim not to have? Contessa what's-her-name?"

Speechless, he stared at her. "It's not like that."

"Then explain it to me," she said, slamming her hands on her hips, uncaring of the curious crowd they were drawing. "Because it sure as hell looks like a bawdy house to me."

He scrubbed a hand over his face. "It's a shelter. My shelter. I own it."

"You own it," she repeated dumbly, staring anew at the facade and seeing the plain bronze plaque affixed to the side of the door: *Prudence Vance, In Memory*.

"For my sister."

• • •

"Your sister?" his wife repeated, pale blue eyes widening.

Winter blew out a sigh. "She died not too far from where you're standing right now. We found her in an opium den. She had no place to go and ended up here in Seven Dials. Daughter of a duke with no way out but death."

"I'm so sorry." Her eyes shone with the glimmer of tears, the scent of honeysuckle curling into his nose and chasing away the ripe stench of the vicinity. "I didn't know you owned a shelter."

"No one does. Besides Westmore."

Winter frowned at the accumulating crowd. He was dressed in a pair of nondescript brown breeches and unassuming coat, while she still wore an obviously well-tailored and costly blue silk and muslin day dress. From the avid looks she was getting, it wouldn't take much for a mob to gather or for the pickpockets to make quick work of any loose buttons, coin or other easily removable possessions. While he could handle himself, he didn't want her in harm's way.

He had no idea how she'd come to be here and whether she'd followed him, but this wasn't the place to discuss it. "Did you come by carriage?" he asked.

She blinked as though coming out of a trance. "Yes, it's just over there," she replied automatically, but when he took her arm and attempted to escort her toward it, she shook off his grasp. "No, I'm not going anywhere with you. Even if this establishment is for your sister, I'm not blind, Roth. I saw you go in with Contessa James." Her voice faltered. "You fought a duel for her, if you recall."

Isobel wouldn't believe him, but he was never involved with Contessa James. She'd wanted to get away from her current protector—a viscount who treated her abominably and had bruised her throat so badly weeks ago that she couldn't perform on stage.

When he'd threatened to cut out her tongue so she could never sing again, she'd come to Winter.

It was why she'd been temporarily staying at the shelter, until she could find new accommodations. The viscount had thrown her out on her ear after Winter and Westmore had paid the man a sinister visit, letting him know in no uncertain terms what would happen if he ever laid a finger on the contessa again. That was the purported duel that had made the papers. But this wasn't the place to clarify that.

"It's not like that," he said again. "I will explain, but it's not safe here, Isobel. Will you please let me get you home?"

She stared at him, and then her glance slipped to the side as if only just taking stock of the infringing throng. "Take me inside."

God, she was a stubborn thing.

"Very well, but it's not what you're accustomed to, and you may see things that might harm your sensibilities."

She firmed her jaw. "You might be surprised, Lord Roth, at what I've seen. I'm not a wilting daisy who swoons at the slightest provocation."

Looking at her, all arctic rage and a spine of pure iron, he could believe it. There were things he was learning about his wife that made him question whether *anything* he knew about her was accurate. He wanted to discover everything about her. And that was a dangerous want. Lusting after her body was one thing; being seduced by her courage or compassion or intelligence was a slippery slope he had no intention of nearing.

With a nod, he took her elbow and unlocked the

door, ushering her into the spare but clean foyer of the building. An enormous man limped toward them, and Winter felt Isobel tense at his hulking appearance. Creighton was a pugilist who had had his jaw broken outside of the ring in an attempt to rig a prize fight, and beaten to within an inch of his life.

Astoundingly, Winter had found him alive in a pool of his own blood, left to die. He'd saved the man's life, and Creighton had been loyal ever since. As porter, he was the only man allowed on the premises, tasked with the responsibility of protecting the vulnerable inhabitants from any forced entry.

"Forgot something, milord?"

Winter shook his head. "No, Creighton. This is… Lady Roth."

The man's eyes popped wide, his huge body forming a clumsy bow. "Milady."

"He's the overseer," Winter explained. "Keeps the riffraff out."

He led her down the corridor to a large staircase. It was a far cry from the dirty streets outside, and instead of rot and unwashed bodies, smelled faintly of antiseptic and clean linen. The soft murmur of voices wafted down the white-painted hallway from the rooms upstairs.

"Is this a hospital?" she asked, her eyes darting into some of the well-lit, clinical-looking rooms off the main hallway.

"No, but a doctor visits on occasion, should the need arise." He drew a breath. "It's simply a place for women and children to feel safe when they have nowhere else to go, or when they need help."

A gasp left her lips. "There are children, here?"

"Sometimes. We try not to separate them from their mothers."

Before she could form a reply, Winter guided her into what appeared to be a small salon. A maid curtsied and dashed out of the room, mumbling something about fetching a pot of tea. Isobel shook her head, but he didn't stop the servant. He was usually the only visitor here, apart from the shelter's constant trickle of residents.

"You fund all of this?" she asked.

He shrugged. "The auctions do for the most part. The money is put in a trust that's managed by Matteo."

"I thought Matteo was your man of affairs?"

Winter shook his head. "He also handles The Silver Scythe and other investments. He does what he wants when he wants basically."

The maid returned with a tea tray, and though he knew Isobel wasn't in the mind for tea, she thanked the girl sweetly. Her hands shook as she poured, though the minute she took a sip, she seemed to settle. She took several more before replacing the teacup on the tray and clearing her throat. "You built this for Prudence?"

Winter flinched, even knowing the question would be forthcoming. "She died from too much laudanum, and no one saw the warning signs. She was depressed, fearful, and had developed an unhealthy dependency. I was too late to help her. Westmore found her in a hovel covered in her own vomit and filth."

Pain brimmed in her eyes. "I am so sorry."

Winter exhaled. "Thank you. She got involved with a fucking opium eater who only wanted her money." He swallowed his fury, though he noticed that Isobel didn't so much as flinch at his oath. "I bought this place so that women like Prue can get help if they need it. To them, it could mean the difference between life and death."

"That's very noble of you."

"It's atonement," he said. "I wasn't there for her when she needed me."

Isobel held his gaze, those pale blue eyes softening. "Is that why you're so closed off?" she asked. "Is that why you won't make this marriage a true one? Or want a family? It's because of her, isn't it?"

This had nothing to do with his sister. It had to do with *him*. If he couldn't protect his own sister, how the hell would he be able to protect anyone else? The only real motivation for this marriage was to protect his inheritance, he told himself firmly. "When Prue died, my heart died, too. There's nothing left of it. Not for you, not for anyone."

He watched her elegant throat swallow back what he could only assume was hurt at his cruel words, but she still reached for him. "Shutting everyone out isn't the answer. Me, Kendrick—"

"Don't," he snapped. "You don't know him."

She advanced on him, not quailing at his temper. "No, *you* don't know him or what he's been through, or what he feels because you don't care to know. You've shut him out just as you're trying to shut me out because it suits you." She let out a shuddering breath. "Well, it doesn't bloody suit me! What about what happened between us, Winter?"

"Your triumphant wager?"

She swore under her breath. "You know damn

well it was more than that."

God, he wanted to kiss those trembling lips, bury himself in her body, and forget for just one moment that his world wasn't cobbled together from broken pieces. Even now, she was undaunted in her passion. One step. That was all it would take to gather her in his arms.

He stepped away instead. "That was a mistake. Go back to Chelmsford, Isobel. Take a lover, have the child you want, I don't care." A lie. Just the thought of it soured his stomach and made him want to break something with his bare hands.

"You wish to be cuckolded?" she whispered, eyes bright with tears.

He made his gaze hard, raking her with it, his voice little more than a sneer. "It should go both ways, shouldn't it?" She recoiled as if he'd slapped her, agony and betrayal filling her expression. Christ, he felt sick to even suggest such a vile thing, the pain on her face mirrored by the savage ache in his chest. God knew he couldn't so much as look at another woman, and the thought of her with anyone else gutted him. But still, he pressed on. "What I truly want is for you to leave. Can't you get that through your foolish little head?"

They stared at each other in fraught, ugly silence, until his achingly beautiful wife squared her shoulders and swept from the room. Head high, she paused at the door, a queen addressing the most despicable of her subjects. "Go to hell, Roth."

CHAPTER NINETEEN

They say hell hath no fury like a woman scorned. I counter that with hell hath no fury like a woman with a purpose.
– Lady Darcy

"You look like a bag of shelled crabs," Clarissa pronounced, barging into Isobel's bedchamber, eyes narrowing at the discarded tea tray that was still full. "That got peed on by a bunch of drunken sailors. And then chewed up and spit out by sharks."

Her best friend's assessment was probably true. Though Winter's cruel words had hurt at the shelter, they had opened Isobel's eyes. Hours and hours of cursing his existence had led to hours and hours of thinking. And the only conclusion she could come to was that her husband was irreparably broken, and that somewhere along the way, he'd convinced himself that it was better to shut out the world than to open himself up to anyone.

Including her. Prue's death had been the feather that had broken the horse's back. And unless Winter wanted to change, no one—much less her—could force him to do so.

"Tell me how you truly feel." Isobel rubbed her sore eyes, knowing they would be rimmed in crimson since she'd spent the past two days sobbing into the bedclothes. She was surprised they weren't more of a tear-sodden mess. "How did I ever get so lucky to have you as my best friend?"

Clarissa propped her hands to her hips. "We promised never to lie to each other, didn't we?"

"True, but a little tenderness never hurt anyone."

"You don't need me to be tender, Izzy. You like that I give the medicine to you straight. And right now, you've been in bed for two days." Clarissa sniffed and wrinkled her nose. "You're starting to smell."

"I am not!" Isobel squeaked, but then lowered her head to give a discreet inhale. "Some of the milk spilled this morning."

"And let me guess…you're crying over it?" Giggling, she dodged the frilled cushion that Isobel threw at her head.

"That's the spirit," Clarissa said. "Fight back, though I'm not the enemy here. That prize goes to your sap skull of a husband."

"I won't disagree with you. Men stink. Especially ones who think they can tell you what to do and when to do it, just because the thought of being vulnerable for once in their lives scares the spit out of them."

"Don't they just!" Clarissa burst out with uncharacteristic venom. "They can be the most clod-brained dolts in creation. It's a wonder God had to give them two heads just so they could function. Honestly, imagine how eternally lost they would be if they only had to make do with one." She rolled her eyes, warming to her diatribe. "Then again, it might make life easier if they only used the one below stairs. No mind games or perpetual misunderstanding. Lady Darcy should do an exposé on the male brain."

"God, no!" Isobel said. "The *ton* would never recover. Nor would Lady Darcy, I imagine. We exercise our minuscule freedoms within a male-dominated world view."

"It's such a double standard, isn't it?" her friend groused. "They want to have their pie and eat it, while we must do the baking, the cleaning, and watch our figure. We women need some pie, too, damn it!"

Despite her tongue-in-cheek tone, Isobel picked up on some underlying bitterness and felt a stab of guilt that she hadn't noticed Clarissa was also in a funk. "Did something happen with Oliver?"

"Oliver who?"

"You very well know who. Your tea-making abettor."

Huffing, Clarissa ducked her head to hide her blush, but injury glinted in her eyes. "Let's just say that anything to do with tea is on hiatus."

"What did he do?"

"The usual hot then cold, typical Oliver. Doesn't know what he wants when it's clear to everyone but him. Must run in the family."

"You deserve better."

"We both do," Clarissa said. "Now get up. We'll get the twins who are bored out of their minds from being stuck indoors all day, and we will take Oliver's new barouche for a turn outside for some fresh air. Then we can all pick out future husbands."

"In Hyde Park?"

Clarissa grinned, faking an affected voice and throwing her hand against her forehead. "What better place to see and be seen, darling. It is nearly five, the fashionable evening hour, after all."

Husbands aside, Isobel did need to get out of bed. Clarissa was right. She needed the fresh air, and she was sure that Clarissa needed a break as well. The twins, too. Being in mourning had to be hard. Isobel had been so caught up in her own drama that she hadn't even thought about how Molly and Violet might be adjusting to London, considering it was improper for them to attend too many social functions.

The last time she'd spoken to Violet, the woman had been complaining about the never-ending amount of needlepoint she'd been doing to stave off boredom. Guilt sluiced through Isobel. Lately, she avoided anything that involved a pair of knitting needles or embroidery hoops, but knew someone like Violet would also abhor the tedium. She should have been spending more time with the twins.

"Good idea," she said to Clarissa. "I'll be ready in twenty minutes. Get the twins and we'll make an outing of it."

It didn't take long for her to have a quick slipper bath and get dressed in a navy riding habit with silver buttons and matching trim. It was one of the fashionable new pieces that she had commissioned from Madame Pinot.

"You look smart," Clarissa said with an approving smile when Isobel emerged from her bedchamber. Clarissa had also changed into a forest-green habit that accentuated her figure, also one of the modiste's creations. The twins waited on the landing, smiles on their faces. Even Molly looked excited at the prospect of going out for a spell.

"Thank you, so do all three of you."

"We look like ghosts," Violet said mournfully. "Drab riding habits are the worst. You and Clarissa look lovely, though. I can't wait for half-mourning to be over, God rest Papa's soul. He would want us to look our best, I think, and gray's just not my color!"

Molly sniffed. "Speak for yourself. I look fabulous in gray."

"You're deluded, sister."

Laughing, they descended the staircase, only to bump into Oliver on the way out. The look he gave Clarissa was downright cold, though Isobel didn't miss the way his blue eyes flared at the snug cut of Clarissa's clothing. He might pretend he didn't want her, but his gaze gave his inner desires away.

Isobel grinned. "Don't mind us, we're off to find a husband for Clarissa."

Oliver opened his mouth, thought better of it, and then closed it, turning on his heel and striding away without a word. But from the rigid set of his shoulders, it was clear that he was furious. *Good.* Isobel ground her jaw. She'd had outside of enough with broody Vance men. A brisk outing would do her and Clarissa good.

"Won't Oliver be angry we're taking his barouche?" she whispered as Randolph brought the conveyance around the front and the twins piled in.

Clarissa's grin was wicked. "Isn't that the whole point?"

Isobel grinned, her friend's mischievous mood contagious. However, as they rode into the park, she found herself to be the subject of considerable attention and fevered conversation. Fans lifted and heads bowed. It was curious…and unsettling.

"Something is wrong," Isobel whispered to Clarissa who nodded, her brow furrowed.

"Why's everyone looking at us?" Molly asked.

"And whispering?" Violet added, scowling.

Clarissa frowned. "I will get to the bottom of this."

Isobel watched in silence as she directed Randolph to steer the carriage over to a nearby throng of people, where she descended and spoke to them for several minutes, and then hurried back over with a handful of crumpled newssheets in hand. Isobel felt her insides tighten with dread as her friend climbed back into the barouche and shared them with the twins. Isobel bit her lip, watching them. Anything in there couldn't be good, not with the pitying look on Violet's and Molly's faces. Isobel had enough experience with the gossip rags to know.

"Izzy—"

"Just hand it over," Isobel said, reaching out a gloved hand.

Violet passed them over with great reluctance, and Isobel drew in a clipped breath. What could be worse than her husband fighting a duel over an opera singer? She smoothed out the crinkled paper, the dark ink smudging. The first thing to jump out at her was the headline.

FORSAKEN ITALIAN HEIRESS TELLS ALL

And then her stomach turned as she took in the rest. It was worse than she had ever imagined, each word like lead ballast to the chest. Not only was Lady Vittorina claiming that Winter had left her broken-hearted after promising to marry her, but she was also saying that he'd left her and *their child* destitute and alone years ago to come back to England out of duty for a forced marriage to one Lady Isobel Everleigh. The newssheets painted her as the villain and Winter as the consummate womanizer.

"Isobel, you know that they print untruths," Molly said.

Violet reached for her hand. "They're full of lies."

White spots danced in front of Isobel's eyes as her fingers fisted in the sheets. Oh, dear God, she was going to be ill. Right in front of everyone watching… with their condemning, scornful gazes. It didn't matter if any of it was true—the *ton* thrived on gossip and this was just the kind of juicy morsel they enjoyed. *Relished*.

"Isobel!" Clarissa said, sounding as though she'd been calling her name for some time. "What do you want me to do?"

She focused on her friend's face, licking dry lips, her heart in pieces. "Get me home, Clarissa."

Clarissa nodded. "Randolph, you heard her ladyship, go."

The short journey back to Vance House passed in a fog, and only when they arrived back at the mews did Isobel realize she was still clenching the creased news-sheets between her fingers. She let them fall, uncaring of where they ended up, before blindly dismounting the carriage and rushing into the house. She could hear the twins yelling, but the thudding of her heartbeat in her ears was too great.

Dimly, she heard Clarissa saying something about fetching some tea from the kitchens and the twins seeing about a hot bath, but Isobel couldn't think. All she wanted to do was reach the safety and comfort of her bedchamber before she embarrassed herself further.

Shouting reached her ears as if from afar. It

sounded as though people were arguing in the study, where the heavy door stood slightly ajar. Isobel was about to turn and go up the stairs when one voice hit her hard…one she instantly recognized.

Her husband's.

• • •

In their father's study, Winter stared at his brother, his eyes tracing the trickle of blood on the corner of his mouth. Fuck, he should have hit him harder. After all these years, it was more than the blockheaded cad deserved.

"You married her to inherit," Oliver said, pressing a palm to his bleeding lip. "Don't pretend otherwise. What's to say that Vittorina's account in the news-sheets wasn't real?"

"It's *not*. You'll believe anything terrible about me, won't you?"

"You earned it."

Winter ground his jaw. "I can't control what the newssheets publish, no more than I can change what happened in my past."

"Like you did with Prudence?"

Blood filled his vision again, and riled beyond belief, he lunged toward his brother, only to be hauled back by the duke himself. Shrugging his father off, Winter's fingers curled around Oliver's neck, his rage pounding between his ears like a bellowing beast. "Don't you dare bring her up, you fucking bastard!"

At his words, Oliver paled, pain flashing across his face before all the fight drained from his body. He went limp with a defeated huff, but Winter's boiling anger blinded him to his brother's sudden paralysis.

"Enough!" Kendrick roared, finally about to tear them apart, but managing to catch a flying elbow in the nose at the same time. He stumbled back and crashed into a small table.

"Your Grace," Simmons exclaimed, rushing in to escort the duke away and guide him into a nearby armchair. He held up a pristine handkerchief to his bleeding nostril.

"I'm fine, Simmons," he said. "Leave us, please."

Breathing hard, Winter felt an unexpected pang as he stared at his bloodied father. His eyes slid back to Oliver, who stalked to the bottle of whiskey on the desk and poured himself a liberal draught, dabbing at his lip with a fingertip. They glared at each other until the duke spoke.

"What in damnation is going on here?" he asked.

They stared at him, but Oliver beat Winter to the punch. "More of the same. The fact that he's always doing stupid things and tarnishing the Vance name, and not caring about anyone else but himself, even his own wife, whom everyone in the *ton* knows he married for convenience."

"Isobel is going back to Chelmsford," Winter said through his teeth. "And you're right. I don't care about anyone, not her, not you, and certainly not some Italian chit hunting for a title."

"Does your dear wife know about your old flame?"

Winter's fingers curled into fists at his side. "This has nothing to do with Isobel," he snapped. "I never wanted to marry her in the first place. This whole farce has been the worst mistake of my life, and with what happened to Prue, that's saying a lot." His gaze shifted to the silent duke and then back to his brother. Something deep behind his ribs stung—the falsehoods stabbing into the heart of him like lethal needles—but he shoved those useless emotions down deep. His wife had been a means to an end. He had to believe she still was, for both their sakes. "I did it for one reason as you both very well know—because of that bloody codicil. That was your doing, don't think I don't know it."

"It was in there for a reason," Oliver said. "The duke could not have a wastrel for an heir. You needed to come up to snuff."

"So you convinced him I needed to marry?"

Oliver huffed. "You were out of control, Winter. You lost sight of your duty and name, and you needed to be reminded of what was important in a way that would get your attention—your pockets."

"Well played, brother," Winter shot back. "So I did as I was bid and wed the chit. What does any of this have to do with her? I don't even know why she's here in town."

"I warned you that your past would catch up to you one day. And now, because of you, this woman from your past is smearing our good name."

Cursing under his breath, Winter walked over to the decanter and poured himself a drink, which he dispatched in one swallow. The brandy burned a path to his stomach, leaving clarity followed by no small amount of guilt in its wake. His brother was right. It *was* his own fault that he'd dallied with a woman of her vile nature in the first place, but he hadn't made her any promises and there was never any child.

"I regret many of my actions, and until Prue's

death, I saw no reason to change," he said with a sigh, raking a hand through his hair and pouring another drink with shaking fingers. "But answer me this, brother—why do you hate me so much?"

Oliver's eyes flashed with resentment, though they darted over to where the duke sat for an infinitesimal moment. "No matter what I do, I can never measure up. Yet, you, the prodigal son, does as he pleases with no consequence. Hate doesn't begin to cover it."

"We are brothers."

"Not so when you're born on the other side of the blanket!" Oliver snarled.

Winter blinked, his brother's odd reaction to being called a bastard suddenly making sense. Holy hell. Was Oliver a by-blow of Kendrick's?

Their stares converged on the duke, who sat silent and ramrod still, his eyes showing no surprise whatsoever. *Fuck, no.* Winter felt a rush of resentment gather inside of him. What more indignities had his poor mother suffered at his hands! She'd confided in a young Winter, eyes glazed with laudanum, that the duke had never loved her and sought comfort elsewhere. But to bring his by-blow under the same roof? That was unconscionable.

"How could you do this?" Winter growled aloud. "To Mother?"

Two sets of eyes fastened on him—one full of regret, and the other laced with shame. "I did it *for* her," the duke said and then turned to Oliver. "How long have you known?"

Winter frowned. *For her?*

Oliver clenched his fists. "Since I was a boy. She told me herself that you were not my father. I've had to live with that shame in silence for years, while he"—he spared Winter with a fulminating glance—"flaunted his name about like filth. A name I could never truly have."

Winter's rage ebbed and flowed in confusion. Stunned, he opened his mouth and shut it. None of this made sense. His *father* was the adulterer. At least, that was what his mother had always claimed. "You're lying," he said.

"About what, brother dear? About your conduct or the fact that I'm a bastard?"

"You're my son," Kendrick said. "Just as Winter is."

Oliver laughed. "None of your blood runs in my veins, Duke."

"Blood doesn't always make a family. Loyalty does, choice and sacrifice." The duke tilted his head back as his nose started to bleed anew, wheezing painfully. "And love, if you can be brave enough to earn it."

The last hit Winter like a fist to the gut. Love—the thing that had sent his mother to madness and led Prue to her death.

"What would you know anything of love?" he bit out.

"I wasn't the perfect father, but you were my children. *All* of you," he added with a pointed glance at Oliver. "Your mother was jealous, inventing liaisons that did not exist whenever I left Kendrick Abbey for my duties in parliament. I loved her, gave her you, but it was not enough. It was never enough. Oliver was simply her way of punishing me."

Winter was reeling at the bald admission from a

man who always shied away from any squeak of scandal. "Who's his father?"

"I am," Kendrick said tiredly. "Who sired him doesn't matter one whit. It never has."

The look on Oliver's face was so fleeting that if Winter hadn't been looking at him, he would have missed it. But for a heartbeat, the man looked dazed.

"She said you cuckolded her."

"I meant my vows."

Winter could not fathom that Oliver wasn't Kendrick's biological son. After all this time, he'd never suspected. Oliver had modeled himself after the duke so thoroughly that he physically resembled the man. Though as Winter compared them as they'd stood there, the differences were clear. Despite their identical stances—hands clasped behind their backs, imperious chins tilted just so—Oliver was stockier than the duke, his shoulders broader. Their hair and eyes were similar shades, but while the duke's mane leaned toward black, Oliver's had reddish tints.

How had Winter not *known*?

No wonder Oliver hated him so much. Where had Prue fit in to all of this? Had *she* known? Hell and damnation, he'd been so caught up in his own life— his own stupid agenda of destroying the Vance name—that he hadn't paid his little sister any mind. Until it had been much too late…until he'd lost her. Winter blamed himself for that, too.

"Did Prue know?" he muttered.

Kendrick nodded. "Your mother told her." He scraped a palm over his face. "You have to understand that the laudanum twisted her thoughts. At first, she took it to calm her worries and then more and more. Prudence, God rest her soul, took the same tincture with your mother's blessing and got her first taste of addiction. I blame myself for allowing that to happen."

"No," Winter said, backing away. "You're wrong. She wouldn't have done that."

"I don't know what she told you, Son, but I have no reason to deceive you."

Winter's emotions were an ugly, jumbled mess. The sorrow and sincerity on Kendrick's face could not be faked. If anything of what the duke had said was true, his mother had manipulated Winter's feelings so completely that her bitterness and resentment had become his. The duke had become the monster in the story…a poisonous narrative *she* had controlled.

God, he felt sick.

He didn't have the time to play back every single time his father had reached out and Winter had rejected him out of hand because of what he thought the duke had done, when the truth was, the duchess had borne a child out of wedlock and had turned his own legitimate son against him.

Christ, his bloody head was spinning.

He needed to think. He needed to *leave*. But he forced himself to sit. Running in the past had not served him well. "Start from the beginning," he said to the duke.

Kendrick did, and Winter listened while his father spoke. For the first time in his life, he considered a side of the story he'd never imagined—that his mother had been fabricating things all along, that his own innocent feelings might have been manipulated, that *his* father might have been the victim in this whole scene. What felt like ages later, Winter hung his head in his hands, his brain spinning with all he'd learned.

It was too much.

The door crashed open and they all stared at a wild-eyed Clarissa standing at the mouth of the study. "Isobel is gone."

"Gone?" Winter asked dully.

A furious and worried gaze met his. "We can't find her anywhere. She was already distraught after seeing the newssheets, so we had the maids prepare a bath to calm her down, but she didn't take it because she overheard you saying that she's the worst mistake of your life! How could you be so callous, Winter?" She jammed a finger at his chest, eyes brimming with tears. "She's distraught and not thinking straight. Violet said she barely spoke before fleeing upstairs, mumbling that she never should have come to London," she choked out. "She wouldn't ride back to Chelmsford, would she?"

"She didn't take her groom, Iz?" he asked.

"She *is*—oh God—" Clarissa cut off, bursting into tears. "She's gone alone and it's already dark."

Grabbing a lamp, Winter bolted to the mews, calling for Randolph. When the old groom came running out from the depths of the stables, his eyes widened. Winter clenched his teeth, worry lashing through him. "Did you see where my wife went?"

"No, my lord. She'd just come back with Miss Clarissa and gone into the house, only to rush out again, calling for her mare. It was a while ago." He hesitated, and Winter waved his arm for him to continue. "She seemed upset, my lord. Her eyes were red."

Fuck. He looked around the yard. "Where the hell is my horse!"

"One of the grooms was tending to him, my lord. I'll get him at once."

Randolph raced back inside the mews, and Winter paced, raking a hand through his hair in frustration. Where would she have gone? Was Clarissa right in that she would decide to ride to Chelmsford? It was over forty miles—several hours of hard riding—and she loved Hellion too much to run that horse into the ground. How could she be so reckless?

He didn't realize he'd muttered that last question out loud when Clarissa replied, sniffing. "Because she's Isobel, and because you hurt her."

A heavy hand came down to grip his shoulder and he turned to see his father standing there. Amidst murmurs of *Your Grace* in the courtyard, the duke turned him about. "Isobel is capable, Son. If she is alone, she won't have left here unarmed."

Winter frowned. Armed? His wife?

"Don't look so surprised," Clarissa said in a scathing tone that he no doubt deserved. "She owns pocket pistols and has better aim than my brothers."

Kendrick nodded. "I taught her. The girl is a skilled marksman."

Winter barely had time to process that his strait-laced, uptight duke of a father had taught his young, impulsive wife to shoot before the butler came running down the stairs to the mews.

"Your Grace?" he said to Kendrick. "It's a message for the marquess."

Winter snatched the grimy bit of paper that was scrawled with an address, one he recognized in Covent Garden near Seven Dials. But that wasn't what made his heart drop to his feet—it was the note at the bottom, written in an untidy scrawl.

Come quickly. Lady Roth has taken a terrible fall.

CHAPTER TWENTY

Dearest Friend, if you intend to enjoy the benefits and pleasures of conjugal love, communication is the cornerstone of any relationship.
– Lady Darcy

Isobel swiped her tears angrily away. Though she swore that she wouldn't shed any more tears for Winter Vance, here she was doing just that. Sobbing as though she was the first girl in history to ever have her heart trampled upon by a cruel, unfeeling man.

God, he was a blackguard. A rotter. The worst kind of scoundrel.

And she was married to him.

"I hate him," she whispered.

Her sister's eyes met hers, compassion swimming in them. "I know it feels like you do at the moment, but you don't. You're just upset."

"Don't patronize me, Astrid." Isobel sniffed. "I hate him enough to shoot him or strangle him with my bare hands. And that isn't love, it's assassination."

The duchess laughed and patted her rounded abdomen. It was only by chance that she'd accompanied Beswick to London, given her advanced state of pregnancy, and had sent a note of her arrival to Isobel only that afternoon. Apparently, Astrid had insisted she was sick of the country, and because the duke was so besotted and couldn't deny his wife, she was here for the week. Isobel couldn't have been more grateful for her sister's presence.

"Trust me, I've felt the same with Thane on more than one occasion. But those we love have a certain knack for getting under our skins."

Isobel blinked. "I don't love Winter."

"Don't you?"

"He's a rogue without a heart," she said. "There's not much there to love, trust me. He doesn't want me here in London. He doesn't want *me* at all. I've lost track of how many times he told me to go trotting back to Chelmsford like a good, biddable pet." She paused for breath. "And let's not talk about that club of his. Goodness, if you only knew!"

"I know about The Silver Scythe," her sister said.

Momentarily thwarted from her tirade, Isobel gaped. "What?"

"It's Beswick's social club of choice. He frequents it for the gambling." A secret smile touched her lips as she caressed her baby bump, making Isobel's jaw drop to the floor. "Though we've visited the private side on occasion. Eight months ago to the day, in fact."

"Astrid!" Isobel's cheeks flushed red. "Did you know Winter owned it?"

She shook her head. "News to me, and I'm your older sister, Izzy, not a nun." Her lips curled with a pointed glance to her swollen belly. "Obviously."

"I don't need to know the sordid details of your love life!" She sipped her tea and pulled a grimace. "Gracious, don't you have anything stronger? I suddenly feel the need to wipe these images of you and Beswick conceiving my newest niece or nephew from my brain."

She was only half joking. Her gaze slid to Astrid's

bump, nearly obscured by the clever design of her dress. One wouldn't guess she was with child unless one looked, but pregnancy made her sister radiant. Isobel was unprepared for the brutal stroke of envy that slashed through her. She'd always hoped for children of her own, but that dream was now well and truly out of reach.

"Shouldn't you be entering your confinement?" she asked, wrinkling her nose.

"Shortly, in a few weeks or so. I feel ridiculously healthy."

Isobel frowned. "What made you want to make the journey to London?"

"No reason," her sister said quickly and reached to pour a fresh cup of tea, though she was impeded by her protruding stomach. Isobel grinned and took the teapot from her, refilling both their cups. "Can't a girl simply want to see her sister?" Astrid asked.

"Not when she's about to pop, no."

The duchess chuckled, though she avoided Isobel's eyes. "I'm weeks away from popping, trust me. I needed a break from the tedium of North Stifford. In any case, Pippa was late in arriving. I assume this one will be as well. I am in no danger, other than being in constant need to relieve myself."

"Where *is* my darling niece?" Isobel asked. "Did she accompany you and Beswick?"

"No, though she was dreadfully disappointed to miss out. She's missed you terribly." Astrid peered at her over the rim of her teacup. "How has it been, besides your errant husband, of course? Have you seen anyone of note? Any familiar faces?"

It was a rather odd question. Who exactly did

Astrid expect her to see? Isobel didn't know anybody. She thought back to the time she might have glimpsed the Earl of Beaumont, and shook her head. It was no use bringing him up—it would only upset Astrid. Even if he *were* here, her sister had Beswick, and Isobel had the protection of Winter's name, if not the man himself.

She sighed and thought about the rest of Astrid's question. "The season hasn't been what I expected. It's exhausting for one. A never-ending carousel of balls and musicales and soirees, all designed to make a girl positively fed up. I miss the country and the fresh air, and being myself."

"And yet, here you are, still in London," Astrid pointed out. "When your own husband is telling you to go back to Chelmsford, which seems to be what you claim to want. So, which is it, sister? Roth or Chelmsford?"

Isobel resisted the urge to stick out her tongue in a childish gesture. Astrid had always been able to cut right to the heart of the matter. "I don't know. Both, perhaps."

Astrid canted her head. "Do you *like* Roth?"

"Sometimes, he's affable."

Her sister's brows rose. "*Affable*?"

"Fine," she mumbled. "On occasion, he's clever and thoughtful, and I enjoy his company. Especially when he doesn't know it's me."

Isobel blushed as her sister shot her a questioning look. She hadn't meant to allude to her secret persona as Iz, but now the cat was out of the bag. And besides, it was probably a good thing, since Iz had supposedly worked for Beswick. In a few short words, she explained how Iz, the groom, had come to be, watching as her sister's eyes grew into surprised orbs.

Staring at her, Astrid shook her head in mute fascination. "Sometimes, you astound me."

Isobel bit her lip. "It wasn't my fault. It just happened. I couldn't well tear off the mask, dressed like a man wearing breeches in the middle of the dratted courtyard!"

"You could have confessed later."

Isobel lifted a shoulder. "I liked it," she admitted. "I liked him talking to me without those walls he surrounds himself with. I saw a side of him that I never expected."

"Does he know about Lady Darcy?"

She shook her head hard. "No, and he will never find out!"

Concern flashed on Astrid's face. "Secrets have a way of coming out, Izzy, you know that. It's better to be truthful before they have a chance to hurt you or anyone you care about."

"There's rather little chance of that, isn't there?" Isobel said, a wave of bitterness cresting through her. His words from the study haunted her: *I never wanted to marry her in the first place*. "Winter doesn't care about me, and if he has anything to say about it, I'll be cloistered away in the country, never to be heard from again. So my secrets are safe."

"Quit being dramatic."

"Well, you're being entirely too pragmatic," Isobel tossed back. "I thought pregnancy would have softened you, but you're as waspish as ever." A horrified sob broke from her at the hurt look on her sister's face. "I'm sorry, I didn't mean that. You're right, of course, you're right about everything."

Astrid reached for her hand, and squeezed. "You need to talk to Roth. One on one, without anger and without agenda. Men are complicated creatures, and unless the question is put to them in a direct way, you will never have the answers you seek and it will drive you to folly trying to read his mind."

She sniffed. "Clarissa has a theory about them having two heads for a reason."

"That girl is outrageous, but she's not wrong." Stifling a snort, Astrid shook her head. "Talk to your husband. If you wish to go back to Chelmsford, I will be leaving in three days. You can accompany me and spend some time at Beswick Park. Pippa will be thrilled to see her favorite aunt."

Isobel leaned in and gave her sister a side-armed hug. "Thank you, Astrid."

"What are sisters for?"

. . .

Steering his mount through Covent Garden, Winter tried to tamp down the maelstrom of emotions coursing through him.

The fact that she'd overheard his cold explanation to Oliver and the duke dug at him. *Tormented* him. This was *his* fault. She wouldn't have left if he'd been truthful…that this wasn't just a marriage of convenience. It might have started out that way, but Isobel had come to mean something to him. The thought of her lying hurt in a ditch somewhere left him cold. Fearful. This was the Garden…not Mayfair. Isobel could be in real danger. The fright that swallowed him made him urge the horse to go faster.

Hell, what if he was too late?

Something inside of him faltered at the thought. Life without Isobel would be…desolate. Impossible to contemplate. No, no, *no*. He'd find her and all would be well. She would laugh about being clumsy and he would berate her for running off without a word. Isobel was alive. She had to be. The alternative was…intolerable.

Winter eyed the brace of pistols tucked into his saddle and moved one of them into his waistband. He'd also tucked a smaller one into his coat pocket and had a knife hidden inside his boot. If he had to take on bandits or ruffians, he wanted to be prepared. All he cared about was finding Isobel and making sure she was safe.

The sense of foreboding settled more firmly over his shoulders, even though his initial alarm was settling. Was she truly hurt? Or was it a ploy? If it was an accident and some Good Samaritan had indeed found Isobel—who seemed to attract trouble like honey drew bees—he would be grateful. But something about this didn't seem right, and his sense of misgiving thickened the deeper he headed into the narrow, smelly streets.

Isobel wouldn't have ridden here alone. She was smarter than that.

Then again, a handful of days ago, she had followed *him* here.

Hell.

Agitation made his muscles tight as he rode. The rookeries were full of rough men and criminals. He wasn't afraid, but he wasn't foolish, either. Winter's hard reputation wasn't limited to the drawing rooms of the *ton*. Those in Covent Garden knew enough not to steal from him or cross him in any way. But at this time of night when crime was rife, he had to be careful.

Gritting his teeth, he cantered ahead toward the address that had been written on the scrap of paper, feeling the eyes on him from various doorways and windows. Thank God he had the presence of mind to shout to Oliver to send for Westmore as well as the Runners if he didn't return in short order with Isobel. Instincts on high alert, he came to a square with several gin-shops, a street or two away from Prue's shelter house.

He normally took care to dress down whenever he visited the area, but today, he was in his usual, expensive kit. Winter was well aware that the lure of a few gold buttons could tempt even the most hardened thief, much less a foxed one. He gave the gin shops a wide berth. His hand slid over the butt of his pistol beneath his cloak when he entered a small alleyway, unsurprisingly in the most dangerous part of the district. This was Russell Street, but it was uncannily quiet.

Too quiet.

His senses tingled, and Winter swung around only to dodge the missile swinging toward his face. Ducking, he slid from the horse. The smell of unwashed bodies wafted into his nose as three footpads surrounded him. They were huge, two of them holding what looked like makeshift cudgels. The other held a blade.

"Give us yer purse, guv, or we'll slit yer throat."

Winter grinned. "Is it going to be like that then?"

"Aye."

"Come and take it, if you dare."

They rushed him at once and Winter only had time to throw his fist out, catching one of them in the nose. Blood spurted as he howled, but Winter paid him no mind as he fought to stay out of reach of the other man's knife. Energy coursed through him as he kicked his leg out, forcing one of the men to his knees, then he brought his elbow up into the man's jaw. A sharp crack echoed through the alley. Thank God for the kidskin gloves protecting his knuckles. With another swift move, he disarmed the man of his blade, and kicked him square in the gut, sending him crashing into a pile of rubbish.

The skirmish with the three was over in seconds… but far from over as a handful more men surrounded him. This couldn't be coincidence. It was too organized, and these men didn't smell like the others. Had they followed him from Vance House? He would bet his fortune that these new arrivals were paid brutes. And given that none of them had guns, they were there to incapacitate, not kill.

Winter had no such compunction, however. He drew the small pistol from his coat and fired a warning shot into the air. To his surprise, they didn't scatter. They were not only being paid, but they were being paid well enough to risk their lives.

By *whom*?

Before he could go for his second gun, a fist the size of a boulder came flying out of nowhere to crunch into his face. Pain exploded behind his eyes as he fought to defend himself, throwing up an automatic left hook that connected with bone. A scream was the only sound as his assailant stumbled backward. Winter shook his head, seeing stars. The momentary distraction cost him greatly as four bodies attacked him at once, taking him to the filthy ground.

He fought with everything in him, but he could barely find purchase. His feet kicked out, and one of the men uttered a savage oath as it connected. Winter could only register one thing—the man had cursed in fluent Italian, and only one person of his recent acquaintance hailed from the continent.

It could not be a coincidence.

CHAPTER TWENTY-ONE

Sometimes, Dearest Friend, white knights are over-rated. Be the storm in the night and stage your own rescue.
– Lady Darcy

"What do you mean he's gone looking for me?" a dumbfounded Isobel asked Clarissa upon her return to Vance House. Though she'd visited only for a brief time with Astrid, her sister was right. She needed to talk to Winter once and for all. They were married, for better or for worse, and unless he had plans to dissolve said marriage, they had to come to some workable compromise. For everyone's sake.

But she'd walked into utter chaos. Amidst shrieks from the twins that she was safe and well, Clarissa was in a fine froth. Her friend blew out a breath. "You told Violet you never should have come to London. I thought you'd gone back to Chelmsford!"

"I did need to clear my head," Isobel said, "but I went to visit Astrid. Goodness, Violet, can you be any more dramatic?"

"I'm not dramatic!" Violet screeched.

"Your sister is in town?" Molly interjected at the same time. "Isn't she with child?"

"When has that ever stopped Astrid? She claimed she wanted to get out of North Stifford for a spell, but my sister rarely does anything without a reason. She asked if I'd seen anyone familiar, which I thought exceedingly strange. I suspect her being here must have something to do with Beswick." Isobel shook her head and focused her attention back on Clarissa. "Wait, what were you saying about Winter before—why on earth would he go looking for *me*?"

Violet's eyes widened. "He received a note, Izzy, that said you had fallen and needed him to come to you."

"But I didn't send any note. And as you can see, I'm perfectly well."

Clarissa let out a breath. "Clearly. Though he rushed out of here like a beast the moment he had an inkling you might be hurt. If I were a betting girl, I'd wager that man has feelings for you. Told Oliver to get Westmore and the Runners if he doesn't come back in an hour."

"It would reflect badly on the duke if anything were to happen to me," Isobel said automatically. "He was motivated by duty, nothing more."

"You didn't see his expression. *We* did." Clarissa ignored Isobel's skeptical look even as the twins nodded. "In any case, I read the note. Number twelve Russell Street. That's near Seven Dials, I heard him say, right before he took off at a breakneck pace on his horse."

Isobel felt a beat of shame for leaving as she had without a word to anyone. He was probably out of his mind with worry, out there searching for her. She gathered her skirts. "I have to find him."

But Clarissa grabbed her by the arm. "Don't be ridiculous," she hissed. "You can't just waltz into Covent Garden. It's dark and it's rife with criminals and prostitutes."

"And if it's a trap, then you should tell the duke and let the men deal with it," Violet put in, her face worried, but Isobel shook her head, her mind already made up.

"You're going to go no matter what we say, aren't you?" Clarissa asked.

Isobel set her jaw. "I can go as Iz. I won't be recognized."

"You're still a lady venturing into a literal cesspool of sin and vice," Molly said.

"I've been there before," Isobel admitted. "It's not so bad."

During the day, a voice reminded her. It was well past dark now.

"What?" Clarissa bellowed. "*When?*"

She bit her lip. "I followed Winter there after that time we went to his house on Audley Street, when you went for an ice with Oliver. I was in the coach and was quite safe," she added, when she caught sight of her scandalized expression. "Roth saw me home himself."

It was a lie. She'd fled her husband's presence after he'd basically given her leave to take a lover if she so wished. Even now, the memory of his cruel words and the sting of rejection caused her chest to burn. But of course, Clarissa knew her well enough to see right through her fib. She shot her a narrow-eyed stare. "You only call him Roth when you're anxious about something."

Isobel didn't have time to argue. "Yes, I'm anxious that he's walking into a snare of someone else's making and that he's going to be in trouble because of me."

"Winter is a grown man, Isobel," she said. "What are you going to do? If you want to help him, it is best to stay here and safe for when he returns. Oliver and the duke will send for the police."

"I'm not going to sit here and do nothing!"

"We are women, that's what we do."

Isobel scowled. "Bite your tongue."

With that, she marched upstairs and started disrobing, calling for her maids to unbutton the long row of fastenings at the back of the riding habit. Clarissa and the twins followed, relief on their faces. But it was short-lived when Isobel shot them a look filled with stubborn determination and called for her breeches. Her lady's maid fetched the garment without comment.

Violet let out a cry. "If anyone discovers you're not a man, what do you think will happen? I'll tell you what. Nothing good!"

"I'll be careful." Isobel tried for a reassuring smile.

Clarissa cursed. "Good God, Izzy! Violet's right. You can get hurt if you put one foot wrong. You think you can hide that face and body with some dirt and rags? Those people are born swindlers—they'll see right through that flimsy disguise of yours. And it's not just women—men there take a fancy to young boys, too." She broke off, her chest rising and falling in agitation, and made a visible effort to calm herself.

Isobel was sure Clarissa was right to err on the side of caution, but there was no way she was going to sit back and do nothing while the police mucked around, figuring out what to do, and with every second that passed, Winter could be in danger. She knew it was risky, but she was well-versed in the persona of Iz. She would not be discovered. Her plan was simple. She would go to the address. If Winter was in trouble, she'd help him if she could, and then ride for assistance. And if he wasn't, they'd return home, no worse for wear.

Easy as pie.

Pinning her lips, she tugged on her breeches and pulled on a ratty linen shirt, foregoing the usual binding of her breasts in wide bands of linen. She didn't have time. The brown waistcoat and coat would have to do. A tweed cap hid her blond curls. Some soot from the fireplace smudged on her cheeks, neck, and brow completed the look. Within minutes of arriving in her chambers, she'd gone from lady to lad, from upper-class to urchin.

"There," she said to her worried friends. "No one will recognize me. I'll be in and out before you know it."

Molly pursed her lips, frowning hard. "Can't we say anything to stop you?"

"No."

Dismissing the maids, Isobel walked over to her wardrobe and removed a case, whereupon she expertly loaded two pistols with shot and tucked them into her coat pockets.

"Isobel—" Clarissa began.

"It's only as a precaution, don't fret."

But she could see that Clarissa and the twins were truly frightened. Their faces were ashen. "This isn't Chelmsford, Izzy," Violet whispered.

"I know and I'll be careful, I promise."

Isobel took the stairs two at a time, skidding into the courtyard and hollering for Randolph to saddle Hellion. The poor mare must be confused by all the times she'd been saddled and unsaddled, but it couldn't be helped. For a moment, Isobel debated on taking another horse, but she knew she could depend on the mare. If things went south and she needed a fast mount, Hellion was the only steed she trusted to carry her safely.

"My lady," Randolph rebuked gently upon seeing her unladylike attire. "I cannot in good conscience allow you to continue to—"

Isobel held up a palm and took hold of the bridle.

"No, Randolph," she said. "I will stop you there. While I understand your concerns, I am mistress here, and you cannot presume to allow me anything. Understood?" He ducked his head but nodded. "Now switch the saddle and please be quick about it. No need for a sidesaddle. I'll ride astride."

Randolph did as commanded, though his face remained tight with disapproval. As she climbed into the saddle, Isobel recognized it as worry for her safety and she relented. "Tell Lord Oliver and His Grace that I've gone to look for the marquess."

"My lady—"

Without waiting to hear what he had to say, Isobel took to the streets of London as fast as she dared, body braced over her muscled mare.

She wasn't as familiar with the roads once she got to Covent Garden, but she tried to recall the path she'd traveled when she'd followed Winter. Her eyes latched onto Drury Lane, the main street that was etched into the stone of one building. If she followed that, she should come to Russell Street.

She blinked as her momentary hesitation and Hellion's irritated posturing caught the attention of several men stumbling out of a pub. Damn and blast. She hadn't meant to draw notice, but they were staring at the mare, their eyes going wide with appreciation. No amount of dust could disguise the horse's pedigree and champion bloodlines. And the tack on the horse would cost more than what many of these men would see in a year.

"Oy, lad, where'd ya get that 'orse? He's a fine piece, innit."

Isobel held her ground as they wobbled closer on unsteady feet. "Stole it from a toff," she said, making her voice sound as gravelly as she could.

The second man cackled. "A wee lad like you?"

"Aye," she asked. "Where's Russell Street?"

"Come closer, and we'll tell it ta ya," one man slurred, his gaze fastening to her stockinged leg hooked into the stirrup strap with an intensity she didn't like. These toads wouldn't help her. Recalling Clarissa's warnings, she swallowed hard and urged the horse into a gallop with the barest press of her thighs. Luckily, Hellion was well trained and took off.

"Wait, boy! Come back."

But there was no chance of that. Those men did not have any good intentions, she could sense it on them. Guiding the mare down Drury Lane, once she'd put some distance between her and the pub, she searched for any sign of Winter's horse, but instead, had the distinct feeling she'd just gone in circle. God, this was impossible. It was like an untidy warren of streets, set up like a spinning wheel, with each spoke leading somewhere else.

No wonder any wayfarers who got lost in the maze of any of these slums were never to be found...

because by the time they would have gotten their bearings, they would have been robbed, stripped of all belongings, beaten to within an inch of their lives, and if they were lucky, killed. If they weren't lucky, well, those were the ones sold into slavery and prostitution. And that was a grim outcome at best.

Suddenly, she heard a man's bellow and what sounded like a scuffle. It wasn't much to go on, but she didn't have much choice. She moved Hellion in the direction of another loud grunt followed by a crashing noise. Her heart climbed into her throat when she rounded the corner, only to see her husband fighting like a devil at the center of a pack of grimy men.

Blood ran freely from a cut on his brow and he was covered in filth, but his sheer strength and viciousness took her breath away. One man flew into a nearby wall, crumpling to a heap at its base. He wrapped one thick arm around another's neck while fending off a third.

A fourth crept closer, a knife in hand, and Isobel cried out.

"Roth! Behind you!"

He whirled, just in time to deflect the strike with his arm. Blood seeped through the light-colored fabric of his coat. Isobel didn't think—she reached for one of her pistols, took aim, and fired. The lead ball caught the man in the leg, sending him howling in pain to the ground. The others turned at the sight of her on the horse, but she didn't waste a second in cocking her second pistol and sliding from Hellion to fire it at the man fighting to take Winter down. The bullet caught him in the side. Her eyes darted to the man who Winter had catapulted into the wall earlier, but he wasn't moving.

One to go.

She started forward and then stopped mid-step. In her haste, she was forgetting something…something important. Oh yes, her mask! She'd stuffed it into her pocket at the house, knowing it would have drawn more eyes riding through London than not. She cursed the few seconds it cost her to tie the scrap in place, but she couldn't expose her secret to Winter, not yet and especially not here.

And then she was off and running toward him, holding pistols high. They were both empty, but maybe Winter's assailants wouldn't know that. Just as she reached them, Winter crumpled to the ground with an unconscious man splayed on top of him.

"Roth? Are you hurt? Can you get to your horse?"

Winter blinked, blood seeping into his eye. "Iz? Is that you? What the devil are you doing here?" He swiped at his bloody face. "Where's your mistress? Is she safe?"

"Yes," Isobel said, shoving the man off of him and half dragging him up by one arm. "Don't talk. We need to get out of here. More will come when they smell opportunity."

Places like these were filled with parasites. Locals protected their own, but God help any nob who wandered into their midst. Isobel could feel the stares of the hidden eyes watching her from the densely packed houses. They would wait until there was no danger to them and then run out to collect the spoils from whatever was left—clothing, coin, weapons, anything that could be reused or sold.

"What are you doing here?" her husband repeated

on a slur as they stumbled toward Hellion where she pawed the ground beside Winter's horse.

"Rescuing you," she said.

Isobel glanced over her shoulder, feeling a prickle on the back of her neck, but there was no one there except for the four bodies…two insensible and two groaning from their wounds. She had to get them out of here before a mob ensued. "Do you have any shot or pistols?"

"One," he rasped. "In saddle."

Good, that was good. It meant they weren't totally defenseless. Propping Winter against his horse, she debated how to get him into the saddle. He was a large man, and built of pure muscle. Even bolstered between her and the horse as he was, he was heavy.

"We need to go," she urged. "Can you get up on your horse?"

Bloodshot gray eyes met hers as he blinked rapidly. "Where's my wife? Need to tell her sorry."

"You will, Roth, but for God's sake, you need to mount that horse now."

She frowned, watching his uncoordinated motions with some trepidation. Why was he so sluggish? Had he gotten hit in the head? Stabbed?

"Roth, please," she begged, forgetting to lower her voice and drawing his stare. His brow dropped in confusion, and Isobel knew what he had heard—her true voice pleading with him. Not Iz's. Perhaps he wouldn't remember. He gave a weak nod and pulled himself up.

Once he was in place, she turned to mount her own horse, only to freeze at the well-dressed gentleman who stood a short distance away in front of a plain black coach, watching her efforts with amusement, a gun held carelessly in each hand. She blinked in disbelief, wanting to shove her cap and mask out of the way. Surely, her eyes were playing tricks on her.

It couldn't be…

"Not one move, boy," he drawled.

That voice. That leer. Bile crawled into her throat as she lunged for Winter's pistol, only to freeze in place at the sound of cocking hammers.

"Not so fast, lad." His gaze flicked up. "Or you, Roth. Unless either of you wants to tempt your odds with a bullet each. On the ground. Now."

Isobel didn't dare glance at Winter, whose body had gone rigid, but he complied, sliding from the stallion with a grunt. She took comfort in the fact that he didn't seem as muddled as he'd been a few minutes ago.

"Don't try anything, Iz," he said, his voice still choppy, but his words less erratic. "Do as he says and you won't get hurt. All will be well, I promise."

But she wanted to scream that it wouldn't be well because she *knew* the man holding the guns pointed at them. She knew exactly what he was and every cell inside of her quaked with fear and loathing. That man had ruined her sister's life, nearly ruined hers, and did not have one drop of integrity in his miserable body.

The Earl of Beaumont had returned to London.

CHAPTER TWENTY-TWO

Dearest Friend, a swift, hard knee to the ballocks will drop any man, no matter how large.
– Lady Darcy

Winter cleared the remaining cobwebs from his brain.

Christ, where was Isobel? Where was his *wife*? The groom had said she was safe, but maybe he had imagined that, too. His head was ringing. His skull felt as though it'd been caved in. He had to get to her… had to figure out where she was…tell her how sorry he was. The notion that the last words she'd heard from him were such untruths tore at him. Ripped his insides to shreds. Fuck, he truly was a cad. The worst kind of cad.

Winter blinked, forcing his fuzzy thoughts into focus. He'd taken a blow to the temple from a bludgeon. If he hadn't dodged, it would have broken his jaw, but as it was, the makeshift club had glanced off the side of his head, making him lose vision for a moment.

He'd been lucky that he hadn't been knocked out. And then Iz, of all people, had come to save his sorry hide. Winter couldn't fathom that kind of courage, though now, he could feel the boy trembling at his side with fear. Who wouldn't, staring down the business end of two pistols?

He focused his attention to the man holding said pistols and forced his mouth to curl into an unconcerned smirk despite his surprise. The former Earl of

Beaumont was a gutter rat. But Winter didn't doubt for one second that the man couldn't—or wouldn't—use those deadly weapons pointed at him and the boy. Had the earl set the ruffians upon him?

Why *was* he here?

Cain had been a part of the Duke of Beswick's war unit in Spain and had defected, causing the deaths of half his regiment. *That* had been the reason he'd lost his title and estate. Beswick was not a forgiving man.

And neither was Winter.

"You're aware that assaulting a peer is a criminal offense, Cain."

The man's eyes snapped with anger at the use of his surname instead of his title, a deliberate slight on Winter's part. He didn't miss how the man's eyes flashed briefly to the coach behind him. Was there someone else in there? Someone who still held him in esteem as an earl?

He let out a growl. "I *am* a peer."

"You were stripped of your title by the Prince Regent, if I recall." Winter canted his head. "And commanded never to set foot in England again. And yet, here you are, with a gun pointed at a future duke."

"You stole everything from me," he snarled. "You and that bitch of yours."

The boy at his side flinched, a frightened sound escaping from under his mask, likely out of concern for his mistress. Winter wanted to reassure Iz, but displaying any care for the lad would only put him in more danger. As it was, he needed to pretend that the boy was nothing more than a mere servant.

"I didn't take a thing from you, Cain. You did that

all by yourself. What are you doing in Seven Dials?" Winter cocked a brow. "Out for a nighttime stroll, taking in the scents of rot and rubbish? Tell me, who's in the coach?"

The door to the coach behind them opened, and amidst a flurry of a gown better suited to a ballroom than the filthy streets of the slums, a woman stepped down. "My, my, so clever, Winter," Vittorina crowed, eyes glittering in triumph.

Winter's gaze swung between her and Cain. It was obvious they were in league with each other. But what was their connection? Had they become acquainted in Italy? The Duke of Beswick had said that the man had been last seen in Rome once Prinny had banished him, but without a name or fortune, he was of little threat. Though that didn't seem to be the case now. And a man with nothing to lose was the most dangerous.

"How do you two know each other?" he asked.

Vittorina gave a venomous smile. "But of course, how remiss of me. You must know my intended, the Earl of Beaumont?"

Winter blinked. *Intended*? Surely, she was jesting. Was *this* the man she'd become betrothed to? "You do know that he's no longer an earl, so I fear your quest to avail yourself of a British title and calling yourself Countess is moot."

Dark eyes panned up to the man at her side. "Naughty Beaumont, keeping such a monumental secret from me. But it's of little import because plans change, you see. Edmund has always carried a torch for your little wife, and I want you back." She grinned, taking one of the pistols from Cain. "Two birds, two stones."

"That's not how the saying goes, Vitta."

A startled sound left her lips at the old nickname, but he needed to throw her off-balance, and playing to whatever misplaced feelings she still harbored for him seemed to be the best angle. If he could distract her enough, he might be able to get to the unspent gun on his saddle or the knife in his boot. Either way, it would take a miracle.

"And I'm married," he added.

She waved a careless arm. "Once we are back in Italy, none of that will matter. You will be mine, and your wife will be his. Everyone gets what they want."

"Bigamy is illegal there, too."

"You worry too much. Italy is not the same as stuffy old England. You'll have new identities. No one will be the wiser." Vittorina nuzzled the former earl's arm. "Edmund has grand plans for his little runaway dove, don't you, *amore*?"

"You will not touch her!" Winter growled. He felt more than saw the boy's stunned stare from beside him at the unguarded possessiveness in his tone. Another instinctive reaction to anything to do with his mistress? The lad was loyal, he'd give him that. "Or the boy."

"Or what?" Vittorina said, her cold laughter echoing in the empty streets. "Nothing, you're going to do nothing. That boy is a loose end to me, but I can see that he means something to you. So, I'll tell you what we are going to do. We're going to collect your wife, who my little birds report is currently ensconced at Vance House like an obedient, spineless, dutiful twit, and then we're all going to board a ship and disappear."

Did the groom at his side just *growl*?

"My father—"

Vittorina chortled. "Your father will receive a note that his son is sick of the stuffiness of London and is going on yet another grand tour of the continent. And then Lady Roth, bless her sweet, demure soul, will run back to Chelmsford, whereupon her carriage will be attacked by highwaymen and she will sadly, lose her life. See? Your worry about bigamy will be solved as the poor dear will be no more in the eyes of English law. Once enough time has passed, the duke will receive a letter of your sudden, tragic death. Lord Oliver will become his heir, and everyone will be happy."

Winter's stomach dropped at the mention of Oliver. Had his brother been involved all along—a way for him to finally inherit the dukedom? "What does Vance have to do with this?"

She rolled her eyes. "That gullible fool. Edmund befriended him, and the sad, jealous sod couldn't stop talking about his dreadful big brother."

The anger that had spiked within him receded on a tide of relief that Oliver hadn't betrayed him after all. "You have it all worked out, don't you?"

She gave a theatrical sigh. "The heart wants what the heart wants."

Suddenly, out of the corner of his eye, Winter saw a hulking shadow creeping against one of the walls. *Creighton*, his man from the shelter! He had no idea how the porter had heard the ruckus or that he was involved, but word traveled fast in these areas. Regardless, he was grateful. When Creighton was in line with the coach, he gave an imperceptible nod and then it was on.

With unnatural stealth for a man of his size, he took out the coachman, before leaping at the liveried tiger standing at the back. The moment of distraction was all Winter needed. He charged Cain, crashing into him and knocking the gun from his hand, and then turned his sights to Vittorina, but she had already raised her pistol and had it aimed at Winter's heart.

"Pull that trigger, and it will be the last thing you do, I promise you." They both turned toward the voice, only to see Iz with Winter's pistol from his saddle in hand. "I'm a much better shot than I am a groom."

But Winter's relief was marred by the sight of the footpad who had attacked him before, about to strike. "Iz, behind you!"

•   •   •

Isobel turned at the same moment that Winter lunged for Vittorina's arm that was holding her gun, only to come face-to-face with one of the men from earlier. The one that Winter had thrown into the wall held a sword. But worse, she recognized him as the man who had cut Clarissa at the exhibition, the one who had told her she would pay. Beaumont—no, Edmund Cain—had sent him.

"You!"

Without hesitation, she discharged the pistol, the noise explosive and making her ears ring. But her aim was true and the man dropped, screaming and clutching his arm. She hadn't been boasting out of turn when she'd said she was a better shot than groom. Kendrick had taught her and she had honed her skill in the many hours she'd spent alone at Kendrick Abbey.

But as deserving as these men were, she wasn't a killer. She'd been careful to shoot all three in areas where a bullet would incapacitate but do the least amount of damage. In other words, they should all live.

Whirling back to where Winter had already disarmed Vittorina, Isobel huffed a breath as Cain unsheathed a rapier and made to slice at the marquess's back.

"Winter!" she shouted, forgetting in her haste to address him as Roth. "Look out!"

The marquess dodged Cain's blade, but his attention was split by the tiger who, unlike the coachman lying in a heap, had evaded Creighton's fists. Cursing under her breath, she flung the spent gun with all her might at Cain, trying to distract him.

Isobel couldn't help noticing that Vittorina had scrambled back toward the coach—perhaps in search of more weapons—but Creighton managed to restrain her. Now that she was without a weapon and in the clutches of one of Winter's men, there was real alarm on her face. But Isobel couldn't worry about her. Cain was rushing toward her with his rapier held high.

She reached for the footpad's discarded sword and held it aloft. While her shooting skills were sound, her fencing skills were adequate at best. But she had no time to dwell on form, using all her strength to counter Cain's down swing. The blow made her bones rattle, but she fended it off and then parried with a strike of her own. Fencing was like a dance, her instructor had once told her—all fleet footwork and lightness of feet. Despite Cain's larger size and strength, she had the advantage of speed. She just had to figure out how to use it.

The strikes came hard and fast, and it was all she could do to keep up her defense. Sweat poured into her eyes and her legs felt like jelly. Isobel heard the sounds of the scuffle behind her and knew that it'd only been a few furious minutes at most, though it felt like she'd been fighting for hours. Her arms shook with the strain of holding the sword up—she was accustomed to wielding a much lighter rapier. This match would not be won by strength, she knew. She had to use her brain, catch him off guard.

"What makes you think Lady Roth will ever want you?" she asked, keeping her voice low. "You're a disgrace."

His face darkened with rage. "Who do you think you are, boy?"

"I know who I am," she said with a short lunge and then danced out of the way of his return strike. "But you apparently don't know who you are. A disgraced, discredited peer. No more of a noble than me."

"Watch your tongue!"

Anger made him clumsy, and as he dove at her, she ducked and spun as fast as she could to shoot her blade out so it caught him on the torso. He staggered back, clutching at his wound and staring at the blood on his fingers in disbelief. "You little brat, I'll slit your throat for that."

"Promises, promises, Earl of Codswallop," she taunted. "That has a nice ring to it, don't you think? How about Earl of Twaddle? Earl of Almost-Had-It-All?"

Edmund Cain used to be handsome, but the past three years had taken a toll on him. Where there had once been muscle, there was now a layer of dissipation that was easily evident around his middle. His face now sported the first sprouting of a pair of pasty jowls.

"I'm going to take great pleasure in killing you."

"You always seem to count your chickens before they're hatched, don't you?"

His eyes narrowed as they circled each other. "Have we met?"

"Sadly, I don't run in the same circles as cowardly criminals." She channeled Clarissa as she let her insolent stare rake down his body, stopping at his hips. "On second thought, maybe Earl of Insignificant Things might suit better." Isobel laughed. "I've heard about you, you know. You're that earl who likes little girls. One wonders why…"

Though they sparked with rage, his eyes fastened on her. "Do I know you?"

"Me? A lowly groom? I think not."

"Take off that mask."

She shook her head, quickening her steps. "But I'm badly disfigured, Lord Little. My face is enough to inspire terror in the most stalwart of men."

"You speak well for a groom." He advanced with a short stab of his rapier. "Who are you?"

Quick as a snake, he lurched forward and it took all her strength to jump out of the way. Despite his wound, he kept coming, and once more, Isobel found herself on the defensive. There was something else driving the earl now—a desperate need to find out who she was. And she couldn't let that happen.

Narrowing her focus, she fell back on the lessons from her fencing master, letting her body remember the movements.

Parry, strike, shift. Repeat.

"You fence well for a groom, too," he panted.

"I do a lot of things well, Lord Beaumont."

Suddenly, the earl pulled back, his face going hard, and Isobel wanted to kick herself for using his old address. Something in the way she'd said it, some minor inflection must have caught his interest, set off a memory. He stared at her. "I *know* you."

"I hate to disappoint," she replied. "But you don't and you never have."

"Show yourself."

Isobel smiled beneath her mask. "No."

Taking advantage of his hesitation, she darted in, bringing her sword down onto the hand that held his rapier. It clattered to the clay-hardened grit of the street, and she used the advantage to drive hers toward him, the tip of it pressing into his belly. "Yield," she commanded.

In a fit of rage, he reached forward and ripped off the swatch of fabric covering her face. Isobel saw the moment he recognized her, even dressed as she was with dirt caked into her skin, his eyes going wide with incredulity. *"You!"*

Thankfully, her back was to the others, but she still couldn't resist replying. "Me," she said in a low voice. "I believe my sister told you once, *Edmund*, no means no. Surely a man of your intelligence would have learned that lesson by now."

His eyes glittered with lust and malice. "When we get to Italy, I'm going to punish you in ways you can't imagine, little one."

"I'm not sure you understand your predicament here."

She wasn't prepared for him to push against the blade and then knock it to the side. Its sharp edges tore through the fabric of his coat, but he paid it no mind. Before he could get a hand on her, Isobel did the only thing she could—she let the sword clatter to the ground, grasped his shoulders for purchase, and then brought her knee up as hard as she could between his legs. He fell back like a sack of shit, cupping his privates and howling.

"Iz, did he get you?" Winter said from behind, and Isobel braced herself.

She drew a breath, not knowing how he was going to respond. Likely, it would not be pleasant, given the danger she'd placed herself in. Not that it was any different for Iz, but the male sex tended to view defending female helplessness as a measure of their own masculinity. It didn't matter that she could fight or shoot as well as any man. She was a woman and by default, delicate. Hogwash, if you asked her, but such was the way of their world.

But before she could quite drum up the courage to turn around and face him, her eyes met Vittorina's, who was standing off to the side in Creighton's grasp. The woman goggled, her mouth falling open in disbelief and then reforming into a hateful sneer. She screamed like a banshee, tearing out of the porter's hold and sprinting toward Isobel, fury in her gaze.

"You've ruined everything!" she shrieked. "You stupid bitch!"

Isobel sucked in a breath, planted her feet, and

waited until Vittorina was in range before drawing her arm back and letting a full-on punch fly. It connected right in the woman's jaw. For a moment, they stared at each other in silence and then Vittorina's eyes rolled back in her head and she crumpled. Isobel moved to stand over her, the pain in her fingers unbearable, but damned if she would let an inkling of it show.

"I'm not spineless," she said. "And I'm not stupid."

"Fucking hell...*Isobel*?"

She swallowed hard and rotated in slow motion, meeting the incredulous eyes of her husband. Fury was quick to light their silver depths as recognition and understanding hit, but she bit her lip and stood her ground. "There's a good explanation, Winter, I promise."

"There better be," he said, "because there's a good chance I'm going to put you over my sodding knee."

Even covered in blood and filth and God knew what else, the sound of his husky voice made every nerve-ending in her body come alive. Isobel gave him a cheeky grin. "Promise?"

As his eyes darkened from silver to slate and a growl broke from his chest, it occurred to Isobel that it might not be the right time to provoke the beast.

Too late.

CHAPTER TWENTY-THREE

Avoid coitus on a staircase. Notwithstanding the ludicrous speculation of having a child born of such a union with a crooked back, the bodily injuries are not worth the trouble. Do the deed outside instead.
– Lady Darcy

Winter's entire body shook. Nodding to a watchful Creighton, who would see to the fallen Cain and an unconscious Vittorina, he throttled his anger. Too many pent-up emotions rioted through him, brought on by a combination of the fight and how much danger the brazen little minx had put herself through... pretending to be a groom, fighting men four times her size, so very nearly being killed. He was torn between fury, relief, fear, and desire.

His blood heated to dangerous levels.

Even as he seized his groom-turned-wife—the little hoyden had truly pulled one over on him—he was busily contemplating pleasurable ways to exact punishment. Putting her over his knee was only the start of it. Tying her up so that she could never leave the bedchamber was a close second. And having her on her knees was a distinct third.

The narrow alleyway he took them to was empty and clear of debris, but Winter would not have cared if it was covered in fifty layers of grime. It was private...and that was what he needed for what he intended to do. The moment they were safely out of sight, he tore off his ruined gloves and filthy coat, and wiped the blood from his face with the clean lining before tossing them to the side. Then he filled his palms with his wife, sliding over her shoulders, down her arms, and up again to cup her jaw before slamming his lips to hers.

She kissed him back with the same ferocity, twining her arms around his neck to tangle in his hair. His tongue dominated her mouth, punishing, punishing, *punishing*, and Isobel moaned her approval. Winter ground his hips against her body, hands dropping to her delectable arse and squeezing, before hauling her up so her legs wrapped around his waist. One step and he lifted her easily around a stack of empty crates, bracing her against the wall.

"*Fuck*," he groaned when the heat of her core rested snug against his hard cock.

Bewildered, lust-filled ice-blue eyes shone up into his. "W-what are you doing, Winter?"

"I need you," he muttered, going in for another kiss, this one no less ferocious than the first before he broke away panting. Christ, her tiny moans made his cock hard enough to crack stone. "Say yes, Isobel. Or stop me now."

"Yes."

With a rumble of approval, he sealed his swollen mouth to hers, swallowing her gasps and cries. She gave as good as she got, nipping and sucking, tugging on his hair. Wrenching her coat open, Winter's hands trembled over the curves of Isobel's body from that slender back to her nipped-in waist to those flaring hips currently clad in coarse breeches.

His fingers went between them to the front,

fumbling for the laces. She moaned into his mouth as his palm slipped into the loosened waistband to fondle the fleshy globes of her backside. Winter groaned into the kiss. No man could ever mistake these for being male. She was all woman. Then again, it wasn't as though he'd been looking at Iz as anything other than a boy. She'd fooled everyone.

God, the moment recognition had hit, he'd nearly buckled, emotions sweeping through him like a tidal wave. Iz was *Isobel*. He should have known. There'd been so many little hints along the way, but either he'd been unobservant or preoccupied with other things. The older groom, Randolph, had slipped up and referred to the younger groom as *she*. And Clarissa, too. In the salon when he'd asked if Isobel had taken her groom Iz, Clarissa had started to say *she is* and then broke off, catching herself at the last second.

Fury and lust roared through him as he unwrapped her legs to wrench those blasted breeches down, then fumbled at his own excruciatingly tight falls. His hard cock fell free and he fisted it. Isobel stared, eyes going wide at the angry-looking appendage, and then she licked her lips as if she meant to devour it then and there. His staff shuddered in his hand. Hell, he wanted that, too, but later. He had other plans for her in that moment.

"Last chance before I take you right here, right now." The words emerged as a strangled growl.

A burning gaze met his. "Tell me what to do."

"Bend over and hold on to the crate," he whispered, biting her ear and moving behind her when she did as instructed. He dropped to his knees to kiss one round cheek of her delicious arse and then gave in to the temptation, biting and then soothing with his tongue, before reaching between her legs. Bloody hell, she was soaked…and more than ready for him. His fingers parted her slick folds, worrying the bead that made her writhe back against him.

"Winter," she whimpered, her back arching in explicit invitation.

He stood, braced one arm around her middle, and notched himself to her entrance. With a groan, he slid in. One thrust was all it took for his wife to clench and erupt around him, her body spasming, her inner walls gripping him. Grasping her hips, he drove into her, grinding into her willing body until his brain went blank. He pulled her up flush against him, tilting her chin up so he could take her lips. One hand slid down to her wet sex while the other kneaded her breast.

"Come one more time," he growled into her mouth.

"I can't," she moaned. "It's too much."

"You can." He worked his fingers against her nub, pinching it between his thumb and forefinger. "Now, Isobel."

With a soft cry of pleasure, she did beautifully, undulating around him, the standing position squeezing him impossibly tight. His ballocks tightened and lightning hit the base of his spine.

"Fuck, *fuck*!"

Pulling out of the hot clasp of his wife's body, Winter's vision went white as the wildest orgasm of his life crashed through him. Panting, he cradled Isobel's quivering body against his while his brain returned from its journey into orbit.

Staggering back, he drew up his trousers and reached for a handkerchief from his pocket. Turning his wife to face him, he gently passed it over her sex and tugged up her breeches before cleaning and putting himself to rights.

"Are you well?" he murmured.

A snicker broke from her, her eyes crinkling and filled with humor. "You just had your wicked way with me in an alley in Covent Garden, Lord Roth. How do you think I am?"

"Sated?"

"Emphatically. Twice, in fact."

Lips twitching, he grazed her bruised lower lip with his thumb, and then looked up at her ugly tweed cap. He pulled it off, watching as her long golden curls spilled free like a waterfall of silken wheat. Winter wound his fist into one long tress and frowned. If that hat had come off at any time during her foray into Seven Dials, she would have been exposed. He didn't want to contemplate what could have happened in a place full of cutthroat criminals.

His amusement faded.

"Don't ever risk your safety like that again," he ground through his teeth. "You could have died."

She stared up at him, eyes glittering like a cerulean sea. "So could you."

"I'm a man."

"And does being male make your life worth any less than mine?" she shot back. "You were in danger, too, Winter. I couldn't let you be alone, not when you were out here because of me in the first place."

"You should have stayed at home."

"Like an obedient, spineless, dutiful wife?"

Her reply was soft, dangerous, but Winter was too far gone to pay any heed. Anger and fear for her rolled into one. Things could have been so much nastier. Couldn't she see that? She could have been killed. Or much worse.

"Yes, devil take it!" His throat worked as he reached for words. "I couldn't countenance it if something happened to you."

Like Prue.

He didn't have to say the words; he knew his shattered expression made that all too clear. And Isobel was not one to miss anything. He adored that about her—that sharp perceptiveness tempered by compassion.

"I'm not her, Winter," she whispered.

He knew that, of course. Isobel was like Prudence in many ways—in her empathy and desire to see the best in people, even him—but she was much stronger than Prue had ever been. The problem wasn't either woman…it was in Winter's inability to protect either of them. He'd been too late to save Prue, here in this very hellhole, and when he thought of what could have happened to Isobel, everything inside of him hollowed out with dread.

"I know, but—"

Her hand slid up to cup his jaw, her index finger sliding across the swollen seam of his lips and halting his protest. "But nothing, Winter. My choices brought me here to you. *For* you. I would make them again without hesitation."

"Why?"

"Because I love you, damn it!" Her cheeks went scarlet at the admission, but she wasn't finished. "And if you weren't so blinded by your own pigheadedness, you would know that."

Stunned, Winter gawked at her. His heart grew wings, beating wildly within his chest as though offered the gift of flight after being caged for so long. The faintest glimmer of hope hummed through his veins…daring him to fly. Fuck. *Fuck.* She loved him.

She. Loved. Him.

Winter's mind spun with unmitigated joy, but then slowed as he rejected the admission in the same breath. She *shouldn't* love him. No, she was simply overcome by emotion, just as he'd been earlier. It happened to the best of men.

"That doesn't excuse the risks you've taken, Isobel. I won't allow you to put yourself in harm's way. I forbid you—"

Her eyes flashed with injury, but she ducked her head swiftly. "To what? Leave my bedchamber? Cross the street? Ride in a carriage? Being female does not make me weak. I made the decision to follow you with my own capable brain. I took measures against possible harm, in my disguise and my weapons."

"A man should protect his wife."

Her chin lifted in defiance. "And should a wife not do the same for her husband?"

He gave a reluctant chuckle. She was the sort of woman who wouldn't need any man to fight a duel for her—she'd do that on her own. Or defend him, as the situation warranted. He'd never seen anything more magnificent as the proud, fierce look on her face when she'd punched Vittorina.

I'm not spineless, she'd said.

No, his brilliant, reckless, headstrong, stubborn

wife certainly was not.

Their heated stand-off was interrupted by the arrival of several coaches in the adjacent square. Isobel bolted from the alley just as Clarissa descended one of the carriages. Oliver was close behind her, wearing the most aggravated look on his face. A slew of Runners followed on horseback, as men led by Matteo and Westmore from the other carriages rushed forward to round up the fallen footpads and take them into custody.

"Oh, good God, Izzy," Clarissa cried, seeing her. "You're covered in blood! Are you hurt?"

"No," Isobel said, protesting with a groan as her friend threw her arms around her and dragged her into a suffocating embrace. "Not my blood. Someone else's."

Winter blinked, his eyes tracking the spots of scarlet on Isobel's tattered coat. He hadn't even checked to see if she'd been hurt. Instead, he'd mauled her like a slavering dog. Self-disgust lanced through him.

"Lord Roth," the head officer said, "should we restrain the lady as well?"

Winter's gaze went to Vittorina, who was cursing a blue streak, where she was being detained beside Cain. "Get your damned hands off of me! Don't you know who I am? I'm a lady, and I'll see you all whipped for your insolence."

"Yes, but not with the others. She will be returned to her father in Rome."

Her eyes grew huge. "No! Do you know what he will do to me? Please, don't send me back, I beg of you. I'll do anything."

He had an inkling of what her father would do,

given that the man had threatened it in the past when confronted with the behavior of his unruly, unrepentant daughter. Vittorina's future had a nunnery in it. "You made your bed, now it's time for you to enjoy the spoils."

"You're a bastard, Roth."

"My father would disagree."

His gaze met his brother's, his sorrow and guilt overwhelming. "I'm so sorry," Oliver said. "It's all my fault. Cain pretended to be a friend, a peer who had fallen on hard times. I knew who his fiancée was to you. I wanted…I suppose I wanted to wound you…" He trailed off helplessly. "But I had no idea who Beaumont was or his previous connection to Isobel until Clarissa explained it to me on the way here. She gave me an earful."

"It's done now," Winter said. "Forgotten. Forgiven."

His brother's damp eyes met his. "Just like that?"

"Yes." Winter clapped him on the shoulder, wincing at the pain that lanced across his ribs.

"Why?" Oliver whispered.

He pulled him into an embrace. "Because that's what brothers do."

A furious shout and ensuing commotion had them both spinning as Edmund Cain burst free from the man securing him and reached for the pistol sheathed in its holster on the Runner's belt. His eyes were wild as he waved the weapon and backed away. Knowing he was cornered as several of the Runners responded in kind with their own guns, he pointed it in Winter's direction.

Suddenly, with a manic howl, he shifted his aim,

directing the muzzle at Isobel, and Winter's heart shriveled in his chest. "Shoot me, and she dies, too," he bellowed.

"Put down the gun, Cain," the Duke of Westmore said. "Even if you get the shot off, we both know what will happen."

He blanched, but curled his lips in a sneer. "I'd rather die than rot in prison, and I'll take her with me." The gun wavered, Cain's crazed stare colliding with Winter's. "She's *mine*!"

"Don't try it!" Westmore warned at the same time that the hammer cocked, but it was too late.

The blast of a discharged weapon filled the air as a wild-eyed Winter lunged in front of Isobel, his single focus her safety, but instead of a lead ball lodging into his chest, the only impact he felt was the muscled force of Oliver's body crashing into his and shoving him out of danger. Pain hammered Winter's skull, a spray of something warm splashing into his face.

"Winter!" he heard someone scream. "Oh God, he's been shot!"

His chest compressed as the breath was crushed from him as his vision went dark. Fuck, was he *dying*?

"No, no," someone else cried. "It's not him. It's Lord Oliver."

His senses returned to make out Oliver's groan from above him. The pounding pain in his skull wasn't from a gunshot…his head had smashed into the packed gravel when his brother crashed into him, taking the bullet that had been meant for Isobel. The one that *Winter* had meant to take.

Westmore bent over the two of them. "Bullet went clean through. Roth, that's a nasty gash. Good news, though, you'll both survive."

"That seemed rather more heroic in my mind," Oliver muttered with a pained wince. "Getting shot bloody hurts."

A weak chuckle slipped from Winter. "You saved Isobel and me."

Oliver nodded, his blue eyes filled with emotion. "Brothers."

"Oh God, Olly," Clarissa wept, descending in a flurry of skirts to pull Oliver in her lap, mindless of his yelp of pain.

Winter blinked. *Olly*?

Isobel crouched beside Winter, her face mixed with worry and relief, her lips twitching at the question in his eyes.

"Don't ask," she murmured. "They've been at it for weeks. How's your head?"

"I'll live."

"What were you thinking, you daft man?" Clarissa was chiding, tears running down her cheeks. "A few inches over and you could have died. Heavens, you infuriating fool, I'm going to murder you with my bare hands when this is all over."

"Let me stop him from bleeding out first." Westmore crouched down, a strip of linen in hand as he wrapped a makeshift tourniquet around Oliver's shoulder to staunch the flow.

"That hurts," Oliver moaned.

"Harden up." Westmore grinned. "Trust me, the ladies will love it."

Winter saw Clarissa's elbow aiming for Westmore's jaw right before he passed out.

• • •

Ensconced in the quiet of the carriage while the head of the Runners spoke with Winter, who had awakened and insisted he was fine, Isobel watched as Clarissa ran her fingers through Oliver's hair for the dozenth time. He was sitting half slumped into her lap on the seat opposite, his eyes closed.

"Will he be all right?" Clarissa asked worriedly.

"Westmore has some field experience with bullet wounds, I think," Isobel replied. "I can't believe you elbowed him."

"He deserved it."

Isobel pushed a smile to her lips, attempting to lighten the air and her friend's tense expression. "Speaking of stories, who would have thought Oliver, of all people, the dashing hero? Think of the fodder we have for Lady Darcy."

"How can you joke at a time like this?" Clarissa cried. "Who cares about Lady Darcy? Oliver's been shot, Roth cracked in the head, and you…don't even get me started on the kind of danger you put yourself in with no care for your own safety. Goodness, my poor heart is a bloody wreck! It's a miracle I haven't collapsed from sheer anxiety."

Isobel bit back her smile at Clarissa's dramatics. "Good thing your brothers taught me how to defend myself. Turns out they were right—a sturdy knee to the ballocks can fell even the largest of ne'er-do-wells."

Clarissa's eyes widened. "You did *what*?"

"Fed the former earl a taste of his own jewels," she replied with a laugh. "Thanks to Lady Darcy's *Ballock-*

Busting, A Handy Guide for Ladies."

"Practical application is always excellent." Clarissa's lips twitched. "Good to know such advice works in the moment."

They shared a laugh, and Isobel rolled her eyes. "Good, I say. The patriarchy needs a bit of shaking up and who better to do it than us?"

"Being Lady Darcy does have its advantages."

Oliver shifted in his seat, his eyes flicking open. A pair of glassy blue eyes focused on Isobel and then on Clarissa. "Was I hallucinating or did I just hear you say you were Lady Darcy?"

Caught like a rabbit in a snare, Clarissa went scarlet. "You're delirious with fever, dear."

"Just tell him," Isobel said. "Or he'll keep asking questions and we'll never hear the end of it."

"One half of Lady Darcy," Clarissa grudgingly said. "The other half is sitting on the seat opposite. Surprised?"

Oliver made a noise that sounded like a reluctant laugh, a rare smile curving his stern lips. "On the contrary, impressed."

"Now I know you've been badly injured," Clarissa said with a grin.

"Rabble-rousers, the two of you," he murmured. Then he promptly closed his eyes and fell back asleep. A tear leaked from the corner of Clarissa's eyes, her fingers feathering down Oliver's cheek and cradling his head.

"So, it's him then?" Isobel asked, noting the tender way she stared at him.

Clarissa gave a small nod. "We'll probably be at each other's throats within the week." She let out a happy sigh. "He's not so bad most days. Then again, I'm not so perfect, either. We make quite the pair, don't we...the vicar and the vixen." She giggled. "All I want to do is lead him astray and all he wants to do is keep me in line."

"Sounds like a match to me."

"What about you and Roth?" Clarissa asked. "The beauty awakened from her long slumber by her forever prince? I thought you looked cozy for a moment. Well, apart from all the bloodshed." She shot her a side glance and lowered her voice. "Don't think I didn't notice you slinking out from that alley with whisker burns on your cheeks."

Isobel bit her lip, her body remembering the paces Winter had put her through in a matter of minutes. He had taken her hard and fast, and she'd loved every second of it. Loved the way his body had bracketed hers, loved the way he'd felt inside of her, loved how unhinged he'd been, as though he could barely control himself. Then again, attraction had never been an issue for them. No, it was anything beyond that...like love.

"He won't ever love me."

Clarissa frowned. "What do you mean he won't?"

"He's incapable of it."

Heart suddenly aching, Isobel stared out the small coach window to where her husband stood in conversation with the head officer. Even at a distance, hair askew with blood and grime crusting his face, he took her breath away. There was something so raw and powerful about him. Despite being surrounded by squalor and filth, he gleamed.

Isobel knew he had buried his heart because he

felt that was what he deserved, but he didn't see himself the way she did. He was a better man than what he gave himself credit for. She'd hoped to be the one to help him find happiness, but Winter didn't want that with her. She'd told him she loved him and he hadn't even acknowledged it in kind. His reply had been more than clear: *That doesn't excuse the risks you've taken, Isobel.*

Not, *I love you, too, Isobel.*

Because he didn't. Their marriage had begun with unrequited love, and that was all she still had…unreturned, one-sided feeling.

Isobel bit her lip, forcing back the tears that stung her eyelids. There was nothing for her here. She would go back to Chelmsford and be content with the life she had. There were many things to be grateful for— Clarissa, the twins, Kendrick, her sister, her niece, the breath in her lungs, the simple pleasures she enjoyed, Hellion… Life would go on, with or without Winter Vance.

"What will you do?" Clarissa asked.

"Go home," Isobel said. "Perhaps help with Roth's charitable endeavors, if he allows it. Try to be content."

"But—"

"But nothing, Clarissa. From the start, I was too enamored and infatuated to see this for what it was… a marriage of practicality. I yearned for the fairy tale that my sister had, but Winter's not my prince. He's just a man and I'm a girl with impossible expectations." She gritted her teeth, burying the pain and the need and the anguish that welled inside of her. "I'm going to go back to Chelmsford where I belong."

Oliver let out a moan, his eyes flickering. "Belong with…him."

"See?" Clarissa said, her own tears flowing freely. "Even the comatose man without a romantic bone in his body thinks you and Roth belong together."

Isobel barked a hollow laugh. "He's incoherent from a gunshot wound."

"I think you're making a mistake, Izzy. I think you should stay and fight for what you want. Fight for your marriage…and for what you both deserve."

What she deserved. Isobel didn't even know what that was anymore. She'd thought it was Winter, but how could a woman live with a man who could never love her? A man whose heart, if he even had one, was enclosed in layers and layers of impenetrable stone? Loving a man who didn't want to be loved was an uphill battle with only one outcome—perpetual disappointment.

"I'm tired of fighting, Clarissa," Isobel said. "I'm tired of losing."

She'd already lost her heart. She couldn't afford to lose everything else.

CHAPTER TWENTY-FOUR

Love is like lemonade, Dearest Friend. It's bloody hard work, but the lemons are worth the squeeze.
– Lady Darcy

"I need out of this bed," Winter groused. "Out of this damned house."

"Soon, my lord," Matteo soothed, plumping the pillows behind Winter's head like a mother hen and bustling around the room.

It'd been nearly a week of forced rest after he'd fallen unconscious again upon return to 15 Audley Street. Westmore had called for the doctor, who checked his pulse, pupils, and reflexes, and diagnosed a minor head injury, prescribing laudanum and rest. Winter had endured the rest but refused the laudanum. Five days later, his head ached, but he felt better. Despite the healing contusion on his skull, Winter wasn't in *that* bad of shape.

And for God's sake, he'd had enough of Matteo's smothering.

The last time Winter had tried to get out of bed, a day ago, Matteo had enlisted the assistance of Ludlow, who took obscene pleasure in throwing his considerable weight around, despite growled threats of being turned out on his arse. Winter's entire household had decided to mutiny, it seemed. Even Westmore, who took it upon himself to visit every day, guffawed each time Winter expressed his displeasure.

"You need your rest, sweet cheeks," the duke had said, nonchalantly chewing on an apple and looking windblown and ruddy as though he'd just come in from a glorious ride. Winter knew he'd done it on purpose to needle him. "Dr. Barnes's orders, you know."

Winter had scowled. "I didn't need to rest that time Matteo rescued us from an angry mob in Venice, and I sustained three cracked ribs and a broken nose trying to save your arse."

"A cracked skull is slightly different," an eavesdropping Matteo had put in. He'd eyed Winter, who'd put one leg over the side of the mattress. "Don't make me get Ludlow!"

A grudging Winter had replaced his leg.

Ludlow, Matteo, Westmore, and the lot of them would pay when he was fully mended. It chafed that Isobel hadn't visited. Matteo as well as Westmore had been surprisingly close-lipped about his wife, other than to say she was recovering. However, he needed to see her for himself.

He'd sent countless messages to Vance House, but had received none in return. Oliver had also come by the day before, his shoulder bandaged and healing, though he'd been suspiciously unforthcoming as well, only to say that he was sure that Isobel was doing well, but he'd been busy of late with managing the duke's estates. And no, Isobel hadn't sent any messages for him.

Upon reflection, Winter frowned. Everyone's responses seemed far too similar and much too carefully guarded. He sat up and swung his legs over the bed. Two days before he'd risen to use the chamber pot and to have a bath and the effort had exhausted him. He felt much better now, and besides, he had a purpose. *Isobel.* There had to be a reason why she hadn't been to see him.

Iz like the verb.

He almost laughed out loud. Winter still couldn't reconcile the fact that she'd been disguised as a stable boy all along and he hadn't recognized her, but little things kept coming back to him at random moments. Like Isobel herself…when he'd noticed that she had smelled like honeysuckle one afternoon in the yard and he'd remarked upon it. The saucy tart had deflected it with a careless *her perfume makes my nose itch.*

Chuckling, Winter slid a pair of trousers on and found a clean shirt. He let out a breath as he tucked in his shirt tails and fastened the falls. Not bothering with a waistcoat or cravat, he shrugged into a nearby coat and found his boots. When he was done, he glanced at himself in the nearby mirror and winced. His gray eyes were bloodshot and a lovely purple bruise that was turning yellow flowered down one side of his temple. A few days' growth of dark beard covered his cheeks. He grinned. Add in a gold earring and he'd look like a pirate who'd gotten on the wrong side of the law.

"Matteo!"

Several minutes later, the man waltzed in, a banyan flowing in his wake, and scrutinized his charge with narrowed eyes. "Going somewhere, my lord?"

"Yes, I need to see my wife. Have Ludlow summon the carriage."

If he didn't know Matteo so well, he would have missed the infinitesimal furrow of his broad forehead, but he didn't. His suspicions heightened. "You're still not fully recovered, my lord, to venture out. I must—"

"It's been days," Winter cut in. "As accommodating as I've been to the doctor's draconian demands, I haven't lost my ability to function. And unless you have something more to say, help me look presentable. I need to see her."

Matteo hesitated. "You cannot, my lord."

"Try to stop me. I'll plow through you, Ludlow, and anyone else."

"You cannot because she's not in London."

It took a moment for Winter to register the full measure of what he'd said. "Where is she?"

"I'm not sure."

"When did she leave?" he asked.

Matteo canted his head. "The day after the attack."

"So you've all been *lying* to me?" he shouted, his fingers curling in powerless rage. He wanted to rail and yell and pummel something—preferably all his so-called mates—but his body probably would not cooperate.

"The doctor said it was for the best, my lord," Matteo said. "And it wasn't precisely a lie. She *is* resting, only not in London. I'm sorry I could not tell you."

Winter closed his eyes, irritation tightening his belly. Of all the bloody nerve. Not only had they sequestered him against his wishes, they'd all been in cahoots to keep him in the dark. And now Isobel was gone. She'd run from him because he'd been too blockheaded to tell her he loved her back.

"Lord Roth," Ludlow said from the doorway. "His Grace, the Duke of Kendrick."

Winter gave the butler such a look of fulminating

fury that the man visibly paled and rocked back, his eyes widening before he gulped and backed away. Winter waited until his father came into the room before turning the force of his anger on him. Because God knew, he'd been part of the deception, too. He opened his mouth, but his father lifted a hand, dismissing Matteo with a nod.

"Before you say something you regret, Son, I gave the order for you not to be told," the duke said. He lifted his hand again as Winter's mouth opened to argue. "Not only was it to allow you the recuperation you needed, but it was also a particular request of your wife."

Winter blinked, his protest forgotten. *Isobel* had asked for them not to tell him?

"Why?" he asked hoarsely.

"I imagine that's for her to share when she's ready," Kendrick said.

He swallowed hard. "Where is she?"

"Kendrick Abbey."

Winter felt his chest squeeze, the withered organ inside batting fiercely. *Fuck*. When had he lost the very heart he claimed not to have? He'd repeatedly ordered her to go back, to return to where she belonged, and she had. It was what he'd wanted…what he'd *thought* he wanted, and now that she was gone, he wanted to beg her to return. The only place she belonged was in his arms.

"She left me," he murmured. "I pushed her away because I don't deserve her."

A long moment passed before the duke cleared his throat. "I loved your mother, but her designation of love differed greatly from mine. In the world of the *ton*, love doesn't have much value, yet it is the most valuable thing we can hope to experience. And it's worth fighting for."

"I—"

"Let me finish," his father said. "I know the duchess turned to you with her troubles—a burden that no young boy should have to bear. But you need to know the truth. She used my love, and yours, to serve her interests. Prudence got the worst of it." Winter exhaled at the mention of his sister's name. "She knew how much you adored that girl, as I did. Like Oliver, Prudence wasn't mine in blood, but she was mine in every other way."

The confession stunned Winter. Oliver's parentage had been a shock, but *Prue*? He'd never suspected, though once more, hindsight was perfectly clear. It'd been in the way his mother had treated both Oliver and Prue—in her reverence toward Winter and her subtle disdain toward the other two. She'd been exacting on Prue, forcing her to play the pianoforte until her nails broke and fingers bled. Forcing her to be perfect. His sister had been treated as though she wasn't good enough, because in their mother's mind, she wasn't.

"I should have seen it," he muttered. "Done something."

"I overheard Prudence once telling her maid that she could never measure up—she wasn't beautiful enough, clever enough, talented enough. And that she was done because she'd found out the truth, discovered your mother's infidelity and her lies, and nothing would ever change who she was." A harsh sound ripped from his father's chest. "I couldn't save her, tell her she was loved and so *wanted*. I failed her."

"We both did," Winter said hoarsely.

His mother especially. He wouldn't speak ill of the dead, but he knew that he had to let go of the darkness that he'd kept clamped around his heart. The past, though not what he'd thought it to be, was in the past. He could only look forward. Start afresh.

"Isobel reminded me so much of her. Nothing will ever replace Prudence in my heart, but she brought so much light back to Kendrick Abbey. I couldn't let you throw away one of the better things in your life, even if you think you don't deserve it." Kendrick's eyes shone with something that looked suspiciously like pride. "And don't think I don't know about your shelter and the good you've done. I'm proud of you, Son."

His chest clogged with emotion, Winter embraced his father, feeling suddenly as if all the pieces of his life were falling into place. All except for one…the one that would make him complete.

"I fucked up," he murmured. "She told me she loved me, and I didn't know what to say."

Kendrick nodded. "That girl has loved you from the start, Winter, and I knew you weren't as inured to her as you pretended to be, even when you left her on my doorstep three years ago. You had to get out of your own way first."

"What do I do?" he asked.

His ever-proper father gave him a look that bordered on exasperation. "You bloody well go and get her, Son."

• • •

Isobel sat on her favorite hill, looking out at the scenic undulating hills of Kendrick Abbey. Tenant farms dotted the horizon at wide intervals, the lush landscape and verdant fields stretching between them as far as the eye could see, her favorite lake twinkling in the distance. Usually the view brought her peace, stunned her with its breathtaking beauty. But today, like all the days she'd ridden out before, her chest felt raw and her heart heavy.

Everything hurt. Everything ached.

She plucked at a piece of thistle on her breeches. It seemed like she'd come full circle. This was the exact spot she'd come to when she'd found out about Winter's opera singer…when she'd read and screamed about every previous one of his exploits. Now, however, she knew better. He was a man who helped the help-less, who gave hope to those who had none. Who hid all his goodness and all his light behind a rakish reputa-tion. He was as wild as the season he was named after, her Winter, but he was beautiful all the same.

No, *not* hers.

A sob broke from her lips and Isobel put a hand up to her mouth to stifle any that might follow. She'd spent every night drowning in a sea of tears, crying for something that would never be. It was a dangerous thing to love the possibility of a man versus who he truly was. But if only he could see himself the way she saw him.

Isobel's heart clenched painfully, wrenching a groan from deep behind her ribs. When was it going to hurt less? Would it ever? People said time healed all wounds, but she couldn't fathom what she felt ever lessening in intensity. More fool her. She'd tried to guard her heart, but she couldn't guard something that had already been given away. It would always be his.

"*Fuck*," she screamed. And then let out a laugh. She missed his filthy mouth, too. His complete lack of propriety, his inexorable amusement, his raw earthiness. *Him*.

"Get over it, Isobel," she said out loud. "You're not the only woman to face heartbreak. You'll survive."

Maybe she might not have the same happy-ever-after that her sister Astrid had gotten with the Duke of Beswick, but that didn't mean Isobel couldn't have her own version of happiness. Hers would just have to include an absentee marquess. Maybe one day he'd become the man she knew he was.

As Isobel stared out at the bucolic countryside, her heart seemed to settle as if its master had come to some momentous decision. She *would* be happy.

"What would Lady Darcy do?" she murmured.

Lady Darcy would prevail. She would love fiercely and wholly, even if there was a risk of loss or the promise of pain because love was always worth it.

Isobel watched the sun descend behind the hills, turning the landscape into a spectacular medley of oranges, golds, and reds. The natural beauty took her breath away. As much as she'd enjoyed the excitement of London, nothing could beat a perfect country sunset. She inhaled deeply, smelling the faint scent of wild roses and freshly turned soil on the light breeze.

Hellion wandered over and knickered softly, as if reminding her mistress that it was time to ride back before it got too dark. That, and she was probably hungry.

"I hear you, girl," Isobel said, tucking her loose braid up into the confines of her cap. She patted the mare's glossy neck as the horse gently nuzzled her. Isobel wondered if the mare sensed her sadness. She wouldn't put it past Hellion—the horse was smarter than most. She stroked her velvety nose, staring into her intelligent brown eyes. "At least, I'll always have you."

A thundering of hooves in the distance reached her ears. Isobel squinted into the dying flares of the sunset. A groom on a black horse galloped up the hill from the stables. Randolph or Mrs. Butterfield must have gotten worried and sent someone out to find her.

She checked Hellion's cinches, tightening the straps and making sure everything was in place before turning to reassure whichever groom they'd sent that she was fine and well.

But when she looked up, her breath stuck in her throat at the sight of one windblown and utterly gorgeous Marquess of Roth. A smile curved his generous lips, those gray eyes gleaming like pieces of silver as he dismounted. It was all Isobel could do to keep her legs locked in place.

She blinked, half expecting that she'd conjured him with her thoughts, but no, when she raised her lashes, he was still standing there. So tall and proud and astonishingly handsome that her anguished heart stuttered.

Her eyes tracked over his fading injuries. The wound at his temple was still a motley of colors, though it was fading. He looked fit and healthy. Why was he here? Why had he come? She opened her mouth to ask but he beat her to it.

"Why, Master Iz. You're just the person I was looking for."

CHAPTER TWENTY-FIVE

Pleasure in the bedchamber isn't the answer to a good marriage, but it is the answer to a mutually satisfying one.
– Lady Darcy

Christ, his wife had never looked more beautiful. Dressed in the finest of gowns or a pair of worn breeches or nothing at all, she was easily the most stunning thing Winter had ever seen. And right now, she glowed, limned in the fading light of the sunset, like the earthly angel she was. He wanted to drop to his knees and revere her as she deserved. Beg her forgiveness for being such a stubborn jackass. Lay himself bare before her and take whatever she chose to give.

"What are you doing here?" Isobel stammered, pulling the cap from her head, her cheeks going an endearing shade of pink.

"I told you," he said with a pointed stare to her breeches. "Looking for Iz."

Something like fire flickered in her pale eyes for a scant second, her chin lifting. "You found me. What do you want?"

"I'd like him to get an urgent message to his mistress. That I, Winter Ridley Valiant Vance, would like to—"

"Wait, Valiant is your middle name?" she interrupted.

He gave a shrug. "No, but I thought it would win me some points of partiality."

"That's not how middle names work," she said in a prim voice, but he could see that she was fighting a smile.

"Nicknames, then?"

"We shall see, though vainglorious comes to mind as a more suitable choice," she said and waved an arm. "Carry on, Lord Valiant. Iz has duties to attend to."

Winter bit back his own smile. God, he wanted to pull her into his arms and kiss her senseless, but he knew that he had to make amends for the hurt he'd caused. Words had the power to build and demolish, and he needed to use his to fix what he'd so stupidly destroyed.

"I would like to beg Lady Roth's forgiveness for being an utter ass, and since you are someone she trusts implicitly, what can I do to win back her love?"

Isobel blinked, her breath exhaling in a rush. "You wish to win her *love*?"

"Yes." He gave a wry smile. "Though I expect I look a fright at the moment with my unsightly injuries. She might find me too hideous to look upon."

"That must have been quite a blow to your ego," she replied. "And to your many toad-eaters."

He shot her a wounded look. "There's only one person's opinion that matters to me, and that is my wife's. Between you and me, she's my favorite toadie. I've missed her terribly."

"Have you?" she whispered.

"Inconsolably."

Her slender throat worked, her teeth sinking into

that lower lip. "Do you love her then?"

Winter stared at the woman he adored more than life itself, drinking in the beautiful lines of her face—those piercing wintry eyes, the barely there golden freckles spattered across that pert nose, her full, pink lips begging to be kissed.

He thought of her generous heart, her easily given compassion, her loyalty, her fearlessness, and her passion. The way she constantly surprised him, kept him on his toes, made him think, made him *feel*. She was his light, his life, his everything.

"With all my wasted heart," he replied softly.

"Good," she said, her voice wobbling and a tear leaking from the corner of her eye. "I shall pass on the message. Though I expect that she will be amenable to your sentiments, but only after copious amounts of groveling."

"Naturally." Heart swelling behind his ribs, Winter laughed and closed the distance between them. "May I kiss you now, Lady Roth?"

"Please."

She met him halfway, her mouth fusing with his, her body lining up in exquisite symmetry, her soft to his hard, and Winter felt as though he'd come home. Her delicious lips parted and she licked at him eagerly, demanding entry. He gave it, kissing her back with helpless hunger, his tongue tasting hers and wanting more.

"God, I've missed you," he groaned against her lips. "Why didn't you stay?"

"You told me to leave," she said. "Repeatedly."

"I was a prize jackanapes."

"Yes, you were. That was my nickname for you

whcn you left me here."

"I must have deserved it."

Smiling, she pressed up against him until there was not a sliver of space between them. Her hands wandered down his back and slid beneath his coat before dipping to cup his backside. Desire drilled through him, hot and relentless, and he could feel his impossibly hard cock grinding into her abdomen. He wanted to pull away, but she wouldn't let him, holding him tight. "But you're here now, and that's all that matters. I'm certain you can think of ways to make it up to me."

He arched a brow. "Here?"

"No one comes out here, except for me." She grinned and unfastened the buttons of his coat, sliding it off his shoulders. "And Clarissa and the twins, but I expect that they already know what would happen if they sent you to find me."

Inexplicably, Winter felt heat climb up his neck. Did the entire estate suspect that he was about to ravage his wife? Did he even care? It was early evening, the sky shifting from blue to shades of red and orange as the sun began its descent. She certainly didn't seem to mind that they were outside.

Carefully spreading his coat onto the grass, he rose once more, standing in front of his magnificent wife. His breath quivered in his lungs—he hadn't felt nerves like these since he was a boy. "Are you certain you don't wish to return to the manse?"

"Yes, I'm sure." Her grin was wicked, though her cheeks bloomed scarlet. "I've been thoroughly corrupted by an unapologetic rake, it seems."

"Have you, Lady Roth?" he ground out as her

nimble fingers made quick work of his waistcoat and untying his cravat. He pulled his shirt over his head and stood there as she stared at him, her jaw going slack and eyes lighting in bold appreciation as they slid over his bare chest and abdomen. His muscles flexed, and her pink tongue darted out to lick her lips. "Like what you see?" he rasped.

"Very much." Her hands dropped to the waistband above his falls, her knuckles feathering over the iron-hard bulge of him. "Grovel and impress me."

This woman. She'd be the death of him. The most glorious, splendid death and he wouldn't regret a second of it. "Sit, love, and enjoy the show."

Her eyes widened, but she did as asked, lowering her graceful body to the ground atop his coat. A smirk rode her lips when she kicked off her boots, stripped off her stockings, and shucked off her own riding jacket, the small acts making his own heart race.

"Is this an auction?" she asked when she was settled, the sight of her bare, pink toes and trim ankles making his body harden to indecent proportions.

"If you wish it to be." Winter drew a shuddering breath, holding her pale blue eyes that were hot with desire, burning like the brightest part of a flame. "The bidding will start at one thousand pounds."

"That's rather high, isn't it?" she commented.

"Keep watching, my lady. I'm well aware of my worth and what this body can do." He enjoyed the blush that spread across her chest and climbed into her already pink cheeks.

Mimicking her earlier actions, he kicked off his riding boots and then his stockings, feeling the cool grass beneath his feet. Feeling like a prized stallion on display at Tattcrsalls, he turned in slow motion, unfastening the first few buttons on his falls so that his breeches hung low on his hips. When he completed the oscillation, her indrawn breath was loud in the silence, her hot stare fastened on the two V-shaped strips of muscle that arrowed down to his groin.

He cleared his dry throat. "Does the lady wish to make a bid?"

"Five thousand," she groaned. "Two more to lose the togs."

He tutted and rolled his hips in an explicit thrust better suited to a bordello than the grounds of a duke's country estate. "That's not how auctions work, darling. Anticipation is half the battle."

Winter almost grinned as he saw her fingers knot reflexively into the fabric of the coat beneath her. "Off. Now. Roth."

The growling command in her voice made him weep his arousal into his clothes. Fuck, he'd never been harder. He was dominant by nature, but by God, the sound of his woman making her demands known in no uncertain terms made him want to kneel at her feet in supplication.

"As my lady wishes."

With one flick of his fingers, his breeches slid to the ground, and the sound of her needy gasp was his undoing. Her lustful gaze fastened to his groin, where the evidence of what she did to him stood thick, erect, and proud. Never had Winter ever had a woman look at him with such need, such blazing desire. It fueled him. Empowered him.

"Sold!" he croaked. "To the lady in the front row."

"You were right," Isobel whispered, patting a spot

in front of her and widening her thighs in invitation. Oh, *hell*. Winter's mouth went dry. "Worth every penny. Now come here."

He knelt on his coat, between her spread legs. "You're a little overdressed," he murmured. "I can help with that." When she nodded her approval, Winter made fast work of her shirt, baring her chest that was bound in linen. He pressed a line of kisses to her hot skin at the top edge of the bandage. "Now this is a travesty. These sweet beauties should not be treated in so rude a manner."

Unwrapping the linen, Isobel let out a moan as the warm evening air caressed her breasts. Their pink tips budded, and Winter's mouth watered with the need to taste them. He lowered his head and took one berry-tipped peak between his lips. His wife arched into him as his tongue curled around the sweetest nipple he'd ever tasted.

"Delicious," he murmured, adoring the other breast with equal attention, lest it should feel left out. He kissed his way down her torso, rubbing his cheek against the soft curve of her hip and feeling her shiver.

"Are you well?" he asked.

"Yes," she whispered, her fingers slipping through his hair. "I'm fine. Just nerves."

"You have nothing to be nervous about." Isobel writhed against his continued downward path until he kissed a line across her breeches. "These have to go."

She offered no protest as he tugged them down her thighs, all the way to her feet and deliberately not staring at her nudity, until he could take her in fully.

Crouched at her feet, awe and love filled him.

"You're the most beautiful woman I've ever laid eyes on."

A pink blush distilled its way through her skin as he stared in mute appreciation, taking in the lush landscape of her perfect breasts, her tiny waist, those flaring hips, and long, lean legs, topped by a tuft of gold at the juncture of her thighs. Once more, his mouth watered.

He gave in, nibbling and biting his way up each leg, taking care to learn the places that made her tremble, and moan, and sigh—like the arch of her foot or the bend of her knee. Her pants increased as he kissed a leisurely path up her inner thighs, closer to his destination.

"Winter…"

"Hush, love," he whispered, settling himself in place, his wide shoulder urging her limbs to part. She was so boldly passionate and yet so innocent. The combination drove him crazy. He wanted to be the one to pleasure her as she deserved, to *make love* to her as she deserved, and she would accept every second of it. He would make her body sing.

"I don't…what are you doing?"

"Loving you," he said before setting his mouth to her center.

His eyes nearly rolled back in his head at the first flick of his tongue. Fuck, she tasted like summer and sin, heaven and decadence. Her hips nearly arched off the ground, a moan breaking from the depths of her that had his own answering groan replying to hers. He loved how responsive and open she was, not hiding, not faking what she felt.

This was a far cry from the explosive coupling in

the alley, but he wanted to take his time. He wanted to worship her beautiful body, to show her with actions what he hadn't been able to say before. She owned every single part of him, for better or for worse.

Winter nibbled and sucked, licked and thrust, devouring every delectable inch of her until she was a writhing mass of need…until she cried out, went still, and then tumbled over the edge.

He crawled his way up her body, meeting her heavy-lidded, delirious gaze as he settled his large body over hers, his elbows bracketing her on either side. Those beautiful pale eyes of hers glimmered. "You're full of surprises, Lord Roth," she said in a sultry voice steeped in sex.

His cock jumped between them, and her eyes widened.

Winter's lips formed a gratified smirk. "Told you, I know my worth."

• • •

That he did. Molten waves of pleasure still undulated through Isobel's satisfied body. He was very, very good at *that*. Extraordinarily good.

Ice sluiced through her and she bit her lip, stilling beneath him. She had to ask, even though this was not the best time to do so, she had to know. "Winter, did you ever…" She trailed off, embarrassed. "With the auctions at The Silver Scythe, was this part of it?"

He had to understand what she was asking: whether sexual pleasure was part of the prize.

"No," he said, those silver eyes of his capturing hers. "Not for me. One time it was to attend a ball with a wallflower. Needless to say, she was engaged within a fortnight after being seen on the Rakehell of Roth's arm."

Isobel smiled. "Cocky."

His hips rolled slightly, his hardness pressing against her sensitive softness, making her gasp. "Indeed," he went on with a wicked grin. "Another time was to make a prospective suitor jealous enough to propose to a lady. Also, no surprise when he did. And the last time, last year, you saw what Lady Hammerton had me do."

Isobel did—that gorgeous portrait of masculine beauty was etched into her mind.

"Why do you do it?" she asked. "The auctions?"

"At first, when I wanted to raise money for Prue's shelter, we started offering items that patrons wanted to donate or get rid of—paintings, jewelry, and whatnot. And then one evening when I was modeling a particularly fetching timepiece, the notorious hellions, Lady Verne, Beswick's aunt, and of course, her partner in crime, Lady Hammerton, called out a ridiculous sum for both me and the watch. And thus, the idea was born." He smiled. "It was fun, made money, and people loved it. The men take it in good sport, some women feel vindicated in having a man at their beck and call, and everyone's happy."

Isobel squirmed beneath him, pleasure starting to build at the lean, hard sensation of him pressing her into the ground. She looped her arms around his neck and drew him down for a kiss. His mouth was warm and soft, and tasted shockingly of her own arousal and a deeper flavor that was uniquely him. She couldn't get enough.

"I like having you at my beck and call," she

whispered when they broke apart, panting for breath. "And right now, I command you to lie on your back. It's my turn to play the adventurer."

"Is it?" His eyes darkened, but he complied when she gave a firm nod. "As you wish."

He rolled them over in a swift motion that made her breath stick in her lungs, and then she was straddling him in the most lewd, pleasurable position possible. Isobel gorged her fill of him, eyes tracing those golden stacks of muscle, his broad shoulders and that chiseled face fit for a Greek God. Handsome was too tame a word to describe him.

Her fingers stroked his chest, making the coiled muscle beneath leap. She circled the small coins of his nipples, watching them tighten, and then bent her head to sample them with her tongue. Winter groaned her name and she smiled. She wanted him to be moaning it, shouting it. Shimmying down the length of him, she dragged her mouth over each tight ridge of his abdomen, licked into his navel—which made his hips jerk—and then went lower.

"Isobel." The whisper was a warning. A plea. A benediction.

She stared curiously at the appendage that interested her the most. Winter's *cock*. Lady Darcy had done an expose on names to describe coitus and its various parts, including the filthier ones. Thank goodness for Lady Darcy, Isobel thought now, or she might not be able to continue. The thought that this part of him had fit into her body made her core muscles warm and clench.

Unable to stop her exploration, her fingers slid over him, not even completing the circumference. His cock was hot and silky-smooth, the lightly furred globes at its base round and tight. She caressed them, too, taking pleasure in watching his every reaction to her touch.

"Do you like this?" she couldn't help asking, stroking from base to tip.

He groaned. "Yes."

She wanted to put her mouth on him. Though she and Clarissa had discussed this shocking act at great, clandestine length, she was still unsure. But if it felt half as good as it'd been for her when he'd kissed her *there*, she suspected it would please him.

A bead of liquid gathered at the top as her fingers slid down his shaft again. Gentle hands fell into her hair, winding into the tendrils that had escaped her braid and tightened when she took the broad crown into her mouth. His essence was spicy with a hint of brine, not unpleasant, but like nothing she'd ever tasted. Inexplicably, she wanted more.

Keeping her hands firmly around his base, she worked her mouth over him, reveling in the indecent grunts coming from him. His grip tightened in her hair and she felt her own arousal heighten at the slight pain.

"Fuck, Isobel," he groaned. "Enough or I'll spend."

Her mouth slid off of him as she met his eyes down the glorious landscape of his sweat-sheened body. "Isn't that the point?"

"How do you even know such a thing?" he bit out when she gave a leisurely lick.

She warmed at the praise, but had to give credit where it was due, though it was kind of self-praise in a way. "Lady Darcy."

"Why am I not surprised?" he said with a guttural laugh. "That harridan lives to corrupt innocent ladies."

Isobel gave a pretend nip, making him yelp. "I think the word you're looking for, Lord Rakehell, is enlighten. Or elucidate. Or educate. Our sex does not appreciate being kept in the dark like forgotten mushrooms."

"Fair point, but I'm forced to concede it given my precarious position at your questionable mercy."

"You doubt me? I'm wounded, husband." She licked her lips and took him deep.

With a strangled noise, Winter hooked his hands beneath her shoulders and dragged her up so she was splayed on top of him like a loose-limbed ragdoll. "Not this time," he growled. "I want to be inside of you where I belong when I come."

In a swift move, he flipped her back under him. Isobel trembled at the savage look on his face. His eyes were almost black with desire, his body coiled and tense like a predator ready to claim what was his. And she was ready to *be* claimed. As much as he played at letting her have control, Isobel loved this side of him when he took charge. She wanted to be possessed by him. Owned by him. Swived to within an inch of her life.

She grinned at her indelicate thoughts, her body drowning in delicious want.

"What were you thinking just then?" he asked, positioning his body between her hips.

Boldly, devotedly, she met her husband's eyes. "That I want you to fuck me senseless."

"*Christ*, Isobel," he grated, his cock jerking wildly

against her, "you cannot say such things to me!"

"Why?" she teased and tilted her own hips to receive him, feeling him notch into place where she was hot and wet. "When you clearly like it so much?"

"I do like it, but I want to be gentle."

"I don't want gentle. I want you as you are."

Winter didn't question her desire. He entered her in one powerful thrust that wrenched a low moan of approval from Isobel's chest. God, he filled her to bursting. But like with his hand on her hair before, the pain of his entry and his girth skirted the edges of pleasure, blurring them into something indefinable. Something transcendent.

"Good so far, love?" he ground out huskily, withdrawing slightly and shoving back in.

"Yes." It was a gasp of need. "I need you to move. Now!"

His laugher rumbled against her. "Patience, little tigress."

When he did begin to move, his huge body owning hers with every deep pull and slide, Isobel could only hold on, wrapping her ankles around the backs of his firm, hair-roughened thighs and digging her nails into the meat of his shoulders. There would be marks left there, she was sure, but she didn't care. She wanted to mark every inch of him as he was marking her.

The pleasure began to build as ribbons of heat cascaded from between her legs to the rest of her body, tethering her to that one spot. To him. To where they were joined.

"Harder, Winter," she commanded.

His eyes widened, but she nodded. She wanted him unleashed. Ungoverned. Wholly *him*. His pace increased as he flung one of her legs over his shoulder, pressing so deeply into her body that she could feel him everywhere. The position made his pelvis drag against her sex, sparks of pleasure bursting every time his body ground into hers.

Her eyes screwed shut when it became too much to bear. "Oh God, Winter…don't stop."

"I'll never stop."

Her orgasm burst from her like an explosion, relentlessly burning everything in its path until there was nothing left but passion and ash. She felt him slow, his body thickening on the verge of his own release, and in that moment, her husband's eyes met hers.

"Winter?" she whispered, seeing the emotion on his face.

Silvery gray eyes seized hers, the unguarded adoration in them staggering. His hands reached up to cup her jaw as he leaned down to press the sweetest, most tender kiss to her lips.

"I love you, Isobel," he said. "And I want everything with you. Children, a future, whatever will make you happy."

And then with a few short thrusts, Winter was there, leaping over the edge into the flames with her, incinerating them in tandem. To Isobel's stunned surprise, her body released again, as her husband emptied himself and his love inside of her.

He gave her everything he had to give.

CHAPTER TWENTY-SIX

If you don't feel like you are about to expire from
organ failure, you're not doing it right.
– Lady Darcy

Not long after their reunion, Winter ensconced his
beautiful marchioness at Rothingham Gable, a short
ride from his father's ducal country estate in
Chelmsford. Neither of them had any inclination to
return to London for the rest of the season, so they
remained in the country.

After several weeks, a gloating Matteo, along with
the rest of his London staff, delightedly followed their
master's swift departure from town. Even Ludlow
wore a ridiculous smile on his face. If Winter had
known getting on the cranky butler's good side meant
bringing Lady Roth home, he might have done it
years ago. Certainly, if he'd known *he* could be this
happy, he would have done it from the start.

Winter felt his sated body stir as he watched his
sultry wife saunter across the room to the breakfast
tray that had been delivered earlier. Breakfast being a
stretch since it was already late afternoon. It had been
a long, and undeniably pleasurable, night…one that
he intended to repeat as often as possible.

Even in a silk robe, Isobel exuded sensuality. The
golden coils of her hair were piled into a loose top
knot, and she wore the look of a thoroughly satisfied
woman.

He didn't miss her slight wince as she sat in a chair near the window.

"Sore, love?" he asked.

The smile she gave him radiant, her cheeks going pink. "A bit."

"I can rub it better."

"If I come near you, we both know what's going to happen," she said wryly. "And my body needs food, Lord Insatiable."

He threw a hand to his chest. "It's not my fault my wife is a ruthless temptress."

"Ruthless, am I?" she shot back. "If I recall, I wasn't the one who was ruthless."

Her blush intensified as she no doubt recalled being restrained while he'd pleasured her until they were both mad with lust. The coupling that had followed had been frantic, swift, and hard. Other times, they'd made love slowly, but for some reason, the passionate ferocity of the previous night stuck like thickened honey in his mind.

His sweet, innocent, demure wife was not as sheltered as she seemed.

And that pleased him immensely.

He rose, dragging on a robe, and met her at the small breakfast table near the window. It looked out upon Rothingham Gable's lush gardens that even boasted an ornamental pond. A few white swans dotted its glassy surface, the late afternoon sun shimmering on the water.

Isobel had fallen in love with it the moment they'd arrived, and Winter felt a stroke of guilt that he'd been remiss in not welcoming her here before. Rothingham Gable had been his sanctuary, and despite the vulgar rumors that surrounded the estate and a few parties that his friends enjoyed, it was his home.

His beautiful marchioness poured him a cup of tea and refreshed her own, her movements both economical and elegant. Every move she made was full of grace...poetry in motion. He could watch her for hours. She sipped her tea and then bit into flaky bit of pastry. He stared, the sight of those lips and the glimpse of her even, white teeth mesmerizing. God, even the innocent act of her eating aroused him.

"You're staring, Lord Roth," she said over the croissant.

"Can you blame me? I've been ensorcelled by my nymph of a wife." He accepted the proffered cup and sipped his tea. "So, about Lady Darcy."

She glanced at him over the gold-edged rim of her cup. "What about her?"

"You've mentioned that you learned quite a bit from her."

She smiled. "I have."

"And I approve." He smirked. "Heartily as it were."

Isobel set her cup down, an odd expression of discomfort crossing her face. She rolled her lips between her teeth and cleared her throat. "I have something to confess."

"You're keeping secrets from your husband, Lady Roth?"

"A few," she muttered.

His eyebrows rose at that, but he waved a hand for her to continue, despite the pinch of worry in his gut. Whatever secrets she had, she was entitled to them, given his part in leaving her alone for so long.

"*I'm* Lady Darcy," she said.

He blinked and nearly spit out his mouthful of tea. *That* was not what he'd been expecting. "I beg your pardon?"

"Well, half of her. Clarissa is the other half."

Winter shook his head. What in the ever-loving hell? "Are you pulling my leg, minx?"

"I wish I was."

And then the rest of the story spilled out of her— how she and Clarissa had met, the start of the correspondence, the interest from her sister Astrid's publisher, the anonymous publication to protect their reputations, and their cosmic rise to success. Winter's jaw dropped. He couldn't countenance a word of it. But the more he thought about it, the more it seemed plausible. Isobel's wit and intelligence were present on every page. Clarissa's as well. His own cheeks warmed as he thought of several particularly irreverent pieces on carnal pleasure.

Good God, his wife's mind was just about as debauched as his.

Dazed, he exhaled and reached for his forgotten tea. "What's the next confession?" he mumbled. Mentally, he prepared himself, though nothing could be more shocking than what he'd just learned.

"I think I'm with child."

This time, the unfortunate mouthful of tea shot across the table and splashed onto the windowsill. Wiping his mouth, Winter blinked at her, the uncertain, tremulous expression on her face driving him to his knees as he crept over to where she sat, his large hands spanning her flat silk-clad waist in wonder. "Truly?"

"I was due to have my courses when we first

arrived here, and well, we've been so busy, I hadn't noticed I'd missed them," she said, her hands falling to his shoulders. "I think it happened when you came to collect me at Kendrick Abbey. Are you upset?"

Upset? Winter's heart was beating so hard, it was about to burst through the narrow confines of his chest and throw its devoted self at her feet. His smile was so wide, it felt as if it might split his face into two. "I am the luckiest man on earth."

"I'm so glad," she burst out, flinging her arms around his neck.

Her lips found his and it was some time before they spoke again. By the time they broke apart, Isobel had joined him on the plush carpet, both their robes had been discarded, and they were both panting from mutually enthusiastic exertion.

"Not that I wish to give myself premature heart failure," Winter said, propping to one elbow. "But are there any more secrets I need to be aware of?"

"Just one more." Her fingers trailed down his damp chest. "That old wishing well of yours works."

"How so?"

"Because you were right. It did know my deepest thoughts and desires, even before I knew them myself. It gave me everything I asked for—it gave me you." Her beautiful eyes met his as her mouth curled into a mischievous smile. "I love you to the stars and back, Winter Ridley *Valiant* Vance."

CHAPTER TWENTY-SEVEN

Living happily ever after is not a fairy tale. The point is to live.
– Lady Darcy

If happiness could be measured in tender looks and kisses, Isobel would be the richest woman in the world. They hadn't tapered in the least, not when she and Winter finally descended from their love nest, not in the carriage on the way to Kendrick Abbey, and not through most of the dinner the duke had hosted in their honor.

Isobel was about ready to melt in her chair from the intense, scorching looks Winter had been sending her all evening. She hadn't been joking when she'd teased him about being insatiable. Not that she was complaining…though it made things highly uncomfortable when all she wanted was to climb onto the lace tablecloth and offer herself up as a dinner course. As it was, her body was dreadfully damp and the scoundrel knew it.

Kendrick stood and cleared his throat, drawing everyone's eyes. "I know that it's proper for the men to retire to the library for a cigar and a brandy while the women withdraw to the salon, but if it pleases you all, I'd rather keep my family and friends close to me for as long as possible."

Mouths practically dropped open in unison. The Duke of Kendrick breaking propriety was a momentous thing.

He laughed, a deep belly laugh that made Isobel feel light. "Come now, it's not as though I suggested mounting a siege to rescue Napoleon."

"Close, though," the Duke of Westmore muttered, and even Oliver nodded.

"Brandy for everyone," Kendrick said. "Or sherry if the ladies are so inclined."

"Cigars, too, Your Grace?" Clarissa piped up from where she sat. She and Isobel had once filched some of the duke's finest to do research for Lady Darcy, and had nearly suffocated themselves in the process.

"If you wish it, Clarissa," the duke agreed benignly.

Winter shot Isobel a bemused look as though he couldn't quite recognize this relaxed version of Kendrick with the father he'd known. It was true—the man was different, even more so ever since he and his son had reconciled. This breach in decorum, clearly, was a consequence of his new philosophy...sometimes, some rules needed to be thrown out the window.

Glasses were delivered, brandy and sherry poured, and cigars distributed. Isobel refused both, given her delicate condition, though she grinned to see that Violet was game enough to try. Molly, however, shook her head at her with no small amount of disgust. Oliver gave Clarissa a defeated look, knowing that nothing he could say would deter her. The two of them as a couple still made Isobel giggle, though she couldn't remember the last time she'd seen Oliver so happy. Clarissa, either. However, when they fought, the world knew it.

"A toast," the duke said, lifting his glass of brandy. "To my daughter, Prudence, who should have been here with us. She is dearly missed."

"To Prudence," most everyone chorused, with the exception of Westmore, Isobel noted. After a moment, he lifted his glass, his mouth shaping something that looked like *Prue*, and then he drank. Within moments, however, his face relaxed back to its casual mien.

"I have an announcement," Oliver said, shoving his seat back. His hairline was dampened and his face had gone the color of thinned milk. "Well, perhaps more of a question. A request, rather, that is if the lady is amenable and if she isn't then, well, there won't be an announcement. Oh, sod it, you twat," he muttered to himself, and then dropped to one knee. "Miss Clarissa Bell, will you do me the honor of becoming my wife? If you'll have me?"

There was dead silence before the table erupted in cheers, Winter banging his fist on the tabletop so hard that all the glasses shook. "Well done, mate!"

"She hasn't answered yet!" Violet said.

Spluttering, Clarissa had gone as red as a tomato as she gaped in surprise at Oliver. "Couldn't you have waited until I didn't have a mouthful of smoke?"

"It's a filthy habit," he said. "You deserve what you get."

She glared daggers at him. "Don't judge me."

"You judge *me* for lots of things."

"That's different."

Winter groaned. "Oh, for God's sake, say yes, Clarissa. No one else can put up with either of you. Yours is a match made in purgatory." Two lethal stares pinned him, but he only grinned and lifted his glass. "To the happy couple? Misery loves company?"

"You're an arse, brother," Oliver muttered.

Clarissa rolled her eyes. "Yes, my lord, I will marry you."

"Hear, hear!" Kendrick said.

They all cheered and drank, Isobel sipping from her water goblet and nearly choking herself when Winter tapped on his glass with a spoon and stood. "I have an announcement as well."

Isobel felt her heart hammer against her ribs. She hoped her husband meant the fact that they were expecting a baby, not the tidbit that she and Clarissa were Lady Darcy, which was no one's business at all and still a secret. Kendrick had been in an agreeable mood of late, but that didn't mean he would take lightly to his daughter-in-law being the author of such a scandalous periodical.

Catching Clarissa's suddenly horrified gaze, she shook her head. "Winter—"

"Isobel and I are expecting, and I couldn't be happier," he said and glanced at the duke. "You're going to be a grandfather, Your Grace."

Relief mingled with love as she stared at her father-in-law's incredulous expression. Then his blue eyes softened and he smiled with so much joy that it made her chest tighten. "Goodness," he said in a choked voice and swiped at the corner of his eye before lifting his glass. "Wonderful news, my dears."

Westmore rose, his affable smirk firmly in place, making Isobel wonder whether she'd imagined his solemnity earlier with Prudence's toast. "Well, congratulations everyone. Sadly, I'm off. Things to see, people to do, hearts to break, and all that."

"You're leaving?" Winter asked.

Westmore winked. "I'll see you when I see you, my

friend. Business doesn't run itself in London, you know. Not all of us have wives to keep us abed every day of the week."

"You know, you could have a wife, if you wanted," Winter said.

"You can't chain this kind of charm down." He grinned and nodded briskly to Kendrick. "Your Grace."

There was laughter as Westmore left the room, before Winter leaped to his feet and followed his friend out.

"Everything all right?" Isobel asked him when he returned a few moments later.

He kissed her brow. "Yes, that's Westmore for you, unpredictable at the best of times."

Dinner culminated soon after that, and she and Winter decided to take a walk through the fragrant gardens. They bade the others goodnight, the duke pulling them both into a remarkably affectionate embrace, and once more saying how delighted he was.

By the time she and Winter had made it into the gardens, they were both in need of a walk. Lamps were lit at frequent intervals along the path. The evening air was fresh, with the barest hint of rain on the light breeze.

"Kendrick is happy with the news," Isobel said, squealing as Winter turned and spun her up into his arms.

"Not as happy as I am, my love."

Her husband carried her over to a bench beneath a wide elm tree and sat down beside her. "Soon I will be too big to carry," she said, smoothing a hand over her middle.

"You'll never be too much for me. You and any

children we have."

She smiled. "Children?"

"I want at least eight."

Isobel giggled and pulled a face. "For a man who didn't want children, you've certainly changed your tune. Two."

"Six, if I must."

"Three, then," she said.

"Four and we can call it even."

Isobel opened her mouth to protest and then he kissed her, his skill and sweetness making her forget her entire train of thought. In fact, when he pulled away, she was hard pressed to remember where she was and how she'd come to be there.

"You are devious, sir!"

Her cheeky husband grinned. "All's fair in love and war, my beauty."

• • •

Winter hadn't wanted to return to town, instead enjoying the idyllic peace—and pleasures—of his country estate, but duty was an unforgiving master, if left untended for too long. Happily, Isobel had agreed to return with him, and as such, it hadn't been as dreary as he'd expected. London was teeming with the end of the season almost upon them, and the Marquess and Marchioness of Roth were invited everywhere.

Besides that, to his immense surprise, Isobel had insisted on learning about the inner workings of the shelter house in the past weeks. She hoped to take over some of the duties from Matteo, specifically overseeing general management duties and fund allocation. It overwhelmed Winter how much it affected him that Isobel *wanted* to be involved. No other society lady of his acquaintance volunteered to work with the poor and downtrodden or get their hands dirty. Then again, his wife wasn't like any other woman. She continued to astound him—in every conceivable way—from the bedroom to business to the ballroom.

He'd just finished meeting with Bow Street that had run quite late. The head of the Runners had wanted to follow up with him to close out the open investigation into his attack. Edmund Cain was sentenced to prison for the attempted murder of a peer, and Lady Vittorina Carpalo had been returned to the care of her father, and rumor had it, he'd sent her to an Italian convent the next day. Winter had no doubt she'd find some way to convince her father that she'd repented at some point, but that was for Lord Carpalo to worry about.

When the coach arrived at Vance House—he'd instructed Matteo to put 15 Audley Street on the market—he hurried up the stairs, handing his cloak off to a frowning Ludlow. "I know I'm late. Glowering at me doesn't make time go any quicker."

"But I enjoy it so," the butler said in the driest possible tone.

"You're lucky my wife likes you or I'd sack you."

Ludlow gave him an unperturbed look. "You're lucky she tolerates you or you'd be sleeping in the guest chamber."

"Touché."

Winter took the stairs two at a time, only to stop at the door to their bedchamber, watching as his wife sat at her dresser, fastening a pair of earbobs. Dressed in a midnight-colored gown, her hair twisted up into an intricate updo, she stole his breath.

"You're a fucking dream."

Isobel met his eyes in the mirror and smiled. "So eloquent, Lord Roth."

Winter slammed the door behind him and proceeded to strip every inch of clothing before prowling toward her. Laughing, she raised her hand, warding off his approach. "No, I refuse for us to be any later than we already are. Go, your bath is waiting."

"A kiss then?" he begged.

But his cruel wife shook her head. "No, because we both know where one kiss leads with us." That was true as they'd learned on many previous occasions. "Furthermore, it took *three* maids to get me into this dress," she went on.

Winter couldn't quite hide his disappointment as he veered toward the bathing chamber and climbed into the waiting tub. He glanced down at his raging erection—how on earth was he to get rid of that? He sighed. Desperate times. Isobel's laughing voice reached him just as he'd fisted himself. "However, if you can hold out and behave, I'll let you rip it off me later."

At that erotic promise, Winter's hand instantly fell away.

"God save great George our king…long live our noble king," he sang at the top of his lungs while washing vigorously. "God save the king! God save the king, send him victorious, happy and glorious. God save the king, send him victorious, happy and glorious. Long to reign over us. God save the king!"

"Who let the feral cats out?" Matteo said, walking into the room and making a show of plugging his ears, even as Isobel convulsed in laughter in the background.

"It's a meditation technique," Winter said. "Now come on, man, help me get dressed before I have to sing it again. The quicker we get to Lady Hammerton's, the faster we return home so I can deal with my evil wife."

"Oh," Matteo said with a grin. "*That* kind of meditation."

"Shut up."

With Matteo's help, Winter was dressed in record time, and soon they were on their way to the Lady Hammerton's mid-season ball. In the carriage, Isobel couldn't stop smiling. Winter would be in a pleasant mood, too, if not for the baton in his trousers. He adjusted himself, watching as Isobel hid her grin behind a gloved hand. Minx. Two could play at this game.

"You'll pay for this, you know," he promised softly.

Her brilliant eyes met his. "I'm aware."

"First, I'll rip that dress to shreds," he said in a low voice. "Next, I'll remove those silk stockings, warmed from the heat of your body, lash them around your wrists, and bind you to the bedposts for my pleasure." Her sudden inhalation made him grin, her cheeks flushing with hot, delicious color. "Then when I'm good and ready, I'll peel your chemise and drawers off with my teeth."

"That all sounds wonderful, Roth," his wife purred. "If I were wearing any drawers to speak of."

Point, set, and match to one Lady Roth.

Winter threw himself back against the squabs and bit back a groan at the thought of his sultry wife wearing nothing beneath her skirts. He almost fell to his knees like a philistine on the floor of the carriage and groveled, begging for anything—a glimpse, a touch, a taste.

"Be patient, my love," she whispered, staring at him demurely from beneath her lashes. "Remember that good things come to those who wait."

He knew because he'd promised her the same while driving her mindless with pleasure.

One thing was for sure, this ball was going to be bloody torture.

EPILOGUE

Two years later

Clarissa and Oliver's wedding breakfast had already broken all manner of wagers for number of quarrels, number of oaths whispered, which of Clarissa's brothers would get into a brawl—the winner said all of them—and whether Clarissa would make herself a widow before the day was done. The wager for the length of engagement had been won by none other than her husband, and considering that the date kept getting pushed out for one ludicrous reason or another, it had been anyone's guess when it would happen.

The wedding itself at St. George's, however, had gone off without a hitch, mostly because of the stern-faced presence of the Duke of Kendrick, whom no one wanted to aggravate or provoke. Even Winter had been on his best behavior, though he'd pulled Isobel into a deserted alcove early on.

"What are you doing?" she had whispered.

"Matteo has brought us presents from his recent trip home to Venice." His voice lowered, his lips caressing her lobe and making her knees shake beneath her gown. "A few silk scarves and feather switches. I can't wait to use them on you."

She'd been properly scandalized. "Winter, we're in a *church*!"

"I know," he'd said. "Marry me, love?"

"We're already married."

He'd stared into her eyes, the moment made profound by the quiet of the beautiful church. "But if we weren't, would you have me, Isobel?"

"With all my heart."

Eyes aglow with love, he'd kissed her so soundly that she'd been bemused for half of the ceremony. In hindsight, Isobel knew why he'd asked the question. It was the same question he asked on occasion, as if to prove to her that he would always choose her as his wife, if ever given the choice again. And her response was always the same: *with all my heart*. Because she would always choose him. He was her wicked knight. Her imperfect prince. *Hers*.

A familiar broad-shouldered figure made her veer toward the balcony doors.

"Hiding out?" Isobel whispered in her father-in-law's ear where he stood just inside the terrace, hands clasped behind his back.

The duke turned, glancing fondly down at the sleeping baby in Isobel's arms. "Just for a minute. How's my lovely girl?"

"She's worn out," Isobel said softly, brushing a kiss to the girl's temple. To everyone's surprise, Juliet had been born with a shock of auburn hair. Winter had shared that Prudence's had been that same color as a child. Her eyes, however, were the exact same shade as Isobel's.

"You were quite terrifying this morning," Isobel said, mentioning his no-nonsense brusqueness at the church.

A slight smile curved the corner of his mouth. "All part of the plan, Izzy dear. Otherwise, my son would have lost sight of the important things."

"Which was?"

"Getting his lovely bride to the altar in good time." He shot her a conspiratorial grin. "Throwing my ducal weight around has its uses. No one wants to mess with the big bad duke."

Lips twitching, she shot him an arch glance. "That's clever."

"You're only realizing this now?" he asked.

They shared a laugh and then walked together to the edge of the huge garden terrace at Vance House. Isobel glanced to the lawns where a game of lawn cricket for the children was being set up by Violet and Molly, while the intimidating Duke of Beswick was trying to teach his four-year-old daughter Philippa how to bowl the ball while he also tried to keep a close eye on his mischievous two-year-old son Maxton, who was supposed to be fielding. Though Max was busy eating a handful of grass at the moment.

"Max, no!" Beswick groaned, bending down to wipe his son's fingers clean.

"But I'm a bunny, Papa," the boy insisted. "And bunnies get hungry when hopping."

The duke nodded and gave him a kiss. "After this game, we'll have a proper snack for little boys. Grass will make you ill, and we don't want to miss out on cakes later, do we?"

The boy's eyes lit up as he nodded enthusiastically.

Meanwhile at the other end of the makeshift cricket pitch, Isobel's husband was showing their fifteen-month-old son how to hit, meaning that Winter was clutching a squirming toddler in one arm while attempting to swing a bat with the other. Unlike his

quiet twin sister—older by a mere twelve minutes—
James Darcy Vance had come screaming into the
world like a warrior with a cap of blond fuzz and his
father's gray eyes. Also blessed with his father's devilish charm, and much like his sister, he already had his
grandfather wrapped firmly around his finger.

"Winter," Isobel called out, trying not to wake
Juliet, though she slept like the dead. "He's going to
get clocked in the eye."

Both her son and her husband looked in the direction of her voice, and her heart filled with an
incandescent joy at the sight of the two male loves of
her life. Her son definitely favored his father in looks.

"He's a natural," Winter crowed. "Going for the
boundaries on this one."

"Careful with my namesake," Kendrick called out
as Violet got ready to bowl the first ball.

Winter grinned. "Perhaps you should come down
here and show him how it's done, then."

Isobel shook her head as the prim and proper
duke discarded his coat and gloves, skipped down the
steps, and joined the mêlée to squeals of delight by
the children. Isobel had the sneaking suspicion he'd
been secretly feeding them sweets all week, much to
the dismay of their parents. That said, it was wonderful how much the twins had brought their father and
grandfather together. They often did things as a four-
some, which delighted Kendrick to no end. And
Isobel knew that he loved seeing his son working at
being the best father he could be.

The children's nanny approached and Isobel
passed the sleeping Juliet off with gratitude. Not that
she didn't love holding her daughter, but she was

heavy. It was time for her nap anyway. Soon, James would follow, though he would battle until the last second before his eyes gave in to sleep.

Her sister Astrid came up beside her where she was leaning on the balustrade and offered her a glass of champagne. Isobel smiled and declined, hiding her sudden blush. "I can't."

Astrid's eyes widened. "Are you…?"

"Possibly. I've only just found out."

"Congratulations," Astrid said. "Does Winter know?"

Isobel shook her head and bit her lip. "I haven't told him yet. I'm a bit afraid to tell him. He's only just gotten comfortable with being a father to a pair of rambunctious twins."

Astrid fought laughter. "Didn't he tell you he wanted eight children?"

"He did, but I think he changed his mind after the first few months of no sleep with James and Juliet. Even with a children's nurse, he insisted on trying things himself."

"He's a good father," Astrid said, her eyes panning from her own husband and children to where Winter stood with Kendrick and James. "How have things been?"

This time Isobel couldn't hide her telltale flush. "Can't complain."

"Goodness, with a blush like that, it's no wonder you're with child." Astrid barked a laugh and nudged her fondly in the shoulder. "My, how far you've come from that little girl who turned her nose up at anything that wasn't proper."

"I guess she grew up."

Astrid met her gaze. "Into a remarkable woman.

I'm proud to call you my sister, you know. Even though at times it's hard to believe that the scandalous Lady Darcy came from that prim head of yours."

"And Clarissa's."

"Oy, wenches, did I hear my name?" Clarissa squealed, edging her way between them and flinging an arm over each of their shoulders.

"Goodness, Clarissa, you smell like the floor of a public house."

She gave an unladylike snort. "I do *not*! I am the bride. I smell like delicious."

"Yes, dear, you smell like delicious." Isobel signaled to a nearby footman and gave Clarissa a glass of water. "Drink this. You'll thank me." Obediently, she drank the water, and Isobel made her drink another. "Don't want to be too pissed for your wedding night, do you? You remember the code?"

Clarissa brightened. "What would Lady Darcy do?"

"Exactly."

Astrid laughed. "You two are ridiculous. Though I admit even I ask myself from time to time, what *would* Lady Darcy do? It seems you've spawned an entire generation of independent female thinkers."

"That was the plan," Isobel said.

Over the past year, she and Clarissa had mutually decided to retire the infamous Lady Darcy, despite her popularity. Her last letter to her adoring public had been equal parts heartfelt and scandalously vulgar, and had ended with an irreverent: *now, piss off and make up your own minds*! Seemed like her readers were vociferously taking her up on that.

Though Lady Darcy had retired from her writing

career, she wasn't totally gone. Isobel had also donated the dowry that Winter had put aside in a trust for her to a handful of women's shelters in poorer districts in London in Lady Darcy's name. She and Clarissa had also decided to set up the Lady Darcy Fund for deserving young women who wanted an education but did not have the means to pay for one.

A sudden wail made all three women perk up. Obviously exhausted and fighting it, James seemed to be throwing a tantrum. Winter made quick work of calming him down, though he hoisted him up on his shoulders and walked toward the house. Isobel met him at the entry, turned her face up for a kiss from her husband, and took the cranky toddler into her arms.

"Nap time," she said.

"No nap, no nap, no nap," he babbled. "Mama, no."

"Yes, nap," Isobel said and hugged him close, humming a lullaby softly under her breath.

By the time she'd climbed the stairs to the nursery, he was out like a blown candle. She tucked him into the cradle beside his sister's, smiled at the nurse, and nearly crashed into her husband who was waiting outside the door.

"Do I get tucked into bed?" he whispered, nuzzling her ear.

As always, her blood simmered beneath her skin at the barest touch of his lips. "You're a grown man and it's not bedtime. And all the guests are downstairs."

"I'll be quick, I promise."

His mouth found hers, and her fate was sealed. Once that man kissed her, she became his willing marionette, his to do with as he pleased. Winter's clever tongue claimed hers urgently, leaving her breathless and wanting. Still kissing her, he scooped her up and walked briskly down a narrow corridor.

"Where are we going?" she mumbled against his lips.

"Somewhere private," he said, dragging his mouth down the column of her throat, biting down and then soothing the sting with gentle licks. Isobel moaned, his mouth returning to drown out the sound before they could be heard.

Somewhere private turned out to be a small room that looked like it had belonged to a governess at some time. Neither of them cared by that point. The room was empty but for a rack that looked like a curious combination between a spinning wheel and a clothes press that stood at one end. Winter directed her to the strange object and spun her to face it.

"Hold the wheel and don't move," he whispered in her air. "And swallow those screams."

Desire unspooled through her at the needy rasp of his command. Her trembling arms reached up and held on for dear life as he lifted her skirts and positioned himself behind her. The air kissed her bare buttocks when one foot edged her ankles wider, her frame forming an X.

"Winter…" she moaned, her body ready and weeping for him.

Without a word, he entered her in one slick thrust, filling her, his hands covering her mouth so her groans would not be heard. She was completely blanketed by him from head to toe, and she loved every domineering second of it. It didn't take long for either of them to reach their peaks—hers following quickly on the heels of his.

"Winter, we're going to have another baby," she blurted.

He kissed her neck and loosened her numb fingers, twisting her around to face him. "I know."

"You *know*?"

His eyes dropped to her swelling décolletage. "I kiss these beauties every night. You don't think I'd notice when a handful turns into two?"

"Are you…pleased?"

"Deliriously, my love." He grinned and kissed her. "Only five more to go."

When their clothes had been put to rights, they crept back downstairs to the wedding breakfast with no one the wiser. No one except Astrid, whose brows were in her hairline when she caught sight of them; Clarissa, who started giggling uncontrollably; Oliver, who spared them a disparaging look; Kendrick, who chose to discreetly look away; and Beswick, whose face showed no emotion whatsoever, but that knowing glint in his eyes said it all.

"No one knows," Winter whispered down to her.

"Our *entire* family knows, you wicked man!"

Her dashing rogue of a husband gave an unapologetic grin. "Tell me then, love, what would Lady Darcy do?"

Lady Darcy would smirk, throw her shoulders back, and own it.

Isobel Helena Vance decided to do just that.

ACKNOWLEDGMENTS

First, I owe a tremendous thank-you to my brilliant editors, Heather Howland, Liz Pelletier, and Lydia Sharp. This time, it's Team HALL for the win! Honestly, thank you so much for everything you've done for this book. To the fantastic production, design, quality assurance, and publicity teams at Amara, with special thanks to Stacy Abrams, Curtis Svehlak, Holly Bryant-Simpson, Riki Cleveland, Heather Riccio, Katie Clapsadl, Jessica Turner, Bree Archer, and Erin Dameron-Hill, thank you for all your hard work. To my agent, Thao Le, I can't thank you enough for being in my corner every step of the way. To my friends and fellow writers who saw me through an incredibly challenging year—Katie McGarry, Wendy Higgins, Cindi Madsen, Damaris Doll, Vonetta Young, Kerrigan Byrne, Brigid Kemmerer, Ausma Khan, Angie Frazier, Lisa Brown Roberts, Jenna Lincoln, Alyssa Day, Jodi Picoult, Jen Fisher, Stacy Reid, Heather McCollum, and my fearless golden girls: Aliza Mann, Sienna Snow, Sage Spelling, MK Schiller, and Shaila Patel—thank you for everything. To all my loyal readers, forever friends, family, fans, bloggers, booksellers, and librarians who spread the word about my books and humble me with your unwavering support, I have so much gratitude and appreciation for you. Thanks, Mom, you've always got my back! Finally, to the lights of my life—Cameron, Connor, Noah, and Olivia—I couldn't do this without you. Love you.

The marriage game is afoot in this clever blend of My Fair Lady *meets* Pride and Prejudice *with a twist!*

THE SPINSTER AND THE RAKE

Edward Stanhope, the icy Duke of Thornfield, likes his life in a certain order. Give him a strong drink, a good book, and his dog for company, and he's content. But when he goes to his library and finds a woman sitting in *his* chair, petting *his* dog, what starts as a request for her to leave quickly turns to a fiery battle of wits, leading to a steamy kiss that could ruin them both if they were caught.

So of course, damn it all, that's when Edward's aunt walks in, and thereafter announces Miss Georgiana Bly is the future Duchess of Thornfield.

Georgiana was content to be a spinster, spending her days reading and working to keep her family out of debt. But now her days are spent locked away with a growly duke, learning how to be the perfect duchess, and her nights spent fighting the undeniable attraction to a man who was never meant for her.

As their wedding day approaches, the attraction between them burns hot and fierce, but is it enough to melt the duke's chilly facade?

*Eloisa James meets Sarah MacLean in this
fresh, fun take on women rising up
and taking what's theirs.*

HER WICKED MARQUESS

by Stacy Reid

Miss Maryann Fitzwilliam is too witty and bookish for
her own good. No gentleman of the *ton* will marry her, so
her parents arrange for her to wed a man old enough to be
her father. But Maryann is ready to use those wits to turn
herself into a sinful wallflower.

When the scandal sheet reports a sighting of Nicolas
St. Ives, the Marquess of Rothbury, climbing out the
chamber windows of a house party, Maryann does the
unthinkable. She anonymously claims that the bedchamber belonged to none other than Miss Fitzwilliam, tarnishing her own reputation—and chances of the dastardly
union her family secured for her. Now she just needs to
convince the marquess to keep his silence.

Turns out Nicolas allows for the scandal to perpetuate
for his own reasons… But when Maryann's parents hold
fast to their arranged marriage plan, it'll take a scandal of
epic proportions for these two to get out of this together.